Unlock the door, wake up the world.

Branwyn smiled. With the knife side by side with the Machine, she could see just what to do. She pinched the lattice of the knife here and there, until she found the heart of the weapon. It pulsed under her fingers, long, slow, hissing beats. She placed one palm on the knife's heart, and touched a finger to the Machine Key. A spark of light ran up her arm, through her chest, and down into the knife. The tangle of lines under her palm *expanded*—

Somebody shook her by the shoulder, hard. "Branwyn! Branwyn, you've got to put that thing away, or we're going to get into even more trouble." It was Marley. But Branwyn was almost done. She ran her fingers over the node she'd created, smoothing it like the inside of a clay pot.

She was still so angry. The knife was a small thing compared to all that Severin had done. She pressed both hands over the node now, the sharpened blade slicing into her fingers. The knife felt her rage, shared it. It felt the mark on her skin as a brand on its own metal and tasted her hunger to even the scales.

It woke up.

Praise for *Matchbox Girls*:

"Lovely worldbuilding and an unusual heroine surrounded by strong relationships and good intrigue kept me reading *Matchbox Girls* until well past my bedtime. Tzavelas has created a winning story universe and I'm impatient for the next book!"

—CE Murphy,
author of *Urban Shaman* and *The Queen's Bastard*

Also in the Senyaza Series:

Matchbox Girls
Wolf Interval
Etiquette of Exiles

infinity key

Chrysoula Tzavelas

dreamfarmer press

ISBN: 978-1-943197-06-4
eBook ISBN: 978-1-943197-02-6

Cover art by Ravven
www.ravven.com

Book design and composition by Kate Sullivan
Typeface: Adobe Caslon

Editors: Kate Sullivan and Sarah LaBelle

Proofreader:
Courtney Swanson

www.dreamfarmer.net

For my husband Kevin,
who wanted more of the kaiju,
and for my baby Killian,
who only wanted more of me.

-one-

What can you do?" he asked. "What can you do that all my people cannot? After all, you're only human."

He didn't mean to be cruel. It was the truth. Her best friend was dying, and there was nothing she could do. In a world where angels and demons and monsters and faeries waged secret wars, what were humans but toys to be fought over?

She didn't like that at all.

Marley threw an agonized look at the clock as she dragged a brush through her hair. "I'm not going to have time to visit Penny today."

Branwyn curled her legs under her on a tattered couch, watching her friend hurry with wry amusement. Marley's hair already gleamed like polished oak. "Don't worry about it. I'll go and tell her all about your double date."

Marley froze mid-stroke, looking aghast. "Going to lunch with two men is not a double date."

"Well, they both want to date you. It's practically the same thing." Branwyn suppressed a smile as she watched the flush creep over Marley's face.

"No. It really isn't. It is in *no way* a date. It is a debriefing. That's *all*." Marley flicked a hand at a tabloid magazine on the kitchen table, changing the subject hurriedly. "Will you remember to take the copy of *Eclipse*?"

"No problem," said Branwyn, her fingers curling into the worn plush of the couch. She was careful to keep her tone cheerful, but Marley stopped again to frown.

"You don't mind?"

Branwyn shrugged and turned it into a stretch. "She's my friend, too. I can't promise to read the damn thing to her like you and her mother do. But I don't mind visiting her, Marley. I just don't like brooding and when I visit Penny, there's nothing else to do."

"Bran, I—"

"Hey, check out the time. You're late," Branwyn interrupted. "As enjoyable as it is imagining what your dates will get up to without you, I think you should probably interfere."

Marley gave her another horrified look, grabbed her purse, and fled the apartment.

Branwyn regarded the closed door for a long moment. Then Marley's calico cat jumped up on the couch and gave Branwyn a meaningful stare. It meant, *Pet me or get out of my spot.* Since the cat was the size of a beagle, and magical to boot, it wasn't an idle threat. So after tickling the cat's nose for an entertaining moment, Branwyn relinquished the couch.

The magazine on the table pulled at her gaze. She squared her shoulders and picked it up. *No time like the present.*

At least it was nice out—a warm September afternoon. The smoky haze of the previous month had been washed away by a recent drenching downpour and the high sky was a brilliant shade of azure blue rarely seen in the LA autumn. But lower down, the smog was already accumulating again.

The private hospital that cared for Penny had a lovely garden filled with blooming white and yellow roses on the walk from the parking lot to the building. Arbors draped with bougainvillea kept the walkway itself cool. Penny's room was just as pleasant. In addition to all the medical equipment that kept Penny's body going, there was a large bay window overlooking a fountain, a plush navy couch, and a matching armchair. There was enough room to throw a party, and for the first few days after Penny had been hospitalized, her friends and family had filled the place, ready to welcome her back to the world when she woke up.

But she hadn't woken up.

Branwyn tossed the magazine onto the stack lying on the round table between the couch and armchair before going to inspect Penny. She was almost as lovely as she'd been before she'd been hurt, except her dark hair no longer shone and there was a pallor under her deep olive tan. Still, if anyone ever held a contest for a brunette Sleeping Beauty, Penelope Karzan would win.

But there were no princes to wake her with a kiss. No magic could repair what had been done to her. No science could save her. There was nothing to be done, except wait and hope for what had never happened before.

Branwyn's eyes narrowed as she scanned the machines attached to Penny. Then she pushed the call button above the bed. A moment later, when a nurse peeked in, Branwyn pointed to a new monitor.

"What's this?" It was attached to some electrodes in Penny's hair and bore the logo of Senyaza, the corporation that owned this hospital. Other than the logo, it was just a beige box, with only five numbered LED lights, each one glowing a steady amber.

The nurse, a tall, middle-aged woman who Branwyn recognized from previous visits, came in and closed the door behind her. "You didn't touch it, did you?"

"No. What is it? It wasn't here last time I visited."

The nurse came over to check the electrodes, as if she didn't trust Branwyn to not meddle. "It's an experimental monitor our technicians are testing. You'll have to ask Mrs. Karzan for more information. She approved it." *Technician* was how Senyaza liked to refer to its wizards. They were the ones who said Penny would never wake up.

Branwyn ignored that. "What does it monitor?"

The nurse assessed her, then sighed. "They're taking special readings on her deterioration. Even though she may not recover, they'll have information that might help them save somebody else." She stroked Penny's forehead and added, "It's a bit like being an organ donor."

Branwyn's fingers curled into her palms. "She's not dead."

The nurse gave her a compassionate look that made Branwyn hate her. "Yes, that's the point. It's a miracle, in a way. All the literature on her condition indicates a much faster decline is typical." She moved to the machines and began checking them over. "Still, she's fading."

Branwyn thought it was bad taste for an employee of this particular hospital to refer to miracles.

Senyaza Corporation, while a superstar in the field of electronics and communication, was also an umbrella organization for the nephilim—crossbreed descendants of angels and humans. Penny was here despite being an ordinary human because she'd been caught up in a conflict between the angels and their children.

Marley had said that Senyaza felt responsible for the situation, but Branwyn, always the cynical one, had thought there must have been another reason—maybe they'd been trying to cover their tracks. But now she knew: they wanted to watch Penny die. They wanted to gather data and use her as a living research subject. She wondered if they were even bothering to try and save her, or if they were going by the "literature" and taking the opportunity to do some extra science on the side.

After taking a slow, deep breath to cool her temper, Branwyn told the nurse, "She wants to live."

The nurse finished checking the machines and gave her a tight little smile. "Well then, maybe that will be enough, dear," she said with false cheer. "We certainly don't know everything here. That's one reason we have this." She patted the new monitor. "Have a nice visit. Make sure to keep your guest pass visible."

Branwyn stared out the window, her face hot, as the door clicked shut behind the nurse. There were other reasons she didn't visit as often as Marley did. Marley didn't need a guest pass to visit Penny. Marley *belonged* there. She was under Senyaza's umbrella. Branwyn was an ordinary human, just like Penny, but Marley was not.

A month ago, almost nobody had known that. Not Marley, not Branwyn, not even Senyaza. Marley's employer and so-called friend Zachariah Thorne did, though, and when he got into trouble, he'd dragged her in after him. But the trouble hadn't confined itself to them, to the nephilim and angels and other supernatural types. An angel had used Penny to get to Marley, shredding their friend's soul in the process. That was why Penny was here. That was why Penny wouldn't wake up.

Marley had tried to keep Branwyn away from the situation. They were best friends and she'd wanted to keep at least one of her friends safe. Branwyn still wasn't very happy about that, despite the good intentions. She preferred to make her own decisions about how much danger she faced in any given week, and her tolerance was high. A lot higher than Marley's, damnit. But she'd tried to be understanding. Branwyn and Penny were as close as family for Marley, and she'd been under a lot of pressure to deal with things she barely understood. People made mistakes in that kind of situation.

Branwyn wrapped her fingers around the rail of Penny's bed. She might be an ordinary human, but she still had a little magic she'd acquired from Marley's technician-wizard friend Corbin. He'd given it to her because Marley asked him to, even though it became clear later that he thought most humans were practically useless. It wasn't very powerful, practically a toy, the kind of magic they gave nephil children to protect them from danger, but if she wanted, she could activate a magical Sight and look at the remains of Penny's soul.

Instead, she turned away. She'd seen it before: a shredded fragmentary glow surrounding Penny, interwoven with strands of acrid light and nodes of washed-out color, burned gray and dead in places. It never changed, never improved, just like Penny. She didn't want to see that it was getting worse.

She hadn't believed in souls before Marley turned out to have an origin story and an angelic parent. Not souls, not angels, not magic, and certainly not fairy tales. Branwyn believed in what was real. Reality was complicated.

She suspected souls were, too.

Branwyn glared at the pile of tabloids on the table. She hadn't liked those much before, either.

Penny had, though. She was always happy to go through a new one. They were full of modern fairy tales, she said. Sometimes they amused her and sometimes she was outraged, but she was always so vibrantly *alive* when she read them. Not like now.

Muttering, Branwyn grabbed the most recent edition and sat in the chair beside Penny's bed. No matter what the nurse said about "fading," she was visiting Penny and she was going to do it right. She flipped through the magazine and read out headlines, just in case one of them sparked the return of consciousness. If the romantic escapades of Hollywood starlets couldn't accomplish that, what good were they?

When she got to the horoscopes, though, she closed the tabloid and tossed it back on the table. She didn't need astrology to tell her, oh dear, things were changing, best buckle down and prepare to face some hard truths. Angels weren't the only supernatural creatures moving around behind the scenes. According to Marley, there were monsters and demons, too. And then there were the faeries. Even the supernatural world itself had to deal with some hard truths about the faeries after recent events

Branwyn had met the faeries for herself. Just like an angel had used Penny, a faerie Duke had tried to use Branwyn. It hadn't worked out like he planned. Or maybe it had. She really wasn't sure. Just like reality, faeries seemed to be more complicated than they appeared. Branwyn thought he'd been on Marley's side in the end, but she wouldn't have bet her lunch money on it. The Duke had gotten what he wanted out of the situation, that much was clear. His kind, bound away from the world for centuries, had a way back again.

Senyaza was very concerned about that, Marley told Branwyn, then promptly assured her they'd kept the angels from meddling directly in human affairs for a long time; they'd be able to manage the faeries. No problem. That the faeries had completely new ways of manipulating the world was just a minor snag.

Even if Senyaza kept a lid on the faeries, Branwyn's life was changing anyhow. It had already changed. Marley couldn't go back to a world where she didn't know about her own parentage and neither could Branwyn. The difference was that Marley was relevant and doing things, while Branwyn was expected to stay home and keep herself safe.

Only human.

Branwyn hurled herself to her feet and kissed Penny on the cheek. "I've got to go, Penny. But I'll be back again, and sooner this time, I promise."

Leaving her thoughts behind wasn't as easy as leaving the hospital, and for a while she drove on autopilot. Only when she realized that she'd navigated back to the neighborhood she'd lived in as a kid did her driving acquire a purpose. Her family was always good for a distraction and with five younger siblings still living at home, somebody was certain to be there.

A few moments later, she got out of her car at the rambling house where she'd grown up. The Victorian her great-grandparents had purchased more than half a century ago had been expanded multiple times. It had been an ongoing hobby of both her grandfather and her mother's second husband, before they both had died, and the result was a functional, if unusual-looking, blue and cream building. A quick scan of the driveway told Branwyn that most of the family was home now, although her mother hadn't yet returned from work and her grandmother was still on her sabbatical. She could hear the noise from the street.

Letting herself into the house, she paused in the foyer to identify individual sounds. From the far side of the house came a piano melding with guitar chords: Branwyn's youngest sister, Meredith, working on her music, with her father's assistance. From the rec room downstairs, the sound of televised machine-gun fire and laughter: Tristan and Morgan, along with some of their friends. And from the office her oldest younger brother had appropriated as his own, a girl shouting: "I just need to borrow it, Howl! For crying out loud, I have to do a *presentation*." That was Brynn, Branwyn's middle sister.

"You should have asked, then," Howl said flatly. He appeared in the doorframe and saw Branwyn. "What do *you* want?" Howl—originally named Howell, but it didn't stick—was nineteen, and in college, and perpetually cranky. That might, Branwyn reflected, have something to do with the way she and his other older sister had picked on him nonstop for the first eight years of his life. But he'd made it so *easy*. When she'd developed a social conscience, around age fourteen, she'd realized it was totally, absolutely wrong to pick on a younger brother just because he was sensitive and serious, and she'd resolved to stop. That resolution lasted a few days, because he was so very Howl. Then she'd decided to only do it once a week, just to help toughen him up. She'd made sure Rhianna kept to the schedule as well and firmly disinvited anybody else from participating. But hey, what was done was done, and he'd turned out okay as far as she could tell.

"Adventure and distraction," Branwyn told him brightly. There was never any point in beating around the bush with Howl these days, not if you wanted anything from him. "What have you got for me?"

"Noise. Please, *please* take some away with you" said Howl. "A *dorm* would have been quieter. Noise and chaos and entropy," he repeated, saying the words like they had four letters each. "Take it all." Brynn appeared around Howl, trying to stuff a tablet computer up her shirt. "And thieves stealing my stuff. Oh, and there's rats in the attic. You can have the rats, too. I'll keep the tablet." As Brynn tried to scurry away, he grabbed her by the ponytail, yanked her back, and divested her of the device. She screamed and kicked at him, but he retreated back to his office and slammed the door in her face.

Brynn kicked the heavy wooden door once, then turned to her older sister. "It's not rats, it's ghosts," she confided. "Rats don't sing. I'm going to get it on video and put it on the internet. As soon as I finish my presentation for History." She kicked the door again.

Intrigued, Branwyn leaned against the wall. "Jaimie sings," she pointed out. Jaimie was Branwyn's mother's third husband and a musician.

"Not like this," said Brynn positively. "This is choral and late at night."

"Why does Howl think it's rats?"

"Because of the scratching and the things moving in the shadows when we're up there. He thinks the singing is just a prank. He says you and Rhianna used to do that sort of thing to him all the time."

"We might have," Branwyn admitted. "We had to entertain ourselves somehow and he was handy."

"Well, you haven't been home in two weeks and Rhianna hasn't been home in months. So it has to be something else." Brynn nodded at her own logic.

"Why ghosts, though? You'd think they would have showed up before now. I mean, we've lived in this house a long time. I'm pretty sure Grandma would have discovered ghosts if we had them. She finds out everything."

Brynn gave her a patient look. "It's mysterious noises in an *attic*, Branwyn. I used to tell Meredith pixies lived up there, but let's be honest. The only thing in a Victorian attic is ghosts and madwomen.

And there's no madwomen." She added conscientiously, "I checked."

As Branwyn put a foot on the staircase, she brightened. "Are you going to see? It's the little room. Be careful of the rat traps."

"Good luck getting the tablet. Try bringing him a big glass of lemonade, then waiting until he goes to the bathroom," Branwyn said in return, and went upstairs.

She remembered the little room Brynn mentioned, although she hadn't thought about it since she was around Brynn's age. It was up on the third floor, beyond a small door in the old attic playroom, tucked under the eaves. These days, the playroom served as storage for elderly electronics equipment. The door was behind a box of speakers, so small that the box completely hid it. Branwyn shoved the box to another corner, avoiding the rat traps, then opened the door.

Beyond was a small room thickly coated with dust. A tiny lamp was attached to one wall, linked to the same circuit as the main attic lights; a narrow window near the low ceiling let in a bar of sunlight. The remains of a doll's adventures in toyland had been abandoned some time ago: tea accoutrements, ponies to ride, dragons to slay. Branwyn recognized a few of the toys as things she'd played with and more as gifts her baby sister had acquired at birthdays and holidays. The dust had been disturbed in a trail leading to another set of rat traps, each one baited and poised to snap.

Branwyn looked at the rat traps in the outer room again. They'd all been set off and the bait stolen, she realized. A flicker of motion caught her eye, and she glanced sharply to the right.

There was a snap from the little room. When Branwyn peeked through the door again, all four of the traps within had been set off. Had one of the dolls moved? She couldn't tell. But she certainly didn't see any ratty pawprints in the dust. She crawled into the room and promptly sneezed, then sneezed again.

The dust settled, but it settled into a familiar shape: the outline of a child's fairy doll, laid out on the floor like somebody had drawn it there.

Branwyn's mouth curved in an slow, pleased smile. The faerie Duke she'd met had first manifested as a doll-like pixie. He'd not only been interested in humanity, he'd been interested in *her*. He'd even sent her a sweet letter after it was all over, written in dusk blue ink on handmade paper that smelled of the ocean, and delivered by magic.

After reading it, she'd felt quite charitable toward him, even inclined to forgive the fact that he'd abducted her. He'd apologized for that, after all, and he'd been acting under—and fighting against—a magical coercion. But despite his assurance that she would have a chance to see him again if she wished, there was no followup.

It was disappointing, because she'd been very much looking forward to letting him make it up to her. As week after week had slid by, the tendency toward forgiveness had faded. But not the curiosity.

Maybe she'd been looking in the wrong places. Or perhaps he'd gotten her address wrong.

That seemed more likely.

She thought about the vague promises the faerie had given her of "making it up to her," and she thought about Penny in the hospital bed, providing experimental data for Senyaza. Senyaza hadn't had to deal with faeries in a very long time, Marley had said. Maybe they knew something the wizard corporation didn't.

She imagined a circle, a triangle, and a square merging, and as they slid together, the second sight she'd been reluctantly granted flickered to life. Lines of colored light sprang across the room, varying in thickness and intensity. According to Corbin, who had given her the ability in the first place, the lines were part of something called the Geometry and manipulating them was the primary focus of modern-day wizards. An expert could identify where various lines came from and what they meant. But they told her little. Cords of light traced the edges of the room and clustered thickly over the storage boxes. A loose knot formed over the main door she'd entered through, and another one tangled in the frame of the miniature door. If there was magic there, she couldn't pick it out from the rest of the room, or any other room she'd looked at. It wasn't enough.

It was pretty, though. She reached out to run her fingers along the knot of the little door. The crimson and citrine glows brightened. Thoughtfully, she crawled back to the outer room and closed the door behind her. Then, without a hint of self-consciousness, she knocked.

The lines of the Geometry rippled in response and the door cracked open.

-two-

The shadows of the boxes in the corner moved as Branwyn pushed the miniature door further open, as if a light she couldn't see streamed from the opening. The tiny room beyond rippled, like it had been painted on a transparent curtain.

"All right!" She exclaimed, recognizing the curtain-like ripple. She'd seen it before when passing into the faerie realm. Hopefully, she crawled through the door. As she did, she had the strong sensation of multiple veils parting around her head and shoulders. Each time the invisible wisps pulled away from her face, the light and color in the little attic space changed. Brown. Yellow. Gold. Red. Purple. And the room grew bigger and bigger; the slats beneath her hands and knees became softer, the air became rich and heavy with jasmine and patchouli.

She rose to her feet in a large, high-ceilinged room draped with fabrics of purple and charcoal, with crimson cushions scattered over elaborately woven carpets. Flames danced in enclosed sconces along the walls, leaving the corners in shadows. Glowing pairs of eyes opened in the gloom, one pair after another, gleaming like a new-wakened predator's.

Still pleased with herself, Branwyn said, "I didn't even need a Drink Me." She recognized the eyes from her previous visit, too, and disregarded them blithely.

"*You* were invited," said the figure lounging in the elaborate chair at the far end of the room. It appeared to be a man, long legs stretched before him in a pose of ready relaxation "Welcome back to Underlight, Branwyn." His voice was deep and clear, with musical undertones. He stretched out a hand toward her, as if commanding her forward.

Branwyn crossed her arms. "I was, but *you* weren't. What are you doing *here?* My family thinks you're rats in in the attic. Why didn't you just come visit me? Admit it, you got lost."

The outstretched hand turned over, the fingers curling into a fist. "Difficulties presented themselves. Fortunately, your great-grand-mother came to our aid."

Branwyn narrowed her eyes. Her great-grandmother had been dead for five years. "Gran-gran never would have helped you. All of her faerie stories were about how to keep you away."

Amusement threaded through that rich voice. "Oh, please, Bran-wyn. She wished so very much for us to exist, her yearning is embed-ded in the very walls of the house you grew up in. In any case, all we needed was a connection point. That was easy enough to achieve."

"Why didn't you just do it at my apartment, then?" She planted her feet wide apart in the deeply piled rugs. She'd come this far, but he wasn't luring her any closer without giving up *something*. She was interested in what he had to say, but *he* was the one who had some making up to do.

"Suspicious Branwyn," said the figure fondly. He dropped his hand and stood up, stepping down from the dais. "Did you only crawl through that door to berate me? And here I thought you *yearned*, just as your Gran-gran did."

Branwyn watched Tarn, the Duke of Underlight, pace down the length of the room toward her. He moved with the lazy predatory grace of a cat, his dark boots barely whispering across the carpet. Black hair curled carelessly over his high forehead and tumbled over the collar of the long, sky-blue satin coat he wore. His smile, too, was that of a cat, one that had a mouse between its paws. She watched him, almost mesmerized for a moment. He was extremely attractive that way. Then she caught herself. "For you to exist? Never."

One of the pairs of eyes emerged from its shadowy corner. They belonged to another male figure, this one short and slender, with wild tufts of chestnut hair and a pointed face. Without saying a word, he fell into step behind Tarn, his gaze never leaving Branwyn. The Duke paid him no attention at all.

"Shall I tell you a story? Once upon a time there was a girl named Branwyn. Branwyn was brave and strong and fierce, and she looked around the world with clear eyes and saw so much that needed to change, and she knew she could change it. One person could make a difference; this was her motto."

His voice entrancing, he went on. "Our Branwyn had many friends, but two who were particularly dear to her. She'd grown up with them and she thought they had no secrets from each other. Imagine her consternation when she discovered that the two of them had gotten into an adventure without her! And what an adventure it was: one of her friends found that she wasn't quite human, while the other discovered her very humanity made her vulnerable. One ended up initiated into a secret world of magic and power, while the other was left with nothing more than a heartbeat. And there was Branwyn, left behind. There was Branwyn, outside. One person could make a difference, but that one person wasn't Branwyn. Wouldn't be Branwyn; she was too normal, too mundane. Too human. Poor Branwyn. Better she should sleepwalk through life than know how meaningless she was, don't you think?"

He paused, then said in a different, more conversational tone, "The young raven wizard of Senyaza offered to teach you mortal magic, but you refused him. Is not something better than nothing?"

Branwyn shook the last traces of his hypnotic storytelling out of her ears. "He only did it for Marley. We stopped the lessons because I'd never be more than a dabbler. I don't have the *aptitude* for more, he said. And that it would take more than a human lifetime for him to teach me anything real, and of course I don't have that." She wondered now if the circumstances of Corbin's declaration should be taken into account—she had just wrecked a day's boring preparations by eating an apple that had happened to be a magic component—then shrugged. It didn't matter if he was angry when he said it, because he was right. "How do you *know* these things?"

"I'm a lord of Faerie. I've had a very long time to learn to read the stories under what I see." He gave her an assessing look. She put her hands on her hips and opened her mouth, but before she could actually say anything, he went on. "You've been granted the Sight and your nodes have been filled with nonsense charms." His hand moved gracefully, tracing out the seven spheres of complex light that she knew she'd see on her reflection if she glanced into a mirror with the Geometry vision activated. They were charms, prepared magical effects like the Sight that could be stored in the nodes the Geometry formed only in living things. If the nodes weren't filled with charms crafted by a wizard, they could be filled with other, darker things by the malicious and powerful. "You've spent time with him, but you are protected as one protects a bystander, not an apprentice. And yet you have the Sight, which would only frighten a bystander. Besides, I saw the way he looked at Marley, and Marley looked at you, when all three of you were my guests."

"They're not quite nonsense," she protested. "Some of them are damned handy."

"Yes," said Tarn sympathetically. "I can see that. You can count a thousand grains of sand correctly and call for help. Practical *and* significant. And yet, you want more. Because here you are."

Branwyn shrugged. "Yes, I do. But what can you do about it? You can't even come visit me in the real world." Then, still irritated, she added, "Would it help if I clapped my hands and believed?"

Tarn smiled. "There's plenty of that already. The world is… amazing these days. It seems that half of all the world dreams of our return."

"But here you are. Trapped. Why is that again?" She put her fists on her hips.

The smaller faerie, still loitering behind his lord, snarled silently at her. Branwyn made a face in return.

"Make no mistake, Branwyn. The door has cracked open and my cousins slip through. That I did not come to you is entirely a different matter, and not particularly relevant now that you have found your way here."

"Tell me anyhow," Branwyn suggested. "I like to know things. Especially when people break appointments with me."

Tarn gazed at her, silent and expressionless for so long that Branwyn wondered if she'd made him angry. She remembered that it was hard to leave a faerie lord's domain without his permission. Last time she'd been here, she'd been locked into a workshop and it flitted across her mind that she should maybe tone down the taunting.

Then she thought, *To hell with that!*. He already had most of the power; she had to take what she could get or be run over by the raw force of his presence. Besides, the way he wanted so badly to make her like him made it almost irresistible to tease him.

He said, finally, "The realm of Underlight is bound to two sovereign Courts and the two power sources they represent. And we are still prisoners, even if one of the chains has been broken. As long as even one chain exists, we are limited to when and where our Courts are the most powerful. The particular land you dwell in welcomes us, but we need more than the welcome of the faulted coast. We need the moon's favor as well. When it is neither new nor full, those of Underlight cannot exit Faerie."

Skeptically, Branwyn asked, "You couldn't even send a note?"

"I did. It obviously didn't arrive. Faerie is full of threats. Need I detail all of them? It will take a very long time." She got the impression he wasn't pleased with this line of questioning.

Despite the temptation, she resisted poking more. Instead, thinking of Penny, she asked, "What can you do, when you're out in the world?"

"Go for walks in the sand. Taste marvelous concoctions—humans are so inventive when it comes to food and drink, did you know that? Go to the galleries..." He sounded almost wistful.

Branwyn's gaze sharpened. "I meant magically. Marley said you have strange magic."

"Ah," he said, thoughtfully. "As to that—many things. Was there something in particular you were curious about?"

Branwyn hesitated, then shrugged. He wanted something from her—she didn't for a minute believe he had invited her here just to chat—and she wanted to find out what that was before bringing up Penny. She didn't want to appear desperate, even if sometimes she felt that way. It was a matter of principle. Desperation did not produce fair deals. "I was just curious. All right. It seems like you have a great, if creepy, grasp of what I want. What do *you* want?"

"Nothing so very awful. You're an artist. I like art, and I've been collecting prizes for a very long time. I'd like you to make art for me." He raised an elegant eyebrow at her.

"I work by commission. That means 'not for free'," she added, just to make things clear. With human clients, you had to be perfectly explicit; from what Branwyn had learned from dealing with Tarn before, it was even more important with faeries.

"We can discuss that. Our mortal income stream will take a while to establish—at least the variety you would find reliable—but I can offer other things…"

Branwyn frowned at the implications, but only said, "And I work with metal. Are you sure?"

Tarn's eyes brightened. "I know. It's one of the things that recommended you to me."

"But aren't faeries allergic to iron and silver and so on?" She was sure she'd heard that mentioned in her Gran-gran's stories. It was usually filed under "how to get rid of them."

"Only in Europe, and even then, not for a long time now," he assured her. "It only happened for long, complicated, and rather sordid reasons. Don't worry yourself about it." He closed his fist, then opened it again. Sitting in the palm of his hand was a polished silver key, small enough to fit on a modern keyring but with the look of an old-fashioned skeleton key.

"I wasn't worried, but fine," she said. She didn't snap, she was sure, despite provocation. "So you want metal artwork and you're going to pay me in some way that doesn't involve cash. Do go on."

"While you're a talented artist, your work hasn't acquired the popular success it deserves. You have to work a 'day job,' I think the term is. We could help with that popularity problem."

A laugh burst out of Branwyn involuntarily as the tension rushed out of her. She'd expected something less clichéd than *that*. "Seriously? My stepfather got an offer like that from a big record label once. He knew enough to stay away, and they were just humans. I think I'll follow his example." She looked around for an obvious way out. The only visible door was behind the throne Tarn had occupied when she arrived.

"Such an independent spirit," Tarn murmured. "Do you know why we of the fae so value artists and musicians?"

"Because you can't make anything yourselves? That's what my great-grandmother said. Hey, where's the exit?" She moved a few steps to the side, as if a new perspective would make a difference.

He padded after her. "There is another reason. Take this," he said, offering the key he still held. It glinted in the lamplight. "A court-key to Underlight. It will let you enter—and exit—my realm as you please. A token of my respect."

Branwyn reached for the key warily, wondering just how solid his "respect" would turn out to be. "Really?" Her fingers closed over something heavy and real.

"Truly." He smiled at her. "The door is behind you."

Branwyn spun around and there it was: a simple mahogany door, looking like it had been there all along. She knew better.

"What's the other reason?" she asked, without looking back at him.

"Because you can shape this prison we've been bound to. It lies alongside the mortal world like a shadow and the dreams and passions of mortals touch it. Those who know how to harness those figments into creative forces have far more control. And a few—" He paused until she turned to look at him "—A rare few, who have honed their skills here under our tutelage, are able to return to the mortal world and shape it directly. The substance of the world becomes malleable under their fingers." He shrugged. "Or so I understand. It has been a very long time since any of these Artificers studied here and desired to return to the world."

Giving Tarn a hard look, Branwyn said, "You know, there's a big gulf between casual chat and a formal offer. So let's bridge that gap. Are you offering to teach me how to do this? In exchange for completing a commission for you? A normal commission?"

"Can you do any other kind yet?" he asked innocently.

Her head whirling with sudden possibilities, Branwyn said, "Golly. You know, I need to think about it. Check my schedule."

"Of course. Go home. Relax. Enjoy your day at work tomorrow. Return when you're ready." He looked around, his eyes bright and his expression pleased. "We should be here for a good, long while."

-three-

When Branwyn got back to the apartment, Marley was already home and cleaning the kitchen like the stove grime represented sin itself and she was determined to hand-deliver the wrath of God.

Ah, not a good lunch, Branwyn thought but carefully didn't say. She flicked a wave as Marley glanced sharply up and hotfooted it to her bedroom. Safely inside, she poked around for a moment while deciding what to do, since Marley was exactly who she wanted to talk to.

Her thoughts were all tangled up between Penny and the angel who had hurt her, and Tarn, locked away from the world, talking about tasting human food with a wistfulness that brought a secret pang to Branwyn's heart. Her own fears of being cast aside as a useless bystander didn't make the knot any easier to work through. And he'd offered her magic! Yet—faeries. Nobody ever said anywhere, "Ach, faeries, they're trustworthy sorts."

But talking to Marley always helped Branwyn sort things out and decide on a plan of action.

Although she'd have to lure her out of her bad mood first, and not by starting the conversation with, "So, I talked to a supernatural man today, quite the sexy beast, oh, and how was your lunch with two more of those?"

When she emerged again from her room, she held the original letter from Tarn. It still smelled of the ocean. She crossed to the kitchen table and threw it down, then slung herself into a chair and waited for her roommate to come to her.

"What's that?" said Marley immediately, dropping her steel wool and coming to see. "Oh, that." She sighed and rubbed her water-pruned hands on a towel. "It's probably for the best that he hasn't followed up. Men never keep promises," she added bitterly. "They can't even pretend to get along for one research-focused working lunch."

"Actually..." Branwyn watched Marley from under veiled lashes, then shook her head and changed tactics. "The twins did something big, didn't they? When they broke that chain. Something big for the faeries. Maybe something big for the world."

Marley settled into the other chair. "That's what people keep telling me, even people who won't speak to each other. That the faeries, locked away for aeons, can visit the world now. Visit, but not stay, not while there's two chains of the Covenant remaining."

"Mmm," said Branwyn noncommittally. "Have you seen any?"

Marley shrugged. "I can't tell them apart from the other celestials. I've seen a few of those, here and there, from a distance. I haven't tried to get closer."

"Were they doing anything particularly nefarious? You'd think a whole class of people so bad they were locked away for eternity with no chance for parole would be absolutely terrifying if they got free."

Marley's gaze sharpened, traveling from Branwyn to Tarn's letter and back again. "Nothing notably awful."

"Ah, must not have been faeries, then," said Branwyn crisply, leaning back in her chair. "Murdering angels, maybe."

Marley blew a wisp of hair away from her face. "Maybe. What's going on, Branwyn?"

Branwyn nibbled on her thumbnail a moment and then a whole slew of words she'd scarcely considered came pouring out. "No matter how I look at it, I can't make it come out square, Mar. Either they're people, individuals, and what's been done to them is awful. Not just imprisoned, but forced to aid their jailors. I saw that angel make Tarn attack you." Branwyn ran her hands through her hair. This was the thread she hadn't seen in the tangle, the one that made the tangle move in unexpected ways. "Or they're a single monolithic force, in which case I still find myself wondering about the motives of the child-murdering angels who locked them away." She placed her palm on the letter. "But you know, I'm betting they're individuals. You said you can't distinguish them from the angels and the others. And you practically made that angel cry and beg for forgiveness when you beat him. He felt guilty. Monolithic forces don't feel guilty."

Marley looked down at the letter again. Branwyn's hand was right over the part where Tarn apologized for abducting her. Softly, she said, "Tarn contacted you again, didn't he." It wasn't a question.

Branwyn shrugged, taking her hand away from the letter. "Yes. And I want to find out more about them. I'm *glad* that the twins gave them a little freedom. I want to see what happens. I feel like something has been stolen from us and I don't know if it's a birthright, or a history, or opportunity, or just the truth."

"I don't know much more," Marley said, still quiet. "I can try to find out."

"I mean, wouldn't that be a good idea? Even if they are the worst of the worst, shouldn't we know more about them? It doesn't seem very likely that the two chains are going to last forever when they thought they needed three. And if they're individuals—" She stopped short of finishing the thought.

"I'll look, I said. Corbin has—" Marley stopped, a faint flush rising in her cheeks. "I can get books from somewhere. There must be *something.*"

Branwyn scrutinized Marley, then offered her a faint smile and said fondly, "You and books. Research Girl." She hopped to her feet, energized by her rant. Corbin and Marley weren't even talking, eh? "Well, you read books and I'll go out and kick some ass."

As she went to the door, Marley called, "Hey—be careful. Even if they turn out to not be as bad as the angels, they're tricky."

"So the stories say," said Branwyn lightly. "Being tricky isn't actually a crime, though. Sometimes *I'm* tricky."

"Not just the stories, Bran. Tarn played me and that angel both, despite wearing a magical choke collar so tight he could barely breathe. I can't even imagine what he'll do now that it's loosened up."

"I'll be fine," Branwyn said brightly. "Besides, this is finally something *I* can do."

Marley regarded her doubtfully. "What makes you say that?"

"Because *I* have an invitation."

Senyaza. Publicly, it was a multinational electronics corporation. Once, it had just been a brand name to Branwyn, but now she knew that it was a nest of wizards and the descendants of angels known as nephilim. Or, as Marley had put it, *angels and other things*. They had locations all over the world, but in LA, the main building was Senyaza Titan One.

Apparently they employed plenty of humans, too, doing the mundane work of expanding an electronics empire, and they were a decent employer, as far as multinational corporations went. Marley had investigated that right after discovering their secret, trying to soothe Branwyn's usual dislike of large corporations. She liked doing that kind of thing. It distracted her from thinking about her problem boys.

Branwyn thought about Marley's problem boys for a moment. Zachariah Thorne employed Marley to protect his two wards and clearly wanted more. There was bad blood between him and Corbin Adair, once his protégé. It was, Branwyn assumed, a wizard thing. Well, and a Marley thing, because Corbin had feelings of his own.

Branwyn would have been on Corbin's side, partially because Zachariah was a manipulative jerk, except that it was Corbin who thought being human meant she should focus on staying safe and out of trouble. But she was better at dealing with misguided and protective than arrogant and controlling, even if sometimes it was hard to tell the difference. And it sounded like Marley wasn't talking to Corbin at the moment, and Branwyn was impatient. So here she was, staring up at Senyaza Titan One.

She dragged her feet walking to the entrance, though. It would be so much easier if Corbin didn't work for the entity treating Penny's illness as an experiment, if he didn't belong to them by birth. She'd quite like the guy if he was just Marley's human boyfriend. He was smart and friendly, with a touch of the nerd and an interesting dash of intensity. And he was patient, and he knew how to laugh, and how to listen.

But he wasn't human, and neither were his parents or grandparents. He was a *third-generation* nephil—that seemed to matter quite a lot to him—and he thought of humans as sheep to be protected, or, very occasionally, trained. That made liking him a lot more complicated.

Branwyn forced herself to get moving. There was no point in brooding about it. That never changed anybody's opinion. Instead, she focused on the bright side.

Bright sides: at least he wasn't the kind of corporate drone who thought his employer could do no wrong. He was usually willing to answer her questions, often at far more length than she was interested in. She'd learned that in their brief, disastrous attempt at training her to do more than just use the charms he'd given her. And because he cared about Marley, she had some leverage if he proved reluctant. She was pretty sure that was true even if Marley and Corbin weren't on speaking terms at the moment. It was all a matter of where you applied the force.

From a distance, the lines of the shining steel and glass building twisted as it climbed into the sky, forming a spiral stretching to the heavens. As she approached, Branwyn joined the steady stream of traffic exiting and entering the building. Inside the atrium-style interior, a waterfall tumbled four stories into a terraced pool lined with green and white tiles, and the air smelled fresh and clean. The first three floors of the Senyaza Titan were dedicated to retail space, with an abundance of restaurants, electronics stores, and a cutting-edge theater. Escalators zig-zagged through the center of the atrium, so that those riding could look out over the whole mall and see how much like a glossy magazine spread it was. It wasn't the sort of place Branwyn generally shopped; it was too expensive, too artificial, too shiny. The waterfall was a nice touch, though.

Following the instructions she'd been given, she took an elevator up to the fourth floor, emerging into a place that seemed far more than a floor away from the commercial sparkle below. Here, it was all business: subdued charcoal carpeting and sterile prints featuring muted colors and shapes far too abstract to ever offend anybody on walls above uniform maroon couches. Even though the reception area was an irregular wedge-shape, it still had the feel of a place that had been designed by a committee determined not to make waves. Branwyn could feel the creativity draining out of her as she looked around, and she longed to take a can of spraypaint to the insipid art collection and free her soul.

The security checkpoint that looked like something from an airport helped her squash that impulse, though. After pausing to sneer at the little attribution card under one of the prints, she stopped at the desk fronting the checkpoint and flashed a smile at the suited professional on the other side. "Hi."

His eyes moved to her green hair tied up in a ponytail and her paint-spattered black t-shirt before he said, his voice cool and unfazed, "May I help you?"

"I bet you can. Corbin Adair is expecting me."

The suit frowned, but before he could say anything, a voice from beyond the checkpoint called, "Branwyn!" A moment later, Corbin himself hopped the low barrier attached to the desk and joined the security suit. The wizard was tall and lean, with untidy black hair and deepset dark eyes. He dressed more like a computer geek than something out of a fantasy movie, in new jeans and a grey button-down shirt. He didn't have a beard or anything, which Branwyn felt was rather letting down the side. He could have at least managed a sinister goatee as a concession to professional standards.

"She's my guest," he told the security guard. "I'm just going to take her down to my office."

The guard pursed his lips—maybe he felt the same way about lax professional standards—and checked the tablet in front of him. "Your office?"

Impatience edged Corbin's voice. "Special Investigations and Threats Department. Still." He pulled an ID card out of his pocket and laid it down.

"Ah, yes, you're full-time now. Congratulations, sir." said the guard, who sounded as if he thought somebody somewhere had made a mistake. "Fill this out." He slid the tablet over to Corbin and pulled out a stack of temporary nametags. First he scanned the bar code on a blank nametag, then said, "Over here, miss." She followed him around the desk and stepped through the security scanner. On the other side, he held out an electronic fingerprint scanner.

She balked. "Is this really necessary?"

"Standard guest security, miss."

She turned to Corbin. "Can't we just grab a cup of coffee downstairs?"

He scrawled something on the tablet and slid it behind the counter. "Branwyn, I've already got charms on you that would let me track you anywhere in the world. What's one thumbprint?"

"Yes, but I trust *you*. Okay, that's a lie. But you're a person. You're not a gigantic faceless corporation."

He gave her a pained look, so she sighed and pressed her thumb against the pad. It beeped, and the security guard pulled the nametag off the device and handed it to her.

"Wear this when you're in the building."

"Thank you, Antonio," Corbin said, joining Branwyn on the other side of the security checkpoint. "I hope you remember my promotion for more than five minutes this time."

"Yes, sir," said Antonio impassively.

"What was that about?" Branwyn wondered, not bothering to wait until they were out of earshot.

Corbin shrugged. "Antonio's very good at his job and he doesn't like me very much."

"By 'his job,' you mean 'being obstructionary'? Because, yeah, I agree."

Corbin suppressed a laugh. "His job is to protect the people in the office, and it's very, very hard to get past his gate by force, even if you're a celestial. He has... special talents. I think he's annoyed at me because of the wild goose chase I let Zachariah talk me into." The laughter faded from his voice. "People got hurt and then I got promoted." His gaze went distant, then he shook his head. "He's right, and I'm trying to be patient with him. He used to bounce me on his knee when I was a kid."

Branwyn glanced back over her shoulder at Antonio. "He doesn't look much older than you," she pointed out.

Corbin gave her the same look he'd given the security guard when he played dumb. "Well, he is. Quite a bit older."

Branwyn thought about that, then decided she didn't want to

pursue that line of discussion.

"You never answered my question. Why couldn't we just meet downstairs?"

"Because you said you wanted to talk about the fae. I don't want to talk about them in public yet."

Branwyn snorted. "If anybody overheard us, they'd just think we were talking about a game. Or have I been misinterpreting my brothers' conversations about an alien invasion all this time?"

He shook his head, but didn't say anything else. Branwyn looked at him in mock astonishment. "No lecture? Come on, don't hold it in. Tell me about video games or something."

He rolled his eyes. "Very cute."

He guided her down the hall to an elevator and jabbed the down arrow. The row of buttons inside had far more downstairs floors than Branwyn expected, going all the way down to S13. But Corbin chose S4, then leaned against the mirrored wall, crossed his arms, and stared at her, his eyebrows drawn together. "How's Marley?"

"No idea. She vanished into the Brazilian wilderness with nothing but her cellphone. Guess you'll have to call her." She gave him a sweet smile.

He scowled. "Never mind." The elevator chimed as the doors slid open. The hall they emerged into had a slightly more lived-in look than the reception area above, with framed horror movie posters on the walls. Some of them were signed. He led her past a darkened lounge and into a large room equipped with four ancient, heavy wooden desks pitted with damage and incongruous with the computers perched on top. There was also a long folding table overflowing with an assortment of technological junk and a dozen or so chairs of various styles, including three different swivel types and a Queen Anne wooden one with torn burgundy upholstery. The office was empty except for a single man sitting at one of the desks, playing a video game of the monster-shooting variety.

"We're still short-staffed. That's Simon." Corbin threw himself into a chair and glared at her as if she was a puzzle he was trying to crack.

Simon paused his game and swiveled around. He had light brown hair and matching eyes, with an Asian cast to his feature, and he looked about the same age as Corbin. After swigging from a bottle on the desk, he said, in a rich British accent, "This isn't your apprentice girl, is it? Her hair seems more... seaweedy... than I remember."

"No," said Corbin bluntly, then added, "She's the friend."

"The unteachable one," Branwyn added. "I don't have the aptitude. No, I'm just an innocent and helpless bystander. You know, a human."

Simon narrowed his eyes at her with an unfriendly, assessing expression much like Tarn's pet goblin, but then turned back to his game and back to ignoring them.

"So where is everybody? Special investigating or threatening?"

"Recuperating. Sometimes it takes more than a month to recover from being practically dead." Corbin spun in his chair to inspect the table. It was covered with various kinds of hardware, and he picked up an LCD screen and started fidgeting with it.

"It's been a bad month," added Simon, still playing his game. Something exploded on his screen and he cursed under his breath. "Why is she here, Corbin?"

"She wanted to talk about the fae and I've got something breakable in progress at my lab."

Branwyn smiled and took her cue. She started with the basics. "Yeah, so they were locked away, and then the apocalypse twins did something, and now they're supposedly not locked away so much. True or false?" The "apocalypse twins" were Zachariah's preschooler wards. Apparently nephilim were especially dangerous when young, and these two were more of a handful than most. Their uncle paid Marley a *lot* for looking after them.

Corbin scowled. "First of all, they're not 'the apocalypse twins' and you're not helping by calling them that. Otherwise... basically true."

"Why hasn't anybody noticed a bunch of faeries running through the streets, then?" Branwyn sat on the Queen Anne chair.

"You've met them. Would you notice?"

Branwyn's breath hissed between her teeth. "Would I notice them? Yeah... but not as faeries. Not unless they were dressed up as pixies."

"There you go then. Some of them are already working their particular form of magic on the world, but they're still limited in how long they can stay out, and when they're drawn back behind the curtain, the magic goes with them."

Branwyn gave him an encouraging nod and squirmed, getting comfortable "Ah, the good stuff. Do go on. What *is* their magic? Do the consequences vanish when the magic does?"

"It's big and complicated, pet. Are you sure you want to fill your innocent bystander head with things like that?" Simon addressed his screen again.

Something of Branwyn's suppressed flare of temper must have showed on her face, because Corbin said quickly, "Simon, you're going to get cut again, and when you sober up, I'm not even going to explain why."

Simon only chuckled, and Corbin added, "Sorry. Ignore him. Where were we? Right. As well as celestial magic, the faeries use their own form of magic, which involves manipulating the matter of the world both directly and via the shadows cast on the Backworld." Branwyn wondered if Corbin was reciting directly from a memorized book. Her brother Howl memorized books and talked like that sometimes. She probably ought to introduce them.

Corbin kept going. "It's not something I've really had a chance to study yet. But I know that before last month, each faerie Duchy could only slip one member past the curtain once a year. When their time was up, they were drawn back through the curtain and any magic they worked vanished. You've heard stories of fairy gold and how it turned to leaves upon the dawn? Well, now that part of the barrier has been broken, more of them can come out for longer periods of time. But they're still ultimately drawn back in again."

Branwyn thought about what Tarn had said. It sounded like what little he'd told her had been the truth. How unexpected! "So things they change magically don't stay changed. Good to know. I'll make sure to spend any fairy money quickly." She paused, thinking more about Penny than fairy gold, then added, "Just my little joke. How long can they stay out now?"

Corbin frowned at her attempt at humor. "No idea. I think it depends on the Courts. There's faerie Dukes and faerie Queens and the power is split somehow. I think that the faerie Queens serve as power converters. But even that's just a hunch." Corbin shrugged. "Up until recently, there was just no reason to prioritize studying them."

Scratching her nose, Branwyn asked, "How dangerous are they now that they're here sometimes? Are they a capital-T Threat?"

He gave her an irritated look. "They're so dangerous that the angels and the demons actually cooperated to keep them out of the affairs of Creation and restrict their access to the Sea of Dreams."

Branwyn looked around at the nearly empty office. "What, each and every one of them? You and your monster-hunter boys are going to have your hands full, then. When they all get back from vacation, I mean."

Corbin ran his hand through his hair. "Senyaza is officially observing the situation for now. The world isn't the same as it was when they were first locked away."

Branwyn tilted her head, then brushed a green tendril of hair away from her face. "How long have they been in the penalty box?"

"Thousands of years," Corbin said flatly.

Branwyn tried to imagine being imprisoned for thousands of years and winced. Then she moved on to the next question in her mental list. "Have—"

Corbin interrupted her, his eyes hard. "Branwyn, what are you planning? You don't ask questions like this unless you're plotting something."

"Hey, innocent bystander here. I've got all these cute little charms you gave me. How could I be more?" She matched his stare until he cursed and looked away. Then she stretched out her legs, resting them on a red swivel chair, "Come on, just a few more answers, Corbin."

He ground his palms into his forehead, then made a frustrated gesture with his hand that she chose to interpret as "Please continue", so she did. "Have you ever read anything about humans learning magic from faeries?"

"No," Corbin said, so fast she was sure he didn't even bother to think about the question. It was hurtful, really. "I mostly hear about humans being seduced and destroyed by them. Or hunted down like animals. Or kept in menageries. Nice little prisons filled with everything they think their pets want."

"Ooh, nasty. How very human. Do they lie?"

More slowly, Corbin said, "As much as any celestial, most of the time. More, maybe. But their rulers, the Dukes and Queens, can't lie within their faerie realms. They're bound too closely together."

Branwyn gave Corbin a dazzling smile and swung her legs down. "Excellent. Thank you very much. I shall be sure to speak kindly of you to others."

"Branwyn, do me a favor and don't do anything stupid."

Simon snorted at his screen. Branwyn ignored him blithely. "You *said* you could track me down anywhere. And you gave me that handy beacon charm, the one for lost children, right? How much trouble could I get into?"

Corbin pressed his hand against his head again. "Oh my God, I can't believe you just said that."

Branwyn leaned over and patted his shoulder. "Don't worry. Marley knows me. If anything happens to me, she'll know who to blame, and it won't be you." She considered. "Or herself."

In a strangled voice, Corbin said, "*What* are you going to *do*?"

Branwyn hesitated, then said, "I'm just going to talk to Tarn again. Relax. Or worry, if you want. Use it as an excuse to call Marley, I don't mind."

"'Talk'," snickered Simon.

Corbin stared at her for a long moment, then turned his attention to the screen he'd dropped, as if changing the channel. His voice chilly, he said, "Use your eyes, and use the Sight, and stay out of the Backworld as much as possible."

"But you said Tarn couldn't lie in the Backworld—"

His voice cut over hers. "He can't. But *you* can't run. Your memory for bad situations is about as good as Marley's."

Branwyn took a deep breath and leaned forward, ready to launch into an aggressive defense, but a hand took her elbow and hefted her to her feet. "Easy now, girlie," Simon warned.

She pulled herself away from the whiff of alcohol. "Keep your hands off me," she said, far more polite than she could have been.

"Fair enough. But I'm thinking that it's probably high time for you to be heading out, eh?" Simon grinned at her.

Branwyn looked at Corbin, who didn't bother looking at her. He glowered at his gadget, as if he couldn't make it work the way he wanted it to.

"Yeah, sure. See you around, Corbin. Thanks for the information." Then, because she couldn't resist, she added, "I'll tell Marley you asked after her."

His baleful gaze slid over to her. "You're welcome. And don't bother about Marley. It doesn't matter."

"And out we go!" said Simon, with the cheeriness of a preschool teacher. He moved his hands as if to guide Branwyn again, pulled them back, then flapped them like she was a wayward cat he was shooing ahead. Branwyn gave him a disdainful look, then left the office.

To her surprise, Simon followed, falling into step beside her. In a more normal voice, he said, "Sorry about that. Got a sense for these things and you two looked like you were heading for a knock-down fight. Normally I'd just place my bets, but it didn't seem like it would pay out. He's been moody as hell since meeting this girl."

Branwyn eyed him, re-evaluating her first impressions. "A sense? Like a charm or whatever?"

"Nah. You hang around enough blood-hungry warriors, you start to learn the signs."

Branwyn laughed despite herself. Blood-hungry warriors. She liked the sound of that.

"So what are you?" Simon went on. "Not a wizard. Not a groupie, I think. And certainly not an innocent bystander."

"*Groupie?*" Branwyn's irritation with the man returned full force. "What the hell made you think that?"

Simon shrugged. "You want to get up close and personal with the fae. And you've already got the scent of monster in your hair."

Branwyn recoiled. "What are you talking about?"

Simon's bloodshot eyes crinkled. "Maybe not on your actual hair, style of thing. But you've got the whiff of kaiju, a big monster, all over you. There's been one very near you for a few weeks at least. Haven't you noticed?"

"Why didn't Corbin say anything?" Branwyn demanded.

"Oh, well, Corbin's a good kid. Owe him my life, as a matter of fact. But he's what, thirty? I've been in this business for at least that long. A lot of skills you just pick up with time."

-four-

Branwyn sat at the table in her dining nook, watching Marley get ready to go to dinner with Zachariah and the twins. She did wonder how Zachariah had managed preserve diplomatic relations when Corbin hadn't. Probably through underhanded means.

It was nice to see Marley getting out of the apartment more, and the kids were adorable, but Zachariah was *not* her idea of a good date. He knew what he wanted and he didn't seem to have any scruples when it came to going after it. This was not, Branwyn felt, a good tactic when pursuing a relationship. No, she couldn't approve. The best she could do was not make a big deal about it, and because it was important to Marley, she did her best.

She focused on her own plans for the evening instead.

She could fit what she knew about the various celestial factions on a Post-it note. The semi-mortal nephilim, with their magic and their big corporation and, most importantly, her two best friends, had interested her much more. She knew the celestials included angels and demons and faeries and the kaiju—maybe even more she didn't know about. It seemed like pop culture existed solely to influence her ideas about the first three.

More specifically, she knew an angel had hurt Penny, tried to kill Marley, and that the faeries had been imprisoned, probably unfairly. She knew they all lived a very long time, maybe couldn't even die as she understood the concept. But the kaiju were only ever described as "monsters," and the only one she'd met had looked very much like a man.

As Branwyn considered him, Marley paused while checking her makeup and frowned at her in the reflection. It wasn't a good frown, a "reconsidering her relationship choices" frown. It was the kind of frown she frowned when she suspected Branwyn was about to misbehave. Marley's personal brand of nephil magic let her see if somebody was contemplating a dangerous course of action, which was sometimes damned inconvenient, but made her a very reliable babysitter.

Branwyn met her gaze and thought hard about the nice bath she was going to take once Marley was gone. Then, because that probably wasn't good enough, she added, "Corbin asked about you when I saw him today."

Marley's mouth tightened. "He thinks it should be so simple. He doesn't know Zachariah."

Judiciously, Branwyn said, "I think he *does* know Zachariah and that's why he's worried."

Turning away from the mirror, Marley said, "I can't just blow Zachariah off. I made a promise to the kids. I can't be there for them and just ignore their guardian."

"You could if he'd let you. That he's not willing to back off and let you figure out what you want makes him an encroaching, controlling bastard, Marley."

Marley sighed. "I know. It's complicated." She scooped up her purse. "What did you tell Corbin?"

"I told him to call you himself."

"Hah. And he hasn't. They could *both* make it easier. The kids are really enough of a handful, you know?"

Branwyn, eldest of seven, assured her she knew.

After she was gone, Branwyn took her bath, mostly to get it out of the way, but she found herself paying special attention to lathering up her hair. Simon had said the "scent" was metaphorical and thus probably not something she could wash off, but she still tried her damnedest. She wondered if he really had been drunk, or imagining things, or just screwing with her.

Somehow, she doubted it.

In the hall, she stopped and looked at a photo of herself, Penny, and Marley that hung on the wall. It was from their high school graduation, in their street clothes but with the tasseled caps still on. Branwyn was between Marley and Penny, and all three of them were smiling, each in their own way. Marley smiled with her eyes mostly, her mouth only curving slightly; it was too used to a pensive frown. Branwyn was too familiar with her own grin to notice it, but she spent a moment looking at Penny's smile. Penny could turn her smile off and on like a light switch, whenever it was appropriate, but Branwyn remembered Penny laughing all day at graduation, overcome with giddiness that she'd made it through high school without disappointing her parents too much.

Branwyn brushed her finger over the picture glass. There was still so much to come for that Penny: college, trips to Europe, an ongoing flirtation with fashion and design and a neverending pursuit of her own identity. Branwyn had never felt as adrift as Penny sometimes seemed to. But she firmly believed everybody found their place eventually. Before, she'd been willing to help Penny find hers. Now she was *determined*.

She paced out to the living room. The Backworld was everywhere, on the other side of a supernatural curtain. Anybody with the power and the skill could be watching from a space just beyond everything she could touch. Moving past the curtain could be a challenge, but being a supernatural peeping Tom didn't seem to take a whole lot of talent. It wasn't the sort of thing that seemed to bother Marley, but the idea creeped Branwyn out.

"Severin? Are you watching me?" She called out the human name of the kaiju she'd met briefly. After a few moments of standing still, listening to the silence while her skin prickled, she swore at herself. Taking a bottle of whiskey from the cupboard, she poured out two tumblers and set one of them down on the table. After taking a big gulp from her own, she cast her mind back to their first meeting. Marley had called him by his human name, too, and he hadn't responded. But Corbin had called him something else.

"Whispering Dark?" The words sank into the stillness of the room, absorbed by the secondhand furniture and all the shelves of Marley's books. It was foolishness. Angry at herself for believing, even for a moment, Branwyn drained the rest of her glass. She was human. Corbin had called and he'd shown up, but what did *she* have other than a burning desire to improve herself?

"A few more like that and you could hallucinate me." A man sat at the table. He had dark brown hair that just reached his collar and a pleasantly attractive face, the kind that always faintly reminded you of somebody seen on TV that one time. He was clean-shaven, with a chiseled jawline and a straight nose and his eyes were—

His eyes were nightmares. Meeting his gaze made Branwyn want to gag and scrub out her brain. If she were to draw him, she'd tear holes in the paper rather than try to channel that brief glimpse. She hadn't remembered this. She hadn't ever had a chance to look into his eyes before.

He smirked, and she realized her fingers were tangled into her hair, her palms pressing hard on her temples. Her glass was on the carpet at her feet, the few remaining drops spilling out.

Picking up the glass she'd set out for him, he sniffed the contents. "You certainly don't have the power to craft an *attractive* invitation like the raven boy did, even if you do share his impatience. If I hadn't been passing through the neighborhood, you'd still be standing here, all alone, begging silence to speak to you. Praying, one might say." He sipped the whiskey. "That *would* be embarrassing for you."

Branwyn pulled her hands away from her head and smoothed them against her jeans. He watched in apparent interest. "Would you like a small, still voice inside?"

I can do that. The silent voice crawled up her spine.

"No! Don't..." The plea escaped before she could stop it.

He put down the glass and stood up. He wasn't particularly large, and nowhere near as tall as Tarn, but the room was suddenly much too small. "Oh, but I want to. Very much." His voice was soft, almost silky.

Branwyn forced herself to think, despite the fear nibbling at the edges of her mind. She'd asked him here. She'd had a reason. Her fear was in the way.

"Look at you, cupcake. You've been fitted up with all the latest pet-management charms from the raven boy. You've even got a call for help installed." He stretched out one hand and traced her outline from two yards away, just as Tarn had done before. His words reignited the tiniest flare of resentment, a flame licking through the fear. "But you know that by the time he got here, there'd be nothing recognizable left of you." It was a promise, not a question. He thought for a moment. "Actually, if you want to call him, I'd wait until he was here. That would be more fun."

"Why would I call for help? I invited you here." There was bravado in the words, but truth as well, and it helped steady Branwyn against the undertow of terror.

"And why would you do something like that? You're not suicidal yet." He winked and grinned. "I can tell these things."

"If you'd wanted to hurt me, wouldn't you have done that by now? I know you've been watching me from the Backworld. Or do you normally require an invitation before you get involved?"

He looked at her for a long moment, then reclaimed his chair and glass. "Every invitation I need is contained in what you are."

Branwyn let herself breathe for a moment before she said, "So why have you been hanging around, then?"

Severin the kaiju settled back, swirling the amber liquid. "I'm protecting you, of course."

"I find that hard to believe," she observed. "But do go on."

"Oh, I am. But the faeries keep trying to get to you, all the same." He smiled. "Tarn's little pets."

Branwyn crouched to pick up her dropped glass, all nonchalant. *Faerie is full of threats,* Tarn had said. "What are you doing to them?"

"You don't need me to answer that, cupcake. You already know." He looked her over like she was a menu. "You're serving as tender, delicious faerie bait. As you may imagine, this is very helpful when you're trying to stem the faerie menace. All I have to do is stay near you, and they come right to me."

Bait, Branwyn thought, and then *Cupcake!* She found herself longing for a crowbar, or her favorite hammer. Something to wrap her fingers around. Something she could use as a weapon, if she had to.

"No, you don't want a weapon," said Severin calmly. "If you had one, you'd be tempted to use it, and while you're interesting, cupcake, you're not nearly interesting enough to bleed for."

"Stay out of my thoughts," said Branwyn firmly, like she was telling a nosy child to stay out of her room. Just like that.

He shrugged. "Don't think, then." He drained his glass.

"Anyhow, you aren't keeping the faeries away from me; I spoke to Tarn today."

"I know. I got bored with the paper shadows. And it occurred to me that you could be even *more* helpful that way. Be my inside man, kind of thing." He raised his eyebrows encouragingly.

"Woman," said Branwyn automatically, then said, "What? I mean—*what*? Are you actually asking me to help you capture and—" She fell silent, staring at him.

"Murder," he supplied helpfully. "Well, kill, anyhow. I don't know if it qualifies as *murder*. It's not like it's permanent. At the moment."

"If you're so hot on this, why didn't you just show up while I was visiting Tarn?" she demanded.

"Oh, you know how it is. All right, *you* don't, cupcake. But in the heart of a faerie realm, invitations do matter. At least for me. It's Tarn's *special* place. He's a bit more powerful there." His glass was full again. So was Branwyn's.

She put the glass down on an end table. "Well, don't look for me to invite you. And I'd appreciate it if you'd stop preying on Tarn's messengers."

Severin shrugged. "I'm no worse than they are."

"This I also have trouble believing," she said flatly.

"I don't know why. The angels created the Covenant to imprison the fae long before the Hush was put in place to inhibit the rest of us."

"Tarn isn't trying to co-opt me into a murder-for-fun scheme," Branwyn pointed out.

"Oh, that's probably true." He raised his glass in a toast to her. "They *would* have a problem with that. I mean, once you kill a human, they're much harder to play with. There's so much else that can be done before death, and the fae like to do *all* of it."

Branwyn slammed the door of her car and glared up at her family home, silhouetted against the setting sun. It hadn't been a good day and she was prepared for the faerie in the attic to make it worse. The conversation with Severin had lingered with her all day through work, like a bad hangover. She'd jumped each time the bell over the garage office had chimed, and she couldn't stop thinking about what he'd said about the faeries and about her. She kept remembering his eyes, too, as much as she tried not to. He was a monster, he practically admitted it, and he wasn't any more trustworthy than the faeries, or Senyaza, for that matter.

Just as she'd finally started to listen to her own lectures on not brooding, a lady had tried to corner her at the garage where she worked, ostensibly making small talk while having her oil changed. And by "lady," Branwyn meant "tabloid reporter." She'd found out about Penny's hospitalization and Branwyn's friendship with her, and she wanted an exclusive scoop about what had happened to the daughter of the famous producer couple Viviana and Tomas Karzan. At first she'd expected Branwyn to gossip freely, and then she'd expected revealing her identity to pry open those gossip channels. Branwyn had locked her in the garage lobby, tossed to keys to José, and gone off to do some paint touch-ups, but the encounter had soured what was left of her day.

It wasn't the presence of the reporter; they showed up sometimes around Penny, and always had. It was the idea that Penny, comatose, was reduced to a minor headline. Penny hadn't minded talking to them, but Branwyn didn't think she'd like this, especially not *these* stories. The tabloids liked the "drugs" angle. But it wasn't any better than what had actually happened.

Branwyn didn't like to think about what had ultimately taken Penny down. Because that was one thing Corbin had been very clear about: to commune so closely with a celestial that one's soul was damaged, one had to voluntarily *let them in.* And now Penny was dying. If nobody did anything, she'd be that minor headline, plus some records in a Senyaza database. And nobody was *going* to do anything, just because they couldn't find anything in their "literature" to do and they wouldn't look beyond that. She *had* to learn more about faeries and their magic, not just for herself, but for Penny.

She slammed the house door, too. Her grandfather, the carpenter, would not have approved, but it warned everybody inside to stay out of her way. She wanted to find Tarn without losing her temper at anybody else.

A head poked into the hall from the living room. It was Jaimie, her stepfather. "It's Branwyn," he reported back over his shoulder. "Come see this, Branwyn. It's pretty cool."

Branwyn hesitated. The smell of sizzling onions and spices wafted through the air. She could hear the low murmuring of a video and the rest of the house was quiet. Whatever it was had pulled all of her family in already, interrupting dinner preparations.

Curiosity overcame her temper and she headed into the living room. Most of her family was clustered around a large laptop on the back table. Her mother, Holly, looked up and then moved to give her a one-armed hug. "Morgan caught this on his phone when he was downtown. Some kind of street performer."

"I want to figure out how he's doing it," said Howl, over their youngest sister's impressed *ooh*.

Branwyn frowned. That was the tone of voice Howl used when he was bothered about something.

"I want one, Mom. Can we go down there? Maybe he's still there." Meredith changed her focus almost immediately to her father, who wasn't as good at resisting her wheedling. "Dad?"

"I'm sure he'll be around again," said Holly. "Don't pester your father, please."

Branwyn stopped trying to peer over heads and shoved closer, bumping Morgan out of the way and sidling past her mother until she was standing directly behind Howl, who sat in the operator's chair.

On the screen, a tall, attractive man with long blond hair stood in a cluster of people. "Who's next?" he asked, his softly accented words carrying over the murmur of the crowd. He noticed the camera and smiled at it before a teenage girl stepped forward.

"Me, please." She was breathless and blushing. She held out her hand.

The man's mouth quirked, and he took her hand and kissed the back of her fingers. His lips lingered against her skin. Then vivid lines traced their way up her wrist and color bloomed inside the lines; when he finally removed his mouth, there was a vivid tattoo of a long-stemmed rose running up her forearm.

"I trust that didn't hurt?" asked the artist.

The girl stared at him, then gave a faint, forced laugh. "It kind of tickled. How—how long will it last?"

He shrugged. "Perhaps a day. Perhaps a month." He smiled again, slow and sexy. "Maybe it will go away when you next wash. It's a surprise."

The girl burbled thanks, and another woman, this one older, stepped forward to elbow her out of the way. "Could you do pixie wings for me? On my shoulders?" She turned to present the artist with a tanned expanse of skin framed by a backless tank top.

The artist laughed. "Oh yes." The camera refocused as Morgan moved to get a better angle. This time, the artist dragged his finger in a rough triangle across her left shoulder and again, color and lines flowed out in a delicate filigree, forming the shape of a ragged-edged butterfly wing.

After he finished the first shoulder and moved to the second, Howl said, "Maybe I'll take Meredith down there tomorrow and see if I can spot the trick."

"Could they be plants? Were there professional cameras around?" asked Jaimie.

"I didn't see anything bigger than a pocket camera," said Morgan. "I should have asked one of those girls for a closer look."

"Even if they were audience plants, how is it being done?" Howl sounded irritated by his own question. "Some kind of invisible ink reacting to something on his finger?"

"Who cares?" retorted Meredith. "It's awesome. I wonder if they really last as long as he says."

Branwyn watched the rest of the video, her mouth set in a tight line. She'd thought she was glad that the faeries had won a little freedom, but seeing magic performed publicly and casually made her uncomfortable. It was a symbol that the secrets of the world were being revealed, but it was also a symbol that those secrets existed at all. And it was a change she wasn't quite ready for. She really didn't want to be one of the giggling girls in the audience, watching passively as the world changed around them.

The video ended before the performance did, when Morgan was tugged away by a school friend, and when it did, her gathered family started to disperse. Her mother caught her hand, though. "You didn't like the video, Branwyn?" She smiled. "If real tattoos were that painless, I'd get one myself."

"They sell temporary tattoos at the store, Mom," Branwyn said absently.

"Not the one I want," said Holly, with a fond glance at her husband. "But tell me why the video made you so grumpy. Do you know something about the technique?"

"I might," Branwyn replied. "But it's just a guess," she added quickly, but not quickly enough. Howl met her gaze.

"Tell us," encouraged Holly, adding, "Did you come for dinner?"

"It's not that I know the technique, just that I thought I recognized the artist. And I'm not in the mood for dinner. I just came by to get something out of the attic."

Howl's gaze sharpened and she gave him a quelling look before kissing her mother on the cheek. "I'll come over for a meal this weekend. I'll bring Marley, too." Then she pulled away and ducked out of the room before anybody else could grab her. She made it all the way up to the attic stairs before Howl caught up with her.

"Branwyn, what's going on?"

"Don't be a pest, Howl," she said hopelessly and bounded up the stairs. He climbed up behind her, closing within two steps. "Hey, don't crowd me."

"You vanished yesterday," he said grimly. "You're going to vanish again and I want to see how you do it."

"I'm just checking on the ghost." Inspiration struck. "I'm also working on an art project behind the small door. It's a secret. You know, private?"

But little brothers never stopped being little brothers, even when they were in college. "You're lying. I *looked*, Branwyn. I'm not an idiot. You vanished and I want to know how."

Branwyn scowled, until it occurred to her that having a lookout could be useful. And with Rhianna, her closest sister, elsewhere, Howl was the next best choice. Unlike her younger siblings, Howl would *listen* to her warnings. He always listened, even if he'd learned to not always *believe* his sisters, and he was cartoonishly cautious. And he could help keep Brynn and her planned ghost documentary out of her way. Of course, the very act of explaining could be problematic and tedious.

Oh well. She could borrow a trick from Marley, who had let her draw her own conclusions at first.

"What do you think is going on?"

"A hidden door?" His hesitation told her that he'd investigated that possibility already. "Those sounds have to be coming from somewhere. I just can't think *where*."

"They are. Yeah, there's a door. But not of wood. It goes somewhere else. Somewhere not here. And I don't know the science, so don't go asking me how. And no, you can't come through with me. But you can watch me go through, if you like. Maybe you can figure something useful out. You can definitely keep Brynn and the other kids from getting involved."

Howl nodded, accepting Branwyn's authority with the resignation of a lifetime of dealing with overbearing older sisters. "What's on the other side?"

"Another world, I think." She watched him blink and narrow his eyes. "Don't believe me. I don't mind. But you know I could come up with a better story if I wanted to trick you."

"You certainly have before," he grumbled. "If you don't want me to go through, how will you prove it?"

"I hope I won't have to. Look, Howl, you know that guy on the video? There's other stuff like that going on. And I think more is coming. Something happened recently and because of it, the world is changing. Street performers who can create body art without using paint are just the beginning."

Uneasily, Howl asked, "The beginning of *what*?"

"I'll find out. And when I do, I'll give you a full report."

"Yeah, right," he said, and she grinned at him.

"Trust me. It's easier this way. You don't want to go getting in trouble. You've got college and everything."

"It'll happen anyhow," he said bitterly. "It's *you*."

"Well, maybe you and me, we can keep it spreading to anybody else." She reached up and ruffled his hair.

"And you won't tell me anything?"

"Watch, instead." And if push came to shove, if she ever had to prove something to Howl, she had ways to do that, too. Marley hadn't had that option at first, and Branwyn didn't blame her for choosing the vague path. Howl, faced with the utterly inexplicable right off the bat, would be easier to convince than Branwyn would have been.

She bounded up the rest of the staircase, Howl close behind. It was going to be really embarrassing if the silver courtkey didn't open the door, she thought.

Fortunately, it did. She waved her arm grandly, making a show of displaying the scene on the other side of the door and how it looked almost exactly as expected. "I'm going to go through the door. When I do, you won't see me on the other side. Now, watch close!" She started crawling through, and only as she felt the curtain part around her did she realize she had nothing but the word of a faerie about where she was going to end up.

-five-

Once again, Branwyn felt the floorboards soften into thick carpets as the wisps of curtain brushed against her face. The light was brighter than she expected, but when she stood up, she recognized Tarn's court. This time she could see clearly the faeries dozing in the corners of the room, and make out the subtle, shimmering patterns of the wall hangings.

Tarn lounged in his chair, reading Penny's favorite tabloid. He rattled the paper. "Do I look like a Taurus to you?"

Branwyn snorted. "I have no idea. Are you?"

"It seems plausible." He turned a page. "Now, Leo, I can get behind."

Branwyn thought of three different questions about celestial horoscopes and then decided they were all distractions. "There's a New Age bookstore a couple of miles from here. Near where I work, in fact. Why don't you move the door there instead? I'm sure you'd be very, uh, welcome. Whatever my Gran-gran believed, they believe about ten times as much."

Tarn folded the paper and looked at her. "But I like it here. I can hear your family down below. They make charming neighbors. Are your younger brothers twins?"

"Everybody makes that mistake." She moved across the piled carpets, watching the way the pattern changed as she stepped on it.

Then she looked up at Tarn. He met her gaze calmly. One of his eyes was walnut brown and the other a forest green. They were striking, but they were just eyes, with a faint tracery of lines around them, and the thick lashes of a newborn baby. Just eyes, unlike the monster's.

Branwyn wondered if he actually knew about Severin's campaign, then decided that if he didn't, she wasn't going to just tell him. Information was all she had right now. Besides, she didn't really like that he was eavesdropping on her family.

He leaned back in his chair, hooking one leg over the arm, as if waiting for something.

She said, "I think I saw one of your friends today. Pretty boy painting pictures on teenagers with just his finger?"

"Is that what you came here for? Real estate recommendations and social gossip?" He raised the tabloid. "It's not your specialty. By the way, how is your friend Penny?"

"Unconscious."

"Just like Sleeping Beauty. A pity." He opened the magazine again.

Branwyn persisted. "So what Courts are the faeries who *are* able to get out part of? Does that affect their magic?"

Tarn flipped back a few pages, as if the answer was in the tabloid. "Oh yes. In your region, most of them are part of a Duchy known as Nightwell, bound to Air and Stone. I believe Nightwell aspires to be the first truly urban fae." Though his voice remained light and neutral, his mouth twisted scornfully.

"Not a fan of the idea, I take it?" Branwyn drew closer to the throne, intrigued by the hint of faerie drama.

"The idea is a lovely one, and inevitable. Your modern cities are something new, with their steel and concrete jungles and all the plastics and the warrens above and below. But Nightwell's claim is... distasteful."

"Why?" Branwyn stopped near the foot of the throne.

"Because I want the urban regions for my own people, silly girl." He swung his foot down and gave Branwyn a look that was equal parts amusement and annoyance. "Faerie politics aren't your specialty, either."

Branwyn huffed. "Fine. Let's talk about my art instead, and what you'd like to pay for it."

"Excellent." Suddenly, he was standing before her, so close she could smell the scent of ocean and pomegranates that clung to him. He was *very* tall. "Let me escort you to your studio." He offered her his arm, which she ignored as a matter of habit. So he took her hand instead, wrapping long, warm fingers around her palm and murmuring, "Sometimes my reasons aren't what you think, Branwyn."

With a tug, the room changed around them, like tiny blocks falling away as new blocks grew underneath. She squeezed his hand despite herself, suddenly nervous about what would happen if she let go.

As the room finished growing around her, she recognized it. It was the stone chamber she'd been locked in when she'd first met Tarn, only weeks ago. It had a brick forge and a tall workbench and a tool rack and a materials cabinet and almost everything she'd ever want to craft the strange yet functional items she sold as art. And the forge was still hot, and the stock she'd inspected before choosing an iron bar during her captivity was still scattered on the workbench.

Branwyn pulled away from Tarn. "Did you make this room or bring us to it?"

"Both. I pulled it out of Underlight the first time you visited me. It remains." He picked up a bronze bar and turned it over, examining it idly.

"Why hasn't the fuel in the forge burned out?"

He smiled at her. "Time is different here. This room was made for you, and it's been waiting for you."

She inspected the heavy door they hadn't arrived through, the door that had once locked her in. He saw her look and said, "Your key will lock or unlock the door as you choose. It is your room."

"Am I the only person here who even uses doors? Do you all whoosh around like we just did?"

He laughed. "No. This is *my* realm. Most of my people learn the paths, just as you eventually will."

"Right." Branwyn refocused. "So tell me if all this blunt talk offends you, but my takeaway from our earlier chat was that you could teach me magic in exchange for my services. Special magic, magic mostly unknown. How does that work?"

"I can teach you to manipulate the raw material of the Backworld, the very stuff Faerie is built from." He reached out a hand to an empty slot on the cabinet and pulled a bar of silver stock out of nothingness.

Then, holding the bar in one hand, he stroked it with his fingers. It curled around itself, as if reaching for his touch. Slowly, it took on the form of a flower, which then became a woman. The little statue stretched. Then Tarn blew on it and it vanished back into nothingness.

"Very nice," said Branwyn dryly. "Are you sure you want me? I have to rely on chisels and molds and fire."

He glanced at her, his gaze appraising. "Are you jealous? I said I would teach you to work as I can."

"What good is it outside the Backworld? Can things I make from dreams and wishing in Faerie last on the other side of the curtain?"

"Not at first," he said slowly. "Maybe never. That depends on you. But there are other benefits. You mentioned a personage earlier, spinning glamour onto children. That is one Earthside manifestation of what we do here. But it comes from our nature, tied as it is to the underside of Creation. In humans, understanding the foundations of the world gives different abilities. The bones of the Earth yearn to be touched by you. They are so often deaf to all but the song of fire, but when you have shaped their dreams, they learn to hear your voice."

"Penny's the one who reads poetry. She reads tabloids, too," commented Branwyn. And then she hesitated. His answer had felt honest, more honest than it needed to be.

Tarn looked at her, steadily, patiently, and she sighed. "I'm sorry. It's not that I'm not interested. I am. But dreams and metaphysics don't mesh well with iron and steel and titanium. I'm still not comfortable with... magic. And Corbin talks about it like it's a science, sometimes." She gave Tarn a hopeful glance.

Gravely, he said, "The way mortals work with the Geometry *is* a science. It is often predictable, usually quantifiable, reproducible. You can learn it from books and it rarely relies on *feel*. Did Corbin tell you the precise aptitude you lacked?"

"Other than a long lifespan? I didn't press him on it. It wasn't a fun conversation."

"If you were to ask me, I would say *patience*. Crafting charms and effects through the Geometry requires research and experimentation and slow, methodical layering of lines."

"Hey, you know what? Still not a fun conversation. Tell me how this is relevant?"

He smiled again, and Branwyn realized her attitude only amused him. She didn't like it. When he reached out for her hand, she pulled away. He said, as if talking to a child, "I can't describe how to touch and call forth the stuff of Faerie. But I can show you how it feels." He turned his hand palm up and waited.

Branwyn took a deep breath. She was as skittish as a stray cat and she knew it. She didn't like the thought of all this magic, didn't like the idea of everything she knew being just a thin layer of gold leaf over the truth. She didn't like how it had hurt Penny. But she liked the idea of ignoring the truth less. She had to learn to accept it, and if she wanted to make a difference, wanted to not be left behind, wanted to find a way to save Penny, she had to learn to work with it. Tarn was not trustworthy, but he seemed to be making an effort to be patient with her.

She thought, randomly, about Severin, telling her she was interesting, but not interesting enough to bleed for. Then she put her hand in Tarn's. She was here. She might as well see what he was talking about.

He took her hand, lacing his fingers through hers from behind, and reached out. His hand, and hers, slipped through an invisible curtain. She could still see it, but it didn't seem part of her anymore.

"Close your eyes," ordered Tarn. "Your eyes will try to make a science of it. Your eyes will lie to you. Listen to your hand instead."

She did so. Layers of delicate fabric draped around her hand. It was as if when she arrived here, she'd stopped halfway through the veils and now Tarn was taking her all the way to the other side. Her fingertips tingled and her thumb grew hot. Tarn bent his fingers, and hers, and the unseen texture crumpled against her palm. It was cold, and sharp points pricked her skin.

"What is it?" he asked her.

"Iron ore?"

"Ah. A good start." He pulled both their hands back into visibility, and Branwyn was clutching a rough lump of rock.

"Great," said Branwyn. "How does this help me? I mean, there's a shelf of ingots right there."

He was amused again. "Baby steps, Branwyn. Once you can touch the foundations alone, we can progress."

She tried, and felt stupid as she waved her hand around. "Show me again."

He did so, over and over again. The iron-bearing stone on the worktable became the base of a tumbling pyramid. Once she pulled out copper, but mostly it was iron, and always, it was with Tarn's hand guiding her.

Finally, she managed to catch the edge of an invisible veil. She *felt* her hand slide past the silken material, felt the tingle of her fingers and the heat on her thumb. But when she opened her eyes, her hand was right there. The sensations faded away.

"We will stop now," announced Tarn. "You're tired. You'll learn better after you've had a chance to rest." She scowled, and he added, "We still haven't discussed how you are to pay for the education I'm providing."

She noticed the change in terms: originally, the lessons were his way of paying *her* for the art she would make him. Now she would be paying *him* for an education? Well, it was the same thing in the end. "What do you want?"

"I'd like you to make me a mirror. With a decorative frame of iron."

"And you want this made of real iron, I assume? Out in the real world? What kind of decoration?"

"Oh yes, definitely made in the world." He smiled. "Although I should like to wait until you've developed your skills here."

Branwyn looked at him for a long moment. He looked back, his handsome face alight with secret enjoyment. "I wish I knew what your angle was. What you're really getting out of this exchange."

"I collect art, Branwyn. And I suspect that the first piece worked by a new Artificer will have a certain... rarity value." He tilted his head. "Would you like to see my collection?"

Branwyn's breath caught. "Other works by other, uh, Artificers?"

"Some. Some by more mundane artists. They are still beautiful."

Branwyn held out her hand. "Show me."

He took her hand, tucked it into his arm, and led her through the door out of the studio.

"We're walking?"

"Yes." The hall was tall and elegant, with wooden beams arching across a high white ceiling. The dark wood widened to become panels on the pale walls, creating stripes that both impressed and disoriented.

Branwyn waited, but he didn't elaborate. "Why?"

"I don't just flit everywhere, Branwyn, especially when I have a guest to show off my realm to."

"Will I get lost if I don't hold onto you?"

He looked down at her. "Your directness is so refreshing. Why are you so averse to being treated like a lady?"

She lifted her hand from his arm. Nothing happened: both the hall and the faerie lord remained reassuringly solid. Sticking her hands in the pockets of her jeans, she strolled along beside him. "Because ladies are treated like children. Although really, Tarn, this is no way to build a relationship."

"You don't think so? I disagree." The hall became an intersection ahead and he took the left fork. "Spending time together, talking, sharing interests."

"Tricks, games, deception."

"Those too, especially in a business relationship," he said equably. "Games to help to pass the time. We have had so much time to pass, after all."

They walked by an open door leading to a large room where figures moved around an extremely large table. Branwyn paused, looking in. A game of some sort was in progress, with dice and blocks and a complex map. The players of the game were as beautiful as Tarn, although some seemed far less human.

None of them had eyes like Severin.

As she stared, the players turned one by one to stare back at her.

She thought she knew why. She represented the world beyond to them. She represented freedom from an imprisonment it hurt her to even imagine. But the undisguised avarice in their looks made her uncomfortable, so she gave a little wave and moved on, trying not to dwell on what she could not yet change.

"My people," said Tarn. "You don't need to fear them. The courtkey marks you as a most precious guest."

Precious. "That's certainly what it seemed like." She added, as an afterthought, "I wasn't afraid."

"Good."

They continued until the hall ended at an ebony door, intricately carved to evoke running water within the grain of the wood. Tarn opened the door and bowed her through.

The room beyond was both museum and work of art. The floor was beautifully tiled in green, blue, and shades of white, producing an effect that was so much like ice and snow that Branwyn was surprised the ground didn't crunch when she stepped inside. Paintings and plinths lined the walls between three archways leading to other rooms, with statues acting as pillars in long rows.

There was a gorgeous wooden seat in the middle of the room, set so that it could rotate on a circular base; like the floor, it was both work of art and functional item. Branwyn went to it first, running her fingers over the wood. Then she looked up at Tarn. "Which ones were made by Artificers?"

He studied her, his pied eyes glinting. "You tell me."

Branwyn set her jaw and looked around. First, she inspected the works on plinths. There was a pair of small jade sculptures: an abstract dragon coiled in a loop around a kneeling woman. Then there was a tiara of green gold hammered into tiny leaves twined around emerald buds, two bronze statues, one of an antler-horned man and one of a winged woman, another jade sculpture, this one of a horse, and a set of toiletries wrought from gold. Somehow, it was easier for her to imagine magic being used in the creation of physical objects. She was a proficient painter, but the medium had never sparked her imagination once she'd started working in three dimensions

So she touched them all, keenly aware of Tarn watching her. She even picked the pieces up, inspecting them for makers' marks.

And she couldn't tell. They all seemed like real objects, shaped and smoothed with mundane tools. She glanced at the pillar-statues against the walls, then went to inspect the paintings. They covered a variety of subjects: battles and bedrooms and behemoths. Apparently Tarn wasn't picky in terms of the subject matter of his collection. Then again, he'd probably had limited choices during the long centuries of his imprisonment.

Branwyn felt another pang of sympathy, which she squashed fiercely. He was too full of tricks to allow herself to be sympathetic in his actual presence; he'd demonstrated that amply. She reminded herself he'd engineered a partial escape for his people already.

Tarn's eyes were slitted closed, catlike. She told him, "They all look natural."

"Hmmm?" Just as with a cat, she wasn't sure if he was paying any attention to her.

Frowning, Branwyn went on another tour of the room. This time, she closed her eyes as she handled each exhibit. When she picked up the jade horse, it felt as if wisps of fiber clung to the edges of the sculpture, catching on the roughness of her fingers. "It's like mold lines," she said wonderingly, and then added, "Why didn't he clean them up? Couldn't he? If using magic means everything I make is covered with invisible spiderwebs, maybe I should cancel my lessons."

"He didn't have the chance before he lost access to the piece," said Tarn. "His other pieces, made later, are cleaner."

Branwyn opened her eyes, disappointed that she hadn't found the way of identifying the Artificer-crafted pieces. "Is there a way to identify those? Without you telling me?"

"Oh yes. That you felt anything at all is a good sign, though. I have great hopes for you." He moved past her and settled into the chair, which had clearly been made exactly for him. "Go, explore the gallery. Enjoy it for its own sake. You needn't view every moment here as work."

"Hah hah." But Branwyn circled the room again, then passed through one of the archways into another room, identical in layout to the first, lacking only the chair and with a different pattern of red and yellow tiles on the floor. After taking in that room, she went to another, and another, and another. Each room was a bit smaller than the previous one, but there was still so much art that it would have taken a collector who *wasn't* locked away from the world decades to accumulate it all. She wondered if he'd acquired each work directly from the artist and what he'd paid them for them. There was nothing from painters she recognized, although there were a few that seemed to be students of the Old Masters.

She stopped in the middle of a room no larger than her bedroom. There were only two arches in this room, although there had been three in every other room. At least, she thought so. She could no longer quite recall. How long had she been exploring the gallery?

But before she could cast her mind back to retrace her steps, her attention was caught by the arch across from her. It was the room beyond that had been calling her. She closed her eyes, and she could feel it from where she stood: the tendrils of unspun magic drifting in a cosmic wind like loose spiderwebs.

Eyes still closed, she moved through the arch into the room beyond. The tendrils whipped at her as the strange wind strengthened. The room around her was incomplete. A plan had been laid down, but not fulfilled. There was something caught in the threads in the unfinished mass, a form she couldn't name that throbbed with heavy potential. Something strange and magical had been left unfinished.

Branwyn raised her hands to try and pull away the tendrils so she could better sense the plan, but they caught around her fingers and wrists. Then they were pulling on her—

Her eyes flew open. A multicolored mist surrounded her, simultaneously gaudy and terrifying. And unlike every other time she'd touched the underlying fabric of the Backworld, unlike all the other times she'd detected faerie magic, this time the sensation didn't vanish when she opened her eyes.

Her hands were still caught, and something no more substantial than the mist was pulling on her. The tug was gentle at first, but slowly it became more insistent as she resisted the pressure. "No," she said aloud. "I'm not coming in. Let go." Belatedly, she added, "Please." But it didn't seem to matter. Whatever was behind the pull didn't listen, or didn't care.

Dread curled within her. She couldn't help but imagine a maw on the far end of the tug, something pulling her in to devour her. But she closed her eyes again, wiggling her fingers. Then she pushed them past the tendrils that caught on them, trying to reach further, past the surface level where the unfinished work rested and deep into the substrate. If she could pull out a bar of metal—or even an iron-laden rock—she'd have a weapon to defend herself against whatever monster waited within. She felt smooth metal against her palm—

A strong hand closed around her shoulder and yanked her out of the room. She fell back into Tarn's arms as the magic holding her vanished abruptly.

"I see you found your way here directly," observed Tarn as he set her back on her feet.

Branwyn brushed herself off as her racing heart slowed down

again. "What did you drag me away for? I was finally making progress there."

A thin smile curved Tarn's mouth. "That room is not a learning experience."

"You're wrong. But what do you think it is?"

"An unfinished project. I've waited a long time for an artist who could see the structure laid down by the original architect and master the power gathered to guide it to completion."

Branwyn looked at the archway behind her. "*I* saw the structure. Well, felt it, anyhow." She looked back at Tarn, her eyebrows raised in challenge.

He looked skeptical. "You? You're just a beginner. That room is a combination of deep faerie architecture, Artificing, and other things you know nothing about. The power there is overwhelming. Maybe when you are far, far more experienced, you might be able to complete that project. If you live that long."

"Oh, give me a break," she snapped. "Whoever started that room was mortal, right? One of your artists? It was a little confusing—and, okay, insistent—but the plan was easy enough to see. All I'd have to do is follow it. It *wanted* me to complete it."

"Is that what you were doing just a moment ago? It looked to me as if you were drowning. I'd rather you not run mad quite yet, Branwyn. That room is not there to teach you."

Branwyn stared at the tall faerie man. Then, brightly, she said, "Fine. How do I get out of this labyrinth of yours?"

He put his hand on her shoulder. "Don't take it so hard, Branwyn. After all, you're only human." His teeth flashed as he grinned at her.

Branwyn narrowed her eyes. Then, casually, she shook his hand off and strolled out of the room, back the way she came. In her pocket, she touched the courtkey Tarn had given her. How useful would it be if she was lost in a gallery without doors? It was another faerie trick. She looked around one of the rooms she passed through and barely remembered it. She'd been in a daze as she explored.

She took an exit at random, and found herself in a room that she was pretty sure she hadn't been in before. Behind her, she heard Tarn's footsteps as he paced behind her. "What happened to the artists?" she asked without turning around. "Are they still here, in a special part of the gallery? Another exhibit for your faerie friends?"

"What a twisted imagination you have. No, none of the artists are still here."

The ground trembled underfoot, just enough to throw Branwyn off her stride. She caught herself on a pillar and looked back at Tarn.

He frowned, and said, "I must correct myself. One of them may be, but by his own choice. You will not see him."

Branwyn said, "Oh, great. Because that's not ominous at all."

Tarn pointed. "Once you go through that arch, take the passage to the left three times. You will arrive at the front room. You may return home, or to your studio, as you wish. I have business to attend to." He looked around the gallery once, then turned and stalked back the way he came.

Once again in the studio, Branwyn looked around. The pile of iron ore was overflowing the worktable, taking up space, so she found a bin and cleaned it up. Then she spent a while rearranging the tools so they were laid out the way she liked. It didn't do much to make the otherworldly studio feel like hers, but she felt better changing what Tarn had planned out.

She no longer wondered why he wanted a mirror. What he'd requested would fit right into his gallery. She even had some ideas in that direction. She'd have to make some sketches. Later. Right now she wanted to work on the Artificing. She *had* learned something from the encounter in the unfinished room, and she wanted to put it to work.

So she closed her eyes and reached once again into the space beyond. This time, her fingers closed over a bar, just as they had in the gallery. It felt as if it was waiting for her, pulled halfway from its storage slot. That was interesting.

She pulled it into existence. It was an aluminum ingot, bright and ready to use. Smiling, she put it on the stock shelf, then settled herself into her chair to explore the foundations of Faerie. She knew what success felt like now, the movements of her hand, the quickness of her breath, the burning of her thumb. The thumb was important in a way she couldn't explain, but beyond that it was texture and temperature and the dreamlike feel of passing beyond everything she knew.

After a while, she was hungry. Something itched at her mind about food and the fae, but it didn't matter. She went and found food, then came back. The wind lifted her hair and she wondered about pulling forth gases and liquids in Faerie. She was sleepy—did she doze at her bench? On something soft? It didn't matter. She reached into the Backworld and pulled out the elements.

Her thumb hurt. She bandaged it. It made pulling out dreams hard, so she abandoned the bandage on the floor. Later, it was gone. Had she pulled the bandage out from Faerie? Interesting.

Eventually, she stretched, cracking her spine and her shoulders. She had no idea how long she'd been in the workshop and she didn't much care. But she knew she needed to look at the Unfinished Room again. She had questions and it had answers.

She stood up and opened the door. The short faerie she'd seen in Tarn's company before stood to one side of her door, as if he'd been guarding it. She remembered that he hadn't seemed to like her very much.

Branwyn generously bestowed a smile on him. "And what are you doing here?"

He scowled back at her. From his pale hair to his expression to his strange, ragged clothing, he seemed decidedly spiky. He certainly lacked Tarn's lazy charm. "I'm here to make sure you don't get lost if you want to go somewhere."

"Delightful. I'd like to go back to the gallery, please. I'm Branwyn, by the way." She raised her eyebrows at him encouragingly.

He looked at her disdainfully. "I know. This way." He strode ahead of her down the hall.

Branwyn caught up. "And do you have a name? Or shall I just call you Fairy Peaseblossom?"

"Oh God. Call me William, if you must."

"What an ordinary name." She watched him stalk beside her down the hall. "So... you and Tarn are...?"

"Eh?" He slid his gaze sideways to look at her, bewilderment briefly chasing the sullen expression off his face.

"Are you an employee? A friend? A jealous lover? A slave?"

"Oh." For a moment, it didn't seem like he'd answer, but then, grudgingly, he said, "I'm one of his changelings."

The term was distantly familiar and Branwyn cast her mind back to her great-grandmother's stories. "You were human once?"

"Yes." The flat answer did not invite further discussion.

Branwyn gave him another dazzling smile. "Fascinating. And why are we so cranky today, William?"

"You smell bad," he said matter-of-factly.

Branwyn sniffed herself. "Oh, darn. Should I shower?"

"Won't help. Won't change things."

"Oh well. I'll try to stand upwind."

He actually looked at her this time, his pale blue eyes glinting. "Downwind."

"What?" He just shook his head, and she smiled to herself. "If there *is* anything I can accomplish to improve your mood, do let me know and I'll absolutely think about it." She lowered her voice confidingly. "Not an offer I make to many, let me tell you. But I'm in a good mood and I've noticed *your* bad mood every time we've met. I keep wondering if you have a cramp." She shook out her hands as if having sympathy pains.

He didn't answer her until they reached the door of the gallery, and then all he said was, "Why do you have green hair?"

"Hair dye," she answered. She opened the door and waved at William before slipping inside.

Navigating through the gallery to the Unfinished Room again was easy. Its incompleteness tugged on her like a draft from an open door. Once she came to its anteroom, she paused. She had every intention of being careful. She knew she couldn't finish it yet. She had only the vaguest idea how to shape the materials she pulled out from nothingness, the way Tarn had turned a silver bar into a flower and then a statue. But it couldn't hurt to look. From outside. Tarn hadn't even warned her against looking, just against trying to shape the unformed room before she was experienced enough.

Looking... Tarn had been so insistent that she *not* use her eyes that she'd never even considered the magic Sight that Corbin had given her. She activated it, keeping her gaze averted from the open archway just in case it *was* dangerous to look that way.

The Geometry in Faerie was... *different* than it was outside. In what she couldn't help thinking of as "the real world," the lines and shapes of the Geometry were everywhere: a dizzying array of designs and clusters of light. In Tarn's domain, there was very little of that. There was only a long, thick line underfoot, more like a road than a line, and several crossing lines overhead. Tiny tendrils from the floor and ceiling lines snaked down to the gallery exhibits, in some cases twisting quite thickly into open circles, but it was as if nothing else in that room existed.

The Unfinished Room beyond was different. A rich, deep light, thick and sweet, spilled out of the chamber, radiating from something lost in the mists. The light shone through the substance of Underlight as if it were glass. The thick line underfoot frayed as it approached the Unfinished Room, like it was being unwound by that light.

Branwyn found herself drawn to it, despite her best intentions. She put out her hand to catch herself on the door frame, and caught at something else instead.

There was cool stone beneath her fingers, worked with a swirling pattern, and the stone emerged from another pattern of dazzling radials that formed a plan, and the plan spoke to the room, spoke to her; it was a container, a passage, leading to—

She didn't know quite what. It eluded her. It vanished through another door, this one in her head. She had to catch it. She felt stone against her forehead, and then nothing.

Branwyn fell into dreaming, running through a maze of lines and light, trying to find the exit. It was fun at first, but then the light changed, shining without illuminating, and she was ready to wake up.

She opened her eyes. A familiar painting of jungle growth reclaiming an abandoned factory hung on the wall opposite her. She was in her own bed, in her own room, in her own apartment. Her coverlet was tangled around her legs, like she'd been running in her sleep, and she felt sticky.

Branwyn closed her eyes, opened them again, and then reactivated the Sight. It was the real world, as far as she could tell. Her real room.

She sat up and realized she'd been undressed and redressed in her sleeping shirt. Her hair hung in a heavy braid on her shoulder, though she rarely braided it. Her clothes were folded neatly on top of her dresser, rather than tossed into the laundry heap near the door.

A deep, convulsive shudder overcame her. Who had brought her home and put her to bed? One of the faeries? Severin? She didn't think it was Marley. Marley wouldn't have undressed her more than taking her shoes off. Marley would have *woken* her. Her brother? Or had she done it herself, under the influence of whatever she'd inadvertently come into contact with in the Unfinished Room?

In the bathroom, she worked on unbraiding her hair. It was ridiculously complicated. Whoever had done this had a sadistic sense of fashion. Afterward, she took a shower. If it went on longer than usual, who could blame her? She'd only ever slept like that, fighting the sheets and trapped in incoherent dreams, after drinking too much while playing terrible video games. And she didn't remember drinking anything at all. She didn't have a headache, either. And, okay, the dreams probably came from the Unfinished Room. Even accepting that, she still had to scrub to remove the prickles from her skin. More than anything, she wanted to know how she'd gotten home.

When she emerged into the living room, she blinked at the bright sunlight and tried to remember what day it was. Marley sat on the couch reading, but looked up when Branwyn moved forward. She frowned in a way that made Branwyn feel an unusual pang of guilt for worrying her.

"Good morning," Branwyn said, striving for cheerful and reassuring, and passed her quickly to get to the kitchen.

But Marley stood up and followed her.

"Bran, you're getting into trouble again."

Branwyn debated asking Marley if she knew who had brought her home, but decided if Marley didn't know, it would probably worry her even more to ask. So she made herself a butter-and-brown-sugar taco, then said, "Maybe a little. Am I going to die from it?"

That didn't improve Marley's mood at all. "I don't know. Do you want me to find out?"

Branwyn almost choked on a lump of sugar. "No. No, I don't." She looked at Marley and sighed. "I don't want to be dependent on you and Corbin for the rest of my life. I don't want to live life as... an ignorant human under Senyaza's benevolent protection, you know? I'm just looking for my voice so I can make myself heard. This isn't any different than protesting downtown."

"It seems more like breaking into a secured industrial building to me," Marley grouched.

"That was just the one time. Why do you always have to bring that up?"

"Your boyfriends are a bad influence on you, that's why."

"Well, that's not relevant now. And it was my idea, anyhow." Marley only looked at her, so Branwyn added, "And I got what I wanted that time, too."

"A criminal record?"

"Nobody pressed charges," Branwyn said calmly. "You worry too much, Marley. It interferes with getting things done."

Marley scowled and muttered something about Action Girl under her breath. Branwyn smiled; if Marley was using that nickname for her, she had to agree with Branwyn on some level. "Have you talked to Corbin yet? I need to check on some things with him."

Marley's eyes tightened. "I thought you said you didn't want to rely on him?"

Branwyn waved a hand dismissively. "I said I didn't want to be dependent for the rest of my life. I've got to get my information from somewhere while I'm learning. And he's easy to reach."

Marley's expression slid from grumpy back into the actively unhappy zone. She threw herself back on the couch. "Hah. He left me—us—a message. He's leaving town. He may have already left town. He's going on a mission to Japan or something."

"That seems... sudden. Did he say when he'd be back?"

Marley gave her an odd look. "He said maybe not for a while."

Branwyn watched Marley adjust one of the couch pillows, then pick up her book. "Do you want him to come back?"

Marley rifled the pages of her book. "No. Yes. I don't know."

Feeling as if she owed Corbin something for his information earlier, Branwyn said, "I wish I'd been here for his call. I would have said, 'Corbin, don't give up! Don't be a loser!' But there's still hope! Fly to Japan after him. Show up at his hotel room wearing nothing but a kimono." She caught the pillow Marley threw as her mind wandered ahead of her words. "Actually, I do wish I'd been around when he called. What am I supposed to do if I want my charms adjusted?"

Marley paused in the act of pulling another pillow off the couch. "Uh. Do you *need* your charms adjusted?"

"I might," hedged Branwyn. "You never know. But they're baby charms, after all. You've been learning magic from Corbin. Can you do it?"

"I can do exactly what you're holding now. We didn't get very far before, uh... we didn't get very far." Marley studied the weave of the pillowcase intensely. "Zachariah and Simon are both wizardly sorts, too."

That pause was suspicious. It was the sort of pause that suggested what Gran-gran had insisted on calling hanky-panky. *When did this happen?* Branwyn wondered. The last she knew, Marley hadn't gotten any farther than chaste kisses with either of her not-boyfriends. She'd get the details later. That kind of conversation was much better late at night, with wine. She refocused on what Marley had actually said. "Oh, Zachariah and Simon, how lovely. I'll keep that in mind."

"Are you going to work today?" said Marley, a little too brightly. Well, that was nice. She'd forgotten all about Branwyn getting into trouble. Boys were useful that way.

Branwyn once again tried and failed to remember what day it was, then shrugged. "If I am, I'd better get moving. See you later."

-six-

Welcome back," said the guys at work, and, "How are you feeling?" but Branwyn didn't really think about it. She didn't think about the date on the invoices she processed, either, or the strange looks Marley had given her, until she opened the door to her family home and Howl immediately grabbed her by the arm and dragged her to his study.

"You have to stop this, Bran. You're upsetting Mom, and the kids are noticing. You didn't even come out for dinner on Saturday, and you promised."

"What are you talking about?" asked Branwyn irritably.

"I know you get into these fugues when you're working on a project. We all know that, but this one is really bad, Branwyn, and I'm worried about wherever you're going. Are they doing something to you there?"

"I've just been busy—" she began, and paused. She remembered working on one of her early twisted metal sculptures her junior year of college. It was her own interpretation of Winged Victory of Samothrace, made from belt buckles and twisted fan blades and toy airplane wings, embedded in soil planted with English ivy. It had consumed her for two weeks and Penny, Marley, and Rhianna had taken turns driving over and making sure she ate once a day. They teased her later about how she'd said, every day, "I'm just too busy to eat."

She probed her memory, looking back before the Unfinished Room that seemed to still occupy such a large space in her mind.

She *had* been busy. It was like it had been with Winged Victory and the other times, but she'd gone deeper than ever before. She'd been calling in sick to work all week. Her memories of working in her Faerie studio, and of visiting Tarn's gallery, were crystal clear, but they swam in a vague sea of traveling to and from her apartment, of her brother's worried face, of brushing off her sisters, and of her mother's concerned looks. Of Marley watching silently as she trudged through the living room to fall unconscious into her bed. All the memories of the real world were ghosts floating over what she'd been learning, less important than exploring the substrate of the Backworld and finding out what she could do.

It was something about Underlight. It didn't feel quite as solid and steady as the real world. It blurred the lines between the inside and the outside of her head.

For a moment, she was angry at Tarn. She'd disappointed her mother and it was his—

But no. That was lying to herself. She knew she got into these moods with projects. Tarn and Underlight may have contributed, but she had to admit there was a chance she was just a huge jerk.

Hm. It was probably a combination of the two.

"I've been busy," she repeated, slowly. "I'm sorry. Is Mom really upset?"

"No," Howl admitted. "She knows you. But she will be when I tell her there's a dimensional hole in her attic, and that you've been going through it."

"Howl, don't do that," Branwyn admonished him. "Is she home now?"

"No. She and Jaimie took the girls out for ice cream."

"Well, good. I'll talk to her later." She disentangled her arm from where Howl was still clutching it.

"You're going back in there," said Howl, sounding sick. "I thought I'd gotten through to you this time."

Branwyn hesitated. There was a time for teasing and distraction techniques, and a time for being gentle. When Howl was this upset, the latter paid off.

"I'm okay," she said. "I'm fine. They're not doing anything to me in there. They've given me the run of the place, and I'm learning a lot, and it's probably the most amazing stuff I've ever learned."

"Then *show me*," he demanded. "Or tell me details. This is creepy, Branwyn, and you're scaring me. And it's damn hard keeping Brynn from asking questions or making her ridiculous ghost documentary."

Branwyn considered her brother. "I'm learning how to work with matter on a basic level. But I can't show you yet because it only works in the special environment they live in. And no, you still can't come in. I need you here on the outside." She reached up to chuck him under the chin. "Thank you for pointing out that I've been acting like a deadbeat."

He scowled. "If you zone out again, I *am* telling Mom. And Grandma. If Grandma comes back from her retreat early, it will be the end of fun."

Branwyn sighed. "I wish you wouldn't. I'm an adult."

"So am I," said Howl stubbornly. "And my adult opinion is that if you zone out again, I'm telling Mom and Grandma."

Branwyn opened the door of the study, saying over her shoulder, "If you didn't learn not to tattle when you were seven, there's no helping you now. I'm going upstairs."

He didn't follow her upstairs, so once she was in the attic, she took a moment to crouch down and gather her thoughts and memories. Especially her memories. The empty spot between the final visit to the gallery and waking up in her own bed remained, even as she remembered other trips home. It was disturbing, but no longer quite as disturbing in context. She'd just been so consumed by what she'd seen in the Unfinished Room that she hadn't noticed *any* of the details about getting home. Simple. Easy. Hopefully true.

Once she had the events of the week sorted and filed, she rose and went to the little door. Then she turned back and rearranged the contents of the attic room, pushing boxes here and there. It was easy to ignore what was usual when she was in a fugue, but having the usual be out of place would help a little. She didn't intend on being caught again by her own obsession, but when magic was involved, every bit helped.

Tarn awaited her on the other side. He hadn't been there every time she'd arrived during the last week, she realized. Sometimes he'd been elsewhere. Once, he'd been in her studio waiting for her. They'd talked about Penny and her family. He seemed to quite like her family.

This time, he said, "You finally used your Sight in the gallery. That *was* supposed to be informative, I admit, although you took it a little harder than I expected." He watched her, his pied eyes cool.

"Did I take a little longer than you expected, too?" She didn't want him to actually answer that, so she rushed on. "Have you been putting the faerie mojo on me? Making me lose track of time? Stay here forever, that kind of thing?"

"You've been leaving every day," Tarn pointed out. "You're hardly staying forever."

"My thoughts have stayed here," countered Branwyn. "I've practically been a zombie outside. And I apparently missed a dinner with my family."

"And has this never happened to you before? I've known other humans prone to… obsession. It's a shame about your family, though." His gaze gentled. "Do you want me to take the blame?"

Angry at herself, Branwyn looked away. The patterned hangings wafted gently, but she barely saw them. The offer was tempting, just like sometimes it was tempting to give up, stop caring, let others dictate her life. It was the easiest path and it seemed like if you followed it long enough, it even stopped hurting. But that wasn't what she wanted when she looked at the world with clear eyes. Letting go of guilt meant letting go of responsibility, and that meant what was wrong never got fixed.

When she looked back, he smiled. "But I'm flattered, all the same. I think about you all the time, too."

That right there was a troubling statement, if Tarn really couldn't lie in his own domain. Branwyn attempted to wave it away. "Me? Or my magic hands? Remember, this is a business relationship." She waggled her fingers. Her thumb tingled. "Speaking of which, I'd like to touch the Unfinished Room again. Would you come with me to play lifeguard?"

Tarn's mouth turned down. "Branwyn, Branwyn. I said you weren't ready."

"If you're there, I'm sure I'll be fine." She cocked an eyebrow. "Or are you saying you can't protect me from your own realm?"

"It's not you I'm worried about," Tarn said, with expansive sadness. "What if you damage the project?"

"You're playing a game again," Branwyn said calmly. Tarn's sadness became a grin, lightning-quick, before returning to a facade of concern. "I want to go back to the Unfinished Room," she repeated. "Will you come play lifeguard or will I go alone?" Then, generously, she offered, "We can call it 'roomguard' instead, if that will align better with your goals."

"And how would that alleviate my concerns?" he asked severely, crossing his arms

"Are you an artist?" she demanded. "Do you make art? Do you make anything real? No? What's this I hear? You're just a pixie playing pretend, afraid of venturing into the big scary real world? Get therapy. It isn't my *job* to alleviate your concerns. It's my job to *make things*, so put up or get out."

"Ouch. Oh, very well. I'll come along and be, ah, roomguard." And he smiled again. This time it was just a seductive quirk of the lips, as if he couldn't help himself. Branwyn found it more than a little distracting.

Cut it out. Client. Faerie. Trickster. She strolled past him to the door behind his throne and opened it with her key. Then she went directly to the gallery, as if she'd been there a dozen times. The room tugged on her soul that much. He followed her, as meek as a kitten.

This time, she asked about the pull. "Why does the Unfinished Room draw me in?"

"It nags like a missing tooth, don't you think?"

She cast him a doubtful look. "Have you *ever* lost a tooth?"

"Well, like I imagine a missing tooth must feel," he amended. "Like an empty spot that you keep encountering and wishing you could solve."

"Missing teeth are solvable," she pointed out. "Trip to the dentist. They *make* you a new one. There's that verb again. Make." She looked around the gallery as they passed through it. "What the Sight told me was that the only real things here are the things made by the human artists. The Artificers. Even the gallery itself, as gorgeous as it is, is just... a dream."

"A dream I maintain," he said lightly. "It should be no less real to you for being a dream. It's as real as anything you feel. I could show you, if you like."

It was true. All a dream had to do was convince all her senses it was true in order to be real enough to be, say, a prison. She considered the tile under her foot, sniffed the scent of pomegranates and jasmine. And she remembered how she'd been trapped in her studio, the first time Tarn had brought her into his realm, before Marley and Corbin had arrived to rescue her.

Rescue. There was a sour word. She shuddered and shook her head. "No, I'm good." She glanced at him in time to catch the look of disappointment on his face, which inspired an unhealthy speculation about what he'd had in mind.

Fortunately, they arrived at the Unfinished Room and she was saved from her own imagination. She stepped right up to the archway and stuck her hand through it to find the plan. She watched the mists drifting closer before she closed her eyes to better interpret the information she was touching.

After a moment, she opened her eyes again. Tarn was leaning against the wall near the arch, watching her lazily. "I can do this," she informed him. "It's not nearly as hard as you said." Then she checked her watch and waded into the mist.

In some places, it was like pulling sheets off a completed sculpture. In some places, it was like sanding and finishing somebody else's work. This, she did, although it was about as exciting as whitewashing a fence. She even found herself thinking of the previous Artificer as "Tom Sawyer," and wondered if he'd convinced other people to do work for him, too.

But in some places, the plan was nothing more than a rough-sketched design: a few concepts and rules were laid out, but the detail work was all for her to decide, and for a while, she lost herself in the joy of creation.

It was a lot of fun, she admitted, to carve a room out of dreamstuff: more like a game than real work. It was a lot easier to do using the plans "Tom Sawyer" had provided, too. It was like filling in an intricate and elaborate coloring book. It was certainly much easier than Tarn had implied. She wondered if she was surprising him, or if he'd just been trying to provoke her.

She opened her eyes to check her watch again and saw that only a few hours had passed. The room's vaulted ceiling soared above her: marble traced with gold and silver. She'd whimsically connected the veins into the patterns of the summer constellations. Below her feet, the floor was warm wood rather than tile, but done in four shades laid out in a herringbone pattern. The walls were made of cloudy multi-colored stone, dark at the bottom and brightening as it rose to meet the ceiling.

Only the far side of the room was still shrouded in the pre-creation mists. That, she felt, was the source of the deep light she'd seen with the Sight. It was one of the more finished parts of the room, which was why she'd left it until the end. Looking at the mists, feeling the plan underneath, she almost wanted to turn away and leave the room as it was. But she'd done that enough as a student. Leaving things unfinished was the mark of an amateur, and she was a professional.

Even if she wasn't getting paid for this.

Dammit! He *had* been trying to provoke her. He'd probably wanted to get this done for free. But she wasn't going to let him get away with that, any more than she'd let a human client. She'd weasel something out of him. Faeries, her Gran-gran had told her, always paid their debts.

Meanwhile, she had work to do.

She reached into the mists and found...

And found a braided edge. The braid was familiar.

It had been in her hair that morning.

Fascinated, she explored the texture. Then she tried to change it, make it something simpler. But it was fixed and solid, unchangeable, and it was the only such thing she'd felt in the whole room. Her curiosity engaged and she worked at the rest of it, pulling away the fog where that was all that could be done and shaping what could be shaped when there was more that she could play with. There were restrictions here, even beyond the braid she couldn't shift. She worked within them. It kept things interesting, until finally, she was done.

She stood there with her eyes closed and her hands by her sides, afraid to look and see what she'd wrought. Then she heard Tarn's sharp inhalation behind her, and her eyes flew open.

In this gallery of open archways, it was a door. She'd made it huge, and slightly rounded, and hewn of white stone. The braid she'd felt encircled the edge, twisted from strands of an unfamiliar black material. The handle of the door she'd shaped as well: a brass lever backed onto a plate molded with a dancing pixie. But the braid intruded here, too, encircling a lock above the handle. She hadn't meant to include that.

She reached out and tried the handle.

It didn't work, of course.

"I recognize that," said Tarn tightly. "The braid. The door that comes with it."

Branwyn looked uncertainly at Tarn. "What is it? It wasn't like the other parts of the room. I didn't make a lock, that's for damn sure."

"It is a marker," said Tarn quietly. "The room's architect wrought *very* well. Great power lies beyond that door."

Skeptical, Branwyn said, "What, like he was digging for iron and struck gold? Does that sort of thing happen often around here?"

Tarn shrugged, reaching past her to brush his fingers over the door. "With power like this, my people were once able to heal the sick, repair the broken-souled, and make the dreams of Faerie come true."

Branwyn's suspicions went from first to fifth gear. She couldn't help but think of Penny when he mentioned broken souls. And she knew he was thinking of Penny, too, because he mentioned her friend almost every time she visited. She was *sure* he'd planned this all, from the first letter.

Sure, and unsurprised. She'd known he wanted something from the beginning. And to be fair, so had she. She wondered if healing Penny would be a fair recompense for finishing the chamber and revealing its magic door. "Well, open it, already. Claim your winning lotto ticket."

He, too, tried the handle. It didn't open for him, either. "It needs a key."

"Locks usually do. Can't you magic one up? This is your realm and all."

Tarn spread his hands. "I can't. The architect tapped into something much vaster than my realm. It requires not just a real key, but a custom-built celestial Machine key. I don't like to touch Machines. Even *looking* at a Machine too closely risks oblivion for me."

"Of course." Branwyn vaguely remembered something about that, when she'd shaped a Machine fragment into a weapon for Marley to use in her battle to save the twins from angelic doom. That seemed relevant, somehow. She thought for a moment. "Could you, just by chance, bring Penny back to us with such power?"

"Oh, certainly. And I would, but tragically, the power is behind that locked door."

Together, they looked at the door. It stood there, huge and pale and impassable.

"Ah, but possibly *I* could make a key? If we had a handy bit of Machine just lying around?"

"Possibly," said Tarn gravely. "You did display an aptitude for interfacing with Machines once."

"Of course," she said. After another silent moment, she said, "And do we have a handy bit of Machine lying around? Ready and prepared, by chance?"

"Alas, I do not. I know where one might be acquired, though."

"Of course," she said again.

"They're here and there," he explained, with an infuriating earnestness "They're dangerous for us, so it's the most dangerous that have them."

"I'm not even going to say it again," she complained, rolling her eyes. "Assume I'm playing along. Who has one, and how do we get it?"

He frowned at her. "Branwyn. You're just a mortal artist helping me expand my collection. Why do you think you'd be involved in acquiring a Machine fragment to open a door to great power? Your job, you said, is to *make* things. I heard you. You were very clear. This would involve a *journey*. Not art."

"It's just this feeling I have," Branwyn said. "Maybe it's because I'm just a mortal artist. A mortal artist with a friend you could conveniently save with the immense power conveniently located behind this convenient door that I just *happened* to help make. How long has this room been Unfinished with a capital U, anyhow?"

"About a thousand years. And you're overtired," soothed Tarn. "You've worked very hard on this chamber, and I'm very pleased— and surprised!—to see how your skills have been developing, and you should rest."

"I'm fine," said Branwyn, but he put his hands on her shoulders and propelled her from the Room. She *was* tired, but not so tired she couldn't have a damn conversation. But he'd surprised her and once they were outside the Room, the gallery itself seemed to slip around her, refusing to provide the traction for her to regain her balance and argue at the same time.

"Can you walk? If you think you're going to stumble, I can carry you," he said sweetly. That galvanized her into moving forward herself. He let go of her shoulders and took her arm, and the gallery immediately stopped acting like a freshly Zamboni'd ice skating rink.

"Tarn," she said, raising her voice. "I'm fine. I want to talk about that lock and whoever has the damn Machine bit that can open it. I want to save *Penny*."

They arrived at the entrance to the gallery much more quickly than she had last time. He pushed her over to the door as it opened. "Not until you've rested. Go see your family. They miss you," he said firmly, and shoved her through.

She fell down on the other side, and when she stood up, she was back in the attic.

Sighing, she went downstairs to spend some time with her family. But she couldn't stop thinking about that door, and Penny, and the idea of making a key herself.

-seven-

Branwyn strolled through the mall at Senyaza Titan One, watching the people rather than looking in the shop windows. Corbin, she'd been informed at the checkpoint above, had already left town. They encouraged her to send him an email. She'd texted him instead, but he hadn't responded.

She wondered if charms could be sent via email. It seemed unlikely, which was a shame. And if Corbin was really on a mission, he probably wouldn't have time to answer her questions, especially since she probably wasn't going to be polite. She'd once tried sending an email disguising her true feelings and it hadn't worked. Penny had explained and explained to her the technique of writing out how one really felt, then deleting all of the nasty things until what you finally had was chilly, formal, and impersonal. But all the same, Branwyn had found her fingers typing, almost of their own accord, something rather rude as a postscript.

This was, Penny had informed her, why she would never succeed in corporate America.

Branwyn sighed as she passed by a boutique window showing off a crimson and gold dress Penny would have loved. She missed her friend. The still figure in the hospital bed wasn't *her*. And even that still figure was running out of time. She wondered, treacherously, if the problem was that Penny didn't *want* to come back. If she'd truly loved her angel and mourned his loss. Corbin talked about damaged souls, but wasn't that just a metaphor for heartache?

No, that couldn't be true. Penny would never leave the people she loved like that, not willingly. She had gotten in over her head, pulled into the secret world of the angels and the nephilim without even knowing it. And she'd held on this far, against expectations. If that wasn't proof, what was?

"Oy, girl—pigeon—Branwyn!"

Addressed thusly, Branwyn considered not responding. But Simon seemed to at least be making an effort. She turned to see him walking down the up escalator in order to stay in one place. He waved at her, his hand clutching a paper bag, oblivious of the people he was inconveniencing.

"Stop fighting the escalator, you idiot," she called, hopping on the same one. He waved again and let himself be carried to the top, where he waited for her.

"Corbin's left town," he informed her when she caught up.

"Yes, I know. He's a pathetic coward."

Simon gave her an unreadable look. "I think he's being rather noble, myself." Then he grinned. "Besides, they wanted him to turn his eye on some old papers in Japan, see if they could shake something loose about—" he caught himself. "About a thing. Happening over there. A Special Investigation-y kind of thing."

Branwyn eyed him. "Right. Is that all?"

He looked hurt. "Thought you'd want to know. Would you like to come down and hang out while I get ready for a mission myself? I've been checking out some stuff that might be, uh, relevant to your interests. I mean, if you're not already bored with the wee sparkly ones." He looked her up and down. "You look like the kind of girl who gets bored quickly."

"Only if you're boring," she said sweetly. "Sure, why not."

In the Special Investigations office, Simon pulled out a bottle of scotch, some duct tape, a box cutter, and a giant-sized bottle of hydrogen peroxide. He began to load all this and more into a heavy leather satchel, oblivious to Branwyn's skeptical stare. The room was scattered with printed paper and opened dossiers that hadn't been there before, including some dreadful-looking photos on the floor.

Before Branwyn had a chance to examine them closely, Simon said, "Mr. Black, he's our boss, he's been riding my ass about the build-up of nasties since that fiasco that laid everyone up. Talked about cutting me off." He paused, trying to cram a spool of wire into the bag. "You think he was kidding?"

"Does he joke like that a lot?"

Simon turned a puzzled gaze on her, then shook himself. "Sorry, forgot you don't know him. Right, I wanted to show you." He turned to his computer, then back again, and grabbed a bag of chips. Tearing them open, he offered them first to Branwyn before digging in himself. He looked a bit gaunt, Branwyn realized.

Back at his computer, he said. "Have you seen this video?"

He had a webpage open to the video that Branwyn's brother Morgan had captured and uploaded to the internet. Branwyn watched again as a handsome street artist drew on giggling women with his finger. "As a matter of fact, I have. Why?"

Simon tapped the screen where the view count was listed. "Three hundred thousand views already."

"That seems like a lot for amateur video of a street artist," she observed. Then she peered at the screen. "But MorganTheGreat307 must be pleased." She snickered quietly.

"It's on a playlist," said Simon. He switched to another window and started another video. In this one, a beautiful woman wearing very little moved down a sidewalk, dancing with trees that danced back. After that, Simon showed her several more.

The playlist was called "Urban Wonder!!!". "The first one is also on a list called, 'HOT STREET PERFORMERS,'" noted Simon.

"Oh? Let's see it, then." Branwyn reached for the mouse.

Simon sighed and clicked it open himself. Morgan's video wasn't the only one in both lists. There were more dancers in the second list, but the video where the male-female pair danced with audience members and the one with the animated chalk painting were both there.

When the playlist was done running, Branwyn sat back. "Well, that was fun. Now what?"

Simon took the half-empty bag of chips back from Branwyn. "They seem so harmless."

Cautiously, Branwyn said, "Are we talking about faeries? Yes?

They're not all faeries, are they? I don't think the kid doing terrible card tricks could possibly have been one. *All* he had going for him was being cute, in a tweeny kind of way. I'm thinking his girlfriend made the playlist."

"Who knows? I'm sure a few of them aren't. What I don't get—and, of course, it all happened before my time—is why they chose to exile those poor buggers instead of the kaiju. They got rid of some guys who mostly seem interested in music and dancing, and let the real monsters run around loose. I never hear stories about the number of corpses faeries left behind." He gave the chips back to Branwyn and splashed some scotch into a mug.

"I don't know, read some fairy tales sometime. But yeah. They've been locked away so long, and it's hard to believe they're all equally bad. Even in stories, there's good fairies as well as bad ones."

"Oh, *fairy tales*," said Simon, in a way that made Branwyn suspect he was thinking about modern cartoons rather than the old stories she'd read with her Gran-gran. "They're scary for the wee ones, I'm sure, but some of the kaiju make Cronenberg look like a preschool teacher."

Branwyn let it go, because she wasn't really interested in arguing *for* eternal imprisonment. She was inclined to think that life imprisonment even for humans was a bad idea. "That reminds me. Is there any chance you could Special Investigate the monster-type you smelled on me?"

Simon's gaze sharpened. "Has he hurt you?"

"Well, no," Branwyn admitted. "He's causing trouble in other ways, though."

"Eh. He does that, that one. Corbin's not real fond of him. But he's not a priority at the moment. There's a lot worse than him out there, simply by scale of operation." He scissored his fingers. "Gotta nip some of those before they show up on the map."

"Well, as long as he's in your queue." Branwyn thought about him for a moment, first his eyes, and then his darkly amused voice, then made herself stop. "With the fae—maybe it wasn't about who was dangerous," she suggested. "Maybe it was about who was inconvenient. Monolithic power blocs don't usually care about problems for anybody but themselves."

"I know there's a lot of old nephilim families with faerie blood." Simon drank from his mug. It had a unicorn on it. "A *lot*. And they don't seem to hate their parents, either. It's like they had forebears who never tried to kill them, or turn them into death machines, or anything. Amazing, really."

Branwyn said, "Is that what you have?"

"Naw. Not like some, anyhow. My dad has mostly stayed out of my life. He never stopped liking my mum, even if I was an embarrassment. I never see him now."

"Yeah, I know how that is," Branwyn confided. "My biological dad suddenly decided he didn't want kids when my mom was pregnant with my younger sister. Got the hell out of Dodge."

Simon glanced at her, smiling. "So you broke your father of wanting more kids. Having known you five minutes, I can't say that's a big surprise."

"I was a very sweet little girl," said Branwyn, with some dignity. "Well, I was a sweet baby."

Simon laughed. "Then you learned to talk, I bet."

Branwyn frowned. "Are you always this bad at making friends?"

He pointed a chip at her. "That's what I mean."

"Hey, I have friends. I don't have to resort to pulling strangers out of malls to watch YouTube videos with so I'm not lurking in my cave alone." She said it without the venom she could have used, but she still watched the smile fade from his eyes.

He looked away. "Yeah." Suddenly his computer seemed intensely interesting to him.

Branwyn tried and failed tried to remember Penny's tips for smoothing over the awkward silences she always seemed to provoke. "So, hey, what can you tell me about Machines? The celestial kind, not the vroom-vroom kind."

"And why would you be worrying your pretty green head about Machines?" he asked absently, closing windows on his computer.

"Oh, come on! You're just trying to be a jerk now. I know I was nasty, but you started it."

He blinked and pulled his attention away from the screen. "What? What did I say?" He seemed to replay the conversation in his head, then put his hand over his eyes. "Right. Modern woman. You don't like that kind of talk. I'm sorry. It's so easy to forget what era it is when I've been drinking. That's kind of a lot," he admitted, flashing a weak grin. "I mean, this era is gorgeous with all the various uses for electricity, very sexy, but the social rules seem to change every decade or so."

It was Branwyn's turn to fall quiet now. She didn't like to think about how *young* she was compared to the circle she kept inserting herself into. Corbin swore to her he was only thirty or so, close to her own age. And while she knew Tarn was ancient, somehow his great age was swallowed up in the fact of his imprisonment, which she couldn't let go of. But somehow she'd thought Simon was also her age, despite what he'd said before.

"How many decades have you seen?" she asked cautiously.

He snuck a glance at the clock on his computer before answering. "Thirty-five? Thirty-eight? Something like that."

Branwyn took a deep breath, then brightened. If she thought of his age like that, it wasn't nearly as intimidating.

"I don't know very much about Machines myself," Simon went on conversationally. "I mean, who does? They're bits of stuff from Heaven that celestials are afraid of. They're rare outside of Heaven, and they do weird things sometimes. When we find them, we stick them in the Repository two floors down and lock the door. Out of my league, really."

"Couldn't you use them to finish off the kaiju? Forge them into arrowheads and spearheads and so forth? I know you guys have some."

"You know, that very topic's been bandied about lately. Used to be we only thought the weapon-shaped ones could be used as such, but for some reason, the idea of changing the miscellaneous bits into weapons has come up just recently. Can't think why." He gave her an inscrutable look. "Consensus seems to be that it's a scary idea to alter something that may still be influencing the nature of reality."

Branwyn gave him a keen look. "And what do the experts think?"

"Who's an expert?" Simon asked with a shrug.

Branwyn was pretty sure she knew one or two, so she put that aside to ask somebody else about later. "Marley said you've got wizard skills. If I need my charms adjusted, can I come to you?"

Simon gave her a worried look. "Oh, please don't. Corbin said if

I inflicted my, uh, my Sunday morning spaghetti omelet on anybody else ever again, he'd curse me so all my booze turned to water."

Impressed, Branwyn asked, "Can he do that?"

"I don't want to find out! When that eye thing of his gets going, there's no telling what he'll do."

"All right," said Branwyn soothingly. "I'll find somebody else." And darkly, she thought about Zachariah.

Zachariah. Before his disappearance had kicked off Marley's discovery of the secret world of celestials and nephilim, Branwyn hadn't minded him. He was a guy Marley knew. He got her out of the house. He had cute kids and a lot of money.

But since he'd returned, things had changed. If he'd been interested romantically in Marley at all before, he'd been taking it very slowly. But now everything was different. He'd come back and officially hired her as the girls' bodyguard-nanny and stepped up the level of his romantic attentions. Right as Marley was maybe, possibly getting something going with Corbin.

Branwyn thought he just didn't like the competition and she didn't like the kind of guy who would pursue someone just to keep her from being with someone else. And that meant she hated the idea of asking him for help. The question was: did she hate it enough to stop playing along with Tarn's silly game? Especially given his offer to help Penny? She undoubtedly did need help with her charms; taking what Corbin had given her on a visit to anybody more hostile than Tarn would be like bringing nothing but a calculator to a gunfight.

She went to see Penny instead. It felt like the right next step.

When she opened the door of Penny's room, she saw a slight figure hunched next to her friend's form, dark hair veiling her face. The smooth brown skin and the expensive suit told Branwyn everything she needed to know, though. It was Penny's mother, Viviana, and she was crying.

Branwyn tried to quietly close the door again, but Viviana glanced up and saw her anyhow. She wiped her eyes quickly and straightened, holding out her hands. "Branwyn. Come in. I'm sure Penny will be happy to hear your voice. Your family is well?"

"Yes, ma'am." Branwyn shut the door behind her and moved into the room, allowing Viviana to take her hands and kiss her cheek. "Has there been a change in Penny's condition?" She glanced at the new machine monitoring Penny's decline.

"No improvement," Viviana said, a sob buried in her voice. "Come, sit down and talk with me." She drew Branwyn over to the couch and sank into it.

Uncomfortable, Branwyn sat down beside her. There was a stack of tabloids on the arm of the couch, more than the ones Marley had been bringing in. They looked like somebody had been reading them.

"The doctors say, if someone is in a coma a certain period of time, the likelihood that they will wake up diminishes. You know this, yes?"

Grudgingly, Branwyn said, "Yes." Viviana had consulted both the ordinary doctors that worked for the hospital and the specialists her connections had let her access immediately. She didn't know that some of the technicians assisting those specialists had been Senyaza's own specialists They hadn't been willing to talk to somebody otherwise uninvolved, except apparently to get her legal permission for the damnable new monitor.

Viviana said, "I have been counting the days. The hospital has set up this new monitor. I let them, because what does it hurt? Penny would consent. But I think they will not get the information they are hoping for." She peered intensely into Branwyn's eyes for a moment, then sighed and looked away. A tabloid slid off the stack into her lap and she replaced it. "My daughter has always been a good girl. Too good to attract this kind of attention, until now. Now I read this trash, because they are trying to find out what really happened to my Penny and I would like to know that as well." She gave Branwyn another intent look and Branwyn held her gaze only with some difficulty. According to Penny, Viviana was famous in the movie industry for getting things done with a lethal efficiency. So rarely was that force of presence turned entirely on her that she was tempted to break down and tell her everything.

Viviana must have seen something in her eyes because she took Branwyn's hand again. "I'm very glad you came by, Branwyn. I've been eager to have a little chat with you. You see, although you say you were there when she fell asleep, I can't help but feel as though there is something you have not shared." Her fingers tightened. "Anything else you could tell us might help, Branwyn. If they knew more—there are special treatments based on what happened, they tell me."

Branwyn squeezed Viviana's hand back, then pulled away. "What else can I say, ma'am? I didn't see any signs of drugs. She didn't have any bruises. She was sick and I went to stay with her, and then this happened." She felt wretched. Not for lying to Viviana—that was just practical—but because she just knew the older woman was going to cry again.

She hated it when mothers cried.

"*This* happened. But what is *this*, Branwyn? Tell me again, because I don't understand. And I do not understand why my daughter won't wake up." Her fist clenched on one of the flimsy magazines, crumpling it.

Branwyn opened her mouth, then paused. Lying was practical, but it wasn't going to help Viviana feel better and it certainly wasn't going to fend off tears, so why waste the effort? Why waste Viviana's time?

Instead she said, "If I knew somebody who could possibly help, but it wasn't... it was a sort of alternative medicine, would you be interested?"

Viviana narrowed her eyes. "You mean such as acupuncture?"

"Could be," said Branwyn noncommittally. "I don't really know the details."

"Your judgment is not always admirable, but I would be interested in meeting anybody you thought could restore my daughter to me." Viviana folded her hands in her lap and looked at Branwyn, the boss waiting for the presentation. It was as if she'd been expecting this for some time.

"I don't have him on auto-dial or anything. I'd need to convince him. And maybe pay him. He's reclusive," she added.

"If I approve of his technique, money will not be an issue," said Viviana, in her crisp producer's voice.

Branwyn's breath hissed between her teeth. "I'm not sure money would interest him. It might require a more... personal arrangement between the two of us." Viviana's expression turned calculating and Branwyn added quickly, "Not sex. An exchange of services, that's all."

The older woman was quiet, her gaze distant. Then Viviana tilted her head. "If you did have to sleep with somebody in order to get them to cure Penny, I think I would condone it. I apologize. I would do it myself, and with Tomas's full approval, I know. But since you see fit to keep the secret of Penny's illness to yourself, I must allow you to also bear the cost of curing her. Do what you must."

"I'll do my best, ma'am," said Branwyn, congratulating herself for averting more tears. She didn't think too closely about what Viviana had encouraged her to do, since an entirely different sort of work for hire was on the table. And it did clarify her feelings about asking Zachariah for help. Her own dislike was a small thing compared to Penny's life.

Viviana's phone chirped and she looked down at it with irritation. "Always, the emergencies. They don't understand the meaning of emergency." She stood up and smoothed her suit. "I must go. You have my number. Please call me when you've persuaded your friend." She then straightened the stack of papers and kissed her daughter's cheek. As she prepared to depart the room, she started flipping through the messages on her phone.

When she opened the door, a voice said, "Ms. Karzan! I was wondering if I could ask you how you feel about your daughter's illness?" Branwyn recognized the clipped, brutally cheerful tones of a reporter. So did Viviana, from the way she rolled her eyes.

The other woman threw a glance over her shoulder at Branwyn, then stepped out of the room and closed the door behind her as she greeted the reporter by name.

Branwyn stood up and moved to Penny's bedside. "Wake up." She paused, just in case this had an effect.

It didn't. She looked at Penny's wan face for a long moment. Then she leaned forward and whispered in Penny's ear. "I can't stand it that you're like this. And I'm going to do everything I can to bring you back. I just wish I'd been there when it started. When that bastard angel convinced you all you needed was him."

She'd play Tarn's game, if it led to Penny's cure. But she wasn't going to head in blind. To Hell with Corbin. She needed to talk to Zachariah anyhow.

Amazing Illusion
Views: 172,098
Check out this great street show I saw!

A noisy crowd in a busy outdoor market. Some men are tossing fish. The crowd noises change. A tall man with golden skin and long, braided white hair is moving through the crowd. He's dressed to stand out, in bright reds and greens, and the crowd moves aside for him. Once in the open space, he bows to the crowd, then bows in particular to a young woman with messy straw-colored hair and freckles. He holds out his hand. She giggles a little, looks around at the crowd, then takes his hand. He gestures as if opening a door and then starts climbing an invisible staircase. At first it's just pantomime, but then he rises in the air. He turns, two feet up, and invites the girl to join him. Hesitantly, she does. Together they climb six feet up, seven feet up. Then the man's head turns as the wind picks up, lifting his hair. He frowns. And then, so quickly the camera doesn't track the event, he vanishes and the girl falls. The camera is lifted high enough to see over the crowd. The girl stands in the middle of several people who leapt to catch her when she fell, looking up at the sky where the illusionist vanished.

Once, Marley had walked into Branwyn's workplace sporting a half-healed bullet hole she hadn't had that morning and she'd refused to explain what was going on. Branwyn had hated that. The truth had been fantastic and Branwyn now had personal experience with the trouble with explaining the fantastic, but she still didn't like Marley's initial evasion. They'd been friends a long time, after all. She certainly didn't want to behave the same way. A friendship like theirs deserved honesty.

On the other hand, Marley worried too much as it was. She wasn't at all pleased to hear Branwyn talk about actually helping Tarn. Apparently learning from him was okay, but taking action was not. *So like Research Girl.*

"If I assist Tarn with a little project, he'll be able to help Penny," Branwyn explained patiently, lounging in Marley's car as they drove over to Zachariah's house.

Marley scowled, keeping her eyes on the road. "A little project, you say. He's trying to escape the remaining restrictions of the Covenant. You know he is."

"Would I help him do that?"

Marley snorted. "In a heartbeat, if you thought that he didn't deserve to be imprisoned. And I don't think you do. What's being done to them is awful, you said."

Thoughtfully, Branwyn said, "That's true."

"Exactly. And he's not in an individual cell, either. It's more like a cattle pen. Even if Tarn is decent, which I have no reason to believe, what about the rest of them?"

Branwyn gave Marley a long, slow stare. "On the other hand, it's Penny. We've been looking out for Penny since we were fifteen years old. You did terrible things to save two kids you've known for a year. Can I do any less for Penny?"

Marley parked outside of Zachariah's home, a Mission-style mansion complete with a walled garden, and dropped her head onto the steering wheel. "Of course not. But—"

Branwyn said sharply, "But *what?* It's not the same?"

"I didn't say that! For all we know, it's *exactly* the same. I certainly can't tell. All I can tell is that you're dancing on the edge of disaster, Branwyn. And I don't want to lose both of you *and* have a bunch of monsters turned loose on the world. And I can't find *anything* that says they're not."

"Yeah. Nobody says, 'Ach, faeries, they're trustworthy sorts.' I was just thinking about that the other day. Look," Branwyn continued.

"You've worried like this before. It's worked out."

"Not exactly like this. I've worried about you ending up in prison, not as a burned-out shell of a person. Not as a faerie slave."

"Close enough," said Branwyn calmly. "I'm going to do this, Marley. And look at the bright side. There are two locks left, right? I'm only going to try to open one. And hey, if I figure out how they work, we can always put them back again. It's experimental research!"

Marley sighed. "I can't stop you. But promise me something. If you get in over your head, ask me for help?"

"Sure," Branwyn replied cheerfully. "I'm always willing to call you for bail money, aren't I?" But Marley was offering something a bit different this time, and Branwyn knew it. Marley's ability to absolutely protect somebody from danger was the primary reason Zachariah left his nieces in her care. But it only worked if Marley was near the person she was protecting, and if they accepted her protection. It wasn't the sort of protection any adult could live under day-in and day-out, because another word for danger was opportunity.

But it could be useful in a fight, assuming Marley wasn't trying to protect too many people, and nobody realized where the magic was coming from. Branwyn didn't want to sit back and live the life of a sheltered child, but she was nothing if not practical, willing to use any weapon she could get her hands on when weapons became necessary.

Marley gave her a narrow-eyed, suspicious glance, then said, "Well, okay then." She summoned a wry smile. "I'll be waiting."

"So, are you going to stick around while I talk to Zachariah?" Branwyn asked as she got out of the car.

The suspicious expression returned. "Is there some reason I shouldn't?"

Branwyn gave her an innocent look. Then the front door of the house burst open and two identical, very small girls raced out.

"Marley! You brought Branwyn! Hi, Branwyn!" said one of them, veering to meet Branwyn. The other one went to grab Marley's hand as she came around the car.

"Hi, grasshopper." Branwyn ruffled the child's hair as she walked past. "Go get Marley. She brought candy."

Ignoring Marley's indignant, "Hey! You—" from behind her, Branwyn walked over to where Zachariah stood in the door, waiting.

He looked like Tarn, save that he wasn't quite as tall or slender, and his black hair was short and neatly cut rather than flowing down his back. And his eyes were an arctic blue, not ridiculously pied. It was, Branwyn observed, like he was a human copy of Tarn. And this wasn't strange, given that, according to Marley, Tarn was Zachariah's father. It wasn't something Branwyn remembered often—neither had ever mentioned the relationship to her—but face to face with Zachariah again after so much time with Tarn, it was hard to overlook.

"Come in," said Zachariah. "Marley says you'd like a favor." He looked over Branwyn's shoulder, a smile brightening his eyes as he watched Marley with the girls.

"Yes, aren't they sweet," said Branwyn. "As a matter of fact, I do. I need some charms suitable for venturing on a vaguely defined quest to convince a powerful being to give up a unique treasure. And Corbin has tapped out or something."

His gaze returned to her. "A bit harsh on Corbin, aren't you?"

"That's rich, coming from you. I'm surprised you're not doing a little jig at having the competition removed. Or maybe a happy slither." She paused, then added, "You know, like snakes do."

He smiled blandly. "You have such a charming way with words, especially for somebody coming to ask for help."

He called for the twins and they ran inside, pulling Marley along by both hands. "Marley is going to come upstairs and play with us," one of them informed Zachariah as they passed by.

"An excellent idea," he said. "I have some business to take care of with Branwyn, and then maybe we can all have dinner."

Marley shot Branwyn a harassed look that surprised Branwyn a little. She didn't usually mind spending time with the kids. And she certainly couldn't be worried that Branwyn would embarrass her. If that was a concern, they would have stopped being friends years ago. Maybe, Branwyn decided, she was worried about Zachariah causing trouble. That's probably what the look meant: *Please have patience with my idiot-male friend.*

Branwyn shrugged in response, then waved as they parted ways. Marley went upstairs with the twins, and Branwyn followed Zachariah. He led her to his office, where once upon a time he'd been stolen away by faeries. It was the sort of room Marley loved, full of books and expensive leather-wrapped oak furniture and dim point lighting. Branwyn thought it needed more color and the leather smelled bad.

"So, I hear Tarn is your father. Do you two get along?"

He paused in the process of settling behind his desk, one hand reflexively clenching into a fist. She noticed he wore a thin silver band around his wrist. "We are cordial, but I wouldn't say we're friends."

"How do you feel about, uh, the Covenant, then?"

"Is this an interview or a request for help, Miss Lennox?" His voice was chilly now. Branwyn could see the Authorized Personnel Only doors clanging shut behind his eyes.

She shrugged and lounged back on the plush couch. "Just curious. I mean, it seems like a complicated situation."

"You're the one directly helping the entity who kidnapped you."

"He invited me," Branwyn corrected. "He kidnapped *you*."

"He prevented both of us from leaving, did he not? Is the difference so significant?"

Branwyn shrugged again. "He was compelled by the angel who hurt Penny. I don't like it when people are forced to do things. It makes me inclined to give them a second chance."

Zachariah laced his fingers together on the desk. "Tarn isn't above compelling people himself."

"Really?" she asked. "He seems more the manipulative type. Offering intriguing goals and reframing situations to suit his narrative. You take after him that way."

His smile was thin. "Sometimes, only pure compulsion will do. Do you want to talk about Marley directly now?"

"Sure." She leaned on her hand on the side of the couch. "Love triangles are a lot less fun when it's your best friend and one of the guys is a thousand years older than her, or whatever you are."

He raised an eyebrow. He looked very much like Tarn, then. "And why should that be relevant? She's an adult, I'm an adult."

"Normally I'd agree, but you've had that much more experience in screwing with peoples' heads. It makes you less sympathetic."

"I don't care about being sympathetic. I need Marley," said Zachariah flatly.

Branwyn twirled a strand of green hair around her finger. "Spoken like a true lover." She watched him as the silence stretched out. His eyebrows were drawn together, shadowing his eyes, but otherwise his face was expressionless. He raised his hands until two fingers rested on his mouth, an absent gesture she wondered if he was even aware of. The silver band stayed fixed in place around his wrist as if glued there, although it didn't look tight.

Finally, he said, "Why should I help you, given your interest in sabotaging my relationship with Marley?"

Bingo. She'd gotten to him.

"Come on, now. You know the answer to that. If you outright refused, Marley would be *so* disappointed in you."

"So I don't refuse. You're full of charms already. Other people's charms are hard to remove."

"Marley's learning magic. Would that excuse work on her?"

"Probably not," he admitted. "But you're the fool that rushes in where angels fear to tread. She won't expect my charms to save you from your own nature."

"Oooh, that's a downright villainous thing you're implying." Branwyn was impressed. If he gave her dangerous charms to dispose of her, or otherwise remove her influence over Marley, she'd be helpless to defend herself. "But it'd be bad for you if it didn't work out. At best, you'd come off as incompetent. At worst, her enemy."

He spread his hands, placing them flat on the desk. "Let's remove Marley from the discussion. She doesn't belong here anyhow. You're not going to buy my assistance by changing your opinion of me. I'm not going to buy your good opinion with a few charms. We think of her because she is all we have in common."

Taken aback, Branwyn could only think to say, "Not the only thing. There's Tarn, too."

Zachariah's smile was so cold it sent chills down Branwyn's spine. "Yes. There's Tarn. And so I am going to help you, free of charge or obligation."

Even more off balance, Branwyn sat up straight. "What? Why?" She had really expected that Marley would play into it somehow: that he'd try to convince her he was a good match for her friend, that she was wrong about his nature. Or even something else, but along those lines.

"I owe Tarn. I should pay him back." She'd never heard that kind of nastiness in Zachariah's voice before. It was enough to make her briefly squirm with uncertainty. But only briefly. "Come." He stood up and moved to the door.

"Uh, now?"

He turned back. "You wish to wait? You've changed your mind? A sense of self-preservation has awakened within you?"

Branwyn bristled. "Look, if I was as blind to danger as you all seem to think, would I be here, making nice with you so that I can arm myself?"

He laughed, clear and loud. "Making nice with me? Is that what this is?"

Nettled, Branwyn said, "I could have a hammer."

"But that wouldn't be polite." His eyes mocked her even as his face resumed its previous seriousness. "Yes, now. Marley is occupying the children, so it will be safe."

Branwyn worked on regaining her composure as she followed Zachariah. She could hear the girls laughing upstairs and Marley's voice raised in amused scolding, and it reminded her of home.

Zachariah's house was larger than her family's even though far fewer people lived there. It seemed like a waste of space, but somehow every room they passed had a clearly defined function. At last, Zachariah made his way to the corner of a large kitchen that smelled of disinfectant rather than dinner and revealed a descending staircase beyond a closed door. "Watch the steps," he said, and went down.

Below the house, Zachariah had a wizard's laboratory. It even looked like one, straight out of a fantasy movie, except for the computer humming in a corner and the concrete walls.

It was tidy, too. There was a complicated set of geometric shapes made of silver and copper and gold, layered on the floor in the center of the room, and many, many shelves lining the walls, filled with… stuff. Glass jars, plastic and metal canisters, cigar cases and security boxes, and the contents Branwyn could see seemed nonsensical: a rag doll, black feathers, ball bearings, poker chips.

"What, no alchemy set?" she asked. "This place really needs some glassware and a bubbling crucible."

Zachariah opened his right hand, showing her his palm. "That's what I have here. It's much more convenient."

Branwyn looked at his open hand, then activated the magical Sight. Just as Corbin did, Zachariah had the seven nodes of humanity along his spine and two more nodes located in the palms of his hands. Activating the palm nodes was advanced magic that a wizard could only perform on himself, so having them was a sign of at least basic competence. Not only was each of his nodes filled with complex charms, there was a web of strands around the bracelet he wore. Some kind of magic tool, she expected.

Seen via the Sight, the laboratory was just as clean. The lines of the Geometry ran through the room in neat bundles. The brightest ones all passed through the supplies stored on the shelves, ringing the room in colored light.

"Step into the circle, please," said Zachariah, gesturing at the diagram on the floor.

"Do I need to take anything off?" asked Branwyn. The circle itself was devoid of any lines outside of the ones making the shape itself.

Zachariah's eyebrows shot up. "Did Corbin ask that of you?"

"Yeah. My shoes and my earrings. He said they'd bring unnecessary influences into the circle."

"Ah," said Zachariah, sounding amused. "No, you don't need to take anything off. I can account for those items."

Branwyn stepped into the circle, then fidgeted as he moved around the room, stopping first at the computer and then moving from shelf to shelf pulling down jars. After a few moments, she sat down on the floor and—

-eight-

Branwyn jerked herself out of a dreamy reverie. She'd been watching Zachariah move around the room, shaping the lines of the Geometry with each component he gathered. Then—what had happened? She felt like she'd fallen asleep and dreamt something already fading away.

"What the hell?" Branwyn scrambled to her feet. She had no idea how much time had passed. Her butt was sore and her feet were tingling from being tucked under her. Zachariah stood outside the circle, regarding her calmly.

"I've installed your charms," he said. He held out an envelope. "And I've prepared instructions for you."

"Why did I fall asleep?" Branwyn demanded.

"So you wouldn't see how I did my magic, or disturb the working. It's built into the circle." He smiled faintly. "A standard precaution. I suppose Corbin didn't do that, either."

Branwyn gave him a flat, cold look. "You could have warned me. I don't like having my will stripped away."

"And yet you're playing with faeries." He studied her and sighed. "It's *standard*, Miss Lennox. I assumed you knew what you were doing when you stepped into the circle. Please believe that I would not have surprised you if I had known you were so..." He shook his head and adjusted his sleeves, his fingers trailing over the band on his wrist.

Scowling, Branwyn said, "How did you get Corbin's charms off? I wanted to see that in particular, since that's supposed to be tough."

"It would require very complex magic to remove a charm spontaneously out in the world, but it isn't impossible. But here and now—well, you went into the circle, and I've made a study of Corbin's magic already. It wasn't hard at all."

Branwyn stepped deliberately out of the circle. "What did you give me?"

"Corbin stocked your nodes primarily with self-defense and personal-assistance charms. I replaced the personal-assistance charms with these." He offered her the envelope again. There were running feet overhead and he glanced up. "And now, I think, it's time for dinner."

Branwyn,

It is important, when spending time in Faerie, not to lose sight of the reason you are there. Corbin has given you one good tool for this. I've given you another. (see attached.)

It's also important to accept that sometimes the only way to survive will be to run away. I thought it might help if you had somewhere to run to, so I've given you two more charms to help you escape from the Backworld when you need to. Try to avoid ending up in a situation where you can't use them. Be aware that they are the most power-hungry of your charms.

If Tarn doesn't ask about me, I'd rather you didn't say anything. I'd like him to be surprised.

—Zachariah

Look At This World
Views: 89,012
Found footage off a lost camera

A camera walks through a downtown city while the cameraman narrates, taking in skyscrapers and boutiques. His voice is deep and sonorous and beautiful, as if added in post-production. "Look at this place. Look what you've built with your hands and your ingenuity. You are an amazing people and we *love* you for it. These dreams! This art!" The cameraman stops and pans across a display of mannequins dressed in the height of fashion. Then he moves into the store, through a window that no longer seems to be there. "And you've been waiting for us. You haven't forgotten us." A brief pan across a display of silver jewelry, and then focusing a startled Japanese girl. "Lovely," the voiceover croons.

"Sir, you ca—" begins the girl, and the voiceover says, "Be at ease, lovely girl. I will return for you when the time is right." The girl's eyes half-close and then she sags against the counter abruptly. An ebony hand reaches out from behind the lens and tangles in her hair for a moment. Then the camera turns away and moves around the store, inspecting the clothing before leaving the shop again. "Yes, we return, and you have multiplied our treasures in ways I never dreamed. Look at this!" and the camera dances over a menu posted outside a restaurant. "Delicacies, available to any who pass on the street. And this camera, so that I may share my experiences with all even without access to my full power. We planted seeds and have returned to a garden paradise. And oh, you love your dreams." The camera pans up to a giant screen on the side of a skyscraper. "Your fantasies, so close to being real. And even now the final barrier is being breached."

Abruptly, the video ends.

"Isn't it rather late on the other side of the curtain?" asked Tarn, relaxing bonelessly in his chair. He put his chin on his hand, watching as Branwyn dropped her backpack to the floor. She wondered if he *ever* sat like he was on a throne, rather than a poorly designed armchair.

"I wanted to avoid any questions. It would really be so much more convenient if you'd move this entrance someplace else, you know."

"What, to a bookstore that would lock its doors every evening? This is much better. You have all the keys you need here." His long lashes lowered as his gaze swept her head to toe. "You've been a busy little bee, I see. I wondered what you'd been up to."

"So let's just confirm things. If you had the power beyond the door, you could wake up Penny, right?"

He shifted position, looked at his nails. "I could."

"And you *would*?"

He looked up at her. "Oh, absolutely. I would very much like to return Penny to you. If the door was open, many, many things would become possible and I certainly would exert that power on Penny's behalf." He quirked a grin. "If you opened the door, how could I do less?"

"Fine. Let's do it."

He looked unsettled. "What, right now?"

"It's Friday. I don't have any other plans for the weekend. So here I am, all gussied up. You said something about a journey. Where do I have to go? What do I have to do?"

Tarn stared at her for a long moment. His fingers tapped on the arm of his throne. Then he stood up and the whole room seemed to revolve around the two of them, changing as it turned.

They stood in another long room. Living paintings lined the walls, but it felt more like a studio containing works in progress, not another gallery. Each painting showed a landscape and she could see the brushwork shift and change as the vision portrayed moved like the view beyond a window.

"You must visit the Queen of Stone and tell her of our project. You will give her a gift and beg for her hairpin." He looked her over again, evaluating what he saw. "If she likes you, she'll give it to you."

Branwyn was startled. "What do you mean, if she *likes* me?"

"If she finds you pleasant, charming, interesting. If she likes you." Tarn gave her an encouraging, sweet smile.

"Oh, that's going to go over well. Why do you need me to go again? If somebody needs to charm this Queen, you've got to have better options. Can't you come?"

"There are things here that require my presence. You are going because you'll be the one to work her hairpin into our key." His smile turned wry. "You'll be the one to interest her, in any case."

"I hope you're sending a really nice gift, then." She looked around. "What are we doing here, anyway?"

A door at the end of the hall opened and William the changeling marched in, followed by eight similar-looking fae armed with spears and shields. William held a small chest in both hands.

"My lord," he said, offering it to Tarn.

Tarn took it and opened it, showing the contents to Branwyn. Inside, snug within velvet padding, were two spheres. One was a glass bubble of the sort Tarn used to convey messages. His letter to her, after the first chain had been broken, had arrived via one. The other was a polished, orange-swirled stone ball. "A message and my gift."

Branwyn regarded the contents of the box dubiously. Tarn had prepared things in advance, despite the surprised act when she showed up demanding to go. Well, she knew he played games. "The Queen of Stone, you said? Is a stone ball really going to impress her? Does she have a collection or something?"

"It's a dorodango. Made of mud, and quite fragile, so do be careful with it." Tarn's smile was faint and absent-minded as he latched the lid closed. "My servants will guide and attend you on your journey." He gestured at William and his friends.

She surveyed the fae. All male, all armed. "A dangerous journey, is it?"

"What makes you say that?"

"It's the nine spears. I think maybe one would be enough for a guide. That's enough for a fellowship."

He walked over to one of the paintings, a Romantic landscape of a road winding around a hillside and past a stark, leafless tree. The road vanished into a narrow valley in the misty distance, while storm clouds tumbled overhead. "The wilds of Faerie are never truly safe, but there's a road between my domain and the court of the Queen of Stone, so you shouldn't be at risk as long as you don't do anything foolish. Don't stray off the path, even if invited to do so. Don't insult anybody you meet along the way. And if William tells you to run, do so."

"A veritable walk in the park," Branwyn said dryly. "How long is the trip?"

"At least one night. Possibly as many as three. My servants have packed supplies that will sustain you without risking your freedom," he added, with a glance at her backpack as if he could see through the canvas to the snacks Branwyn had packed herself. She'd heard from her Gran-gran's stories that Faerie food could be dangerous. Apparently her great-grandmother had been right.

She knelt by the backpack and slipped the small chest inside, making sure to nestle it carefully amidst the energy bars and bags of dried fruit so that it would stay upright. Then she stood up and settled the pack over her shoulder. "So, deliver the box to this Queen of Stone. Be nice to her. Get a hairpin. Come back. Make a key. Save Penny. Am I missing anything? No? Let's do this."

"Indeed." Tarn pressed his palm on the surface of the painting. His hand sank through. "The door is open. The way is clear. The journey is yours."

Branwyn pushed her own palm against the painting. She encountered less resistance than expected, and stumbled forward as a result. The painting passed around her and her booted feet came down on an old, moss-covered road. A moment later, the armed fae streamed around her.

Orienting herself, she looked over her shoulder. Behind her was a rounded hill with a thin silver spire perched at the summit. A great wooden door closed in the hillside a few yards away.

And the hill was odd. She walked closer, touched the grass, and it felt like grass. But it looked like the painting. The colors were unreal and the lines were simplified. The clouds moved overhead as if caught in a fast and playful wind, swirling and changing like ink in water.

William said, "If you look at the sky too much, she'll look back at you. That wouldn't be wise right now. Come along this way."

Startled, Branwyn looked away from the hypnotic sky. The wind ruffled the grass on the slope beside the road ahead, and she realized she could see the wind itself as curls of dancing blue light. The land was like a dream or a story.

William touched her arm and she shook herself. "Give me a minute." One of Corbin's charms might be useful here. She closed her eyes, visualized the activation symbols for the reminder charm, then said, "I am going to visit the Queen of Stone." Just as had happened when she experimented after first getting the charm, she felt the words settle into her consciousness. Any time her thoughts wandered, her own voice would echo in her head: *I am going to visit the Queen of Stone.*

Then, hopefully fortified against the distracting landscape, she shifted the weight of her backpack and set out after William and his troop of faeries.

Around the curve of the valley ahead, the country opened up. In the distance off to the right, another hill dominated the landscape. On top of the hill, an enormous stone woman arched her back, her hands flung out.

I am going to visit the Queen of Stone. "Is that where we're headed?" Branwyn asked hopefully.

William glanced at the sculpture only briefly. "No. My lord made that centuries ago to memorialize a girl that escaped him. Her majesty is a touch more distinctive."

Branwyn noticed the *escaped him* but only said, "Distinctive how?"

"Ah, well, the Queens all live in deep Faerie. They *are* deep Faerie, really. They get a little… odd. You'll see."

"Fair enough. Hey, why did he send so many of you if obeying rules is the key to safe travel here?"

"Safe travel for you, lady. There's little here that would risk the displeasure of both the Queen of Stone and the Duke of Underlight for stealing you away. But there's those that wouldn't hesitate to waylay a single guide and leave you stranded."

Branwyn frowned. "Why would I be safe while you, Tarn's actual servants, wouldn't be?"

William shrugged, his gaze roving watchfully from side to side. "Faerie is but part of the Backworld, and not everything that roams the Backworld is my lord's ally. And the rules are different for my kind and yours."

They passed by a large, leafless tree that held a stringless violin in its branches. The blue curls of wind played over the instrument, teasing impossible music out of the emptiness. Branwyn stared curiously as long twigs moved, finger-like, over the neck of the violin.

I am going to visit the Queen of Stone. The music was beautiful, though. It surged against the reminder at first, then changed, weaving the words into the song.

But the view from the other side of the tree drove the music out of her head. The giant lady enjoying herself on the hilltop was gone, replaced by a distant raised highway built from stacked stone, lined with lights glowing against a purple twilight sky.

Branwyn stopped, then backtracked to the other side of the tree. The enormous sculpture dominated a hillside. Somehow, passing the tree had changed the entire landscape.

Branwyn lifted her foot to walk around the tree from the other side.

I am going to visit the Queen of Stone.

Don't stray off the path.

Branwyn put her foot back down again on the road, then backed away from the edge. The troop of changelings watched her impassively, although William looked impatient.

She adjusted her backpack self-consciously. "Right. Very interesting. Let's move on."

The twilight on the right didn't change, but after a time, the storm clouds on her left vanished and a rainbow shimmered across the blue sky. It jumped between the tops of the hills as if pacing them, before coming to earth in a crystalline pool at the base of a jagged white cliff. A unicorn rested beside the pool, looking away from its reflection at them as they went by.

Branwyn opened a bottle of water from her backpack and didn't go investigate the pool, despite the tinkling waterfall. Despite the *unicorn.* "My baby sister must never come here," she announced. William gave her a blank look and she sighed. "You're not much of a traveling companion, you know."

The lead fae, ranging ahead of them, turned and jogged back. William left Branwyn's side and met him halfway. After conferring briefly, William gave a hand signal and the entire troop stopped. Branwyn looked at them, then kept going until she caught up with William. "What's up?"

"There's something else moving on the road. Better to meet it here, in the open terrain, than ahead in the canyon."

"Ah," said Branwyn. "Should I get my hammer ready?"

William looked at her as if he was seeing her for the first time. "You brought a hammer on a visit to the Queen of Stone?"

"Well, it seemed more practical than a big knife, and I wasn't going on an adventure unarmed." She slid her bag off her back and glanced at his shocked expression with amusement. "I brought some duct tape, too."

"I don't think that will be necessary," he said, his expression sliding from shocked to worried.

Before she could say anything more, a silver birdcage came around the bend, carried on the shoulders of four men garbed in loincloths. At first she thought they were distant, gigantic figures, but she blinked and scale reasserted itself against the odd, slightly forced perspective of her painted surroundings. The bearers were very tall, and very muscular, but not beyond human-sized. The birdcage on their shoulders was a palanquin, fitted with sheer curtains. A barely visible feminine figure lounged within the silver lattice. To Branwyn's admittedly inexpert gaze, it did not seem like a hammer-requiring situation.

Atop the palanquin was another latticework, this one an actual cage, and inside a doll-sized man sat playing a recorder. The lonely tune warbled through the air, sounding almost familiar, and Branwyn thought of her stepfather practicing folk songs with her sister.

As it got closer, William glanced from the palanquin to Branwyn and back again. Each bearer was a magnificently beautiful man with mahogany skin and dark green hair. Branwyn touched her own green ponytail self-consciously even as the bearers came to a halt on the other side of the road.

"Oh, charming," came a voice from the palanquin. The tiny piper atop the palanquin fell silent and a slim hand lifted the curtain away. A woman, white of hair and gown, looked out. "Where are you taking her, servant of Underlight?"

"She is an envoy to the Queen of Stone, Lady of Nightwell," called William, his eyes on the bearers, not the woman.

"Ah," said the woman, with undisguised disappointment. A pale hand gestured languidly. "Come to me, mortal child. Let me look at you."

Branwyn looked questioningly at William, who shrugged. Mutual curiosity winning out, she moved closer to the palanquin.

White of hair and white of gown: the description lingered in Branwyn's mind like the refrain of the piper's song. Her skin barely blushed with life, but the woman had shockingly blue eyes. Her hair was cropped close to her head, except for a topknot and two locks hanging in front of her ears. Her satin gown was simple and form-fitting in the bodice, with an extremely full skirt pooled around her curled legs. It reminded Branwyn of a basic wedding dress. She wore a large silver ring set with a shimmering black gem on her left middle finger. It seemed to leave a trail in the air as she waved her hand again. "Closer, please."

Branwyn obligingly crossed the last few yards to stand beside the palanquin, passing right beside one of the bearers. He was huge, with rippling muscles and shining skin and features so gorgeously chiseled that Branwyn thought sculpting them would be cheating her way to fame and fortune. While the four weren't identical, she thought they might be brothers. She could smell the earthy scent of their sweat and she smiled at the one closest, the smile she always shared with others of unusual haircolors. His eyes didn't flicker from their fixed-ahead position.

Branwyn's smile faded and she transferred her attention to their lady. "Hello."

"You have a striking coloration, child. Most uncommon among mortals." The woman reached out to touch her hair and Branwyn could feel the cold of her hand as the white fingers stroked her ponytail.

She just barely resisted jerking her head away. but she did say bluntly, "It's dye."

"Oh, but that's even better," said the woman. She withdrew her hand, her sapphire eyes glowing with enthusiasm. "Your willingness to change what you were born with to suit your true nature—also unusual among mortals. So many are obsessed with letting their birth define them." Her small nose wrinkled with distaste at the thought. "Will you tell me what you are called?"

"That's true," Branwyn conceded. "My name is..." she caught herself, remembering more of her Gran-gran's stories. "Uh, I'm called Branwyn."

The lady in white smiled. "And I am the Lady Rime, of Nightwell." She clasped her hands together. "This is lovely. I do like mortals."

Branwyn hesitated, then went ahead and asked, "Are your bearers mortal?"

"Not anymore," said the woman in white, looking fondly at the two in front. "I've colored them to suit my tastes." When she saw Branwyn glance up at the tiny piper caged above her, she asked, "Did you like the music? I'm very fond of song myself. I find it opens so many doors." Her smile became radiant. "If you bring music, everybody is always pleased to see you."

"That does seem to work for my stepfather. As long as he doesn't want paying," Branwyn said absently, trying to decide if the piper was a mechanical creation of some sort. When it wasn't playing, it didn't seem to be moving at all, even to breathe. But it looked very much like a tiny man.

"Oh, I always make sure they pay the piper. Or rather me, since the piper is mine." Lady Rime returned her brilliant gaze to Branwyn. "When you have finished your duties as an envoy, I would very much like for you to visit me. My bearers would enjoy getting to know you, too."

Branwyn glanced again at the lead bearers, who showed no sign of hearing the conversation. "Uh, I'll keep that in mind." She took a step backwards. "Thank you for the invitation," she added, remembering Tarn's admonition to be polite. "I should probably go back to my envoy work. You know how it is. Busy, busy."

The Lady Rime looked at her with the same fond, pleased glance she'd turned on her bearers. "Of course. I look forward to seeing you again. We'll have fun."

Branwyn beat a retreat back to William and his troop as the piper atop the palanquin picked up his lonely song again. The bearers carried their burden down the road, the curtains once again shielding the lady within from view. The troop of changelings waited until the palanquin was out of sight before moving out to the center of the road again.

"Is it just me, or was that an extremely creepy encounter?" Branwyn asked William.

"I suggest you don't accept her invitation," William said seriously. "Unless you want to lose yourself in pleasure beyond reason."

A wave of profound alienation swept over Branwyn. She was in a place where *that* was being presented as sensible advice, in the shadow of giant statues and endless bridges and magical waterfalls and unicorns. Even her tolerance for adventure was being tested by the strange journey, and for a moment, she felt a long way from home. "Okay, now you're being creepy, too. Don't do that."

William shrugged again. "That seemed like a mild exchange to me," he said. Branwyn blinked, then realized he was responding to her initial description of Rime as creepy. "A different faerie Lord might have been more dangerous, but the March of Nightwell draws on the Court of Stone just as Underlight does. She gained no advantage from waylaying you, even if her Duke and mine are rivals."

"She isn't actually expecting me to visit her, is she?"

"I can't begin to guess at the workings of Lady Rime's mind. But you didn't obligate yourself to visit her, if that's what you're asking."

"Good," said Branwyn, relieved.

William glanced at her one more time, then nodded to himself and called out for the troop to start moving again. Branwyn fell into step in the middle of the group. After a moment, she found herself whistling the piper's song. When William turned back to look at her, she stopped, considered, then switched to one of her stepfather's favorite songs instead. After the first verse, the troop of faeries joined in on the chorus.

Huh. She hadn't expected that from the reserved changelings. The Lady Rime was right. Music did get you into unexpected places.

-nine-

So how do we know when to stop for the day?" Branwyn asked William as he stalked along beside her. "I mean, 'day' seems like a place, not a time, here."

He looked her over. "Are you tired?"

Branwyn flexed her feet. "A little. Not as much as I would expect, given how long it feels like we've been walking and when we started."

"Ah, well, let's see where the road takes us in the next few bends. It could be we'll need to camp quite soon." He moved to the head of the troop to confer with the changeling in the lead.

A few moments later, he jogged back. "Night is coming. We'll stop here."

Branwyn looked around. "Right in the middle of the road?"

He gave her a scornful look. "Of course not." Kneeling down, he placed his palm on the cobbled surface. A mild electric shock passed through Branwyn, and then the ground trembled. As she stumbled and tried to catch her balance against the earthquake, William stood up, swaying like a tree.

"You see," he said, and she did. The road bulged into the forest on the left, the cobbles duplicating themselves to expand the surface with a sound like falling dominoes. After a few moments, a large semi-circle on one side of the road had formed like a bud on a stem. "Just in time, too. Night is coming faster than I expected."

Branwyn glanced up at the unchanging sky, then scanned the horizons. With a start, she realized that night was literally moving down the road, a vast, dense cloud obscuring the daylight. As the darkness crept down the track, the landscape on both sides changed. The trees of the forest became skeletal, while the fields across the road sprouted misshapen hillocks oozing eerie, faint glows.

Branwyn took a step backwards, glancing questioningly at William. Left to her own devices, she'd retreat rather than let that strangeness overtake her.

"It will pass," he said. "And our campsite will keep us safe from most of what travels the night road. Come."

"Only most?" Branwyn remembered Tarn talking about just how *long* the list of dangers in Faerie was.

"Only most." He turned away.

"You're not going to elaborate, I see." Branwyn sighed and started after him.

He shrugged one shoulder and said, without turning around, "The most dangerous denizens of the Backworld hear their own names. Use your imagination, if you enjoy being afraid."

The rest of the faerie troop had already started work converting the circle of paving into a real camp. Two of them were building a fire while several others constructed three pavilion tents. One planted a banner into the paving stones and stood guard next to it.

"What exactly is the night here?" Branwyn asked instead, following William. "It isn't a time, it isn't a place, it's a…?"

"A traveler," William supplied. "If our need was urgent, we could travel through the night and it would pass faster. But there are things that travel in the night that are best avoided if possible."

Fascinated, Branwyn asked, "Where is it going?"

William raised his eyebrows, taken aback by the question "I've never asked. It's the night."

"Oh." She frowned, remembering what he'd said before about the sky looking back at her.

Bowing, William said, "The lads have your pavilion finished. You're welcome to rest there until we've finished preparing dinner."

Branwyn started to decline the offer, more interested in watching the moving darkness. But the weight on her back reminded her of something she'd been planning on doing once they took their break. So she nodded to William and went into the silver and green pavilion he'd indicated.

It was already furnished with matching pillows, quilts, and a low table, none of which she'd seen the faerie troop carrying. She wasn't sure any of them had been carrying the pavilion, either. But William had just caused the road itself to bud off a campsite for them so they could rest through the traveling night, so it wasn't really first on her mind to wonder about.

It's magic! That was such an annoying answer. It was an answer that required faith; it was an answer that suggested there were no rules. Branwyn didn't have a problem with breaking rules, but she *did* like to know when she was doing it.

She set the backpack down on the table and thoughtfully attempted to reach through the curtain into the substrate of the Backworld. Her fingers closed over cool metal and she withdrew a silvery rod.

After regarding it for a moment, she put it down on the table beside her backpack and stared off into space. Then she pulled out the small chest Tarn had given her and flipped the lid open. There were the two balls, glass and polished mud. She tapped her finger on the polished mud ball, then reached again into the substrate.

This time, she pulled out an orb, swirled grey and green like the pavilion silks. She weighed it in one hand, then picked up the mud ball in the other. It was not the same; the one she'd conjured was probably actually stone.

It would be easier, she thought, if she could just say, "Soapstone," and get soapstone. But while that seemed possible for the faeries, she was still a beginner and it seemed to be a lot more complicated than just wishing.

And, she reminded herself, it wasn't even the end goal. Shaping the substance of Faerie was a neat party trick, but it wasn't useful in the normal world. It wasn't useful like Corbin and Zachariah's magic, and useful was what she was after. Learning to shape Faerie was like learning to draw perspective, or so she'd gathered from Tarn.

She flicked the stone ball, then turned her attention back to the mud sphere. No matter what Tarn had suggested, she didn't believe that he was sending a bit of dirt to his Queen, even if it had been shined up. He used the glass orbs to carry messages, so it seemed to fit his style to encase a more solid gift inside a more solid sphere. He'd even said it was fragile.

She remembered how the Geometric Sight had been useful in the gallery, and activated it. Right away, she saw that the ball of dirt was one of the few real objects in sight, and the only one she hadn't brought with her from home.

The dense lines radiating from the mud ball dwarfed the ones coming from her own supplies. They formed a complicated web that didn't respond when Branwyn poked it with her finger. Of course; she could only see the Geometry, not interact with it directly.

She brought the dorodango closer to her face, studying it. There was something familiar about the complexity of the web. It reminded her of something she'd seen before somewhere. That it was a spell, she had no doubt, but she wasn't sure where she could have seen a spell embedded in an object like this. Most of the magic she'd seen had been charms stored on people. This was like the precursor to a charm, like the knots she'd seen Corbin crafting when he constructed her charms.

This was tightly woven—and strange. She brought it even closer, until her eyes were crossing, then closed one eye to try to see what was bothering her. The knot wasn't embedded in a node, but it was attached to something all the same.

It was something within the dorodango, she decided. There was magic spun about the orange-swirled orb, but most of the lines originated within it. She could just make out a shape, simply because the lines were so dense.

It was a thin band, larger than a ring, smaller than a collar. It was, in fact, very much like the silver band she'd seen on Zachariah's wrist the previous day, right down to the web of magic containing it.

Branwyn stared at it, but before she could decide what she wanted to do, there was a cry from outside, distant and full of pain. The fae started shouting.

Abandoning the orb in its case and pushing her way through the tent flap, Branwyn found the fae troopers with their weapons ready, clustered on the edge of the campsite. She counted, and realized one of them was missing.

"One of the bad ones?" She joined William, who was the only one of the fae who'd left his spear on the ground. Another agonized cry came from the forest and Branwyn flinched.

William's fist clenched and unclenched. "He was lured outside the circle. I did say it was less safe for us."

"What has him? You said you had safety in numbers. Can't you go after him?"

"That's probably what he wants," William muttered.

"Who?"

"Our enemy," William snapped. "Our lord's enemy."

Now that the night had fully engulfed them, Branwyn thought it seemed almost ordinary, if your idea of an ordinary night involved a haunted forest and a field full of graves. The moon hadn't risen, but stars glittered overhead, cold and bright. There was even the distant sound of crickets and the hooting of owls.

Branwyn ducked into her tent and pulled out both her pocketknife and the hammer she'd packed. Then she paced past William and the others, deliberately stepping off the paved campsite into the forest itself as another shriek shattered the night. She looked over her shoulder at the fae. "Well? Let's go get him. Perhaps it won't be so bad if I come along." She summoned up a faint smile, which wasn't easy against the memory of the scream. "I can invoke diplomatic immunity or whatever it is."

William stared at her. "You're insane." Then he kicked his spear into his hand and joined her at the forest's edge. His men darted after him, flowing around them in a practiced pattern.

The wind sparkled and moaned through the interwoven branches of the forest. Even in leaf, the trees seemed like strange skeletons in the dim starlight, and the darkness writhed and breathed around them. *In an ordinary forest, that would just be small animals*, Branwyn thought. But in an ordinary forest, her companions' eyes wouldn't be glowing like cats'.

She followed William, watching the ground before her feet rather than the forest, until she ran into his back. He stood stiffly, facing a still-living fallen tree. Soft whimpers came from the other side.

"What's over there?" she whispered.

He shook his head. "Him. Are you sure you want to do this?"

The changelings' fear was palpable, and contagious. "I thought you said you guys were the ones in danger."

"He's unpredictable. And we've left the road..."

A familiar voice from beyond the fallen tree called, "Oh, stop whispering like children. It's not like I can't hear you." Branwyn stiffened. The voice was like the shock of a cold shower: she should have expected it, she realized, but she'd had other things on her mind.

She climbed over the fallen tree, pushing wet foliage out of her face. On the other side was a clearing. Silhouetted against one of the ghostly grave-born fires was a figure crouching over something on the ground. "Hello, cupcake. Oh, you've brought tools," said the figure. "Splendid. Hand me that hammer."

The lump on the ground moaned, and Branwyn unclenched her teeth enough to snap, "No! Stop it!"

"No? How about the pocketknife? Is there a corkscrew? I know a few good tricks with a corkscrew." Severin looked up at her, his grin a ghastly jack-o-lantern smile. "And you brought the rest of them, too. How considerate."

Branwyn felt sick. "You can't have them. And let that one go."

"After I worked so hard to lure him out here? Not a chance. These guys are quite the challenge, you know. If you go too far—" and then Branwyn rushed him, hoping like hell William's troopers were still behind her.

She brought the hammer around as she moved, trying to catch him by surprise. But a hand like steel caught her wrist as Severin bent backwards to dodge her blow. Then his foot came up, catching her in the solar plexus and knocking her away. She landed on her shoulder and rolled to her feet, then fell to her knees again and threw up her trail mix.

"Damnit, cupcake," complained Severin. "You broke my concentration and look what happened. I lost him."

Branwyn peered up through streaming eyes, then rubbed them clean. What had been a pile of tormented changeling was sublimating into a cloud. Severin waved his hand through it a few times, then tilted his head to watch as it streamed up into the sky. "Back to his master for a new body." Severin chuckled. "If he's lucky. If Tarn cares enough."

He stood up and looked around. "But here are all the rest. That saves me some time." The other eight changelings, William included, stood in a circle around Branwyn and Severin, spears pointed inward.

"Which one would you like to keep as your guide, cupcake?" Severin laced his fingers together and cracked his knuckles.

"All of them," wheezed Branwyn.

"That's not a choice," chided the kaiju, and he darted forward and grabbed one of the spears. Quicker than Branwyn could process, he'd hauled the spear's owner in, twisted him around, and broken his neck. Then he flung the body to the ground as it, too, began to sublimate.

After a shocked heartbeat, the others surged toward him, shouting. For a moment, Branwyn could only make out bodies and flashing spear points. Ignoring her painful breathing, she scrambled up on the fallen tree and watched the battle for a moment. Severin moved like a sapling, bending and swaying to avoid some thrusting spear points, slapping others out of the way. His foot snapped into a trooper's knee and the faerie collapsed. His palm hit another one in the face and that one reeled away with blood streaming from his nose and mouth.

The kaiju stepped out of the circle through the opening he'd created, then jumped up onto the fallen tree beside Branwyn. "You see, it's not as if they're real. I kill them and they just fly along home to Tarn again. It's nothing but a message for him."

"Go to hell," snarled Branwyn.

Severin waved a finger. "Tsk, tsk. So, who will it be? I think they'll all be equally good for getting us in to see the Queen of Stone, so the real question is, which one pleases you the most?"

"Us? *Us?* There is no 'us.' Go *away*," said Branwyn, shoving him off the tree. He flipped midair and landed on his feet. She'd hoped the fae would take advantage of the situation and go back to stabbing him, but they hung back. A couple of them wore grim expressions, but others were obviously frightened. They might not be *dying*, but whatever was happening after they were defeated wasn't comforting to anticipate.

Severin looked annoyed. "Should I just kill all of them and leave you here for the night to consume, then?" He reached behind him and one of the grim-faced fae stumbled forward as if pushed, right into his hand. The kaiju held the smaller figure by the throat without taking his nightmare eyes off Branwyn. "What exactly was your intention in bringing them all out to me, if not this?"

Branwyn shook her head, not biting on that bit of guilt. He'd already acquired one of them. He would have acquired more through the night, and this way, they at least knew what they were facing.

She glanced around the clearing for ideas and met William's gaze. Alone of his troop, he seemed angry rather than frightened. Angry, but resigned. Branwyn didn't like that at all.

She had to do *something*, but what could she do against Severin? She couldn't fight him, that was clear. She couldn't argue with him. She couldn't even barter with him; she had nothing that he wanted. She was *helpless*. And she hated it.

His hand squeezed the changeling's throat. Another one started forward, but William stopped him. The changeling's eyes bulged and his brown skin purpled.

"Please," Branwyn whispered. "Please don't."

Severin cocked his head. "What's that? Did you say something?"

Branwyn swallowed, her chest hurting. "Please don't hurt them."

"Oh, cupcake," sighed the kaiju. "Begging for the lives of some videogame characters? Are they really worth hurting your pride for?"

"I'm not beg—" Branwyn started to say, then stopped. She was. She would, no matter how hard it was to get the word out. "Please."

The kaiju's hand relaxed and the changeling collapsed onto the forest floor. To Branwyn's relief, he didn't dissolve into mist.

But Severin wasn't done. He sprang back up on the fallen tree, closing on her. His eyes glittered in the darkness.

"They aren't worth it, you know."

"I know *you* think that. I disagree."

"You are naive." He cocked his head to one side. "Or maybe you're right. Maybe it isn't costing you anything. Maybe you're just manifesting your true nature. Something small. Something sweet and helpless. Perhaps begging comes naturally to you." His hand twitched and Branwyn scooted backwards. "You'd enjoy losing control. Letting somebody else pull your strings."

"No," Branwyn gasped. Even from a few feet away, he was

crowding her. She couldn't look away from his eyes. He could see her darkest fears: that he was right. She was weak. She felt so much better trusting somebody else's judgment. She'd been lying to herself all this time, trying to live up to an image she'd imagined. Begging really was the best she could do.

I am going to visit the Queen of Stone.

Branwyn jerked out of her reverie of self-loathing and scrambled down off the fallen tree, away from him "No," she said again. "I really wouldn't."

Severin chuckled. "I didn't think that would last long. But it was delicious while it did."

"That's what's important to you, isn't it?" Branwyn said suddenly. "You wouldn't like me saying 'please' nearly as much if it came easily."

"Oh, there's always some appeal." The kaiju sounded positively cheerful as he swung himself off the tree after her. He waved his hand at the remaining changelings. "I'll let you live for now. The mortal has successfully purchased an extension on your pretend lives. Run along back to your camp."

"What?" Branwyn suddenly felt very tired. It had been such a long day already. "Really? God, Penny always talks about the power of being polite but I never thought it went this far."

The jack-o-lantern smile came and went. "You're much more interesting to play with than some animated soul-patterns, cupcake."

Branwyn eyed him, caught between asking what the hell he was talking about and getting away. She finally opted for at least a token effort toward self-preservation and turned to William and the changelings. "Let's go, before he changes his mind."

The changelings tried to fall in around her, but she shooed them ahead of her. She noticed, as she walked, that they weren't leaving Severin behind. She could hear him following them, his feet crunching dead things with every step.

She stopped. She turned around. She peered into the darkness. And there was nothing to see. Nothing to hear.

Something was breathing behind her. She turned around again, but there was only William, a little ways ahead, watching her with some concern.

"This is ridiculous. I know you're there. You can't frighten me if I know you're there."

"Can't I?" His voice was right in her ear.

Branwyn didn't turn around again, but she did pick up her pace, staring fixedly ahead and hoping she didn't fall over anything in the darkness.

It really did sound like Severin was walking over broken bones. Snapping, with occasional squelching.

The firelight of the campsite became visible through the trees, not an instant too soon, and Branwyn broke into a jog. The bone-walking faded behind her. When she burst through the foliage and jumped back onto the bricks of the campsite, she felt a sense of triumph. It was quickly followed by another wave of tiredness, and her body complaining in detail about sore muscles and bruises.

The remaining changelings conferred together. Branwyn sagged onto the ground near the fire, trying not to wonder if she'd made the right decision, trying to rescue the original victim.

"This *is* cozy," remarked Severin, stepping into the campsite. "Which pavilion is mine?"

"What?" demanded Branwyn, starting to her feet, her heart thumping. "Go away. You let them go!"

"Relax, cupcake. I want to visit the Queen of Stone, too. I'm sure I said." In the firelight, he almost seemed like an ordinary man, except for his red-stained hands and the way he moved like a wolverine hoping for a fight.

She narrowed her eyes and he added, "I'll be tagging along one way or the other. If you'd rather have me behind you...?"

"You won't see her," said William. "We don't have the power to fight you, but *she* is guarded by those who would send you howling back into the night."

"We'll see," said the kaiju. He crossed to the firepit with long strides, then crouched beside it. Holding a hand out to the flame, he said, "Have you made up your mind, cupcake? With you or behind you?"

"I'm trying to decide," said Branwyn. "Which one you'd enjoy more. Which one I *want* you to enjoy more."

"And I bet that's a *fun* line of thought." He grinned at the fire.

It wasn't. Branwyn gave up trying to see the point of view of a monster. She was tired and frustrated "Actually, I don't care. Do what you want. It's going to be awful anyhow."

"Lady—" began William, in an alarmed voice.

Severin turned his head slowly to look at her, his eyes glittering again. "I don't need permission, but getting it is somehow… inviting." With one of those lightning-fast moves he was standing right in front of her, once again too close. His hand closed on her arm, and he leaned forward to whisper in her ear, "But not as much fun as doing it my way. Be careful, cupcake. Say that to one of the *fae* and they'll claim you just gave yourself to them."

Branwyn kicked him.

The action wasn't driven by a measured rationality. She was tired, she was cranky, she was frightened, and she was pissed off. And he'd grabbed her.

It didn't work to hurt him, because he was too fast. But it worked to make him let go of her as he dodged away, and that was good enough. "I'll remember that," she said sweetly.

He stood just a few steps away, like a leaf come to earth. As he stared at her expressionlessly, Branwyn's heart climbed into her throat. But he'd done something wrong, not her. As the moment drew itself out, she whirled around and stalked into her pavilion.

Once the silken door was closed behind her, she knelt in front of the table where she'd been working earlier that night. Staring blindly at the dorodango and the low-quality duplicate she'd made, she waited for him to come after her. When that didn't happen, she waited for the sound of conflict outside.

Instead, there was only silence. Branwyn dragged in a deep breath as the adrenaline ebbed away. What did you do, she wondered, when the man-eating tiger you'd just escaped from followed you home, apparently no longer hungry? Apparently, you let him curl up beside the fire and do as he pleased. Even knowing he'd eaten some of your friends.

Branwyn's insides squirmed at the thought. She hated being helpless. But that was why she was on this path. She'd known this would be dangerous when she started. She wasn't going to break and run now, no matter how terrifying it became.

She blinked, shook her head, and focused on the dorodango again. What had she figured out about it? Oh yes, that it contained a band just like the one clamped around Zachariah's wrist.

Frowning, Branwyn washed her face and hands in the bowl of water one of the changelings had left for her. Then she picked up the dorodango, went to the pavilion exit, and listened. There was only the low murmur of the remaining fae troop at first. They spoke another language to each other, something that sounded vaguely Gaelic.

Then one of the voices was raised in song. For a few moments, Branwyn listened to what was almost certainly a dirge while staring at the polished ball in her hand. Whatever Severin had said, whatever he'd meant, the fae certainly acted like they'd lost friends.

And yet...

When the singer finished, she unhooked the pavilion door and stepped outside. The changelings all sat on one side of the firepit, staring across it at Severin. The kaiju had returned to the position he'd been in before, crouched with one hand out to the fire, as if he was alone in the camp.

"William," Branwyn called. Everybody looked at her, even Severin, but she kept her gaze on the leader of the changelings. "Do you know what's inside this?"

She held up the dorodango and couldn't help but notice that Severin pivoted to watch her, smirking.

William loped over to her. "It's a gift for the Queen of Stone," he explained, as if she was a child who'd forgotten.

Branwyn didn't appreciate it. "That's not what I asked. Do you know what's inside?"

"No, I don't." His eyes didn't even flicker.

Branwyn scowled. "Let's find out." She flung the ball at the ground. William moved to catch it, but she'd surprised him and he was too slow. The orange-swirled sphere thudded onto the cobbles and cracked in two.

"Are you mad?" William demanded. "Have you utterly lost your wits?"

Branwyn stepped past him and scooped up the remains of the orb. Silver metal curved out of one side, and as she picked it up, the ball further crumbled until nothing was left but a pile of dirt and a silver bracelet.

She shook the dirt off the bracelet. "Do you know what this is?"

"No!" William looked just as angry as he had when he watched the kaiju strangle one of his men.

"I know what happens to bad boys who lie," said Severin cheerfully as he joined them beside the tent. "It's me! Care to try again?"

William hesitated, looking furious, then admitted, "Yes, I know what it is."

"Tell me," commanded Branwyn. She wasn't happy that Severin was involving himself, but she also wasn't happy that William was lying to her after their experience in the forest. After she'd *begged* Severin to spare the lives of his men.

"It's a control band for my lord's son," William said sullenly. "My lord gives his son's service to the Queen in exchange for the Machine fragment."

"You mean for Zachariah?" Branwyn asked sharply.

William nodded, then volunteered, "When my lord held him captive, the man fell into a black mood. A bargain was struck. My lord promised information in exchange for his son submitting to the control band."

"But Zachariah was released after Marley defeated the angel. So why is he still wearing it?"

William looked at her like she was speaking another language, and Severin said, "You misunderstand, cupcake. The band wasn't part of that captivity. It's the result of a prison yard deal. Trading cigarettes for sex, that kind of thing. The band makes sure Zachariah can't back out." Severin grinned. "Makes sure he—"

"Shut up. I get it," interrupted Branwyn. "What can the band make him do?"

William shrugged. "Many little things. One important thing."

"Importance measured how?"

With a thin smile, William said, "By my lord's son. The information he wanted was *very* important to him at the time."

Branwyn stared down at the silver band. Through the Sight, she could see the magic spun around it. It was astonishingly complex. She remembered Zachariah saying, *I need Marley,* and she wondered if the silver band and its compulsion was why. What if the band turned him into a weapon against the twins? What would the Queen of Stone use him for?

Quietly, she said, "And you didn't see any problem with this? Neither you nor Tarn nor any of your people?"

William's expression became puzzled. "No...?" He cast a glance down at the band. "You destroyed the sphere, which destroys the symmetry of the gift, but the Queen of Stone won't mind that much. I hope."

In her head, Severin's voice whispered, *You don't even like them, but you saved them from me. Would you like to change your mind?*

"No," whispered Branwyn. She curled her fingers over the band. It was one thing to make a fair deal, but a bargain struck under duress for an unspecified payment wasn't fair. Adding in an irresistible compulsion only made it worse. And this deal was probably contributing to Zachariah's interference in Marley's relationship with Corbin, which made it personal.

And yet she was carrying the tool of this coercion to somebody who could provide the key to saving Penny.

Poor, helpless Branwyn, crooned the kaiju. *You'll beg for the lives of strangers. What will you do for your friend?*

"Not this," said Branwyn. She wrapped both hands around the silver band and bent it until it, and the magic bound to it, warped.

"You *are* insane," said William flatly.

"Shut up," Branwyn muttered absently, turning away and further working the silver between her fingers. She'd use the hammer to finish the job. "Don't convince me he's right."

"So now what?" demanded William, ignoring her advice. "Do we turn around and go home?"

"Mortal scruples," said Severin happily. "Don't you love them? The way they consistently put their enemies before their friends. It's beautiful."

Branwyn looked up. "What are you talking about? I'm very eager to meet the Queen of Stone."

Acidly, William said, "You don't think she'll notice the missing orb in the gift chest? Or are you not planning on giving her anything at all? She'll take that poorly, I promise, Lady."

Branwyn's gaze was caught by Severin's again. This time, it was less traumatic. He looked like a child anticipating Christmas. Without even his mental voice, she knew his own thoughts toward the Queen of Stone weren't friendly. And she knew he still considered her a means toward his ends.

She shook her head. He was playing her against them, and against herself, for his own purposes. She had to remember that.

"I can make another of those balls, then. Tarn said she'd want to meet the artisan who would make something of her Machine. Maybe she'd like a piece of art from me as well." And she scooped up the powdered remains of the dorodango and went into her tent.

-ten-

It was two sleeps and one night later that they arrived at the mountain home of the Queen of Stone. The solitary peak towered above the gentle hills and rolling fields that had comprised most of the recent scenery. The road they were on dead-ended at an almost cartoonishly abrupt slope of tumbled stone and loosely rooted grass.

Branwyn looked up at the summit apprehensively. "Do we climb it?" She was in decent shape, but the walking was starting to get to her. Weren't there supposed to be faerie horses? She couldn't ride, but surely they could pull a carriage. And why weren't there cars, anyhow? With the gates of their prison cracked open, it was a golden opportunity to update their technology, especially if the faerie allergy to iron was a myth.

Oh well.

"No," said William grimly. "We go under." His black mood had barely changed since the confrontation over the control band, although he had admitted the replacement dorodango Branwyn had created was quite nice. She'd made some thematic improvements on Tarn's idea.

William dropped to his knees, then pressed his forehead against the slope of the mountain. His lips moved in what seemed very much like prayer. Uncomfortable, Branwyn looked away.

"Most of the other leadership positions among the Backworld

exiles have moved around," said Severin conversationally. "The Queen of Stone is the only one who's held her position since the Fall." The kaiju has been as good as his word when it came to tagging along, and much to Branwyn's surprise, he hadn't done much to cause trouble, either. He'd seemed distracted, although not so distracted that he'd allowed the changelings to sneak up on him when the fire dimmed.

Okay, so there'd been a little trouble, but Branwyn couldn't say he'd initiated it, even if he was the root cause.

"Is that supposed to mean something?" she asked.

"It means she's been here in her mountain since the faeries became faeries. Isn't that interesting?"

"Sounds dull to me."

"That too. But just think about how Faerie would quake and shiver if she emerged from her hole. Why, the whole thing might collapse without this pillar, this bastion."

Branwyn regarded him narrowly. "That's not a metaphor, is it?"

"Nope." He grinned. "If she moved, more than just Faerie would quake."

As if on cue, the ground trembled. Then, as William scrambled to his feet, the mountainside split apart. A tall man in ruby armor stepped out of the darkness beyond and surveyed them.

It was literally ruby armor, too, as far as Branwyn could tell. She stared at it in fascination. His breastplate was a giant, faceted gemstone over a black tunic. Plates of ruby made up the rest of the suit, some faceted, some only polished. Whoever had made it had invested a lot of time into it, even if it had been made by magic. It was very attractive. And sparkly. Branwyn approved.

The armor's owner was also attractive, with dark skin, a smooth scalp, and deep brown eyes. But everybody in Faerie seemed to be beautiful, so Branwyn didn't find him nearly as interesting. She wondered if a mortal had been involved in the armor's creation, and if she'd be allowed to inspect it without somebody wearing it.

"The emissaries from Underlight are welcome to the Well of Stone," the gatekeeper said in a light tenor voice. "The Destroyer is not. Depart from here."

Severin looked the ruby gatekeeper up and down. "Are you going to make me? Because I really don't think you can."

In answer, the other man held a gauntleted hand to one side. With a rush and a hum, red light gathered and elongated in his grasp. Then with a snap, the light solidified into a lance that matched his armor. The very tip of the lance was black, though, and its heart seemed to burn.

"Depart from here," said the gatekeeper again. This time, his voice had echoes that made the ground shiver. He spun the lance and slashed the air in front of him. "By the manifest power granted by the Queen Eternal to hold the door, I say a third time: depart from here. You are not welcome." He spun the lance again, then slashed the air twice more in a complicated and lovely drill.

The black tip of the lance seemed to chime as it moved, like a fingertip on crystal. It rose in pitch as a distortion appeared in the air at its point, like the fracturing of glass previously unseen. With a shattering sound, the warp rushed toward Severin.

"Oh, for f—" he began before the warp hit him and he vanished.

"Come along," said the gatekeeper impassively, as if nothing unusual had happened. He gestured with the lance for them to precede him into the darkness.

The hall beyond the mountain door was vast and pillared, dotted with distant flickers of light that only served to make the darkness deeper. The ground was worn stone, and after walking for a moment, they came to the curve of a stream that washed over luminescent gravel. By that light, Branwyn could make out galleries above, each one hosting a single flame. The cavern looked as if it could easily handle the foot traffic of thousands, but Branwyn saw nobody else throughout their walk.

They rounded a gentle bend, and the glowing creek flowed into tall radiance. At first, Branwyn thought it was a vertical lake. Then she realized it was another hall, this one filled with light. Without hesitating, the gatekeeper led them into it as the stream vanished underground.

The light tinkled. As her eyes adjusted, Branwyn realized that the walls glittered like the crystalline interior of a geode. Near the top of the chamber, the milky crystals grew long and spiky, so long that crystals from both sides of the room intersected to form stone rafters. The floor was polished amethyst, dark as night underfoot and fading to lavender at the walls. Out of the corner of her eye, Branwyn thought she saw the glowing stream running deep in the stone.

But she didn't have time to look more closely, because *this* room was occupied. Tall figures wearing strange, upright hairstyles and adorned with scraps of fabric lounged along the walls, draped over chairs. Each chair, Branwyn noticed, was unique: ancient carved wooden antiques, twisted metal deck chairs, even several varieties of upholstered armchairs. And the inhabitants were quite willing to stare.

Branwyn didn't check her own curious gaze, although she had only a little interest in the people. Her previous encounter with a random lady of Faerie had been more disturbing than fun. But the fashions in this mountain court were very, very different from anything Branwyn had seen outside of a music video. The wearers even posed like models in a video, only their heads turning to follow her as she walked past them. She wondered what Penny would make of them.

Beyond the lounging courtiers, a number of stained glass panels were arranged every which way. Each one bore a classical representation of people engaged in everyday modern life. Each image was animated, moving with a delicate crackling sound. The gatekeeper paused before them and called, "An emissary from Underlight."

For a long moment, there was no response. Branwyn shifted her weight uneasily, but nobody else moved.

Then the stained glass panels parted, gliding this way and that like they were on invisible rails. Beyond was an enormous throne; it was by far the most elaborate chair in the hall. Eight feet tall, it was carved from a single block of milky white stone with dark flecks on the surface and an opalescent fire in its depths.

The woman who occupied it had hair of obsidian and basalt, glossy and matte, with a huge, spiky crystal comb holding it to one side. Stabbed through the middle of the comb was a tarnished copper splinter. The Queen's elegant face was weathered grey stone with a black flaw running from her scalp to her chin, and her eyes were the blank eyes of forgotten statuary. She wore a gown of cabochon moonstone, with a star sapphire sash and a truly astonishing number of pleats and folds. It moved as she raised her hand to gesture them forward, the material sliding over itself with a sound like steel over stone.

The gatekeeper stepped aside and Branwyn waited for only a moment before she realized that nobody else was going to approach the throne.

"Right," she said, and moved forward. "Hi," she said. "I'm Branwyn." Possibly more formal speech was expected with faerie Queens. If so, nobody had told her about it, so she figured that it probably wasn't that important.

The Queen stared at her for a long moment, giving Branwyn enough time to wonder if maybe her approach had some flaws. Tarn *had* said something about not insulting anybody.

But she was being perfectly polite according to her own standards.

She pulled off her backpack and started to open it.

"A free human," said the Queen in a flat alto voice. "Welcome, Tarn's human."

"No, I'm Branwyn. But I *have* come on behalf of Tarn. He sent this." She pulled out the chest, dropped her bag on the ground, and moved forward to present it.

A low wave of noise swept down the hall, scratching and hissing and grinding rather than murmuring. Branwyn gritted her teeth and kept walking forward. A few feet before the throne, she gave a small bow and held out the chest.

The Queen took it in one large, long-fingered hand, her face still expressionless. She opened it and first picked up the clear bubble. As Tarn's bubbles did, this one popped. Instead of a physical letter, there was only a musical fall of notes and the scent of pomegranates.

The Queen's blank gaze fixed on a point somewhere over Branwyn's head for a long moment. Branwyn took the opportunity to peer at some of the stained glass screens to the sides of the throne. The animated scenes illustrated really did make them look like medieval television sets. There was a pastoral scene, and a scene of an elderly woman in a tiny, old kitchen.

The Queen's gaze lowered to Branwyn. She took the other orb, the one Branwyn had fabricated, from the chest and crushed it between her fingers without even glancing at it. Branwyn felt a pang of annoyance. She'd worked for hours to produce something beautiful, even knowing that it was a wrapper. Details were important.

Inside the dorodango, she'd nestled a sphere of silver conjured from the fabric of the Backworld. She'd liked the metaphor: reality surrounding a dream.

"Ah," said the Queen, and delicately extracted something wound around the silver sphere and trailing in the dust. "Tarn makes me an offering and hopes I will send back to him the ornament in my comb, so that he may make something wondrous for us all."

"Actually," said Branwyn, "I'll be doing the crafting. That's why I'm here."

The Queen tilted her head. "Will you? Then why was Tarn's offering this?" She held up the long strand of Branwyn's hair that had gotten caught in the mud as she worked it.

Oh *crap*. There was a moment's silence while Branwyn's mind raced.

"That's just a marker that I'm empowered to negotiate on his behalf for the Machine," she said finally.

"Ah," said the Queen again, and fell silent. The whole room was silent, except for a quiet crystalline hum, and the chime of the walls.

Branwyn shifted uncomfortably. It was a smooth explanation, but now what? She wasn't used to interacting with anything as impassive as the Queen of Stone; it unfocused her. And she had the nagging urge to refinish the Queen's surfaces. She'd really enjoyed her art restoration class in college. That was probably going too far, though. She was pretty sure that was the case, even if she pitched it as a makeover.

Casting her gaze around for inspiration, she noticed the stained glass again. "Your screens are lovely. What do they portray?"

"Images from the world," the Queen said.

"That's what I thought. Do you enjoy watching them?"

"They entertain me." Not a flicker of expression crossed the stone face. The distant hum seemed to grow louder.

"You're not the only one. Reality television is big right now." Branwyn hesitated, then added, "If those screens show you the modern world, you've seen televisions, right?"

A pause. Then: "Yes. Tell me about reality television."

Branwyn brightened. "Well, basically, some or all of a group of people's lives are broadcast for anybody to follow. Sometimes it's about their job, sometimes it's about their family life. Sometimes it's nastier things." Her nose wrinkled. "Some people will watch anything." She looked around again. "Maybe we could get some televisions down here for you. There must be a way to get cable into the Backworld." She smiled. "If that's what you'd like in trade, I can commit Tarn to it."

The Queen stared at her until Branwyn's smile faltered. Then, slowly, like an owl, those stone eyes blinked. She said, with awful majesty, "Not television. No. I think what I will take is *your* vision. Human. Mortal. Full of life."

Branwyn took a step backward, then looked around for her fae escort. William and the others stood back outside the cluster of screens, looking utterly unmoved. They weren't, she realized, at all interested in helping her.

Flushed with adrenaline, she took a deep breath. She still had options. She didn't know what her escort would do if she canceled the deal, but she bet they'd have a reaction then.

She played for time. "What do you mean?"

"I wish to see your life, through your eyes. Branwyn vision. Reality vision. All of your life." The Queen of Stone reached up to pull the giant comb from her hair, which tinkled like glass as it fell from the coil the comb had held in place, tumbling over her shoulder and into her lap.

Branwyn froze. That was so much more *reasonable* than taking her eyes. So reasonable and so deeply horrifying. "How?"

"I will put my blessing on you. All of your nodes are filled, so you must choose something to give up." She raised a hand as if ready to do magic right there.

"Wait, wait. Let's lay this out. In exchange for the Machine fragment Tarn wants, you're going to put a charm on me that will let you see out of my eyes?"

"A blessing," repeated the Queen. "Charms are human magic."

"Just sight? One way, you always silently looking over my shoulder? It won't harm me? I need you to say it, your Majesty."

Again, there was a scraping from the courtiers. Overhead, one of the giant crystals cracked half-through, with a sound like thunder. In the wake of the snap, the crystal sang against itself. Branwyn glanced up at it apprehensively, but then returned her gaze to the Queen, striving for the same endless patience.

"I will lay a blessing on you, human Branwyn, enabling you to serve as my eyes to the outside world. I will control when and how I use that vision. You will not know if I am watching or not. I will not know what you are thinking. It will not physically harm you, or take away any physical capabilities." She looked up at the half-cracked crystal. "I will not vouch for the integrity of your heart or mind. If those break, that will also be... entertaining. In return, I will transfer this—" and her fingers brushed against the copper splinter driven through the comb delicately "—Machine fragment to your safekeeping, for you to courier back to the Lord of Underlight."

"You could just come out into the world yourself, you know," Branwyn said reproachfully. "Everybody's doing it." She wasn't happy about that statement about her future mental health and well-being.

That flawed stone face frowned. "I do not wish to."

Branwyn sighed. "How long would I bear your blessing?"

"For as long as you have eyes, of course. It won't be long. You *are* mortal, after all."

Scratch that; Branwyn wasn't happy about *any* of this. She'd freed Zachariah from coerced service to this Queen in a fit of temper. *And*, she thought, *because it was the right thing to do*. Now she had to take the consequences. She had to let this entity watch everything she did, probably for the rest of her life. No matter what she did, she'd always be aware of the gaze over her shoulder. It made her skin prickle just thinking about it. That kind of invasion seemed like the first step towards even more uncomfortable things.

She could still walk away. Nobody had moved to stop her. They all seemed to move pretty slowly here. She could run if she had to, get to the doors, burst out, find help, she had charms—

No.

Human Branwyn. Mortal Branwyn. They expected so little of her. Except for Tarn, who seemed to expect so much.

"All right," she said. "It's a deal."

"What charm shall I remove?" The Queen's free hand flexed.

Branwyn laid out the charms in her head. Not including the ones Zachariah had given her specifically for working with the faeries, she had the Sight, a beacon, the reminder charm, and a charm for turning her fingernails into weapons. It was a harder choice than she expected. Her ability to see magic, her ability to call for help, her ability to stay focused amidst supernatural distractions, and a last-ditch ability to defend herself. She realized, too late, she should have considered what she was giving up magically, as well as personally.

She thought about it a little more. Then she said, "The beacon."

"Very well," the Queen said, and held out both her empty hand and the comb to Branwyn.

Branwyn took the empty hand in her own. The Queen said, "And my comb." Puzzled by being offered the entire comb instead of just the hairpin, Branwyn took it. A tingle ran up her fingers and down her spine.

"It is done," the Queen announced.

"What, already? You removed the charm and everything?"

In answer, the Queen waved a hand. One of the stained glass screens reconfigured its colored panes with a clatter. It showed a dizzying picture of itself.

With a sudden rush of fear, she activated the Sight. It was an instinctive action, useless except to tell her she still had that charm. Without a mirror, she had no way of checking the rest of her charms.

Right. Next time, pack a mirror.

"I guess it doesn't take you very much to remove a charm," she commented, staring at the glass screen. When she turned away, she caught the movement on it out of the corner of her eye. "Uh, are you going to keep that up there? Wait, don't answer that. I don't need to know."

She looked at the thing in her hand. "It's this splinter here?" She tugged it out of the heart of the comb. It was cold and very hard, but it slid out from the comb as if it was barely held. Up close, she could see that what had appeared to be a single shard of metal was made up of many tiny jointed layers. Inquisitively, she touched one of the joints with a fingernail. It unfolded.

A cool, silent presence studied her. She stroked the length of the shard and more joints unfolded, as if following her touch.

For a third time, the hall hummed with noise.

The Queen's head moved back fractionally. "Oh, you *will* be interesting."

Branwyn flinched at the reminder. Then she smiled down at the Machine fragment. "Yes, I will."

-eleven-

Branwyn stood outside her family home and looked at the construction of it. Her childhood memories were full of the constant sound of the remodeling and additions that her grandfather and first stepfather had collaborated on. It was a mixture of styles extended from the Victorian foundations. The porch was especially pleasant.

She wondered if the Queen of Stone was enjoying the view.

"When," the Queen had asked, "will you be back in the mortal world?" And when Branwyn's answer wasn't "within half an hour," that previously patient personage had taken steps.

It seemed the rules Branwyn had been taught didn't apply to Faerie Queens. It was uncanny. Corbin had assured her that having her magic slots full was proof against being cursed by a celestial. Even Zachariah had required her to willingly step into a magic circle. But the Queen had just waved her hand once and *poof*, all Corbin's hard work was stripped away.

And when her new Branwynvision wasn't going to be tuned to an interesting channel soon enough for her tastes, she'd waved her hand again, and her gatekeeper had opened up another warp in the Backworld. "It will take you home," the Queen had announced.

And so it had, although not the home she'd hoped for. Apparently her great-grandmother's stories and memory, embedded in the blue and cream house, attracted *all* the fae portals. Or maybe she'd just sent Branwyn back to Underlight's Earth entrance.

Slowly, Branwyn turned away. As had become usual when she couldn't get a ride from Marley, she'd taken the bus here from her apartment so her car wouldn't give her presence away to her family. She wanted to go home and take several showers, very badly. But making the walk to the nearest bus stop wasn't something she was looking forward to.

"Hey!" called Howl from the front door. "How did you get past us?"

Us. Branwyn turned back again. Howl stood on the porch, scowling. A familiar but unanticipated figure stood beside him.

"Rhianna!" said Branwyn. "What are you doing here?"

Branwyn's oldest younger sister came down the porch stairs, her dimples showing. "I had some unexpected time off from work, so I decided to visit. Turns out I'm just in time for a celebration. And so are you!" She hugged Branwyn, then pulled back, her nose wrinkling. "What have you been doing? Nevermind, tell me later. Jaimie's band just got a new fan—hell, patron, really. They want to pay for a whole new album. Independently wealthy, too, not part of a corporate outfit." She grinned. "There's a party on."

Too tired and puzzled to argue, Branwyn let Rhianna draw her up the porch stairs and into the house. Howl's scowl never wavered, and she wondered what exactly he'd told their sister. Rhianna herself wouldn't give anything away until she was ready to do so or until Branwyn had worked on her for some time.

The noise of her family in full celebration mode hit Branwyn like a physical blow as soon as she stepped into the house. Everybody was home except for her grandmother. Jaimie's bandmates and a few of their friends practically doubled the noise. Branwyn's mother, already excited for her husband's good news, had been sent into delighted raptures by the impromptu visit of her second daughter from the other side of the country.

Branwyn did her best to take part in the festive atmosphere, but she was too aware of the Machine fragment she'd tucked into her pocket, and too aware of the silent observer inside her head, spying on her family's happiness. And, although she hated to admit it, she was *really* tired.

Howl, she noticed, barely made an effort. He clapped Jaimie on the back and drank a celebratory root beer with the kids. Then he glowered in a kitchen chair until Branwyn was compelled to leave her three sisters talking music with Jaimie's keyboardist.

"What's wrong?" she asked, dropping into a chair beside him.

"I don't want to have a party," he said. "I want to find out if you're all right, and I can't tell."

Branwyn didn't blink, because she'd known her brother for nineteen years. "You could ask," she said gently.

"That's no good," he said curtly. "You'd lie. You don't look like you're all right."

"I'm tired. I've had a long few days. Uh, it's only been a few days, right?"

"Yes. Have you slept at all since last time I saw you? What have you been doing? I know you went through the door again, and you didn't come back out this time."

"Yes, and I meant to ask, how do you know that?"

"I'm not going to tell you," he said sullenly. "You're keeping enough from me. Why won't your dimensional portal work for me?"

"Did you try?" Branwyn rubbed her eyes and thought about splashing water on her face again.

"When you didn't come back at all for a day? Yes!"

Branwyn narrowed her eyes. "Did Rhianna come back because of you?"

"I didn't call her and tell on you, no. Although I would have today if she hadn't shown up on her own." He'd been staring off into space throughout the conversation, but now he cast his gaze over to her. "What have you been doing?" His voice was pleading, reminding her of a little boy who desperately wanted to understand.

"I—" she began, and then she realized that the cool presence of the Machine fragment in her pocket was gone.

She looked across the living room to where Rhianna perched on a chair, head tilted as she listened to Brynn gush about her new girlfriend.

"I'll get back to you," she said, standing up.

He began to curse her bitterly, but she ignored him and stalked across the room. Rhianna looked up and met her gaze, eyes dancing.

"Excuse me, Brynn. I need to take Rhianna and have a little chat. No, you can't come." She reached down and pinched Rhianna's earlobe. "Come along, little sister."

Rhianna let Branwyn pull her to her feet, then pirouetted out of Branwyn's grasp. Light-footed, she dashed upstairs, all the way up to Branwyn's little attic door.

"Howl was sure you'd come out of this," she said when Branwyn caught up with her. Rhianna was crouched down, examining the door. "I checked him for a fever but he fought back." She stood up gracefully as Branwyn shut the outer door and tucked a red curl of hair behind her ear.

"Give it back," Branwyn demanded.

Rhianna slipped her hand into the pocket of her grey slacks and pulled out the Machine shard. "This?" She turned it over. "What is it? Some kind of art multitool?"

Branwyn held out her hand imperiously. "What it is: not yours."

Rhianna curved her fingers over it for a moment. "Oh, don't be like that. You're just provoking me." But then she opened her hand and dropped it into Branwyn's palm.

"Whatever possessed you to pick my pocket?" Branwyn demanded, inspecting the shard. It was exactly as it had been before. Then she peered at her sister, wondering if Rhianna had detected anything unusual about it. The sense of *presence* radiated by the shard was so strong.

Rhianna shrugged. "Howl and Brynn's pockets were boring." She smiled a self-satisfied grin.

"Why are you picking pockets at all?" Branwyn asked hopelessly. She knew that look. Rhianna liked her secrets too much. She asked another question anyway. "Why are you really here?"

"I said. Unexpected time off. Some kind of construction mix-up at the office."

"The office."

"Yup." Rhianna stared at her with guileless green eyes.

Branwyn sighed and rubbed her eyes again. She remembered the day that Rhianna had come home from junior high and announced that she wanted to be a spy when she grew up. The very next day, she'd changed her mind and announced she wanted to be an actress. She'd joined the drama club, and worked very hard. And then she'd gone to college on the East Coast, majored in political science, and been recruited out of college into... an office environment. Where she did things. Involving data. And talked brightly on phone calls home about her hopes for a foreign assignment someday.

"Have you taken a close look at Jaimie lately?" Rhianna inquired innocently. "He's looking well. I'm glad he finally quit that grocery store job."

Branwyn frowned. Then, with a horrible sense of realization, she activated her magical Sight and looked at Rhianna.

Every one of her nodes was filled with a softly glowing orb. Six of the seven contained featureless glowing circles, while the seventh, at her crown, had a pattern of eyes. She'd never seen a charm with imagery embedded in it before.

"And how do I look?" Branwyn asked.

Rhianna pursed her lips. "You look tired. And stinky. And like you've been getting into a *lot* of trouble. Are you going to tell me all about it?"

Branwyn gave her a wary look. "I don't know if that's a good idea. I have to think about it." She hesitated, feeling the unaccustomed twinge of worry. "Did you get sent—er, come back to visit because of me?"

"Well, not just you—my goodness, Branwyn, so self-centered! I came back to see everyone. Plus, it's great to see the place again. There's always something exciting going on."

Branwyn ground her teeth. "Rhianna, do you *have* to use your cute little spy-speak? We're alone."

Rhianna twinkled. "But why? This is so much fun, and I know you can work out what's important."

Branwyn released her frustration in an exasperated sigh. "What you think is important and what I think is important are probably not the same thing."

"I don't know if that's a good idea. I have to think about it," Rhianna quoted Branwyn from before. Then she clasped Branwyn's hand. "It's okay, though. I'm just here to hang out for a while. Well, and maybe stick some pins in that big head of yours."

Branwyn hugged her sister, then said, "I have to get home and get cleaned up. I can't think straight until I get some sleep."

"You do that. I'll take over the Howl-needling." Rhianna grinned. "He's missed me so much!"

Branwyn went back downstairs, hoping that Tarn was smart enough not to let Rhianna into his realm. She peeked back into the main room to say goodbye to her mother, then paused, arrested by the sheer number of people in the room and all the nexuses and vertices of the Geometry manifesting in them.

As she tried to process what she was seeing, her mother came over to her. "You look like you want to leave already. Jaimie's new producer is supposed to be dropping by later, you know."

"I've been working hard, Mom. I feel like a zombie. The new producer shows up, I'll probably eat her brains. That would make everybody sad."

Her mother looked Branwyn up and down. "Ready to talk about your new project yet? We've all been pretty curious."

"Not yet. But when I'm done, believe me, you'll hear all about it. Hey, can you get Jaimie over here so I can say goodbye to him?" Ignoring her mother's strange look, she leaned against the doorjamb and took a ten-second nap.

"Hey, Branwyn, you don't have to go, do you?" Her mother's husband stood in front of her, grinning. She could never even think of him as "stepfather," not really. Her mother had married him when Branwyn was fourteen and it had been Holly's second husband that Branwyn had thought of as "dad." But Evan had died when Branwyn was thirteen.

Losing Evan had been hard, but accepting Jaimie had been much easier than she'd expected. He brought out an enthusiasm in her mother that she'd never seen with Evan. Even after twelve years of marriage, he still made Holly giggle like a schoolgirl sometimes. Evan had been responsible, conscientious, careful, and incredibly devoted to both his children and stepchildren. Jaimie was absent-minded, light-hearted, and boyish even at forty-five.

He also had charms in three of his nodes. Each one had its own motif: a four-petaled flower, a cupped hand, a crescent moon.

Branwyn looked around the room wildly. Now that she'd had some time and really looked at Jaimie, she could better make sense of the confusion of lines and nodes that overlaid the other people in the room. And she could see that the rest of Jaimie's band had the same nodes filled.

"Branwyn?" said Jaimie, his smile fading. "You alright?"

"Yeah. Yeah, I'm just really tired. Burned out. You know how it is."

He studied her. "Yeah. Yeah, I do."

Branwyn summoned a grin. "I just wanted to say congratulations. I'm really looking forward to hearing the new album."

His expression softened. "I've already started putting together a list. We'll be able to get the mastering done properly this time." His faraway gaze returned to her. "But you get out of here and get some rest."

She nodded, and made her escape out the front door. As she walked to the bus stop in the warm night, she thought about Jaimie and Rhianna's charms. More likely blessings or curses, she thought. Both times, she'd been shocked, but that reaction didn't make sense. Corbin had given her the kindergarten charms to protect her from having unwelcome charms and curses placed on her, since she was so insistent on staying involved with the supernatural world. There was no real protection for most people, no way to stop them from being hurt by the attentions of a celestial or a tricky wizard except the checks and balances that already existed in the supernatural world. The relationships between the nephilim and the angels and the others seemed to serve as a shelter for most of humanity.

But the things that went bump in the night were still out there. That balance hadn't helped Penny. And what had always existed was already changing. Branwyn shook her head. That was why she couldn't turn away from the world Marley had moved into. She was going to make herself a place where she would have influence. That was why she'd traded her privacy for a bit of living metal fallen from Heaven.

She looked at the Machine shard, then closed her fingers over it. It was hers now. She'd paid for it, not Tarn.

She wondered what else it could be used for.

Weird horse freakout!
Views: 27,890

A large plaza paved with small white stones, with a fountain and a statue in the center. On the far side of the statue, two mounted police officers sit, observing. A man with a waterfall of chestnut hair walks up to the mounted officers and begins to pat one of the horses. The mounted officer says something and moves his horse away a few steps. The camera moves closer just in time to see the chestnut-haired man tilt his head. Then he starts singing, his gaze focused on the horses. The horses shift restlessly and then, without any other warning, both of them start bucking wildly. The chestnut-haired man starts laughing as the two officers are both thrown off. Then the horses, wild-eyed, start to rear over the officers as if trying to trample them. The camera falls to the ground for a moment and when it is picked up again, the chestnut-haired man is gone and the two horses are calm, nuzzling the two officers cowering on the ground.

-twelve-

A **shower** and a night's sleep and a day in the familiar environment of her garage left Branwyn feeling much more like her
old self. Marley fussed over her at lunch, and the crew at work
teased her about her mysterious boyfriend—which they believed was
the only possible excuse for her sudden vacation—and she felt the
weight of the Machine shard in her pocket. She did her best not to
think about the watcher behind her eyes.

It had been hardest that morning when she'd woken up. She'd had
a dream. It was the kind of dream that she did not want to ever tell
anybody about, and half-awake, she'd wondered if the Queen of Stone
had seen it. It had been in her head, sure—but she'd seen it, too. Felt
it. It had been so *real.* The idea that even her dreams weren't her own
had almost driven her to tears. She didn't even post on public social
networks, and now every aspect of her life was being broadcast to a
faerie court.

But she didn't know what she could do about it, so she tried not
to think about it. There was filing to be done at work, and quotes to
finish, and customers to call. And at lunch, there was Marley, who
scolded and sighed and laughed against her will at Branwyn's jokes.

After work, she thought briefly about visiting Tarn, and about
turning the Machine into a key. But she found she wasn't in a hurry.
She wanted to take time for herself after her trip through Faerie.

And she was mildly curious what he'd do if she didn't show up right away. Would he send his changelings out after her? Would he come himself? Or would he sit on his throne and fume?

That was a fun thought.

She went by Zachariah's place instead. When he answered the door, she looked him up and down. He looked just as he always did, except that the silver band on his wrist was missing.

"What happened to your bling?" she asked.

His eyebrows went up. "My bling?"

"It was pretty weak-ass bling, it's true." When his eyebrows stayed raised, she said patiently, "Your bracelet."

A guarded expression crossed his face. "It cracked and fell off."

"Huh. That's mysterious. Does your jewelry do that a lot?"

"No, not usually. Did you want something, Miss Lennox?"

"I came back alive," she said sweetly. "I thought you'd want to know."

"Hmm." His gaze raked her up and down. "So I see. Not unscathed, though."

Branwyn's smile faded. "No."

"Do you think it was a fair trade?"

She cocked her head. "What do you think?"

"How would I possibly judge?" It seemed like an honest question.

It was her turn to say, "Hmm." Then she added, "You should meet my family sometime. If I'm not around for some reason, get Marley to introduce you."

He studied her. "Of course."

She flashed him another smile, then backed away. "That's all! Go about your business!" Then she turned and ran back to her car. Once she was safely inside, she turned back to look. He stood at the door, looking after her in faint puzzlement. He turned to go back inside, then paused and stooped down. As he picked up the mangled remains of the bracelet Branwyn had destroyed, she smiled to herself and drove off.

Next, she went to see Penny.

"See what I've got?" Branwyn waved the Machine fragment in front of Penny's closed eyes. "It's a strange little thing. It feels like it wants to be used. I've never felt anything like it before. And in the Geometry... it's weird. It's like something real in front of a TV showing the rest of the world." She fell silent abruptly, then said, "TVs... I bet you would have handled this better than I did, Penny. You've always been able to talk anybody into anything when you put your mind to it." She paused again, in case Penny wanted to argue that claim. She so often did.

But there was no argument, no movement except that of breathing. No *Penny*, Branwyn feared.

She stood up. She'd meant to make a long visit this time, just as she always did. And she couldn't. What was the point of sitting with somebody who didn't know she was there? It would only be for Branwyn's own comfort, and she'd much rather be doing something. She'd much rather be working directly toward Penny's restoration. Action Girl, that's what they always called her when they were growing up, Branwyn and Penny and Marley. Always the one wanting to move, wanting to *do*. Every time she came by, she did so hoping it would be just in time to see Penny's eyes finally open. But instead there was the monitor, watching her slowly die. Her eyes weren't going to ever open again unless somebody *did* something.

"See, this little toy might literally be the key to bringing you back to us. I want you back. I'm not the only one, but nobody else has any idea what to do." She tossed the Machine fragment into the air and caught it. "The thing is, it's going to unlock more than Tarn's ability to save you. And I'm not sure I like those other things. They've got good points, but then again, they've got bad points." She kissed Penny's cool forehead. "But don't worry. I'll figure it out."

Then she fled the silence, back into the busy life of the greater Los Angeles area.

She went to her studio, her real-world studio, where once upon a time, she'd bent and hammered metal that somebody had dug out of the earth. It seemed like a long time ago. Tarn hadn't lured her in with promises to heal Penny, she remembered. She'd been looking for anything she could find, with only the vague hope that it might be useful for Penny, and he'd promised that learning to work the substance of the Backworld would pay off in the real world.

Sitting down at her workbench, she picked up a half-finished piece of filigree work and turned it over in her hands. It was a bracelet, the sort of thing that she could easily sell for a good price to pay for some of her stranger projects, like the baroque wrought-iron box fans. She looked at it for a few minutes until she remembered what she'd been aiming for, then started working on it.

Time passed, as it did. She focused. When she was a child, she'd embraced art as a way of making a private world for herself within the noise and distractions of a large household. Even for less inspired works, when she threw herself into a project, she lost time. It didn't take faerie assistance. She worked until she was done or until pain—whether hunger, bladder, or joint—made her stop.

This time, she finished the piece before pain set in. Out of habit, she glanced at the clock, noting how much time had passed, then studied the bracelet. Working with the wire for filigree usually involved mistakes here and there that needed correcting; she'd made fewer of those than she would have expected after her time away from the project. But if that was the magic Tarn had promised, she was disappointed. It was nothing more than the nimbleness of a few more years of practice. She might even have just gotten lucky.

She pursed her lips and activated the Geometry sight, hoping for *something* more.

This time she wasn't disappointed. The lines of the Geometry were noticeably thicker around the half of the bracelet she'd worked on that night. Rather than just intersecting, several of the crossings knotted together. It was interesting. She had no idea what it *meant*, but it was new and different. Her trust in Tarn, what little she had, was restored.

Suddenly she was very eager to get back to her other studio, in Tarn's realm. The more she practiced there, the more she'd understand those knots. But returning to Tarn meant she had to decide what to do about the Machine fragment. He was probably standing by his locked door, waiting impatiently. He was probably even annoyed.

She indulged herself in the image of Tarn striding up and down angrily, then sighed. It wasn't a hard decision when she came down to it. All she could do was make decisions for herself. If other people didn't like what she was doing, they could get involved. They could come up with better options, instead of sitting on their hands and hoping for things to change on their own. Or, she considered, hoping that things wouldn't change at all. Both hopes were futile.

After getting a bite to eat, she went back to her family home. It was late, and the house was mostly dark. She expected Howl was lying in wait for her anyhow, possibly with Rhianna.

Oh well. It was Tarn's brilliant idea to camp out in her family's attic. She wondered if he realized just how obstructionist a determined pair of younger siblings could be.

She opened the front door quietly and stepped into the darkness.

The darkness on the other side wasn't her house.

Tarn had moved the portal.

"Goddamn it," she shouted. The lights along the walls of Tarn's throne room flickered to life, but the throne was empty. "Tarn!" When there was no response, she stomped through the hall to the door behind the throne and threw it open. This time, the door was connected to what probably served as a bedchamber for a faerie lord. There was an enormous round bed on the far side of the room, with mussed sand-colored sheets and a teal coverlet. A collection of luxurious couches with raw silk upholstery in matching marine colors were arranged around a steaming pool set directly into the floor. Other accoutrements like mirrors and desks and wardrobes made sure the oversized room didn't seem empty, but Branwyn barely noticed them.

Tarn was in the process of gracefully lifting himself out of the pool, stark naked. His body was just as beautiful as his face, with a muscular chest and a tapered waist and long, taut legs and—

For a moment Branwyn flashed back to her dream of the morning, but it was somebody else's bare chest, somebody else's hands—then she shoved the memory away, because sleeping dreams were meaningless, nothing and this naked celestial was real, right here and distracting *enough*.

He wrapped a silken dressing gown loosely around himself, and Branwyn found herself wondering where his companion was. That wasn't the sort of bath one enjoyed *alone*. Not if you were a faerie lord. She felt certain of this.

She growled under her breath; whether or not he had a companion, he certainly wasn't as annoyed and grouchy as she'd been imagining.

"Branwyn. I see you found the shortcut. Howl was having trouble defending the attic." He looked amused. "He's a good boy, but you have *insistent* siblings. Rhianna schemes and Brynn dreams and little Meredith is full of pleas. She's got them all wrapped around her finger, especially your parents. Do let Howl know he's been relieved of his tiresome burden." His hair was wet, curling tendrils clinging to his forehead. The dressing gown clung, too.

"I don't like the change. I don't like you spying on my family either," she said. She sounded like a sulky child and she knew it, but she also desperately wished she hadn't charged through the door. She could have taken a different exit directly to her studio. She could be working on the key right now, instead of staring at dripping wet, nearly naked, divinely crafted male flesh. He was her employer, and he was trouble, and he'd kissed her to save her from death when they first met, and she *really* didn't need to be thinking about that right now. Fighting was better.

"They're very loud. I can hardly avoid it." He had a fond, distant look on his face.

"Move out of the house, then!"

"I can't," he said. "For better or worse, that entrance to Underlight is fixed until—until certain matters change."

"What matters?" she demanded.

He gave her a long, cool look. She waited him out, trying to keep her thoughts focused on how he was invading her family home, and not thinking at all about things she was absolutely not going to think about. At last, he said, "The door you were so eager to complete acts as an anchor on Underlight. It *drags*. If I move the entrance now, the silken curtain will slip away in tatters and shreds, exposing Underlight to—" He paused, his expression changing. "Is something wrong? You seem out of breath."

"I'm going to my studio to make your damned key," she snapped, backing out of the room. Once the door was safely closed, she let out a deep breath. Then, after a moment's thought, instead of going to her studio, she went to the gallery chamber where the locked door waited. Her studio provided nothing to her except a place that was nominally her own. The door was everything. She stared at it fiercely until she'd calmed down, then pulled the Machine fragment from her pocket.

She'd changed a Machine once before. It was called the Lullaby Plaything and it had been used as a sort of diagnostic toy. It had been a gentle thing, before Branwyn had touched it. She had turned it into a spearhead for Marley to use in a fight with an angel. For all its gentleness, it had made a good weapon. The nameless thing in her hands now felt harsh in comparison with the Lullaby Plaything, like it had been part of something dangerous once upon a time. But it wasn't dangerous now, and it had no interest in hurting people.

Branwyn hoped she was never asked to explain those certainties. All she could point to if so was a vague feeling, as if her mind was assembling personality traits from the textures under her fingers. It was hard to analyze, and normally she'd resist anthropomorphizing a hunk of metal. But given the circumstances, she allowed herself some leeway.

Plus, listening to the fragment made it easier to manipulate it. She sat leaning against the door, passing the fragment from hand to hand. One of the little joints clicked out, and she tugged on it. It stretched under her fingers, then folded when she bent it. It *really* wanted to be of service.

Soon she was lost in a reverie of work, comparing the rod forming under her fingers to the lock she could feel within the door. It was related to the braid decoration that trimmed the lock and door. And the lock itself was huge; if it were mundane, it would require quite a large key.

She couldn't make the Machine fragment stretch enough. It wouldn't make a complete key. When she finally stopped in frustration, she had a smooth shaft, without the toothed bit that would actually turn a lock. Time and again, she pulled out a bit that matched what she felt within the lock, then inserted the key. The key would turn smoothly, without engaging the tumblers. When she withdrew it, the bits had receded back into the shaft.

This was, she reasoned, probably why the door needed a special material for the key. The lock resisted being opened. It needed to be overpowered. But thinking reasonable thoughts didn't soothe her frustration and anger. She had a celestial Machine fragment, the very definition of "special material," and it still didn't work.

She found Tarn in his throne room, speaking with William and another of his servants. He raised a hand to pause the conversation when she burst through the side door. His gaze traveled from the metal shaft in her hand to her face, then he gave a tiny, unsurprised sigh.

"It doesn't work," Branwyn stated. She narrowed her eyes. "And you knew it wouldn't. You *knew*. That's why you didn't care when I didn't bring it here right away. That's why you didn't care when I went to work on it. I thought you'd be hovering over my shoulder, ready to throw that door open, but you're sitting here instead."

Tarn flicked his upraised hand and William and the other servant left the room quickly. Once the door closed behind them, he said, "I suspected, but I did not know."

Branwyn sneered. "That's a damn fine line."

"It is the truth," he said calmly. "The Machine is not powerful enough alone, I take it?"

"No, it's not," said Branwyn. "And I don't know why, or how to fix it. I don't know enough about what 'power' means. The material is very hard when I'm not working it. Do different fragments have different amounts of power, different qualities?"

He smiled faintly. "Oh yes. That is why some Machines can destroy me with a touch, while others are far slower and more insidious in their devouring."

"The Queen wore this in her hair," Branwyn said.

"Embedded in a comb, I think, but yes. I personally would not choose to spend much time in such close proximity to that little piece, but even if I held it for an extended period, its effect on me would be creeping rather than shocking."

"Pity," said Branwyn sourly. "Devouring, eh? They eat you? Vampire machines?"

"They absorb us, rather. "

Branwyn thought about that for a moment. Then she said, "Okay. If you suspected this Machine wasn't going to be powerful enough to overcome the lock, why did you send me to get it? Just for kicks?"

He looked exasperated. "No, I did not send you to the Queen of Stone for 'kicks.' My other options were far more dangerous, and if there was a chance that the Queen Eternal's hair ornament would work, then the goal would have been achieved at relatively low risk and small cost." He paused, his multicolored eyes scanning Branwyn. She looked away. He went on. "It was unlikely, but it was a thing that could not be known until it was tried."

"Are these other options more powerful?" She closed her eyes, wondering if the Queen of Stone was amused.

"Not significantly. But I believe they could be combined with the one you've already acquired to create something stronger than either is alone."

He leaned on the arm rest of his throne, looking at her for a long moment.

"Well?" Branwyn frowned. "What are these other options?"

"Dangerous," he said briefly. "Perhaps if I take some time, I'll be able to find better ones."

Branwyn shifted uncomfortably. Tarn's expression was inscrutable and he seemed more serious than he'd ever been before. His eyes, dark and light, slitted half-closed as he watched her.

"How much time?" she asked.

He shrugged. "Years, perhaps. I've waited centuries for that door to be finished, let alone opened. I'm in no hurry."

Branwyn was surprised the ground didn't shiver underfoot like it had when he'd falsely claimed all the other artists had departed his realm; he'd certainly seemed like he was in a hurry before. "Penny can't wait years," she said sharply. "Let's discuss the dangerous options. I'm tough."

Tarn stood up and walked across the hall to her. He was barefoot, wearing dark, loose pants and a fitted dove-grey jacket he hadn't quite finished buttoning. She took a step backward as he approached, and he stopped. "Tough? You run even from me, Branwyn. You are exquisitely fragile, beautifully mortal."

"Shut up," she said, and stepped forward, back to where she'd been standing before, two arms' lengths apart. She had to tilt her chin up to meet his gaze, which was better than staring at the poorly buttoned jacket.

A light touched his eyes. "And earlier, in my chamber?"

Branwyn scowled. "Sensible people lock the door when they're taking a bath. Or whatever you were doing."

"I was, yes, taking a bath," he said, and she could hear laughter unexpressed in his voice. "Alone, since I noticed you wondering. I happen to like baths."

Her skepticism must have shown on her face, because he sighed and said, "Do you know what our crime was, those of us exiled from Heaven, cut off from the Sea of Dreams, bound to Earth, and locked away in Earth's shadow? What terrible thing we desired that made us the most hated?"

Branwyn hesitated, then bit down on her sarcasm. She'd been wondering about this for too long. "Not really."

"We wanted to *enjoy* the world." He paused, letting that sink in. "Yes, Branwyn, I enjoy baths. I enjoy silk under my fingers. I enjoy lovely things." His hand half-lifted toward Branwyn, then dropped. "I very much enjoy having a body, even if I *am* locked away from the vast world I gave up my name for."

Subdued, Branwyn said, "Faerie seems like a pretty nice prison. It's a bit bigger than I imagined."

"It's a sandbox full of dreams. Appealing for a vacation, but after a few centuries, one starts to notice the difference. We can change the furnishings but the walls are always, always there." His voice was neutral, but the light had fled his eyes.

"Do you even notice time? I thought that was a mortal thing." This had been preying on her thoughts. How could anyone endure centuries, let alone millennia, of even the nicest prison without becoming a pile of mental goo?

He hesitated, then said, "We notice change. It comes so rarely here, and always brings destruction." A deep weariness flashed across his face and was gone. "When the Covenant was enacted, I was not the Duke of Underlight. I was an individual. I believed the Creator made the world, the infinite universe for us to enjoy, no matter what the first wave of angels said."

"Believed? Not anymore?" The last of her acid irritation fled in the face of his timeworn sadness.

"When he—and do not ask, for we do not speak his name—destroyed our names, it disconnected us from the Sea of Dreams, which is the womb from which all celestials are born and reborn. It might have been the final oblivion. They didn't know. Many did not care. But the Earth embraced us. We'd already started learning to draw on her powers: to pull magic from the tide and the tectonic plates, from the rise of the sun and the change of the seasons and the howl of the storm. And when the first of us fell after the Covenant, he rose again from the energy field surrounding Earth."

"That sounds good?" Branwyn said uncertainly.

A smile touched his mouth but not his eyes. "So many have said. But to answer your question, no, Branwyn. I no longer believe the Creator made this world for us to enjoy. It seems possible the Creator made *us* for the *world* to enjoy. I have had many centuries to think about it and I have no good conclusion, save that the centuries have been very long and we have had precious little in the way of change that has not come hand in hand with destruction. We war and die and are reborn merely to relieve the tedium. And each cycle, the few Machine weapons we have claim more lives that are lost forever."

Branwyn scowled, now angry on Tarn's behalf. Nobody deserved that, to be locked away from the world for so long that death was just an end to the tedium. "The locked door is connected to your prison, isn't it? You're getting me to make a key to your cell door."

He opened his mouth to say something, then closed it again. After a moment of consideration, he simply said, "Yes. Another Artificer crafted it long ago, but the craftings of Artificers sometimes take time to mature." Then he added, "It is not the only lock. Even if it were open, we would not truly be free."

"Then why, after all this time, are you hesitating on sending me after the more dangerous Machines?"

"I don't want you to get hurt." His voice was low. "I should not care, and yet I find I do."

Branwyn ran her hands through her hair. "I'm mortal, that's what happens. Beautifully mortal, right?"

"That's what happens. And yet you're risking that mortality on a dying girl. I can't believe you welcome it." He caught her hand in her hair, untangled her suddenly nerveless fingers and laced them with his own.

Branwyn's answer vanished in a mouth gone suddenly dry. When had he gotten so close? He regarded her calmly, his palm warm against hers. She stared up into his eyes for a long moment, then remembered herself and managed to whisper, "We have to take care of each other. I never believed in you, but I always believed in us."

"Yes," he said softly. "Beautifully mortal."

She'd knotted her fingers in the lapel of his half-buttoned jacket, her knuckles just brushing his warm skin. For a long, breathless moment they looked at each other. The air between them seemed electrified.

Then his other hand slid down the curve of her waist, and she woke from her daze. "Um," she said, and he promptly removed his hand from her hip. Their fingers seemed fused together, though. Then he pulled his hand away from hers. His intent gaze never left her face.

She stumbled backward again, both embarrassed and worried. Then she remembered the Queen of Stone looking out through her eyes, got even more embarrassed, and banished the feeling with anger.

"You don't need to seduce me or spin me sad stories," she said coldly. "I'm already helping you, despite the advice of almost everybody I know."

He looked blank for a moment, then his face shuttered. "So I see. I do appreciate your efforts."

"Well, your appreciation doesn't need to go that far," Branwyn said firmly. "Teaching me magic and saving Penny is enough."

"Yes." He held out his hand to her again, the same formal gesture he used to escort her through his court. When she didn't take it, his smile was chilly. "Would you like me to make arrangements to acquire the next Machine on my list? Despite the danger?"

"Yes! That's what I've been saying." Relief surged over her at the topic change. Danger? It was *dangerous* to let herself be attracted to him. Or to—to any of them. That was the true mortal peril: to be swept away in their strength and power and forget that which made her Branwyn. She thought something like that had happened to Penny. And she couldn't help believing Tarn knew that, that he was trying something devious. But she couldn't figure out *why*.

She needed to think about it. She needed time.

As if reading her mind, Tarn said, "It will take some time. A few days. Run away, Branwyn, while you can. Stay away." He turned away, dismissing her from his attention.

Without argument, and without hesitation, Branwyn departed.

-thirteen-

After a restless night's sleep, Branwyn was less confused. She still didn't know Tarn's motivation, but how could she? He was ancient, and probably a little insane after being confined for so long—imprisonment did that to people, after all—and trying to understand his motivations was like trying to understand the motivations of a thunderstorm. A sexy male thunderstorm who wanted to kiss her.

No, what was best was just putting that aside. She was going to learn her magic and save Penny and go from there. Maybe she'd alleviate an injustice, too. And it would all work out very well, as long as Tarn kept his hands to himself. And didn't look at her with that odd mix of hunger and tenderness in his eyes, an expression that would make *anybody* attracted to men weak in the knees. And she could do it, too. She could resist being charmed. It might be a different matter if it was—

No. She wasn't going there. There was stupid, and then there was suicidal.

It didn't matter anyhow, because it was Tarn, and Tarn could make her weak in the knees, but not in the head.

And it wasn't to prove this to herself that she went to her family house after work and used the silver key Tarn had given her to open the front door to his realm. She had to practice her magic, after all.

She was ready to interact with him on a purely business level.

The door opened directly to the studio set aside for her in Tarn's realm. Nobody was there but her.

That was… frustrating. But, she quickly realized, probably for the best. It let her focus on what was really important. So she spent some time reaching into the substrate of the Backworld and conjuring up materials. This time, with her experience in her earthly studio to guide her, she paid attention to the details of what she was summoning. She was doing better, she thought. She still wasn't quite sure where this was leading, in concrete terms, but it was an interesting road.

When she opened the door of her Faerie studio, it led directly into the front hall of her family home. That was going to end up as inconvenient as the previous arrangement, she predicted. But at the moment, nobody was waiting for her, and that was a pleasant change. From the living room, she heard Jaimie playing his guitar softly: the gentle strumming he occupied himself with while other people were talking. She also heard her mother, and another voice. Curious, she wandered down the hall. At first, she didn't recognize the new voice, and then she couldn't place it. When she did, she froze midstep.

Howl appeared in the doorframe. "Hi, Branwyn," he said, more cheerful than she expected. "Come and meet Jaimie's new producer."

Hoping she was wrong, Branwyn went into the living room. But she wasn't. The Lady Rime of Nightwell sat on the nice couch drinking a glass of iced tea. Her white gown had been replaced by pearl grey slacks and a dusky rose blouse, but her hair was just as it had been when they'd met on the Faerie road. Jaimie sat beside her, his fingers moving lightly over the strings of his instrument.

Branwyn's mother looked up. "Branwyn, lovely. Come meet Rime Nightwell. Rime, this is my eldest daughter."

Rime looked at Branwyn with sapphire eyes and smiled. "Hello, Branwyn. I was hoping to meet you."

Branwyn stared at the faerie woman. "You mean meet me again. We've met before."

"Yes," said Rime, sipping her drink. "You have a lovely family."

Branwyn let her mother tug her down to the loveseat beside her. Howl hovered nearby, his gaze fixed on the faerie noble as if she was the most lovely thing he'd ever seen. Branwyn grudgingly admitted to herself that he might be right. She'd probably looked the same way at Tarn the other day.

"Where did you two meet?" Holly asked. There was an odd edge in her voice that made Branwyn actually look at her. Her mother was smiling, and it was genuine, but there was a wry twist to it that only those who knew her best would recognize, and even then only if they were paying attention.

"Um, while I was working on my latest project. I encountered her on a trip to pick up supplies."

Rime said, "That's right, you said. Although you didn't tell me anything about your current project. I'd love to hear about it."

Branwyn still had the half-finished Machine key in her pocket. She wondered if Rime was after it, then remembered that it was dangerous for her kind to even touch. "Maybe later, when I'm done. What made you decide to help Jaimie with his album? Things seem to be moving so quickly."

Rime shrugged her slim shoulders gracefully. "It was an easy decision. He's an excellent musician. I always look about for excellence in the arts when I arrive someplace new." Her mouth curved. "Song has long been an interest of mine. There are so many possibilities here and now. So much to finally be achieved. The internet is amazing, don't you think?"

Holly took up the conversational thread, asking Rime about the far country she was clearly from. Branwyn let out a deep breath. She couldn't help but think of her great-grandmother's stories of fairies — or faeries—who sucked the life out of artists and poets. But Tarn, as irritating as he was, wasn't sucking out her life, and she had no reason to expect that from Rime, either. Unless one of the other factions took steps, the faeries were here to stay, and they deserved to be treated as individuals. Innocent—or at least inoffensive—until proven guilty.

She'd have to tell Howl what Rime was, though, when she told him everything else. That would be amusing.

Rime gave her an unreadable look and Branwyn realized she'd smiled at the thought. Then Rime looked away, complimenting her mother on the house and guiding the conversation away from her own origins. It was something Branwyn had never been able to do. She sat back and let the words flow over her, thinking about her mother's discomfort.

"Hello!" said Rhianna from the door, and then, "You," with a hostility Branwyn had rarely heard in her sister's voice. "You don't belong here."

Startled, she looked up. Rhianna's emerald gaze was fixed on Rime. Jaimie's strumming stopped.

Rime looked amused. "But I was invited in."

Branwyn's mother gave a tiny sigh, then rose to her feet. "Rhianna, don't be rude to my guests."

"Mom, I told you, she's bad news."

Holly said, "And I told you, I have—" and she glanced at Rime. "Excuse me," she said brightly. "I just want to have a word with my daughter." Then she grabbed Rhianna by the arm and tugged her out of the room just like she was a child. Curious, Branwyn stood up to follow.

Over her mother's shoulder, Rhianna said, "You stay here, Branwyn. Don't let her do anything." Then they both vanished to the hall beyond.

Rime tilted her head, still smiling faintly, listening to the indistinct sound of hushed voices. "Does she think I'm going to steal the silver?"

"Your kind does have that reputation for theft," Branwyn said, settling on the couch again and keeping the conversation vague.

Jaimie smiled to himself as he started picking at the guitar again. "I warned you my family was energetic. It's nice to see Rhianna feeling protective of me for once. I remember when I first started dating Holly, she reacted almost exactly the same way to me."

Branwyn remembered that, too. She'd been left in the living room the exact same way, while Holly dragged Rhianna out to plead with her to behave. "So, is it just coincidence that you met Jaimie after meeting me?"

"Of course," said Rime, and Branwyn remembered that it was only faerie rulers that couldn't lie, and only in their own realms. Rime went on. "I'm glad I did, though. We've been looking for someone like Jaimie for a while. I'm hoping to talk him into helping out with a special project."

Branwyn narrowed her eyes. "What kind of special project?"

Rime put a finger in front of her lips. "That would be telling." Something chimed and she reached into her designer purse and pulled out a smartphone. "I love these things," she said absently as she tapped the screen. "Aw, it's a video of a kitten. I used to have to work really hard to set up situations like this, and now here they are, available to everybody with an internet connection. Look." She proffered the smartphone.

Warily, Branwyn took the phone and watched the small screen. It was a video of a kitten being enormously cute. She'd seen it before. She was pretty sure *everybody* not locked in a shadow world had seen it before. But maybe it was a rule about kitten videos: there was always somebody new to appreciate them.

Holly entered the room again, looking harried. "Branwyn, your sister wants to talk to you." She squeezed Branwyn's shoulder as she moved past and settled into her previous seat. "So, Rime, you were telling us about your company."

Branwyn hesitated. She wanted to hear about Rime's so-called company, which she assumed was the faerie court called Nightwell. She hadn't forgotten that Nightwell was Underlight's rival in moving into the urban regions. But her mother gave her a pleading glance. It was enough; she hated seeing her mother with that look.

Out in the hallway, Rhianna was leaning against the wall, looking like a kid sent from the classroom for misbehavior. She gave Branwyn a dark look. "Grandma's going to be pissed if she comes back from her trip and *that* is still hanging around."

Branwyn tilted her head. "Would she even know? Mom grew up on Gran-gran and Grandma's stories and she's clueless."

Rhianna shook her head. "She knows something's off. She can't see the details, though. Seriously, Branwyn, what were you thinking?"

Stung, Branwyn said, "Me? I didn't bring her here."

"But you're *fraternizing* with the guys living in the attic."

"They've moved to the front door now," Branwyn said absently. "And really? Fraternizing?"

"They ought to just keep moving straight out of the house, then." Rhianna ran a hand through her hair. "Grandma is going to *disown* us."

"I've told him that, yes. And since we're discussing fraternization, who exactly are *you* fraternizing with?"

"That's classified," Rhianna said sweetly. "But I know you got your knacks from Marley's new boyfriend."

Knacks, Branwyn thought. *I wonder how much she actually knows.* And she thought, *Which one is she calling Marley's boyfriend?* She almost asked. But she looked at Rhianna's pleased expression and remembered the Queen of Stone looking out through her eyes. "You're right," she said. "You probably shouldn't tell me anything if it's important." She felt an unexpected urge to cry.

Rhianna's eyes widened in shock. "What? Why?"

From the other side of the hall, Jaimie said, "Thanks for stopping by, Rime." Holly echoed her husband's thanks and Rime made pleased noises. Then she appeared in the doorframe.

"I'll be leaving now, ladies. I hope next time we meet, I'll have earned a better opinion from you, Rhianna." Rime's smile showed her perfect teeth.

Branwyn glanced between Rhianna and Rime, still a little bewildered by the shift in her little sister's behavior. She was normally the one to smooth-talk the people who Branwyn could barely stand to speak with. The world had turned upside down.

Then Rime swept down the hall and out the door. Rhianna caught Branwyn's arm and pressed her head against her sister's shoulder. "God. I don't know how you can stand looking at her."

Branwyn blinked. "She looks normal to me, Rhianna. I mean, like she stepped out of a magazine, but... human."

Rhianna peered up at her, confused. "Not like a living rave?"

Frowning, Branwyn tugged her into the music room. "Not unless I turn on my, uh, knack. And even then, it's not that bad. No worse than anybody else, just... different." She stared at Rhianna. "You can't turn it off? Whoever gave you the charm didn't give you a way to *turn it off?*"

Rhianna's eyes widened. "You *can?*" Her gaze went distant, and she straightened up. "Right. Thanks."

Warily, Branwyn said, "Are you okay?"

"Oh yes," said Rhianna brightly. "I need to talk to some people, but it'll be fine."

"How about talking to *me?*" Howl said plaintively from the door. He'd been so quiet in the living room that Branwyn had forgotten about him.

She looked between Rhianna and Howl. Then she gave up. They

were adults. Sometimes the best thing a big sister could do was provide information other people wouldn't.

Settling in the comfy chair, she began to tell them the story of how she discovered that the supernatural was more than just a fantasy. "Once upon a time…"

It took a while. And when she was done, she met Howl's disbelieving gaze and sighed, right before he silently turned and left the room.

"I'm Vardaris"
Views: 952,031
Some kind of game or movie promo?

This video has been produced in a semi-professional manner. A tall, devastatingly attractive man with ebony skin, light eyes and wild violet hair sits in a wooden chair in front of a burgundy velvet curtain. He's wearing quite a nice suit, with an open jacket and his shirt unbuttoned at the collar.

"Once upon a time," he begins, in a deep and sonorous voice that sounds like chocolate-covered cherries taste. It's entirely too nice to be real. "Once upon a time, a race of dreamers were stolen away from the world. Their cousins were jealous of what could be accomplished with dreams, you see. The jealous cousins followed the rules and rose at dawn and worked hard and wanted what they were told to want. They never understood why they felt so hollow inside. But the dreamers knew the secret was to break the rules and follow their hearts." The storyteller presses his long fingers over his heart. "The dreamers understood true happiness, and they shared it with all who followed them. The jealous cousins invented more rules to try and control the dreamers, but the dreamers paid these rules no attention either. But the jealous cousins were very good at rules, and eventually they created a rule so powerful that the dreamers could no longer exist without obeying it. And so they were stolen away from the world. The world knew the value of dreamers, though. It saved a place for them, even as the hollowness of the jealous cousins spread throughout everything. Occasionally the dreamers could fill the hollowness from beyond the world, but the sickness went deep."

The storyteller spreads his arms. "But there is hope. The dreamers still exist, and they can bring happiness again. I am Vardaris and I will lead you on this journey. Be ready, and do not be afraid!"

After the main video there is an outtake. Vardaris laughs at something somebody off camera says, his suit buttoned up properly. A woman with white hair, white skin, and a blue minidress moves into the frame and unbuttons his jacket and shirt. She reaches up to the wild violet hair as if she wants to tame it, before he pushes her away and swats her on the bottom. Then he smiles at the camera, before the video cuts to black.

-fourteen-

Branwyn wasn't surprised Howl didn't believe her at first. She *was* surprised that he would be so persistent in telling her he didn't believe her after his initial silent withdrawal. He didn't write the whole thing off as a prank, possibly because she'd vanished in front of his eyes a few times. But he wanted more proof, and he promised that he'd make her life a living hell until she either provided it or recanted. The thing about Howl was that when he said that kind of thing, he wasn't making an idle threat. He had resources. He delivered. A day was enough for Branwyn to first regret telling him, then regret declaring that she didn't care if he believed her.

She thought about her stack of charms. She had two that had a demonstrable-to-others effect that didn't involve opening portals: a charm Zachariah had given her to "remove that which was unwholesome, intoxicating, or simply toxic from food and drink," and Corbin's self-defense charm. She wasn't excited by the thought of drinking something toxic just to prove she could, even to escape a life of little-brother-inflicted Hell.

Instead, she met her siblings on the front porch and activated Corbin's self-defense charm. Her fingernails extended from her fingers like claws and she dragged them lightly along Howl's arm. Despite her gentleness, spots of blood bloomed where the claws broke the skin. Howl jerked at first, then held very still.

"Ooh," said Rhianna, perched on the porch railing.

"I can't cut through steel or anything," Branwyn cautioned. "They're still nails, just thick and hard and sharp. And it feels really weird when they change."

Howl stared at the beads of blood. Then he said coldly, "That's pretty unimpressive magic," and went into the house.

Branwyn called after him, "It's still magic."

It was enough, apparently, because he stopped haunting her voicemail and her email, and for the next three days when she went to the house, he wasn't waiting on the porch to ambush her. She missed him, to her surprise.

On the third day, Rhianna waved at her through the front window as she approached, then slipped out the front door. "Let's see if your elf can stop me from coming through with you. As an experiment."

Branwyn shook her head. "He's been prickly lately. I don't want to drag uninvited guests into his house. Not before I've sorted things out, anyhow."

"Even if his house is in our house?" Her sister smiled sunnily.

Shrugging, Branwyn said, "It was a duplex once before, now it's a duplex again. Look, I'll ask him sometime if you can come visit. He might say yes. Don't you have to go back to work at some point?"

Rhianna made a mournful face. "Alas! A rogue squirrel got into the roof in my building and chewed through several very important wires. They're still tracking down the extent of the damage."

"A squirrel." Branwyn loved her sister and missed having her around more, but she wasn't pleased by the news; Rhianna was too wicked and inquisitive to be trusted, especially with Howl around to help her.

"A really big one!" Rhianna pantomimed giant incisors with her fingers. "There's some vicious wildlife on our campus. Absolutely no fear of humans." She paused as Branwyn snorted, then added solicitously, "Branwyn! Are you choking?"

"No, I'm laughing. Since you ask."

Rhianna gave her a prim look. "Anyhow, I'll be here for at least another week." Then she turned and flounced inside the house.

Instead of following her, Branwyn used Tarn's silver courtkey on the door. Then she opened it and stepped through to Underlight, looking over her shoulder to make sure that Rhianna wasn't trying anything sneaky.

Because she wasn't looking where she was going, she put her foot down wrong and slipped when one of the carpets moved underfoot. She went sprawling onto the floor, banging her knee and her hip. It almost felt like the ground had shifted under her, jumping to throw her off balance.

When she looked up, Tarn was gazing down at her. His expression was as chilly as it had been the last time she'd seen him, when he'd told her to stay away for a few days. "My apologies. My realm has been acting out recently." His words were crisp.

"Is it that drag from the door you mentioned? Or something else?" She thought again of the tiny earthquake that occurred in the gallery.

"That is not your concern. Why have you returned?" he demanded, as if she hadn't been stepping through the door directly to her workroom for the last few days. Maybe that had been the realm compromising between his wish and her courtkey?

Irritation flashed through her, all the same. What game was he playing now? "You told me to," she pointed out, rising to her feet and wincing as her knee twinged. "We have unfinished business. A locked door for a comatose woman, a mirror for some magic."

A ripple moved the tapestries, and then Tarn let out a breath. "Very well." He moved to his chair and she realized he'd been standing quite close to the door, like he'd been waiting for her. At his throne, he picked up a small, thick book. "The Machine we seek is in the possession of one of the Lost. He was once very closely aligned with my kind, on the verge of joining us—"

"Wait," Branwyn interrupted. "What are the Lost?"

"The Lost Ones, the Destroyers. One of them slew several of my servants on the journey to the Queen of Stone, before you... distracted him." Tarn's mouth twisted in a sneer that automatically set Branwyn's back up. But she behaved; it was an accurate description.

"Right, them. The monsters, the kaiju. Go on. Wait. Slew? He said they'd return to you and you'd remake them."

"Their essence and their energy did return to me. I will, in time and at need, give them new bodies. May I go on?"

Branwyn thought about asking more but decided now wasn't the time. Penny would have been proud of her restraint. "Go ahead."

"As it pleases you, milady," said Tarn, sweeping her a sardonic bow. "This particular Lost One was once close friends with my kind. He does not remember it now, because he's been reborn several times since those days. But the truth endures. He will be eager to see the door unlocked if approached correctly."

Branwyn gave Tarn a wary look, remembering exactly how well her attempt to negotiate with the Queen of Stone went. "And what's the correct way?"

"Once again, you are to be my courier. You will deliver a gift and a message and return with the prize." He hesitated. "Do not try to alter the terms of the agreement this time, Branwyn. Do not... improvise. This Lost One would be very happy if you did, because then he could claim you instead."

Branwyn met Tarn's pied gaze, then looked away. "What's the gift this time?"

"A trinket," Tarn said blandly.

She looked back at him, scowling. "A trinket representing the ability to coerce yet another person into service?"

He studied her for a long moment, then said, "Yes. Me."

Branwyn blinked. "What?"

"I'm offering him a future favor in exchange for assistance now. It is how we work, Branwyn. Barter and favors." His mouth crooked up. "We're not civilized enough for a proper currency, I'm afraid."

"Why didn't you do that with the Queen of Stone, then?" Branwyn knew she sounded accusing, and she couldn't help it.

He spread his hands. "She's my Queen. Without her, Underlight wouldn't exist. I couldn't offer her what she already had."

"Oh. Right." Branwyn tried to shrug off her embarrassment. "What's this Lost One's name? Where is he?"

Tarn shrugged. "I never knew. But these days, he calls himself Hunter. He lives on Earth, to the north of here."

"Oh, wonderful," Branwyn muttered under her breath. "Is there a hurry? Do I have to leave right away? I'm not really ready to go."

He almost smiled again. "The journey must be soon, while the moon is new, or else we must wait for the full. Only then can my servants walk the world beside you. And I do not think it would be wise for you to go alone." Then, almost as if he couldn't stop himself, he said, "How is Penny?"

"You know the answer to that," Branwyn snapped. "But thank you for the little needle. I'll get ready as fast as I can."

Tarn spread his hands. "We'll be here." The world dissolved around Branwyn and she found herself on her family's porch again, blinking foolishly at the door.

Hunching her shoulders, wondering why Tarn was acting so mercurial all of a sudden, she curled up in the porch swing and pulled out her phone. She flipped through her contact list for a few moments, absently switching between three different numbers while she went over her previous interactions with Tarn. At last she decided that he didn't like that she wouldn't indulge him in all his games, and, that settled, she straightened up and pushed the Call button on the active number.

The phone rang and rang, until finally it reached voicemail. Branwyn frowned, then redialed the number. This time, after six rings, Simon answered. He sounded harried. "What do you want, Branwyn?"

"Can I come by the office to chat? I have a proposition for you."

"I'm not at the office right now," he said shortly. Something tore on his end of the line.

"Oh? Where are you?"

"I'm working. I did say. Everybody's laid up or run off to avoid a girl, it's just me, I'm swamped. What's this proposition of yours?"

"I'd rather meet in person. How about I meet you somewhere and buy you a drink?" Branwyn tried her best wheedle.

There was a squelching sound and a growl. In a lowered voice, Simon said, "You think you just have to wave alcohol and I'll come running, eh? I've got plenty, thank you."

Branwyn rolled her eyes. "Dinner, then. Everybody eats dinner."

"Hold on." There was a thud, then another growl so close to the phone that Branwyn jerked away. After a moment, she gingerly put the phone back to her ear. Something whirred and ticked on the other end.

"Simon?" When there was no answer, Branwyn started planning what she'd do if he never responded. She could find somebody to track down his phone's location—

Her reverie was interrupted by a crash, then Simon said, "Yeah, okay, I've thought it over. You're a pretty girl, I haven't eaten in a couple of days, it all makes sense. I'll just clean up here. Meet me in forty-five minutes at the Brown Bull on Colorado." Without waiting for her acknowledgment—or, more likely, her annoyance—he hung up.

What The Heck? Burned Down House
Views: 120,231
Abandoned house in my neighborhood caught on fire. Went up like an explosion. Saw this weird chick there after.

The burning wreckage of a house at night, all orange and black. The camera zooms in and there's a woman silhouetted against the flames. There's a lot of noise as fire trucks pull up and the video cuts to black. When it returns, it's closer to the fire and the woman. The firefighters are nowhere to be seen, but the house is still blazing merrily. The woman turns to the camera and smiles. "These fall nights can get a little brisk," she says. She holds up her hand and sparks seem to dance across her fingers. Cut to black.

The Brown Bull was a steak joint, the sort that catered to meat-and-potatoes businessmen. It wasn't quite as expensive as Branwyn expected and it wasn't crowded, either. Simon was waiting for her outside when she walked up. He looked trashed; he'd clearly washed his face and his hands, but soap hadn't been involved. Branwyn sniffed as she joined him, but didn't detect anything other than dirt and sweat.

Maybe he hadn't actually been fighting something when she'd called. Maybe he'd been… chopping wood. Assisted by a very large dog.

And maybe she was Little Red Riding Hood.

Simon gave her a cocky smile. "I've been waiting ages."

"This isn't a date," she warned him as she glanced around. "It isn't that kind of proposition."

"Course it isn't." But he kept grinning at her as they sat down.

As they waited for their drinks, she said, "So what exactly were you doing when I called?"

He ran a hand through hair that was already standing on end. "Ah, well, there was some spawn camped out in a delayed construction project down on—well, never mind where. Predators. They needed dealing with."

Branwyn wrinkled her nose. "Spawn? Like, offspring?"

He gave her a puzzled look, then took the glass a waiter delivered and gulped its contents. "Right, you're new. The kaiju can make a deal with willing humans where the human gives up their soul in exchange for a portion of the kaiju's power. The human is remade as a servant of the kaiju. It's a messy process, though. Kaiju aren't exactly sane, so it never goes well for the human. You know how in stories there's a master vampire, doesn't really have much in the way of weaknesses, and then there's other vampires who are afraid of the sun and so on? This is where that comes from."

"Wait, there are vampires, too?" Branwyn couldn't hide her dismay.

Shrugging, Simon said, "There's a couple of kaiju who shape their spawn into creatures of that flavoring, sure. They're nasty, but they're not the worst."

Branwyn thought about that for a few minutes. After the waiter left with their order, she said, "What do the kaiju do with the souls?"

"How the hell would I know? Maybe they eat them. Maybe they store them. Maybe they fold them up into origami and show them off to their friends. But why are we talking about this? This is work. I don't want to talk about work." He grinned at her again. It was a little disturbing how a few fingers of scotch and water had improved his color.

"But I do. I wanted to talk about kaiju in specific. Sorry."

His grin turned into a scowl. "You're not really sorry," he accused.

"Well... no. But it seemed the thing to say. I *am* buying dinner, though."

"Oh, fine. But you'll have to let me buy you dinner sometime, too. And we shan't talk about work at all then." He gave her a sly, smug smile.

Branwyn hesitated. Normally that sort of proposal would irritate her. But somehow, with Simon, it didn't. He was probably lonely, she reasoned. And she didn't feel like he was hitting on her, despite him calling her a pretty girl earlier. Oddly enough, that hadn't annoyed her, either. She wondered if she'd mind if he *did* hit on her. She decided the stench of alcohol would probably get on her nerves eventually. But she could be a friend.

"Sure. But after I get back."

He narrowed his eyes. "Where are you going?"

She took a deep breath. "Tarn is sending me on another quest. This time, it's to a kaiju he called Hunter."

All remaining cheerfulness fled from Simon's face. Slowly, he pushed his chair back on two legs and rubbed his mouth, his gaze intent. "Now I see why you wanted to talk to me."

"Do you?" asked Branwyn, pleased. "Good."

Simon continued as if she hadn't spoken. "You want me to tie you up so you can't go. Wise, very wise."

Stiffly, Branwyn said, "I was actually hoping you'd come with me."

Almost gently, he said, "I'm not suicidal, girl."

"What's suicidal about it? You kill kaiju, don't you?"

He laughed and all the good the scotch had done him vanished from his face. The bread arrived and he started toying with a roll. "I've got no idea how to even talk to you. You've got it into your head that the kaiju and the angels and, yes, probably the faeries are like tigers. But the beasties I fought tonight, the spawn of a kaiju, they're a lot worse than a tiger, and their maker—" He shook his head. "We don't fight kaiju by showing up on their front doorstep and ringing the bell. Ambush, that's the way. Ambush and luck and I've still seen more hunters go down for good than I ever like to think about sober. You think because they talk to you that they're like humans, or even like the nephilim, that they operate on the same scale. But you're a kitten to them. A fuzzy mouthful, with big eyes and a nice purr."

Branwyn took a deep breath, keeping a tight leash on her temper, and Simon waited in silence. Finally, she said, "And yet, there's you."

He frowned. "What do you mean by that?"

"There's you, there's Corbin, there's *Marley*, for crying out loud. You had a father and a mother, and you said they had more than a one-night stand. So we're not just fuzzy mouthfuls. We're people and so are they."

Bleakly, he said, "Is that the route you really want to take on this mad quest of yours? I didn't think that was your style."

"It's not," she snapped. "And I don't. I was just pointing out that there's enough of you bastards running around that there's got to be a reason for their attraction to us. Something that makes us a bit more valuable than you think."

"Sex isn't enough?" he asked dryly.

Branwyn resisted the desire to wrap her arms around herself and close herself off. "I doubt it. They don't strike me as perpetual teenagers. Why are we talking about this again?"

"Because you're trying to convince me that the kaiju known as Hunter isn't going to eat you alive," he said promptly. "By the way, he's a bad one to be applying this particular line of reasoning to. Angels, I'll grant. They're tempted by more than just flesh. But the kaiju are destroyers, one and all. You mustn't even dream of protecting yourself by interesting him."

The meal arrived, but Branwyn's appetite was gone. "I wasn't. Not him, anyhow." She closed her mouth abruptly, before she said something she didn't want to even think.

Simon cut into his steak. "The faerie fellow, then? Could work with him. I guess it has so far, eh?"

"It's not like that," Branwyn muttered. "It's an exchange of services." She pushed the food around on her plate, then made herself eat some grilled tomatoes.

"All right. But Bran, I've got to make sure you're clear on this. I'm a kaiju hunter, not a kaiju social worker. For every sweet story like my mum and dad—and it's not as sweet as maybe you think—I've seen *thousands* of victims. Tens of thousands. We're eating. I don't want to ruin the meal, so I'm not going to go into details. But I don't hunt them because I'm eager to risk my neck. I hunt them because my mum was a good person." He paused, chewed, swallowed. "And, admittedly, because I'm not good for much else. But that's not the point. Stop distracting me with those big green eyes."

He shook his fork at her. "The point is you've been playing with fire with the fae and maybe you're going to burn the house down, I don't know. But Hunter is an inferno. And that's enough strained metaphors for the night. Where the hell's that waiter with my drink?"

Quietly, Branwyn said, "I have to do it."

"Why? Your comatose friend? There's—"

"There aren't other ways," Branwyn interrupted. "Corbin said he was sorry enough times that I'm sure there aren't. They've given up. They might not have even bothered trying."

"Corbin's just a young sprat most of the time," Simon grumbled, but Branwyn remembered that Corbin had successfully forbidden him from doing magic on other people and ignored his comment.

"It's Penny, but it's not *just* Penny. Penny's the here and now, but what you want me to do is roll over and go to sleep even though I've heard an intruder in the house. It's—"

"Ah!" He raised a finger. "I'm sorry, we've now exceeded the metaphor limit for the evening." At her look, he finished off his drink. "It's true. You wouldn't want to confuse a sloshed mind, would you? It'd be wasting the money spent on this fine dinner."

"Fine," she said flatly. "I want power of my own. I don't want to have to rely on people who may decide I'm a little too short-lived to be worth caring about. Fuzzy, with a nice purr." She felt a vicious satisfaction at Simon's startled look. "Besides, I've never backed down from anything in my life. Giving up now would be like suicide."

"Suicide or murder, you're dead all the same." A peculiar expression crossed his face and he added, "And there's worse than death, too. They can keep people alive a long, long time. Changing who you are in the process. It's grim, Branwyn. What are you actually getting out of this that's yours? What power can you have, other than... being like my mum?"

"Oh, I'm getting something. Maybe when I understand it better, I'll show you." Branwyn attacked her mushroom risotto determinedly. After she'd eaten half of it, her appetite returned, and she finished it off. Simon ventured a few comments on the food while she ate, but she didn't say anything until she was done. Then, leaning back, she said, "Thank you for the warning. Do you really think I'm in this much danger if I'm visiting a kaiju as an emissary for a fae? Tarn seemed to think that as long as I didn't, uh, improvise, I'd be fine."

Simon looked at her from over the dessert menu. "No idea. If you trust him, you trust him. But you definitely don't want me along if you're trying to stay within the lines."

"Well, I suppose when you phrase it that way... But can you tell me about him? Something other than 'phenomenally dangerous'? So I know what to expect? The only kaiju I know is—" She shook her head, suddenly certain that if she said his name, he'd show up. "Not what I expected. Honestly, I don't understand why these guys are running around."

"We've got to prioritize, girl. I told you that before. They come back if killed. We don't, not even as ghosts." Simon studied her and his face softened. "As far as I know, he lives in a compound up near Seattle, which is a bit out of Titan One's casual jurisdiction. He's on our radar, but when we're pushed into taking him out, it isn't going to be an assassination—it's going to be a war. He keeps a lot of servants and spawn around him. He's called Hunter for a reason; that's what he does. People, animals, concepts. It's not the only horrible thing he does, but it's what he's notorious for. I think he's old, but I don't know how old; he didn't really appear in his current incarnation until about thirty years ago. What exactly is your faerie fellow sending you to him for? And why can't he go himself?"

Startled by his sudden switch to asking questions, Branwyn said, "We need to get another part for our project. A project he wants to succeed even more than I do, so I don't think he's playing games there. I think he's stuck in his realm until we're done, honestly."

"And he thinks Hunter is just going to hand this thing you need over?" Simon looked as though the thought disturbed him.

"Well, yes." Branwyn almost said more, but then reconsidered. "In case he doesn't, though, doesn't this Hunter have any weaknesses?"

"His mortal form is vulnerable to all the same things I am. A guy like that, a bullet to the head is favorite as a short-term solution. But you're asking for shortcuts and no, there aren't any special shortcuts to killing a true dreamborn kaiju. It's all hard work, doing the things we do. Are you actually thinking of stealing from him?" He gave her a look that she couldn't read.

"Nah," said Branwyn. "I'm ambitious, not crazy. But I'd like to get away safely no matter what he decides. Can't use a gun very well, though."

"Be smart, girl. That's your safest bet."

"I'm always smart," she said crisply. "It's just, sometimes people don't realize it until much, much later." She gave Simon a smile, and dug her spoon into her chocolate ice cream.

Vlog #17
Views: 2,013
Response to ***Amazing Illusion**

A girl with messy straw-colored hair and freckles faces the camera in a darkened room. "I— I can't stop thinking of him. I keep watching that video of him." She looks down, fiddles with some paper. "It wasn't an illusion. I don't know what it was. I don't know what he was. He had the most amazing eyes. I don't think anybody saw them but me." She crumples the paper up. "I haven't been able to concentrate in class since then. Yesterday, I thought, why bother going? So I didn't. I went down to the wharf instead, in case he came back again. I looked at the water. It was pretty, out away from the wharf... It made me think of his eyes. I kind of wanted to jump in." She shrugs helplessly. "Instead I came back here." She pushes herself away from the computer. "This is dumb. I don't know why I try. I'm going to bed. Maybe then I won't feel so alone. I keep hoping I can catch him before he slips away." She reaches forward and turns the camera off.

-fifteen-

Marley insisted on driving Branwyn to her family's house after she'd packed for the trip, yanking Branwyn's backpack away from her and carrying it down to her own car. It was once again night, and the lights flashing on and off Marley's profile as they drove matched what seemed to be dark and distant thoughts. Branwyn could feel the tension radiating off of her, but Marley didn't say anything at all until she'd parked the car.

"I want to come with you this time."

Taken aback, Branwyn said, "You do?" While she'd dragged Marley along on some of her adventures in the past, her friend almost never volunteered.

"Yes!" said Marley, almost defiantly. "I can keep you safe while you do whatever you have to do."

Branwyn grimaced, then softened. "I'm not five years old, Marley. You know how you didn't tell me what was going on when Zachariah vanished? How you wanted to protect me? I'm doing this so you don't ever have to feel that way again."

Marley bit her lip. "I don't want to lose Penny *and* you."

"I don't want to lose me, either," Branwyn said calmly. "Hopefully you won't lose either of us."

"Can I beat up Tarn again if you don't come back?"

Branwyn sighed. "Feel free."

Marley tried to smile and failed, and Branwyn wondered what her friend saw with her magic catastrophe vision when she looked at her. But she only wondered briefly. It wasn't anything definite or Marley would have made that clear and Branwyn would have listened.

That was comforting, actually. She leaned over and hugged her friend, then slid out of the car. "I'll be back, and better than ever. It'll be awesome. Hey, call Corbin while I'm gone. That will take your mind off me." Listening to Marley's muttering brought a grin to her face as she walked up to the house. Her next obstacle awaited her and she hadn't even made it to Faerie yet.

Rhianna sat on the porch, only her eyes and a few strands of her red hair glinting in the light from the streetlamp. "Who's that tromping on my bridge?"

"You make a terrible troll." Branwyn rested her bag on the railing as she stood lightly on the steps. "Do you sleep out here every night, waiting for me? Or do you and Howl take it in shifts?"

"Howl is still sulking. And not everything is about you. I thought I told you that already."

Branwyn said, "Lies!" then added, "But tell me what's not about me this time?"

"Mom came back from an after-party without Jaimie because she had a headache. I'm waiting for him to come home."

"Why?"

"Because he's not home yet, and that… unwoman was at the party, too."

"Unwo—oh, Rime." Branwyn frowned, then chided her sister, "Rhianna, you can't call her that just because you don't like her."

"Well, calling her a woman suggests she's human and she's not."

"Faerie," Branwyn suggested. "It's what they call themselves."

"Whatever. I don't know how you can be so relaxed about her hanging around. She's dangerous."

Branwyn laughed. "Everyone I know is dangerous now. Even you."

"Yes. I am," said Rhianna, with some satisfaction.

But Branwyn kept talking over her. "Everything I know is dangerous now. She's pretty mild in comparison."

"I saw another one of them today. It looked like a teenager, hanging out on Colorado. He was showing off to a group of other kids, making some coins dance across his hands, then showing the girls how to do it. He just touched them and they were as good as he was. Until the wind changed. Then he vanished and one of the girls sat down and cried, right in the middle of the sidewalk. And her friends just left her there, walking off like they didn't remember what had happened."

"What did you do?" asked Branwyn, intrigued.

"Watched," said Rhianna irritably. "A security guard helped her up and used her cellphone and then one of her friends came back and acted surprised to see her there and took her home. Do you know what that was all about?"

Branwyn shifted uncomfortably. "Magic, I suppose."

"So, no, then. And neither do I. You said the other day that they're here now and we're going to have to learn to deal with them. That's what I'm doing. Learning."

Headlights appeared at the far end of the street. Branwyn peered out, then picked up her bag again. "That's Jaimie now. I'm off before he gets here. We're going to talk about this more later, though."

Rhianna only shrugged, and Branwyn unlocked the front door with the courtkey before Jaimie could see her on the porch. She stepped through.

Only William waited on the other side of the curtain, standing at ease in front of the throne. "My lord is in the gallery," he said before Branwyn could ask.

"Is something wrong?" she asked, but William only stared straight ahead. Muttering, she stalked past him toward the gallery. As she walked down the fixed corridor, she noticed that there were lines on the elegant black and white walls, starting at the floor and spidering upwards. At first she thought it was new ornamentation: painted black vines. But when she peered closer, she realized that the lines were cracks that seemed to narrow as she looked more closely at them, until they were just hairlines of blackness. She brushed a finger over one and felt the draw of the Backworld that lay under Faerie. She almost reached through it experimentally, but then stopped, self-conscious. She'd ask Tarn first. She wasn't actually into wrecking things without a reason, despite what her most recent ex-boyfriend had claimed.

She found Tarn standing in front of the locked door, his hands clasped behind his taut back, his eyes half-closed. He didn't seem to notice Branwyn's arrival, so she said, "Hey, what's up with the cracks in the hall?"

Distantly, Tarn said, "The door drags against the domain, as I've said. I'm doing what I can to stabilize it, but the pressure must be relieved soon."

"Oh." Branwyn thought about that for a moment. "Well, we're wasting time, then. Are you ready for me to go on our little errand?"

He focused on her. "Are you?"

"Of course! Although I am curious how we'll be traveling. I heard this guy is in Seattle, which is a bit further north than I was expecting."

He raised an eyebrow. "Did you? Well, your informant is correct. The Backworld is smaller than Creation, but touches it everywhere. There are shortcuts for those who have had the time to find them."

"Oh yeah? How short?"

He gave her a speculative look. "At your walking pace, several hours."

Branwyn sniffed. "No faster than flying, then."

"Your mechanical flight has far too many people poking their noses into places they shouldn't. And speaking of machines.... it would be best to leave the partially completed Machine key here. There's no point in providing the Hunter with temptation."

Branwyn fished it out of her backpack and looked at it wistfully. "I thought it might come in handy."

Tarn moved his long fingers and pulled a soft suede pouch out of thin air. "In here, if you would. I don't even want to imagine how you thought it might come in handy."

Branwyn tipped it into the bag. "You never know. That's the point, really. Shards from Heavenly Machines seem like they might be useful for almost anything."

He drew the bag closed, twisted his hand again, and sent it away. Then he withdrew a box from nothingness and opened it. Like the previous casket Branwyn had delivered to the Queen of Stone, this one contained a message bubble. It also contained what looked very much like a diamond the size of Branwyn's fist. It sparkled invitingly. Her jaw dropped and she glanced up at him. He was watching her with a faint smile.

"Okay, I know you just made that like you made the bag, but it's gorgeous," she said defensively. "I still can't do anything other than raw materials. I'm jealous."

"It'd be no good to send a gift that I created from Faerie," chided Tarn. "It would fade with the dawn, or when the wind changed, or the moon turned."

Branwyn gave him a skeptical look. "You're not telling me that you somehow got your hands on a real diamond larger than anything ever mined by man?"

He laughed. "This is Underlight, bound to the broken earth and the sea-washed shores. If I wanted to find a natural diamond to carve into a throne for my Queen, I could." He paused, then added, "But this is not that, no. It is a crystallized fragment of my own essence. The gift I mentioned." He snapped the box closed and offered it to Branwyn. She tucked it into her bag thoughtfully, then followed Tarn as he returned to the throne room.

William was waiting there, along with his troop of changelings. Branwyn recognized each of them, and noticed that the ones Severin had killed had not been replaced. She pursed her lips. "You have non-changeling fae, too, right? Can't you send any of them along? In case we run into… trouble along the way again? The Queen of Stone had a servant who kept everything neat and tidy."

"My servants draw on my power just as the Queen of Stone's servants draw on hers; it matters only a little whether the servant is changeling or dreamborn. The trouble you refer to is no more than an inconvenience at the moment, and it is less of an inconvenience if he disrupts one of my changelings than if he disrupts one of my dreamborn fae." He spoke with a measured distance that seemed at odds with their earlier conversation and Branwyn wondered if it was because of the distraction of the door.

Then she processed what he said and balked. "An inconvenience? He killed some of William's friends! I know you can bring them back, but—that's got to be more than just an *inconvenience*. At least to them." And she glowered at Tarn with all the force she could.

Tarn tilted his head. "Do you still wish for me to save Penny?"

Branwyn's fingers tightened on her backpack. "Yes. What does that have to do with William's friends?"

"You've never asked me how I planned to restore her to you."

Blowing her breath out in exasperation, Branwyn said, "No, I didn't. I assumed it would be *magic*," she wiggled her fingers, "just like what hurt her. But *do* tell me, how will you save her?"

Tarn nodded toward William. "I will make her into one of my children, just as once I made William into my child. Oh, it isn't the same as the process that produced Zachariah. It is," and Tarn smiled his old smile, "less enjoyable. But they are my children, just the same, born from my desire and my essence. William and the others were dying on a hillside when I found them. I took them into myself, then fashioned them new bodies from my own power and placed their minds within."

Branwyn the crafter seized on a detail. "Why did you have to make new bodies for them?"

"Their existing bodies were badly damaged," said Tarn, and paused, waiting for the question he seemed to know was coming.

"But Penny's body is just fine. Can't she keep her body? She's very attached to it."

"Her mortal body will not support a mind without a soul. That's why she's wasting away despite your doctors' efforts. Celestial magic is required to support a body without a soul."

"She has a soul, it's just damaged," Branwyn protested, then dropped her eyes rather than meet Tarn's sympathetic gaze. Subdued, she added, "What does this have to do with trouble along the way? Trouble you consider only an inconvenience?"

"Edward and Alfred and Harold are all still here," he said, tapping his chest. "They endure as long as I do, or at least as long as I hold Underlight." He turned a brooding glance toward the gallery. "Restoring them is only a matter of energy. I have not done it because that energy is reserved for Penny."

Branwyn looked between William and Tarn. William's gaze was fixed on the middle distance, like he wasn't listening. Then her eyes narrowed. "Did you *mean* to say that? Because it sounds like you just said you don't need the door open to save Penny."

"If only it were that simple." His shoulders slumped. "I said I would save her if I could. Until I try, Underlight keeps me to my word; it holds the power in trust—and it is more power than merely embodying a changeling would take. But I cannot try until the door is open; it requires too much of my attention."

Branwyn regarded him suspiciously. Then, softening, she said, "Poor faerie Lord, caught by your own game." He didn't even look at her, although she waited for a long moment. Then she shrugged. "Fine. It sounds like a plan. Let's do this."

As if released from an invisible cage, Tarn went to one of the pictures on the wall and touched its gilded frame. The fairytale castle contained within grew larger, and the point of view swooped through the castle's golden gates. Light gathered within the frame and grew so bright that Branwyn could no longer make out what was beyond.

"Follow me," said William, and stepped through the frame.

Branwyn moved to follow him and Tarn caught her hand as she drew close. "Branwyn. It is important that you come back."

Without thinking about it, Branwyn squeezed Tarn's hand. "It's important to me, too."

As if the tightening of her hand was an invitation, Tarn brought her fingers to his mouth and brushed his lips over them, then released her before she could pull away. "Make sure he accepts the message as well as the gift. I'll know when that happens. Now go," he said, turning away.

Without letting herself hesitate, she stepped into the light.

Her foot came down on a hard surface. As the dazzle faded from her eyes, disorientation swept over and she flailed her arms instinctively.

William caught her shoulder. "Steady. Look down at your feet for now."

Branwyn did more than that, dropping to her knees to hold onto the ground. "Where the hell are we?" she whispered. She was kneeling on stone steps about five feet wide. One side clung to a wall, while the other had nothing remotely resembling a banister or guard rail. Before she'd fallen to her knees, she'd seen the dizzying drop off the side. She'd seen more, too.

"Why," she started, then cleared her throat and tried for a more normal voice. "Why are we upside down?"

"We're not upside down. The castle is." William moved in front of her and offered her a hand up.

"That isn't helping. *Why* are we *here?*"

William quirked an eyebrow. "Are you afraid of heights? I wouldn't have guessed."

"No," Branwyn snapped, and stood up, keeping her eyes on William's face. He smirked and she narrowed her eyes. "Lead on. Just remember I'll be behind you on this death staircase."

"Of course. And my men will be behind you. Don't worry, they'll catch you if you stumble and fall." He started climbing the stairs. Branwyn glanced up carefully, bracing herself for the vertigo that came at seeing the floor of the castle far, far above her. A chandelier on an impossibly long chain reached toward the sky, the candles in it burning upside down. The pale flames were only barely visible, because there were windows in the curving wall that the staircase hugged and sunlight streamed in, making the polished silver fixtures of the lamps and chandeliers shine brighter than the flames. As they passed one window, Branwyn glanced out and saw clouds drifting by below.

One of the changelings behind her caught her shoulder again, and she shook him off. "I'm fine." She stopped at the window, though, and took a good long look out. It was true that the castle was upside down, because far, far below, under the drifting clouds, she could see the green of a verdant land. She took a deep breath, feeling a breeze on her face, tasting the tang of rain. Then a rainbow arched past, translucent but far more solid than any prismatic reflection she'd seen on Earth. She looked at it wistfully, remembering childhood stories, then sighed and turned back to where William was waiting. Sometimes being a grownup wasn't nearly as much fun as being a kid.

Not only was the ridiculous structure upside down, it was also far larger than even a fairytale castle had any right to be. The climb went on for nearly half an hour and Branwyn's legs were burning by the time they turned at a landing and entered a long corridor. The surface they walked on was both curved and tiled with a flowered mosaic, and it was scarcely easier to navigate than the stairs had been. Still, once she got the hang of it, she found she had breath to talk. "Why aren't we on the road? I liked the road. It was scenic. It was *flat.*"

"That road is for travel within Faerie. We're traveling between two points in Creation right now. It's different."

"When are we going to leave the castle?"

William glanced back at her. "When we get to where we're going."

Appalled, Branwyn said, "This entire trip is going to be in the castle? How big is it?"

"Much, much bigger than we'll see," William assured her.

The corridor ended in a courtyard roofed by a thin wooden lattice wound with grapevines. Roofed, which meant that would serve as their ground. Branwyn stared at the delicate-looking network of twigs and rods, and the spaces between them. They weren't very large, but the sticks didn't look very strong, and Branwyn was certain that if she lost her footing and fell, she'd crash through the lattice and fall into the sky below.

William was watching her. When she noticed, she asked brightly, "Any special rules for crossing this?" When he shook his head, she sprang out onto the lattice, felt it sway underneath her, and sprang again, half-running, half-jumping until she got to the shaded arcade on the other side. Then her wobbly legs gave out beneath her and she sank into a heap. Several of the changeling guards were laughing and cheering for her, and even William wore a faint but genuine smile.

They bounded after her, far more sure on their feet than she felt she had been. They didn't collapse once they reached the other side, either. It was probably because they were professionals.

"Do you need a rest?" asked William, offering her a canteen.

She pushed herself to her feet. "I'm good for now. Maybe after the next challenge. What *is* next, by the way? Do I have to walk a tightrope across the sunset? Fly? Because I can't fly, let's just get that out there. At least, not unless you're handing out wings. Are you handing out wings? Do we get to slide down rainbows?" Then she took the canteen and drank from it, just to stop her own babbling.

"Down, yes, but more stairs."

"We're going higher in the castle? Well, that will be easy. Yay!"

But going down endless flights of stairs was almost as exhausting as climbing them, at least in the number of flights they descended. "Why do they call them flights?" Branwyn wondered aloud. "It's a bad word for stairs. It raises one's hopes. I disapprove."

Eventually, they did take a break, on the flat ceiling of a high and narrow tower. The stairs continued up one floor, but a tapestry dominated the far wall of the tower and. like them, it was upside down compared to the rest of the castle. It showed a dark, wet forest, full of tall pine trees and tangled, fern-strewn foliage. A modern lodge lurked amid the trees, completely unlit.

"That's it?" When William inclined his head, Branwyn added, "Are we going to hike through the forest? Or shall we end up in the lodge, upside down?"

"Very droll. Have you rested enough? Are you ready to face the Hunter?" William put his hand on the side of the tapestry and pulled it aside. It covered a large hole in the wall that led into absolute darkness.

Branwyn stood up. Her legs had stiffened during the brief rest and she could feel the beginnings of a deep ache that was going to make walking torture tomorrow. "I'm not going to get any more ready than this."

"Very well." With no more warning than that, the darkness of the hole reached out and swallowed the room. The floor vanished beneath Branwyn's feet and she thumped down on an uneven surface. Wetness tickled her ankles and cool dampness invaded her lungs. She couldn't see a thing.

"William?" she called, as she fumbled in her backpack for her flashlight.

Somebody near her groaned, and William swore. There was a sick thud and a cry of pain and a moist squelching. Something moved past Branwyn's arm and she swung violently with the flashlight as she turned it on. A hand caught the flashlight, fingers obscuring the beam, and somebody whispered, "Shh," too close to her ear. Then the flashlight was released and the shadow that had caught it moved on.

Flashlights aren't very useful in dark, wet forests full of strange sounds and pained cries . The darkness became darker, and the points illuminated by the beam of light seemed to be nothing more than shadow and glare. William growled, "You wo—" and trailed off in a gurgle, which in turn faded into silence.

Trees rustled in the wind. Branwyn turned her flashlight onto the ground and didn't look directly at the spot of light, waiting for her eyes to adjust even a little. It was moonless and cloudy above; without a flashlight, she wouldn't be able to move until dawn. With one hand, she scrubbed moisture off her face; a tree branch must have flung droplets at her in the scuffle. "Severin? I know that's you."

"Yes," he said, right behind her. She was expecting that, so she managed to limit her reaction to her breath hissing between her teeth.

"What have you done?" She tried to control her emotions. *They're okay, they're okay, they just took a shortcut home. I need to worry about myself.*

"I only meant to do one or two, but I got bored waiting and waiting and waiting. I thought you'd be here hours ago." He sounded accusing, as if it was her fault he'd gone overboard on the whole "murder" thing.

Branwyn looked up at the sky. It was brighter than she expected, even with the clouds and no moon. "How did you know we'd be coming here?"

She could feel his warmth on the back of her neck as he murmured, "I've been at this a long time, cupcake."

When Branwyn looked around the forest again, carefully not turning around, this time she saw some lights distantly through the trees. She fixed the direction in her mind, then looked down at the flashlit ground and started picking her way across it.

Severin crunched behind her, humming under his breath. *Oh, William,* Branwyn thought. *I'm sorry.* The dampness of the air seemed to blur the distant light, but when she blinked, it came back into focus again, steadily growing larger and, she hoped, more welcoming.

She meant to ignore Severin for the entire hike, but after a while he stopped tromping behind her and glided up to walk beside her, his steps becoming as silent as a ghost's. If she didn't look at him, he barely seemed more than a voice in her ear. "What's he trying to bargain with? Not you, I hope."

"None of your business. Go away."

"Oh, I can't do that yet. Hunter knows I'm here. Saying hello is only polite."

Branwyn stopped, digging her heels into the pine-needle carpet. "Why are you so obsessed with Tarn? There's fae running all over LA now that you could be stalking."

"Perhaps I'll get to them eventually. Would you like that, cupcake?" She could just make out his eyes, wells of blackness in the shadowed planes of his face.

Refusing to be drawn in, Branwyn said, "Why Tarn first?"

"I owe him," said Severin easily. "Don't push, Branwyn. You won't like the result." And there was a note in his voice that gave Branwyn pause, like he meant what he was saying.

Even so, she almost pushed further—but she was here on a mission. She had a different monster to get something out of. So, as much as it galled her, she turned her gaze back to the uneven ground and resumed her trek. Severin drifted beside her, silent.

As she got closer, she realized she was approaching the house from the back, and in front was a proper driveway that extended out to a private road. Scowling, she circled the house. She understood from one of the charms Zachariah had given her that it was easiest to enter and exit the Backworld from specific locations, but it was annoying that she'd had to hike through the woods in the dark.

Annoying, and worse. *Oh, William.* She hoped she'd understood what Tarn had been telling her, that it was just an inconvenience, that the bastard beside her hadn't hurt them too much first. They could be hurt, oh yes, she remembered that from before.

She couldn't stop going over how helpless Severin made her, in so many ways. In ways she usually tried to avoid remembering. She was just an accessory in a game he was playing with Tarn. He could hurt and kill her companions, then walk alongside her, and she could do nothing about it. He got under her skin and into her subconscious. It was intolerable; it barely stood thinking about, but here in the darkness, wrapped in a fear she couldn't contain, she couldn't escape it.

The shadow beside her shifted, became something with footsteps again. He sighed and touched the back of her neck lightly. "Don't."

She shied away and lost her footing on a tree root, landing on her hands and one knee. The flashlight fell onto the same root, half-illuminating Severin. He stood with his hands in his pockets, his head low as he watched her without expression.

"*You* don't," Branwyn snarled, rising to her feet again. "Don't touch me."

He didn't answer, but somebody else did. A voice called from the front of the house, "I hear somebody lost in the woods." It was a sing-song, anticipatory cry, meant to carry to prey. Several figures appeared around the edge of the house, bringing with them the scent of cigarette smoke.

"Do you think it's Hunter's guest?" asked the same voice.

"That would be a disappointment," said another voice. The third figure moved into the woods, obscuring several of the house lights. He was very large.

Severin moved just a little, so he was between Branwyn and the three figures. "It's me," he said, very quietly.

From the sudden stillness, the complete cessation of movement sounds, they heard him just fine. For a moment the night was dead silent, and Branwyn instinctively paused in the act of brushing herself off in case her hands on her jeans broke the calm.

Then the first speaker said sullenly, "You."

"Me," Severin repeated lightly. "And an envoy for your master. Be a good dog and show us in."

"Right," muttered the first figure, and all three of them withdrew. Severin strolled after them without a backward glance. Branwyn took a deep breath, exhaled out her fear, and followed behind. She passed by the edge of the wood where they'd been standing and noticed a half-smoked cigarette still smoldering in the layer of dead leaves. Scowling, she ground it under her foot until it was nothing but char and dirt.

-sixteen-

Hunter sprawled on a long, leather couch in the large front room of the lodge. Although he was only one of several men giving advice about somebody's woman problems, he was immediately recognizable as the lord and master of all he surveyed. When he saw Severin, he stood up. "My brother," he said warmly.

He was as tall as Tarn and built like a tank, with closely trimmed dirty blond hair, a mustache and goatee. When he strode forward to clasp Severin's hand, Branwyn thought he would loom over the leaner, smaller kaiju. But something odd happened as Hunter bore down on them: the world seemed to ripple. A pulse both visible and painful passed out from the two of them as they gripped each other's wrists. Suddenly physical size didn't seem to matter at all. Both of them bared their teeth at the other; there was no way to describe what passed between them as a smile. For a moment, red and black static danced across her vision and an enormous hand seemed to be pressing down on her.

Branwyn leaned against the door and exhaled. The pain arrived between her eyes like a needle and passed out through the base of her spine. The others in the room shifted uncomfortably as well, which was a small consolation. It wasn't agonizing; she could cope, but she didn't like it.

Then the two kaiju parted and the pulsing pain faded. "Welcome to my home," said Hunter. "Sit down. One of the boys will get you a beer." Severin smiled, as if amused by the thought, but moved to an occupied armchair that almost magically became unoccupied as he approached.

Hunter turned to Branwyn. She straightened up, embarrassed that she'd been letting herself hide behind Severin. Simon's warnings had gotten to her, made her expect the worst. But this didn't look like the set of a horror movie. It had big picture windows and large speakers high on the walls and a bearskin rug in front of a subdued fire at the far end of the room. A few men were repositioning themselves in Severin's wake, some giving up their chairs to others and leaning against the walls. It looked like, at worst, a frat house. And she'd met Severin's terrifying gaze more than once; how bad could Hunter be?

But Hunter didn't meet her gaze at all as he said, "I've been expecting you. Tarn's little friend. Come on in, missy. You look like you've had quite a hike." Instead, his gaze roved up and down her body before settling on her breasts. "We've got a shower if you want to get cleaned up." The other men in the room snickered.

Branwyn clenched her jaw and she heard herself say distantly, "Thank you, I'm fine." *At worst, a frat house.* She'd been steeping herself in the dangers of magic too long. She'd lost perspective, and a new fear coiled in her stomach as a result. No, not a new fear. An old fear. One of the oldest.

Hunter grinned. "Well then, take a seat. Annalise will get you a drink." Branwyn scanned the room for an unoccupied seat she wouldn't have to share, then jumped as Hunter barked, "Annalise! I said get the nice lady a drink!"

A dark-skinned teenage girl with curly brown hair stood up slowly from where she'd been sitting on a piano bench with her back to the others. Without a word, she walked out of the room. "My daughter," confided Hunter. "Come on, there's room on the couch." He returned to his place and Branwyn reluctantly followed him. It was a large couch, at least. She forced herself to sink deep into the cushions so that she wouldn't look as tense as she felt.

Hunter continued talking about his daughter as he settled into place. "I wanted her to inherit the family business, but she threw the most ridiculous tantrum over it. Even ran away for a while. I said, fine, but I figure she can at least make herself useful." He paused as Annalise returned with a tray of bottles and plunked it on the coffee table where her father's feet rested. She stole a quick glance at Branwyn, then averted her gaze and moved stiffly back to her piano bench.

Her host picked up a bottle and showed Branwyn the label. "Local microbrewery. Pretty good stuff." He opened it, handed it to her, then popped the cap off one for himself. The rest of the bottles vanished as Hunter's companions claimed them. One was offered to Severin, who snickered and waved the man off. He'd placed himself, Branwyn realized, so that he could watch Annalise as well as Hunter.

Hunter was still talking. "It's a shame, really. Her mother was the prettiest little thing. Good genes." He gave that not-actually-disarming grin again. "I still have her around somewhere."

Across the room, Annalise's curls bobbed as she lowered her head.

Branwyn's stomach flip-flopped. *What the hell*, she thought. *Why tiptoe?* "This is the family business of... hunting things?"

His eyebrows went up. "Things?" He smirked. "But nah. That's really just a hobby." His expression darkened. "Can't enjoy myself too often or those self-righteous half-breed bastards start sniffing around and things get awkward." He gave Branwyn a measuring look, as if wondering if she was going to defend Senyaza. When she remained silent, he leaned closer to her and said, "Don't tell anybody I said so, but it's kind of been a good thing. Forced me to think bigger than my immediate gratification. Develop what you might call a business plan."

"Yeah?" Branwyn said without enthusiasm, and tried to steer the conversation toward the purpose of her visit. "Tarn said you were almost a fae once."

An ugly expression passed across Hunter's face. "Was I? I don't recall." Without taking his gaze off Branwyn, he raised his voice. "Annalise, get my brother a whiskey, since he rejects my beer." Slowly, the girl stood up again.

Lazily, Severin said, "Yes, AT, get me some whiskey." The girl half-turned, raw pain on her face, then lowered her head again and left the room.

Branwyn sat back, stunned. She knew the name AT from Marley's stories. AT was the nephil girl who'd helped Marley rescue Corbin, who'd fought monsters beside her and held off a living nightmare until she'd finally been overcome. Severin, Marley had said, had returned her to her father for healing. And Marley had been moody and concerned about it, but Marley was often moody and concerned and—

Fury swept over Branwyn and she turned a blazing glare on Severin. But he was looking at Hunter instead, smirking faintly.

Hunter complained, "Why did you call her that ridiculous nickname when you know it makes me angry?"

"Did I?" asked Severin. "I must have forgotten. Sorry."

There was that horrible, painful clash of auras again, even though the two kaiju were on opposite sides of the room now. The other men in the room shifted their weight, drawing closer to Hunter and farther from Severin. Then AT reappeared, holding a tumbler full of amber liquid. She stalked across the room, apparently heedless of the headache-inducing tension, and offered Severin the glass.

He took it, inspected it, then made a big show of sipping and savoring.

The pulsing pain vanished, and Hunter turned back to Branwyn again, as if nothing had happened. This time, he looked from her breasts to the untasted beer she held in her hand.

Branwyn responded by activating the charm Zachariah had given her to prevent tainted food and drink from affecting her, then took a swig. "Good stuff," she said. "That reminds me. I have a present for you from Tarn." She withdrew the casket from her backpack and handed it over.

Hunter took it and glanced inside for only a moment, disinterest plain on his face. "Looks like work. I'll take a look at it later." He saw her expression and laughed. "It's just a formality, missy. Like signing the papers after negotiating a contract."

Branwyn didn't waste her time trying to reconcile the contradiction. "We're in a bit of a hurry, actually."

"Well, that just means if I finish the deal, you'll run off, and I'll miss a chance to spend some time with the first green-haired girl I've ever talked to." One of the peanut gallery muttered something to a companion and there was general laughter. Hunter chuckled and added, "Returning today or tomorrow isn't going to make a difference to Tarn's plans, believe me."

This was it, Branwyn realized. She could get up and walk out without the Machine part she'd come for, and she was almost sure they'd let her go without chasing her. Almost sure. Or she could put up with this bullshit until she got what she wanted from the situation.

Her gaze was drawn to AT, back at her piano bench. Could AT just walk away?

Branwyn looked back at Hunter and bared her teeth in a smile. "I *am* tired," she said. "These midnight trips through Faerie take a lot out of a girl. But I'm pretty worried about Tarn. There was an... incident when we arrived. Your, uh, brother made a mess. And poor Tarn is already having—oh dear, maybe I shouldn't say that." The line sounded fake even to her, but it seemed important to get Hunter to accept Tarn's message before doing anything else. Tarn would know, then, that she'd delivered it. No matter what happened, Hunter couldn't claim ignorance.

Besides, anything Hunter wasn't in a hurry to do seemed like a good idea to Branwyn.

He looked at her sharply, yellow eyes running over her face before meeting her eyes. She gasped preemptively and ducked her gaze, playing up nervousness and uncertainty. But his eyes weren't like Severin's. They didn't stay with her when she looked away. Hunter wanted to own her, and would be delighted to break her in the process. But that was him, not her.

He frowned and she wondered what he saw in her eyes. Was the Queen of Stone looking back? Would that make a difference to a creature like him?

Probably not.

The frown faded from his face like it had never been there. "Well, go on, missy. Tell me what Tarn's problems are. Maybe I'll be able to help out more than I already am."

"Oh, I couldn't. I don't really understand them. But I think maybe he put something in the message bubble?"

Severin was watching her. Even without looking at him, she could feel it. She hated that she couldn't be herself and just be direct and she thought he must be enjoying her self-hatred.

But it wasn't herself she hated, she realized. She hated Hunter, hated the men who followed him. She hated the situation. But she didn't hate herself for doing what she had to do to survive and achieve her goals. She looked up again and saw Severin's flickering smile out of the corner of her eye.

He was pleased. She didn't want to know why.

Hunter considered her, then hooked the casket on the floor open with his foot. Without looking down, he picked up the message bubble. It popped.

Once again, Branwyn only saw the reaction to the bubble, not the message itself. Hunter scowled, then actually growled under his breath. When his gaze refocused on the here and now, his scowl didn't change.

"Nothing's changed. He's weak, as he's always been. Lacks the conviction to maintain his position." He reached down and picked up the diamond, then sneered. "Hardly worth the trade. With time there might be something, but now—" He shook his head. "Pfah."

Without thinking, Branwyn said, "You know Severin wants to kill him, right?" She couldn't help it. She didn't *like* the way Severin always knew what was in her heart.

Hunter looked at her like she was a small child who'd just done something precious. "Missy, my brother wants to destroy *everything*. That's just his nature. Mine too, really. Doesn't mean we can't enjoy ourselves along the way."

The other men in the room chuckled and nudged each other. Hunter's gaze swept them coldly, almost scornfully, before settling on his daughter, watching her clinically as she shifted uncomfortably. For the first time, Branwyn realized just how much of a game Hunter was playing and started to get scared all over again. She still didn't know where she fit into this new world, except as a victim. She had to find a better place.

"So can I see it? The Machine you're trading to Tarn? I'll be the one working with it, you know."

He turned that cold gaze back onto her again. "Yes, I know." Then the facade snapped back into place. "Sure thing, missy." He nodded at one of his men, who left the room. "Yeah, it's a little treasure. Got it off an angel who was trying to return it to Heaven after it escaped. She thought she could clean me up, too, but I showed her a thing or two. I heard she came back from the Sea of Dreams nuttier than a fruitcake.

I guess there's some things that outlast even death." And he laughed and his men laughed and AT hugged herself and Branwyn promised herself she'd come back again with something more dangerous in her bag than a hammer.

Hunter's man returned, holding a slab of clear acrylic with something embedded in it. At a nod from Hunter, he brought it to Branwyn and then retreated again. Frowning, Branwyn turned the slab over. The Machine fragment inside was a toothed wheel on a stem, like a flower plucked from a mechanical plant. The acrylic encasing it was smooth and seamless.

"Can you extract it?" said Hunter, leaning forward, his eyes glittering.

"Of course." Branwyn gave him a puzzled look.

"Right now? I'd just love to see a little demonstration of your skills."

Frowning, Branwyn looked down at the acrylic again. There were a half-dozen ways of getting something out of an acrylic block, but they all required tools other than what she had with her. Something about the way Hunter said it, though, made her want to take the challenge. She activated the Sight and looked at it more closely. The acrylic itself was nothing more than a faint and fuzzy line, but the toothed wheel was vibrant, making everything else fade around her. She stroked the acrylic and watched the fuzzy line quiver. Rubbing her fingers did little more; she wasn't going to cut or melt the acrylic with her bare hands any time soon.

She realized suddenly how quiet it had become and glanced up, then recoiled at what she saw. She knew there were people in the room other than Severin and Hunter, just like she knew there were objects in the room other than the Machine fragment. But they were just shadows compared to the two fallen angels. *That's what they all are*, she thought distantly. *Severin, Hunter, Tarn, Rime...*

She looked down again, less worried about appearing intimidated than actually being overwhelmed. She didn't let herself think about Severin's skeletal wings and the black vortex over his head. She didn't think about Hunter's cloak of blood and broken bones. She thought, instead, about space. She thought about how small Earth was compared to the sun, and how small the sun was compared to other stars, and how small any star was against the endless expanse of the night sky.

And yet here *she* was, dreaming of vastness. She could hold the universe inside herself. Perhaps it was a power reserved for the very small. The thought made her feel better, bracing her against the intensity of the kaiju presences.

Protected by the shell of her own ego, she slowly let out her breath and focused once again on the acrylic-encased Machine fragment. When she held still, she could feel the faintest vibration. Even within the plastic, the fragment longed to move. It had been part of something once and wanted to be part of something again, and instead it had been locked away. It trembled, as if hurt by the rejection.

It was far more *real* than the acrylic encasing it. Branwyn put both hands on the block, framing the fuzzy line between her fingers. Then she pulled her hands apart, fuzzing the line further. She'd never fuzz it enough on her own to break through the block, not with her current skills. But she wasn't on her own.

"Come on, then," she whispered. "Time to work."

The block grew warm in her hands. With a creak, the toothed wheel began to turn. At first, the motion was infinitesimally small. Branwyn bent closer, working on the Geometric line. The block's vibration became more noticeable, the creaking louder. They could do this. It was going to be easy.

Large hands came down and pulled the block away from her. Branwyn looked up, indignant. Still sheltered in her bubble of ego, she scowled at Hunter and stood up. His cloak of blood and broken bone was frightening, but he'd asked her to do some work and then he'd yanked it away from her. There was no way she was going to put up with that.

"Now, now, missy. You were about to injure yourself. No need to push things. I've seen enough. Tarn is very lucky to have you." Blood dripped from his cloak onto the wooden floor, and the face that gave her a wide smile wasn't the one he'd worn before. There was something almost lupine about it. If he'd licked his chops, Branwyn wouldn't have blinked.

He lowered his voice and added, as if reminding her of something she'd forgotten, "Best turn that off before you see something that hurts you." The cloak flared around his shoulders like crimson wings, then swept forward. Branwyn fell backward onto the couch, the psychic protection she'd conjured for herself vanishing as droplets of blood burned on her skin. "Off, I said," Hunter commanded again, his voice half an animal's growl.

Branwyn banished the Sight, half-terrified, and slid out from his shadow, trying to get to the other end of the couch so she could bolt for the door if panic took over entirely. She scrubbed frantically at her arms where the drops of blood had landed, even though there was now nothing to see. Beyond the kaiju looming over her, she saw Severin leaning back in his chair, swirling his whiskey. AT, too, was watching her, half-turned on her stool, her hazel eyes swimming with compassion.

"Hold your horses, missy," drawled Hunter, looking like he had before. "I can see you're in a hurry to get back to Tarn, but it's far too dangerous to let you go alone and my brother *did* make a mess, as you said. Best spend the night here. I'll put you on a plane back to LA tomorrow, with the package in hand."

Severin said, "And here I was, looking forward to escorting her back through the Backworld."

Hunter grinned broadly. "She's not that kind of an idiot. And even if she was, there are predators no man would let her face."

He chuckled, and under his chuckle, Branwyn heard one of his... yes, his *pack*... whisper, "More fun when they run."

"Take me to the airport and I can get my own flight tonight," Branwyn suggested. She didn't expect it to work, but she felt an almost academic curiosity about how he'd respond.

"You're far too tired for that. I could see it as you worked with the Machine. These things," he tapped the block, "can take over the unwary. But really, let's not argue about it." He flashed a huge smile. "The fact is, I wouldn't feel right if I let you go before morning. So it's not going to happen. But don't be such a worrywart. We have plenty of guest rooms and you'll be just fine as long as you don't go wandering the house alone at night." He winked. "Predators here, too."

-seventeen-

After another fifteen minutes or so, Hunter personally escorted Branwyn to a guest room. She felt she could have done
without the privilege. AT trailed behind them, and several
of Hunter's pack followed behind her. When Hunter tried to draw
Branwyn's arm through his and she refused, as she always did, one of
the pack muttered something nasty. But Hunter only smiled, as if she
was a child to be indulged.

"Here we go," he said, opening the door into a room. "There's a
private bathroom through there. Toiletries and all." He grinned. "I
host parties sometimes. Anyhow, I'll send somebody for you in the
morning. Don't leave before then or I can't be responsible for your
wellbeing."

Another door closed down the hall and Branwyn realized that AT
had vanished into the room next door with a murmured, "Goodnight."

Before she could say anything, Hunter gave an elaborate bow,
gesturing her into the room. "Sleep well, missy." He closed the door
behind her.

Branwyn put her backpack on the bed and waited for a click
that didn't come. She tried the door and the handle turned freely. Of
course he hadn't locked her in, she thought. What fun was that? There
was a lock on her side of the door, though, and Branwyn turned it.
She had every reason to distrust his assurances of her safety. While a

lock wouldn't stop a determined assault, it might at least give her a bit of warning.

That done, she turned to inspect the room. It was a combination of rustic and lacy: a heavy, rough-carved four-post bed with a delicate lace coverlet; a doily on a primitive dresser that would have done a log cabin proud. There was a rocking chair in one corner, with a large rag doll propped up in it. The bathroom, though, was thoroughly modern, with a luxurious jetted tub and a marble basin. Branwyn backed away; the bathroom felt like a baited trap.

The bedroom had no television, no clock radio, and no phone. It did have a pair of floor-length windows with frothy white curtains. Beyond the windows was a small balcony. When Branwyn slid her hand along the window frame, she found the latch and opened the French doors inward. A cool, damp breeze lifted tendrils of her hair.

She regarded the balcony warily, then stepped outside. It was made of wooden planks and smoothed split-rail timbers, and no larger than a closet. Similar balconies ran along the length of the house at this level, with a larger deck below and a single expansive balcony on the floor above. The lodge really was more like a hotel than a home, and she wondered how many of Hunter's guests left again. It wasn't a productive line of thought and she was only lured into it because she was much more tired than she'd realized. The wind freshened against her cheek, sending a shiver down her spine, and she shook herself out of the thoughts.

Back inside the room, she latched the French doors closed and sat stiffly on the bed. After stretching out legs that ached from all the climbing she'd done that day, she looked around again. Then, methodically, she worked her way through the contents of her backpack and her collection of charms. She had snacks. A wallet. A cellphone without a signal. Her hammer. An assortment of odds and ends that didn't seem useful here: paracord, matches, a bungee cord, a handful of tiny LED flashlights. A tiny stuffed frog, crayons, and a coloring book, because she was the eldest of seven and children could break out at any time. A dozen thin metal rods, some hairpins, and a pocketknife. A multitool. Duct tape, twist ties, baggies. She was *set* for being stranded in an urban environment with a lot of time on her hands. What she wasn't prepared for was the chance of fleeing supernatural predators through a dark, wet forest.

Her charms were a bit better. With Zachariah's poison ward, she wasn't worried about being drugged. She could feel the direction of the nearest weak spot in the curtain between Earth and the Backworld— back into the forest—and if she made it there, she could open it. Of course, that only meant she was in a new place, not that she was safe.

She'd sacrificed her ability to call for help in exchange for providing the Queen of Stone with BranwynTV. Somehow she didn't think the Queen of Stone would provide the same benefits. And what could she do if BranwynTV was unexpectedly cancelled? A letter-writing campaign, Branwyn felt, probably wouldn't help.

Oh well. She'd have to use her wits if Hunter turned out to be the treacherous scumbag the presence of his nasty pack suggested he was. She needed the Machine no matter what and she wasn't going to back out or back down just because her gut clenched up every time Hunter touched her or his pack opened their mouths. Her gut did not understand what was important.

A sound caught her attention, so quiet that it rang in the silence. A gasp, or maybe a sob. Branwyn went to the French door again and looked out. The balcony next door was lit by its room, and the door was half open; the sound had come from within. Branwyn frowned, went back inside, tucked some things into her pockets, then returned to her balcony. It was about seven feet from the other balcony, well beyond her ability to safely jump. But there was a thin ledge connecting the two, no more than six inches wide. The drop from the ledge to the deck below was at least fifteen feet.

She leaned out and inspected the ledge, then the slanting roof the balconies jutted out from. Then, with a single practiced blow, she drove one of the metal rods from her backpack into the roof just above head level, an arm's reach out. She squinted, activating the Sight just long enough to stroke the rod, compressing its Geometry line, rolling it between her fingers until it shone, then twisting it around the line of the roof until the two merged. When she dropped the Sight again, the rod seemed darker.

Pleased, she turned her attention to the paracord. It was basic survival equipment: a woven nylon cord with a removable core of yarn. The yarn was useful anywhere string was, but the paracord itself originated with parachutes, and was immensely handy. It was an old friend. This time, she fashioned it into a simple harness and line. Then, tying herself to the rod she'd embedded in the roof, she swung herself over the balcony rail and onto the ledge. After a moment to catch her balance and feel the ledge under her feet, she quickly paced across to the other side.

Easy. Not much worse than the balance beam in her childhood gymnastics classes. And she'd had just enough cord. It was lovely when things worked out.

She climbed onto the other balcony, then peeked in the French doors. AT sat on a black and white coverlet on a bed just as rustic as Branwyn's, her knees pulled to her chest as she stared warily outside.

Branwyn grinned at her. "Knock, knock. I was just wondering, can I borrow a cup of sugar?"

AT visibly relaxed, releasing her knees to rub her face. "How did you get here?"

"Oh, I walked. We're right next door."

"I know, but—" AT began, then stopped and shrugged. "Father said you were special."

"Hey, it's just paracord, you can buy it off the internet." She paused, then added, "May I come in?"

"All right." AT watched her as she entered the room and looked around.

It wasn't much like any teenager's room she'd seen. The basics were very similar to the room she'd been assigned, except the frills were more subdued, there was no rocking chair, and AT had a TV and game console. Except for a single frame containing nothing but black pigment, the walls were bare. The dresser had a few personal items on it and there was a shelf of books that looked like they'd never been opened. Branwyn didn't look at either too closely.

AT pointed a remote at the TV and turned it on, raising the volume. Then she beckoned Branwyn closer, scooting over on the bed to make room for them both to sit.

"We have a mutual friend," Branwyn ventured as she perched on the edge of the bed.

"Is Marley all right?" AT rested her chin on her knees, her eyelashes veiling her expression. "And the kids?"

"Oh yes. All fine." Branwyn studied the girl, then added, "From what I hear, it's only thanks to you, though. You saved all of them."

AT brightened, lifting her head. "Yeah? That's something. That's worth it." Then she sighed and dropped her head again. "I wish I could have done more."

Branwyn watched her for a moment. "Are you going to come back and visit sometime? I know Marley would be really happy to see you. Corbin, too."

AT turned her head to the TV, but her gaze was far away. "Probably not. Will you give them my love?" There was an odd strain in her voice.

"Nope," Branwyn said cheerfully. AT's head turned toward her, her big hazel eyes full of surprised hurt. "You're going to have to do it yourself." She winked and said, "I make it a policy to not enable people wimping out."

"I'm not wimping out," AT protested, then added sullenly, "You don't understand."

Branwyn raised her eyebrows in a silent invitation for explanation, and after a moment, AT said, "I got away once. It's not going to happen again."

"Have you tried?"

"He let me go the first time," AT said bitterly. "He won't do it again. Not when I screwed everything up so badly."

When Marley had related the full story of her fight to save the twins from heavenly injustice, she'd mentioned that AT, when faced with the living nightmare spawned by the children's fear and unearthly power, had fought it to a near standstill, then called on her father's power for assistance. Severin had appeared in her father's stead, finished the fight, then carried the badly wounded AT off to her father.

"Why does he care so much?" Branwyn finally asked. "I thought they didn't like their children."

"I wasn't some accident. Some one-night stand. He wanted me. He *bred* me." AT's voice was flat. "To be his chief monster."

Branwyn regarded her. "Please, take it personally when I say that it seems like he failed there. You seem like a pretty decent kid."

AT's face froze and she buried it against her knees so that her words were muffled. "My father seems like a nice man, too."

"Only to anybody who doesn't listen to their gut. I've met a double handful of supernatural types by now, and, AT, nobody scares me quite like your dad." Branwyn hated admitting to fear, but there were times and places where it could be productive. "I can't see how a girl who sacrifices herself to save people she barely knows is going to end up as a monster."

AT sighed again and lifted her face. "I hope you're right. But sometimes it feels like there's nothing else I can do. If I let myself be what he wants me to be..." She trailed off. When she spoke again, there was a liquid throb underlying her whisper. "It's just so tempting."

A prickle of alarm ran down Branwyn's spine and her words tumbled out. "Sure it is, here. Surrounded by all these assholes, stuck in this godawful forest. And I'm guessing you don't train a baby monster with cupcakes and athletic meets." AT shook her head weakly, and Branwyn added, "Hell, do you even go to school?"

"N-Not since—not for a couple of years."

Branwyn scowled. "That's bullshit. Anyhow, how 'tempting' was it when you were in LA?"

"Not very," AT admitted. "As long as I didn't—" She shook her head. "It doesn't matter, though. All I know how to do is fight, so that's what I end up doing and that's what he *wants*. I wanted to throw myself at the twins' nightmare, just lose myself in rending it. The only reason I held on was because I knew that after it killed me, it would go back for everybody else. And I couldn't beat it on my own. Father says that with him as my master, I'll be unstoppable, but if I insist on acting like a lost little girl, I'll be alone *and* incompetent, just like I was then."

Branwyn stared at AT in consternation. This wasn't something that could be unraveled with a light chat after introductions. The kid needed therapy, or at the very least not to be under the roof of a supernatural creature who regarded her as property, as a material to shape as he chose.

AT apparently misinterpreted Branwyn's expression, because she forced a cheerful expression on her face. "It doesn't matter. I'll be fine. All kids have problems with their parents, right? So why are you here after one of his treasures?"

Branwyn let her change the subject, even though she wasn't done with it. She needed a few minutes to let the situation simmer in the back of her head before she made a decision. "My friend Penny is very ill. Tarn will heal her if I help him out."

Real pleasure chased away the artificial cheerfulness on AT's face. "Penny survived too? I hadn't realized that. That's wonderful!"

"'Survived' is the only way to put it," Branwyn said darkly. "That bastard burned through most of her soul, and she won't wake up."

AT frowned. "What can a faerie do about that?"

"Oh, he says he's got some way of adopting humans and lending them his essence. Basically, he'd make her a changeling." Branwyn shrugged. "It seems a lot better than letting her die. What's a soul, anyhow, eh? Especially a badly damaged one?"

A look of horror transformed AT's face. "A soul is *everything*." Hastily, she took control of her expression and sat up straight, dropping her knees for the first time in the conversation. "I mean... that's what it seems like to me. Nephilim don't have them, you see."

"And look at you," Branwyn pointed out. "You're just fine. Debating ethics and morality and everything."

AT shook her head. "That's not what souls are about." She bit her lip, eyeing Branwyn as if wondering if she was capable of understanding. "Souls are immortal."

Impatiently, Branwyn said, "Yes, that's what practically all religion says. And you nephilim are immortal in your own way. Frankly, I'd rather be alive than dead."

Shrinking back, AT said, "But nothing can hurt a soul unless the owner consents. *Nothing*. When I die, that's it. I'm gone."

Branwyn's lips tightened. "When my stepfather died, he was gone, too. Frankly, I'm not convinced souls really exist. If Corbin hadn't given me magic spells, I'd think you all were crazy."

AT caught at Branwyn's hand. "Sometimes souls do go away, but it's not—not the same as oblivion. Not for them. And I'm not crazy. My mother died and my father... Souls can be caught, you see. Claimed. If they consent while alive. And they continue to exist; they can feel and remember and even communicate."

Branwyn took a deep breath, trying to calm the blood pounding in her head. "So... if a soul doesn't, uh, consent to being destroyed in exchange for physical immortality, or being caught, what happens to it?"

Still holding Branwyn's hand, AT glanced up at the ceiling. "Somebody told me there's a tear in the sky they vanish through."

Dryly, Branwyn said, "Wow, that sounds dramatic. What's on the other side?"

AT finally released Branwyn's hand and shrugged. "Nobody's ever come back and the celestials can't get through. There's a lot of theories, but souls are key. They're that important, Branwyn," the girl finished earnestly.

Branwyn stared at AT for a long moment before abruptly relaxing as a manic cheer chased off her tension. "Well, Penny's soul has been mostly destroyed. Where does that leave her?"

"I think any soul is better than none. But I've never had one to give up. Was your friend particularly spiritual?"

"Not until she met an angel." She patted AT's shoulder. "Thanks for letting me know. I'll definitely keep it in mind. Meanwhile, do you have anything in this charming chamber that you'd like to take away with you?"

AT blinked, as so many people blinked at Branwyn's sudden topic shifts. "What?"

As gently as she could, Branwyn said, "Do you *want* to stay here?"

Her breath catching, AT said, "I wish I could—I don't want to be here, no. But after what happened, I don't think anybody's going to help me get away again." She searched Branwyn's face anxiously.

"Wrong!" said Branwyn brightly. "I have an escape plan for you. It may be a little tricky, but if everything goes well, this time tomorrow you'll be in California again. What's wrong?"

Halfway through Branwyn's explanation, AT's gaze darted to the door, and she touched Branwyn's foot. Then Branwyn heard the thudding footsteps outside, too. They stopped nearby.

Branwyn held her breath. For a long moment, silence gobbled up her thoughts. Then the same aura that had been painful in the lodge living room flared again. This time it radiated an obscene smugness that made Branwyn feel like she'd been dropped in filth.

A heartbeat later, somebody—something—howled. It sounded for all the world like a wolf, and AT raised her head, her eyes widening and her throat moving silently.

After the howl faded, Hunter caroled, "She's gone and run off, boys. Out the window, it looks like. Time for the hunt!"

Her heart in her throat, Branwyn met AT's eyes. Before she had time to do anything else, AT's door was flung open.

"Well, I'll be a monkey's uncle!" exclaimed Hunter in exaggerated surprise. "Here you are, missy." He shook his head. "Tsk, tsk."

Branwyn stood up slowly, her stomach roiling with fear she barely understood. "Here I am. I didn't run off, as you see."

He grinned. "You still left your room. That's the big no-no. And if you won't obey the rules, why should I?" He tilted his head to one side and there was a burst of static from the television. "Conspiring to steal my most precious possession, too. You just don't know how to stay out of trouble, do you?" He lunged and had Branwyn by the arm before she could get out of the way. "That's all right. I know *just* how to keep you under control."

"Get your hands off me," Branwyn snapped, and kicked him as she thrust her free hand at his throat and activated the charm to grow her claws.

It should have worked to get her free, at least for a moment.

Instead, something snapped and Branwyn screamed as a red haze of pain swept over her. Somehow, with one hand and barely any leverage, he'd broken her arm. He shook her by that arm and the red pain became white flashes against blackness. Distantly, through a miasma of agony and nausea, she felt his mouth press up against her ear. He licked her, then whispered, "I knew you'd end up here."

"Father!" cried AT, standing up. "Oh God, Branwyn, why—" Branwyn forced herself to open her eyes. She was on her knees beside Hunter, still held by her broken arm.

Hunter glanced at her. "One way or another, you'll serve me, my daughter. If not as part of my pack, then as bait for the prey." His smile was wolfish.

Horror chased shock off of AT's face. Then something else chased the horror away. She stared at her father, lowering her head but not her eyes, which brightened with yellow highlights.

"Oh, don't get my hopes up," growled her father. "It's damned *depressing* each time you let your weakness win." He hauled Branwyn up to her feet and she did her best not to scream again. But something must have escaped, because AT flinched and the light fled her eyes. "You're right, by the way. Nobody is going to help you escape again. And anybody who tries is going to end up..." He looked down at Branwyn, "Well, not like her. I have something special for her. But the dogs need feeding, eh?"

"Tarn," croaked Branwyn.

"What about him? You think he'll miss you? But he understands these games. I'll make sure he gets his Machine and, well... you wanted to steal my daughter. It's only fair I get you." He turned to the door where his pack crowded, scooping up Branwyn and dropping her over his broad shoulder with a slap on her butt. "Easy as pie, boys. Two counts of being exactly the dumb bitch I expected her to be."

AT whispered, "I'm so sorry. So sorry." Branwyn tried to struggle, to show AT she wasn't beaten. She tried to mouth something reassuring. But her limbs wouldn't obey her. She felt as weak as a kitten, the pain using up all her available energy. All she had left was hate, and hate alone didn't mean a thing.

-eighteen-

Hunter carried her to a room in the basement and dumped her on a futon on the floor. While fireworks of pain lit up the red-black darkness behind Branwyn's eyes, he moved back to the door and waited until her whimpering faded. "Now, I've got to go exercise the boys. You got them all riled up. I'll be back for breakfast in the morning. If you're a good girl, I'll send somebody down here to splint your arm." He flashed that horrible, hateful grin. "If you're bad, I'll splint your arm and break your leg."

The door closed while Branwyn was still struggling to work up enough saliva to spit with. Alone, she turned her face to the futon, letting the pain wash over her and carry her away from hatred and fear into true darkness

She woke smelling the unfamiliar scent of perfume that lingered on the futon. It seemed like only a few moments since she'd let go of consciousness. Perhaps it was; she heard feet moving above her, possibly Hunter going to "exercise the boys." She had a watch, she remembered. If only she'd thought to check her watch when she was assaulted, or at any time since she'd arrived in this monster's den. She giggled, then sighed. *If only.*

The footsteps above went away. Carefully, she sat up. The room she'd been placed in—well, let's be honest, the *cell* she'd been placed in—was stripped bare. It had nothing but the futon, which was blue and stained in places, tossed haphazardly on a grubby white tile floor. The light above was an old-fashioned fluorescent tube. The door was made of heavy wood. It didn't have a handle.

There were some marks on the floor that suggested that a table and a chair had once been bolted to the floor. Branwyn wondered if they'd been removed for her sake, or because of some other prisoner's peccadilloes.

Her arm didn't hurt as much as it had. As long as she didn't move it, it was a dull, distant ache. But when she did move it, even just by bending her elbow to try to see her watch, the pain exploded. So she fumbled with her watch strap, unbuckling it awkwardly and painfully, then checked the time. She thought she still had a few hours before dawn. Nobody ate breakfast before dawn, did they? She had time to come up with something.

She *had* to come up with something. If Hunter had taken his pack out of the house—and the silence above suggested it—she would never have a better time to escape.

Dropping the watch onto the futon, she emptied her pockets of coins and keys and a pebble and a penknife. She still had her hammer dangling from a belt loop, which she told herself was lucky and not a trap. She added them all to a pile, staring at it. Then she inspected the futon for buttons and a zipper. Surely she could make something from all of this stuff. She was learning magic. She'd influenced the acrylic casing of the Machine even if she hadn't actually broken it. She'd coaxed the roof and the metal rod into clinging together. This would be a learning experience.

She realized her teeth were chattering and she was freezing, which was ridiculous. It wasn't cold. She didn't think she had a fever, and the bone fracture hadn't broken the skin—there was no way she could have acquired an infection so soon. She activated Zachariah's poison ward charm again, just the same. Infection was a kind of poison, wasn't it? She didn't have time for being hurt or sick; she had work to do. She could probably make a splint herself by tearing up the futon and—but that was stupid. By the time she finished it, Hunter would be back, and *he* would splint it. No, she had to be out of here, preferably in an ER with a police officer writing a report, before he showed up again.

The chills faded and she felt warm.

She woke up again, her face pressed against the tile floor, her knees on the futon. She stumbled to her feet, her arm screaming at the jarring movement. Her little pile of pocket junk was untouched. She'd lost half an hour this time.

She moved slowly to the door. She didn't use wood nearly as much as metal, but she had a penknife and if she could access the lock mechanism for the door—

Severin's unwelcome voice said, "What are you going to do when he breaks your leg? Crawling doesn't seem like your style."

Branwyn said without looking over her shoulder, "Have you come to splint my arm?"

"Now, why would I do that?"

She did look at Severin sharply then. He leaned against the wall in the corner of the room near the futon, like he'd just stepped out for a cigarette. "Hunter said—never mind. Obviously not."

"I'm no one's errand boy, cupcake."

"Could have fooled me," Branwyn muttered, and tried to concentrate on the door. He'd just come to torment her. She could ignore him just like she could ignore her arm.

But he straightened up, mouth thinning, and took a step closer. There was still the width of the medium-sized room between them, but her stomach clenched all the same.

"You're in a bad situation, cupcake." His voice was soft, insidious. "You thought you could go toe to toe with the big boys, you thought you could matter." His words seemed to resonate off the walls, surrounding her. "And you know what? You're right! He'll break your legs and your spirit, but he'll fix your arm so you can work and you'll matter *so much* to him. And that'll make you matter to others. They'll want to kill you if they can't steal you. A ragdoll, torn apart between rivals."

A gurgle of bitter laughter escaped Branwyn. "That won't happen. Shut up and go away."

"You want me to go? Find him? Send him here right now to see what a naughty girl you're being? All right." But he didn't vanish immediately, as she knew he could.

"Of course not," Branwyn said. "Stay here then." She caught his smile out of the corner of her eye and wished she hadn't.

He moved closer. "Just think, you wouldn't be down here if you hadn't fallen for his bait."

Branwyn whirled around. "Oh, come on. He was never going to voluntarily let me leave."

He laughed. "Oh, but he would have. He's a sportsman. And taking you this way involved his daughter. That was important, too." Conversationally, he added, "He used to beat her, until he realized she'd never fight back."

Branwyn clenched her fists and immediately regretted it as pain flared up her broken arm. "Have you *ever* cared about anything? Or were you born this monstrous?"

"You think this is monstrous? How precious," he drawled.

"I think dragging an abused girl back to her abuser is unforgivable." She turned back to the door, blinking to hold back unexpected tears. She stared at its wooden surface, trying to remember what she was doing.

Right, she was escaping. Escaping and–

"Leaving her behind," said Severin softly, too close to her. "Leaving behind the Machine, too."

She pressed her head against the door. "No. I'll get them. I will."

"You won't. You'll fail in every way." She could feel his breath in her hair.

Branwyn gritted her teeth and tried to focus on the door, but her vision was too blurry. Since he wouldn't go away, she had to ignore him. But he was making everything worse.

"I could help you," he whispered. "Save you."

Horror and shame surged through her and she half turned around. "No!"

A feral smile flitted across his face. "But here you are, a helpless princess in a tower."

"No!" she said again, raising her voice. She caught herself, forced herself to speak to him calmly. "It's a basement. I don't want your help."

Severin gave her an amused, disbelieving look. "Your actions say otherwise." His foot moved, pushing aside the penknife Branwyn had dropped at some point.

Branwyn ran her hand through her hair. "Look, if you're having some kind of charitable impulse, get AT out. I can take care of myself."

A finger and a thumb wrapped lightly around the wrist of her injured arm. "Liar."

"That's nothing—" she said, before pain crashed over her at his lightest tug. "It'll heal," she gasped, and made the mistake of meeting his dark eyes. The pain became a tide of self-loathing. She was an idiot. She was a stereotype. She was nothing but a dreamer—

—but then the tide crashed and parted against her glittering core. She would make her dreams real. She always had. She was Branwyn, and that was that.

She used the tools she had. But she couldn't accept Severin's help. She wouldn't be his pawn.

She caught her breath and blinked away the blur. Her back was pressed against the door. "If you rescued AT, that would be enough. A distraction. I can get through this door—"

"I'm not going to steal AT away from Hunter," said Severin calmly. "I'm going to steal you." The fingers around her wrist moved up her arm, a warm light touch against the red throb.

"No," she repeated, frustrated. He watched her like a cat watching a bird. "I don't want that. Just listen—"

"But it isn't about what you want, cupcake. It's not up to you." He dipped his dark head, his mouth brushing her ear. "It's up to me. I can save you, or not. My choice."

He rested his head against hers. "You've never understood that I can do whatever I want to you." His voice was a barely audible murmur that ran down her spine. "And if I bothered to make the effort, I could make you *love it*."

A dark feeling she dared not identify roiled through Branwyn, mixing with bitter loathing and a boneless, rubbery fear into a poisonous black cocktail. She tried to speak and her voice came out as a whimper. She tried again. "That wouldn't be fun for you." Her voice was small and weak and the shame added its own cherry to the black cocktail.

He pulled his head back and regarded her with a wry amusement. "Oh, the idea has a certain charm." *Making you scream*, she felt rather than heard him add. Then he tilted his head. "But I can exert myself to resist even the sweetest temptations when I want to. You wouldn't last long, and I have plans for you yet."

Her breath came quick and shallow. "I—I can't go without the Machine. I'd rather you broke me, killed me now." She struggled to resist the terrible intoxication of the black cocktail; it led only to oblivion.

Very gently, he lifted her injured arm, inspecting it. "Oh, of course," he said absently. "How else will I get my hands on Tarn? But first we have to deal with this." Coolness and heat spiraled up her arm in turn, followed by a tingling that became the jolt of a thousand needles. It hurt in a whole new way, like shards of crystal were growing inside her arm. She made an animalistic moan and tried to squirm away.

"Shh," Severin said and dropped his mouth onto her skin between her collarbone and shoulder. At first she thought he was going to bite her, but if he did, she couldn't tell. A cool numbness spread out from his lips, flowing down her arm and taking away the needling pain. It faded as it reached her elbow, and by the time tendrils of coolness reached her wrist, she could move the fingers of that hand without wanting to sob. She hardly even felt like wincing.

Blearily, she craned her head to look at her arm. It looked almost normal: a bit swollen but already visibly better. She tried to figure out if she should be doing something in response. But the pain had only masked exhaustion and Severin's head close to her own was disorienting. She could no longer remember if she needed to pull away or cling to him.

It was important, she recalled, that she make sure he knew she wasn't enjoying this. She was still herself.

"Asshole," she said weakly. "I'm going to remember this." And the black cocktail was an ocean she teetered over.

He pulled back and regarded her. Drunkenly, she met his eyes, but they were different now. Shadow-grey and fathomless. They'd never had a color before, other than "evil."

"Yes," he said, almost gently. "You will." And the soul-devouring darkness flared in his eyes again before she lowered her gaze. "We'll go now." He closed his fingers around her wrists and tugged her sharply toward him.

She fell against his chest and the world changed around her

like a window sliding past. Her few things, abandoned on the futon, hovered in the air. They were in front of a display case. One of Severin's hands moved and glass cracked and splintered. The shards joined her belongings in a glittering spiral dance around them as an alarm screamed.

Severin caught something up in his free hand and yanked Branwyn again somehow, despite the fact that she was already pressed against him. The picture window of the world changed again. Images of several places spun around them, beyond the backpack she'd left in the bedroom and the hammer and coins and a nebula of broken glass. For a moment they floated freely at the center of a maelstrom of *place* and *thing*. Then one of the windows darted in and dropped on them.

Severin let her go and she fell into a heap amidst her belongings. The shattered glass darted to his hand and hovered there, gathering itself into a sphere.

She was on her own worn, familiar carpet. They weren't alone. Marley and Simon were both there, and they looked startled.

"Am I ruining something?" inquired Severin, solicitously. "Something heroic? Oh dear. Well, I must be off. Can't play with *you*," he said to Simon. "There's bigger hunters to tease." As he spoke, the sphere of shards above his hand acquired a red gleam. Orange light beamed out of it as it fused into... something else.

With a lazy smile, Severin vanished.

"Branwyn!" Marley dropped to her knees beside her and started checking her over. Through gritted teeth, she said, "I am going to *end* him."

Branwyn thought she ought to explain, but instead she felt the carpet on her cheek and inhaled the familiar smell of her home. Some part of her had been sure she'd never be here again.

Corbin's voice emerged from Marley's phone, sitting on the counter. "What just happened?"

Slowly, Simon said, "Whispering Dark just appeared, deposited the girl, and left. You know, Corbin, I'm starting to see why you dislike the fellow so."

"He brought back *Branwyn?* Marley, is she all right?"

Branwyn ignored Marley trying to coax her into accepting her shield, but let her best friend hold her close. She ought, she thought hazily, to show them she was fine. "Hey," she managed. "You called Corbin just like I said. Way to go!"

But she was very tired. And there was something else she had to do. She looked around the floor, trying to catalogue the fallen items.

"She doesn't seem injured, but there's this mark—Branwyn!" Marley fell back as Branwyn lunged away from her, scooping up the acrylic-bound Machine part. He'd brought it. She had it. It had cost her more than she had hoped, but she had it.

She curled protectively around her prize and, laying her head in Marley's lap, relaxed the tiny amount required to pass out.

-nineteen-

Branwyn woke up in her own bed, sunlight falling in slices across her face through half-closed blinds. Her mouth was dry and she had to pee, which was always an awkward combination. Her throat hurt and her eyes felt gritty, too. Other than that, she felt only the ache of a long hike in her legs. Her broken arm might have just been a nightmare. But the acrylic-bound Machine was on the nightstand.

Marley sat in the corner, in Branwyn's comfy chair, her legs curled under her, a book on her lap. Instead of reading, she was regarding Branwyn. Marley's gaze was shuttered in a way Branwyn had only seen when she was acting with great restraint. For a moment, they looked at each other. Then Marley offered Branwyn a folded bath towel in silence.

Branwyn rolled out of bed and took the towel. "Thanks." She hesitated, then added, "Don't go anywhere, okay?"

Marley's closed-off expression became one of a deep, sad, *disturbing* sympathy. "I'll be here."

Branwyn hurried to the bathroom and took a long shower, scrubbing herself down, then letting the heat seep into the places that had been chilled by her encounters the day before. She felt almost normal as she stepped out of the shower. She was angry about the past but excited about the future and ready to get to work on finishing the key. Art had always given her something to move toward in the wake of any relationship yuck or deeper shock. It was almost like... magic.

But she defogged the mirror and peered at herself, wondering what had inspired Marley's expression. She wasn't exactly sure what Marley's nephil magic told her, but she thought it was about what might happen, not what had happened. And even if she somehow knew what Branwyn had gone through, it wasn't *that* bad.

She shied away from that line of thinking and looked at the bags under her eyes. More sleep was definitely called for. She'd get it, eventually. Her gaze slid down to her arm, and all the psychological good of the shower was undone as her blood froze in her veins. Right between her left collarbone and shoulder was a black mark shaped like a stylized pair of skeletal black wings.

I'm going to remember this, she'd said, but she'd been willing to remember in a distant, fuzzy way.

He wanted the memory of his assistance to linger.

Branwyn dropped her towel and went back into the shower. Rationally, she knew it wouldn't scrub off, but she just couldn't help trying. Instead, it felt like the black mark was spreading all over her. She recalled Marley's sympathetic expression again and bit her lip so hard it bled. Eventually, the hot water ran out. When she emerged this time, she toweled off without looking in the mirror, then padded out of her room and went to the acrylic-bound Machine part beside her bed.

She picked it up, then looked around as if she had the tools to liberate it in her bedroom.

Marley, still in the chair, said, "You wouldn't let it go when you passed out. Not until you started having dreams."

"I don't remember any dreams." Branwyn put the Machine down and went to her dresser.

"*Good,*" Marley said fervently.

Branwyn gave her a sharp look, then remembered the poisonous black cocktail of emotions she'd felt as Severin held her, along with some other dreams she'd had lately. She looked away. "I was tired. The brain does funny things when you're that tired. Don't worry about it." She stepped into some denim shorts and added, "Dreams like that don't mean anything unless you let them."

"Tarn sent me dreams when he wanted to manipulate me," Marley pointed out gently.

Branwyn laughed without any humor. "Nobody is sending me these dreams except my own subconscious."

"How do you *know*?"

Branwyn concentrated on her zipper. She really didn't want to talk about this. Talking about it felt like giving the dreams power, making the attraction real. But Marley sounded more troubled than she had since Branwyn had first walked into Underlight. "Fine. Three reasons. First, this isn't the first time I've had embarrassing dreams about somebody I didn't even like. My sleeping mind is stupid, what can I say? Second, when he wants to manipulate me, he just shows up and pokes me with a sharp stick. He's not exactly subtle. And third, Corbin said that having my charm slots filled would specifically prevent things like how Tarn got into your dreams. It was just a dream. Okay? Are we done?"

Marley was silent for a moment and Branwyn looked for a clean shirt in the interim. Finally, she said, "What *happened*, Branwyn?"

Once her head emerged from the paint-splattered t-shirt, Branwyn said, "The guy I went to see is AT's dad. She was there. He's an asshole. I tried to get her out. It went poorly."

Marley looked startled. "AT? I thought... no," she shook her head. "I hoped. I was stupid." Her expression changed as she processed what Branwyn hadn't bothered to spell out. She looked grim and dark-eyed in a way Branwyn had only seen once before, when she'd used her nephil power to push *pain* into Tarn. "So how *does* Severin figure in?"

Branwyn shrugged, quick and tight. "He wants me to help in some game he's playing with Tarn. I couldn't do that locked up in Hunter's basement."

Marley's eyes went to the black mark now mostly covered by Branwyn's shirt. "You owe him now?"

Branwyn snorted. "I owe him, but maybe not in the way he's hoping. I didn't exactly agree to a bargain." And then, because she didn't want to continue that line of conversation, she said, "Did I dream that you were having some kind of meeting with Corbin and Simon when I got home?"

Marley gave Branwyn a look that said *I know what you're doing,* but said, "We were talking about you. I knew something bad had happened to you and Corbin said you'd lost the beacon charm he gave you."

"Oh, that was days ago. I exchanged it for a different kind of beacon."

"Not a very useful one," Marley said sharply.

"Well, no. But it did get me a step closer to saving Penny." Branwyn furrowed her brow, trying to remember the thought she'd had on that topic. It had come in the midst of basement rooms and tormenting kaiju, but in the wake of AT's warnings, there'd been something… "Speaking of Penny, I have work to do." Something in the air changed and Branwyn glanced at Marley. "Thank you, by the way. I'm sorry I worried you."

"We would have come for you," said Marley fiercely. "He wouldn't have kept you."

Branwyn summoned up cheer she didn't feel. "I know." Cradling the Machine part again, she left the room and tried to leave introspection behind as well.

Sexy bastard!
Views: 67,019
Thought this guy was hot but damn!

A man with spiky red and black hair, dressed in a blue t-shirt that clings to his muscular torso, walks down a street. He passes by a sidewalk cafe and pauses. The camera zooms in and focuses. The man is looking at a woman and a small child eating dessert. He smiles at them, and reaches out to tousle the child's hair. Both of the diners stare at him in surprise. He reaches out and takes the spoon out of the child's hand and licks it. The camera shakes a little. Then the man reaches out and takes the plate and the mother's fork and starts walking down the street again while eating the dessert. The mother and child stare after him in silence.

It was late in the morning, the autumn sunlight bright and unfriendly. Once upon a time, Branwyn would have been at work at the garage by now. She wondered if she still had a job. Every day, almost without fail, it was the smell of metal and paint and coffee and counter cleaner, the yawns and yells of the mechanics that had anchored her days. It wasn't her dream job. It was just earning a living doing something that she liked. What she was doing now was more important. It was a pity there wasn't a paycheck in it, though.

But Marley was making enough for both of them now, and Branwyn had paid the bills for months while Marley was unemployed. This was fair. This was working on the future.

She turned the stereo up loud enough to rattle the windows and drove first to her studio, where she stayed just long enough to break the acrylic casing. Then, with the Machine in a bag so it wouldn't distract her, she went to the house.

Thankfully, since it was a weekday morning, the house was utterly empty. Branwyn spared a moment for a childish burst of gratitude that her grandmother, the ultimate authority in the family, was away on a sabbatical. If she was home, not only would she be there, she'd have *questions* for Branwyn that would revert her back to a little girl trying to squirm her way out of trouble again. Holly was her mother, but Tara was her mother's mother, and even when her great-grandmother had been alive, Tara had ruled like a queen. When she got back, there was going to be trouble. Branwyn imagined it and realized she was imagining being a little girl again, hoping for her grandmother to fix everything—

She burst into Tarn's court as if she could leave her thoughts behind that way. The hall was dark after the brightness of the morning, and she stood still where she arrived, squeezing her eyes shut, unwilling to advance until she could see what she had gotten into. Tarn's entry hall wasn't always the same.

Before her vision had adjusted to the dim light, hands closed on her arms. "Branwyn!"

She instinctively flinched away, even though her arm no longer hurt, and Tarn's grip loosened, sliding up her arms to rest on her shoulders, then cup her face. "Branwyn. You're safe. The souls of my servants returned to me—" Abruptly he let go of her, giving her space.

"Aw, you worried?" Branwyn flashed a grin. "I was fine."

"I was... concerned." His voice had cooled. Branwyn's vision cleared up enough that she could finally make him out. He looked... tousled. His hair was wilder than usual, and his clothing lacked the usual careful crispness. "And you recovered the Machine."

Branwyn tilted her head, wondering at the shift in his manner. Then she remembered the mark beside her collarbone. Obviously he recognized it.

She rejected out of hand *explaining* it. She hadn't wanted it there. She hadn't asked for help. And she wasn't going to let Severin use his unwanted act of kindness as leverage over her. It was a non-issue, as far as she was concerned, except as a cosmetic concern. And if Tarn couldn't figure that out, that was his problem.

"Yep. I'm ready to get to work, too. I've got a good feeling this time. This little bit of Heavenly trash is eager to do some good."

Tarn sighed. "Of course." But he didn't move out of her way.

She gave him an amused look. "No backing down, bub. I open the door, you step right out and save Penny. Right?"

"And then? After that?" he asked.

"What, are you worried? I thought you wanted this."

He eyed her. "You don't care what happens after you get what you want?"

"Should I?" She put on her most cheerful voice. "You don't have any... dubious plans, do you, Tarn?"

"No," he said flatly. "But I am not the only one who will be affected. Perhaps you have noticed: I have many, many cousins."

"Oh, I've noticed." She thought first of the Queen of Stone and then the Lady Rime, and all the videos she'd seen lately of strange people and happenings. "Some of them get out more than you, too."

Tarn spread his hands. "I've observed," he said simply, but there was a greyness in his voice that frightened Branwyn.

That spike of fear drained the last traces of cheer from Branwyn. "Don't do this. Don't tell me you've changed your mind. You want this. Underlight needs this. You said you were committed. You're just worried about Severin picking on you while you're distracted. Don't be."

"Branwyn—"

"Tell me!" she commanded. "Say it!"

"I want this," he said in a low voice, and the yearning under the words seemed to make the room tremble.

Her own voice shaky, she said, "Don't worry about other people's choices. I've seen enough of you to realize that you're all individuals. And what has been done to you is terrible." As quickly as it left, her manic cheer returned. It wasn't as if she didn't have options. "Besides, this isn't the only lock. I was there when the first one broke, you know. There's three. You admitted that yourself."

Tarn looked away, a complex expression shifting across his face. As the silence dragged out, Branwyn wondered if she wasn't supposed to talk about the door, or parrot his own words back to him. Perhaps she'd broken some kind of unspoken rule.

Oh well.

"Now. I'm going to get to work, if you don't mind." She made as if to move past him.

Still looking away, he waved a hand absently. "Carry on. The Machine key is in your studio."

"Practice your soul-charming or whatever. Pack for the beach," she said encouragingly, then frowned, reminded again of AT's opinions on the changeling procedure. "See you later."

The detour to her studio to get the key took no time at all. Once in front of the great door, she took the unfinished key from its suede bag and ran her fingers over it. The sense of the Machine sank into her again. It seemed to fill her up, this partial *thing*. It had tendrils into her, oh yes. She wondered if it was possible to work a bit of Heaven without being changed in turn.

Carefully, she put it aside and picked up the toothed wheel Machine fragment that Hunter had claimed. The emotional signature traveled up her fingers and into her spine. It was eager, as she'd noticed before. It yearned to be of use. It had a crisp attentiveness compared to the rod's ancient harshness that made Branwyn wonder if they were

from different ages. Or maybe just different full Machines. Nobody
seemed to know very much about those, after all.

She spent some time with the two emotional signatures,
analyzing the hooks of light stretching from the Machines to herself
and thinking about how to align them. They'd become a new single
thing. An alloy, she hoped. Something strong enough. But working
with these Machines wasn't like blending copper and tin. They had
personalities instead of just qualities. And merging personalities
seemed like it would require a skill she wasn't sure she had. She
wished she had something she could practice on, but all she had was
the models she'd constructed in her head.

After some consideration, she couldn't see how it could work.
They didn't fit together the way she thought they had to. They needed
to mesh, and instead they just clanked. She might be able to jury-rig
something, but she didn't think she could build something that lasted.

She had to try. She picked up the Machines, one in each hand.

They weren't the same. They'd *changed.* Not substantially, but the
sharp, clearly defined personalities she'd sensed before had softened.
They were softening further, as she held them in her hands. Her
breath came fast, wondering. The spirit tendrils they'd reached inside
her chest throbbed. She didn't feel as if they were *taking* anything
from her, but at the same time, she was *giving* them something. The
difference was slight but significant.

You are the forge. The knowledge traveled through the tendrils, and
Branwyn felt dizzy and tired.

"Of course," she muttered. She brought the two Machines
together. As they touched, their substance softened just like their
personalities had.

She fell into the fugue of twisting and shaping the metals. Even
through the haze of creative effort, something nagged at her. The
pieces were mobile, willing to serve. But—

But—

Her face hurt from her scowl. A sound impinged on her
consciousness and she looked up. Tarn stood in the corner, watching
her. His expression was reserved, but he was not calm; he shifted his
weight and he didn't seem to know what to do with his hands. When
she caught his eye, he started forward. "Did it work?"

Branwyn goggled at him, wondering how he could think that. Then she followed his gaze, looking at what she held in her hand. The toothed wheel had locked itself at one end of the rod. They'd merged into a single piece, singing with one voice a song of structure and excitement. The key itself shimmered like it was coated with wet satin paint and a soft blue glow radiated from it. It was beautiful.

It was also a failure.

Carefully, she rose to her feet, clenching her fingers over the flawed Machine.

"It *did* work," breathed Tarn.

"No. No, it didn't. Why would you think that?"

He frowned at her. "You merged them."

She offered it to him. "Try it, then." When he hesitated, she wanted to throw it at him. Instead, she turned away and walked stiffly over to the great door. She put the key into the hole, smooth end first. It was the only way it would fit; the toothed wheel was too large. It made an excellent grip. But while the grip would magnify the power of the turner enormously, the key itself still couldn't get leverage on the hidden tumblers of the mystical lock.

In the same stiff, controlled way, she withdrew the key. "Doesn't work. *Doesn't work.*" She thought of Severin's mark on her, and wondered if the Queen of Stone was laughing as she looked on this failure of effort. This waste of energy. Oh, the Queen had gotten her money's worth. But Branwyn hadn't.

"Take it," she said again to Tarn. "Take it and go away. Find yourself a locksmith or something." She knelt down and put the key on the floor in front of her. "Leave me alone."

Tarn's breath came rapidly. "What does it need?"

"What does it need? It needs *more*. More than one life. More than I have." She thought again of Penny.

Tarn knelt across from her, the key between them. He took her by the shoulders and shook her gently. "What does it need?"

The words hurt like salt in a wound. "It needs another Machine fragment."

He just nodded. Of course he just nodded. He'd known. How could he not? He'd had centuries to understand the lock. Maybe it couldn't be opened. Maybe this was nothing more than entertainment.

She knuckled her eyes and jerked away from him. He stood up again. "I'd hoped..." and the world shuddered around them. Only the great door seemed unmoving. Tarn ducked his head, muttered something about threes.. Then he raised his head again. "Will you stop now?"

Branwyn glared up at him. "Is it possible to make a complete key?"

He stared at her for a long moment, and she held his gaze until finally he said, "Yes. It is possible."

"You're sure?"

"There was a time when I wasn't. But now... it is vulnerable. If it wasn't, you wouldn't be permitted to access it, to study it as you have. It demands the third part, though. Threes are powerful, especially here."

She pressed her hands against her head. She wanted to scream. She'd come so far. If she backed down now, she'd lose everything. "I can't stop. Even if it takes seven. I hear seven is powerful in fairy tales, too."

He said, "Acquiring another fragment may be... challenging."

"Challenging? Because everything else has been a walk in the park. Please go away. Go find another one, go dance, go take a damned bath. Just leave me alone." She didn't look up at him. She looked at the key, shimmering quietly on the floor. So eager. So useless. Like her. They both had to do this in order to justify everything that had gone before. No matter the cost.

After a long moment, she heard Tarn's footsteps receding. Once she was sure he was gone, she buried her head in her hands and let the tears she'd been holding back spill over.

-twenty-

Too soon, Branwyn heard Tarn returning. She tried to drag her heart out of the black pit it had fallen into, but Tarn's hand fell on her shoulder before she managed to lift her head from her knees.

"Branwyn," he said in an unfamiliar tone. "Wake. You are needed."

Urgency. That was a note of urgency in his voice. She raised her head and glared at him. "I know. You don't need to pester me."

There was something odd in his eyes. "Your mother is crying."

"What?" Branwyn shot to her feet. "Why? How do you know?"

He made an impatient gesture. "We are neighbors. Your mother is crying and your sister has sent your brother to find a way into my realm. They bid you come home."

"Right," said Branwyn, and scrubbed at her face again. Tarn gestured and a steaming washbasin and a towel appeared on a low marble pillar. "Right," said Branwyn again and went to wash her face properly. "What's she crying about?"

Tarn didn't answer, watching her with a face like a stone. Branwyn shook her head. "Be that way. I'll be back." She went back through the gallery and opened the door out, stepping into her front hall.

Howl rose from his seat on the stairs, a grim expression on his face. "Come on." He led her upstairs to her mother's room and took up a station just outside, as if standing guard. Or as if he was afraid to go inside.

Branwyn wasn't afraid of the room. But she didn't like to see her mother crying, so she lingered a moment, trying to get her bearings after the transition between worlds. She could just see her mother sitting on her bed, Rhianna's arms wrapped around her. Her mother was weeping and murmuring softly, and Branwyn averted her gaze.

But Howl gave her a shove, and Rhianna noticed her. "There you are, Branwyn." There was a steel in her voice that Branwyn never wanted to be on the receiving end of again. She was the eldest, damnit.

Holly glanced up and saw Branwyn, then said, "Oh, no!" and tried immediately to cover up the fact that she'd been crying. Branwyn felt a guilty pang that went straight to her core.

"Mom—"

"Don't, Mom," said Rhianna. "What's the point in hiding it?"

"Branwyn always gets so upset—" Holly said weakly.

"Mom!" said Branwyn. "I'm an adult. I can cope. Why are *you* so upset?"

Holly's lower lip trembled. "He's left me. I didn't even realize we were having problems and I came home and they were here and he said goodbye—" She covered her face with her hands.

A chill ran down Branwyn's spine. "They?"

In an awful voice, Rhianna said, "Jaimie and Rime." She stroked their mother's hair while giving Branwyn a fierce, meaningful look.

Branwyn stared at the two of them, then stared past them. Holly hugged herself, clearly trying for control. "We have a party on Friday and I have no idea what I'm going to say—"

"Right," she said, and left the room. Then she poked her head back in. "Mom, don't write Jaimie off yet. He may not have left you willingly."

"Oh, Branwyn, that's so," she gulped, "sweet, but he seemed... very enthusiastic." She blew her nose on a tissue Rhianna handed her.

"Well, he's a musician," said Branwyn vaguely, as if that explained everything. She'd found it often did. "I'll just go talk to him."

"Branwyn," said Howl, in a low, urgent voice. Branwyn closed the bedroom door and went to where he leaned on the wall looking at his phone. "Lots of people have been vanishing." He turned the phone toward Branwyn and she read the headline on *Eclipse* magazine's website blaring about a starlet vanishing from her home. Then Howl tapped the screen and brought up another tabloid site, this one earnestly declaring that a wave of alien abductions had swept across the LA area.

Branwyn glanced at Howl and he said hastily, "I wouldn't ordinarily pay any attention to trash like this, but a friend of mine posted the second link because his girlfriend's cousin is also missing."

"And he thinks aliens took her?"

"He thinks something's going on." He glanced at the phone again and added, "It's not like they're wrong, is it? Just the wrong damned abductors. Is he going to come back in a century, the same age?"

Exasperated, Branwyn said, "He didn't stumble through a fairy circle. We'll get him back."

"You have a plan?" asked Rhianna, closing their mother's door behind her.

Branwyn frowned at her. "Why are you leaving Mom?"

"She's taking a nap. She wants me—I know you'll laugh at this—she wants me to stop you from doing anything *unfortunate* to Jaimie." Rhianna gave a grim little smile. "Howl, I'm going to have to delegate that to you. You can keep his head from bouncing on the ground as Branwyn drags him home. I'll be busy."

"Doing what?" said Howl, the words dragged out of him.

"Ripping that b—" Rhianna caught herself and showed her teeth. "Having a nice chat with Ms. Rime."

Howl looked between Branwyn and Rhianna uneasily. "I'll let the kids know we're going out, shall I?"

"Good idea," said Branwyn and Rhianna simultaneously.

"Street fight"
Views: 3,407
I was testing out my new camera and
caught this. Freaky.

A man with spiky red and black hair walks down

the street eating something off a plate. As he passes
in front of an alley, he trips and somersaults forward
like a cat, landing on his feet again. A hand off-
camera grabs him and the camera adjusts its scope.
An older man with a neatly trimmed white beard
has taken off a suit jacket and rolled up his sleeves.
He looks big, like the kind of man who works out
regularly. The younger man surges forward, pushing
the older man, and the older man starts to smack
him around. It isn't entirely a one-sided fight, but
the older man is visibly sneering at the younger
one. Finally he catches the younger man by the shirt
collar, then twists him around with his arm behind
his back, nods at the camera directly, and both men
vanish in a puff of smoke.

"Why exactly do you think she didn't just take him off to
fairyland?" Howl inquired, wiping up some crumbs from Branwyn's
fried mozzarella with a frown.

Nearly an hour and many phone calls later, they were sitting in a
booth at a bar and grill Jaimie's band frequented, waiting for someone,
anyone, to respond with a lead on Jaimie's location. "Because she was
imprisoned in fairyland for centuries. She's not going to go back until
she has to."

"And when's that?"

Branwyn made a face. "As far as I can tell, each group of faeries is
limited by a specific set of conditions. Tarn's people are bound by the
phase of the moon, for example. Currently, they're only paroled here
during the new or full moon."

"But *she's* not from your friend's group, right?" Rhianna ate a
cherry from the bowl of Maraschino cherries she'd convinced the
waiter to bring them. "What's she attuned to?"

"No idea. But it's probably not something we can really influence."

"I think I saw something," said Howl slowly. "I was coming

home one night and I saw one of them—they're so tall and pretty, they're hard to miss," he added defensively. "Anyhow, I saw one with this group of girls following him. He was encouraging them, almost herding them sometimes, down the sidewalk. The girls were giggling and stuff; it wouldn't have looked strange at all except it was one of *them* doing it, and he kept circling them. Then something happened and he swore and vanished. Straight into thin air. I had no idea what had happened, but I knew I'd seen it. But now I remember: the wind changed."

"Hey, I saw something like that, too. What did the girls do?" asked Rhianna with interest.

Howl snorted. "Giggled and looked for him, then argued and split up to sulk. None of them believed he just vanished, even though they saw it. Idiots."

Branwyn reached over and flicked him in the forehead, hard. "Don't. And like I said, I don't think we're going to be able to send her off that way. But I have some ideas." She looked around, then stood up. "Man the phones. I'll be back in a bit."

She went to the restroom. It was relatively nice: clean, with a faded old couch against one wall under a papering of old band posters. Branwyn met her own eyes in the long mirror placed over the two sinks. "You might not like what you're going to see, Your Majesty. But if you wanted, you could get involved." She paused a moment, expecting no response and getting exactly that.

Her gaze fell to her collarbone, and the mark mostly covered there. She sighed and loosened the lid on her reservoir of useless thoughts. After the last week or so, it was quite full. Hatred rolled out first, the foam on a tide of helplessness. She squeezed her eyes shut. Her arm twinged with an ache that wasn't physical, and she heard the sound of the bone breaking. She remembered AT's expression.

That did it.

Severin's voice whispered in her ear, "Delicious cupcake."

Branwyn opened her eyes. She could feel his presence behind her, but there was nothing in the mirror except the bathroom stalls. She could even feel his hands on her hips, stopping her instinctive attempt to turn around.

Her mouth dry, Branwyn said, "You're not actually here."

She felt his breath in her hair and couldn't stop a shiver. "Smart girl, too. I'm almost here." *Almost,* his mental voice echoed. *Almost there. Always.* "Did you want something in particular, or were you just putting on a show for fun?"

"I want to pay you back for saving me," she said breathlessly. He didn't say anything at all, although she thought the pressure on her hips increased just a touch. She closed her eyes again; it was easier than the confusion presented by the mirror. "You want a faerie to, uh, play with, right? I'll give you one."

A lazy coolness had entered his voice when he spoke again. "Oh. Tell me more, do."

"Lady Rime of Nightwell. She's causing problems."

Severin laughed, low and full of genuine amusement. "Of course she is, cupcake. That's what they do."

"I want her gone," said Branwyn fiercely.

"You mean you want her free. Isn't that what you're working toward?" He leaned forward so that his breath was in her hair again and said conspiratorially, "I don't mind."

Branwyn's own breathing sped up. "I know what I'm doing. And it isn't right to punish the innocent along with the guilty. But that doesn't mean the guilty can't be punished."

"They're all guilty. All of them." His voice changed, became flat and threatening.

Branwyn tried to turn around again and couldn't. Panicked helplessness rose in her throat and she thrashed for a moment, whimpering.

Severin dropped his mouth to her ear and made a sound that was disturbingly like a purr. The sound seemed to roll across her skin and somehow, the panic receded. She *wasn't* helpless here. She'd decanted her own buried despair, dangled it as bait to lure him to her. When she let it overwhelm her, of course he came closer. She could handle this. She just had to keep control.

That in mind, she promptly opened her eyes without meaning to. He stood behind her in the mirror now, watching her with glittering eyes. He was, she realized, probably listening to her thoughts right now.

"Look, you want a faerie," she began, and realized she she'd already said that. "If they're all guilty, why won't you go after her, even if I help you?"

"And give you the feeling we're square? Nah." His reflection smiled at her. "I want Tarn. I owe him. It's personal. But getting to him is the only thing that will taste better than what brought me here tonight. I'm afraid Rime Nightwell just isn't the same." His smile changed into the jack-o-lantern grin and he added, "Besides, I'm very interested in her project."

Branwyn scowled, but before she could say anything, the bathroom door opened and Marley stalked in, followed by Rhianna. Once again Branwyn tried to turn, and this time Severin let her, although he didn't lift his hands from her hips. That made it worse, not better. Much worse. Now she was practically in his arms. He smelled like blue smoke and burnt sugar. She remembered being tugged against his chest and dreams she didn't want to have—

Marley glared. "What is going on in here?"

"Why, hello there, sweetheart. Come on in. There's room." The kaiju extended a hand.

Murder in her eyes, Marley said, "Branwyn, come here." Branwyn had a fuzzy memory of Marley threatening to *end* Severin and wondered if she had any way of doing it.

Almost gently, Severin said, "She doesn't want your protection, sweetheart. None of your friends do. We could talk about why, if you want."

Branwyn saw the anguish rise in Marley's eyes. That undazed her. She moved away from Severin, interposing herself between the two of them. "Go away," she told him coldly.

The kaiju's eyes narrowed. "You invited me here, cupcake."

Branwyn snorted. "That's like saying blood in the water is an invitation to a shark."

The grin he flashed was, in fact, shark-like. "Isn't it?"

"Fine! Come along and help us deal with Rime, then."

It was his turn to snort. "Nice try." He moved forward, passing by Branwyn and Marley and Rhianna. But he turned as he opened the door. "Oh, by the way. I've made a deal with Hunter that he won't try to recapture you. Isn't that nice?" And then he was gone.

Marley's fingers closed over Branwyn's. "What were you *doing?*"

"Asking for help," said Branwyn tiredly. "Just like I did with you. Except I don't know his cell number." She met her sister's wide gaze and braced herself for more questions. But no more questions materialized. Rhianna just looked at her with a faintly interested expression that Branwyn knew she'd practiced in the mirror when she was seventeen years old.

Marley got her attention again. "Are you okay to go back out again? I want to make sure he actually left. Simon's out there."

"I'm fine," Branwyn said, irritated. "Did you and Simon show up together?" She headed out of the restroom.

"Yes. He found the faerie you mentioned, too. Oh, God—" Marley tried to brush past Branwyn to rejoin Simon and Howl. Tried and failed, because Branwyn had longer legs and Severin hadn't actually left.

He'd settled into the booth across the aisle. He watched the hostess notice him, a faint smile on his face. He didn't seem to be paying any attention to Branwyn and her friends at all. But Simon was standing beside their booth, looking both puzzled and annoyed.

"Hey," said Branwyn, moving into his field of view. "You found Rime?"

"Oh, yeah," he said absently. "At a studio downtown."

Branwyn frowned. "What kind of studio?"

"A recording studio," said Simon, stepping around her. "What's he doing here?"

"Being an asshole," said Branwyn. "Ignore him. He hates that."

"It's true," Marley confirmed.

The hostess stopped by Severin's table with a menu and a smile. The smile froze as she stared down at him. He reached up and laid his fingers on her wrist.

Simon gave Branwyn a look of disgust. "That's not my job. I'm not going to sit by while even the mildest kaiju hurts people in my presence."

"Mild?" said Severin softly. The word shouldn't have carried, but it did, bouncing off the walls like they'd been plunged into a fishbowl. Abruptly, Branwyn once again felt a massive pressure all around her, as if something was trying to drive her down to the ground. This time, blackness seemed to lap around her feet. The dining room actually seemed darker. It was like a black diamond rain, hard and sharp and painful.

Simon staggered, then scowled and straightened up. He muttered something under his breath and started forward.

The kaiju continued speaking, but this time soft words remained soft, meant for the hostess's ears only. When Simon said, "Oi," he glanced up in mock surprise.

"Coming out to play after all?" He stood up, holding the hostess's wrist.

Quick as a flash, a knife, long and split down the center, appeared in Simon's hand. Just as swiftly, Severin moved his free hand and his foot. Simon flipped into the air but caught himself and landed like a cat. Lightning crackled from the knife, searing a jagged afterimage onto Branwyn's eyes.

She blinked and then, while they fought, she ran to the hostess and grabbed her free hand. The woman stared at her, dazed, tears in her eyes. Branwyn pointed at Marley. "She can help you. When he lets go of you, run to her." She wasn't sure if the woman understood, but Branwyn couldn't actually yank her out of Severin's steel grip. "Marley," she shouted.

"She doesn't want help, damnit! I'm trying."

There was a thud as Simon went down badly on his back. The kaiju stomped heavily on his knife hand and the lightning crawled up his foot. The heavy, dragging pressure intensified.

"Of course she doesn't want help," said Severin conversationally. "She knows how treacherous she is. She's betrayed everybody who's ever loved her, in some fashion or another. Her justifications— amazing." He shook his head and twisted his foot on Simon's hand. The lightning played around his knee and Branwyn smelled something metallic burning. "And she's never felt bad about it until tonight. We have a lot of work to do, don't we, princess?"

The hostess shuddered and started crying. Branwyn looked frantically between Marley and the woman, and saw only Marley's frustration. She yanked on the woman, hard.

Then Severin caught her arm and dragged her close enough to rasp in her ear, "I could take your sister instead. Or Marley. The little darlings aren't here to protect her now. I could take this pathetic excuse for a monster hunter. Just say the word. No?"

Branwyn tried to think of something, anything she could do. But the only person she could offer was herself, and that wouldn't save Jaimie, that wouldn't save Penny. While she was arguing with herself, handicapped by the terrible dark weight the kaiju radiated, Severin continued. "Of course not. Besides, she wants to come with me." He brushed his mouth across her forehead. His lips burned. "Be a good girl and go back to your friends, cupcake. You've caused them enough trouble."

Then he stepped swiftly away, hauling the hostess after him. The crushing pressure vanished as soon as he walked out the door.

"Ah. I don't mean to be rude, but could you get off of me, Branwyn?" Simon said, and Branwyn realized with a start that she was standing on Simon's chest. She stepped down and ran to the door, looking for Severin and the woman. But there was no sign of them in the parking lot.

"Regular bulldog, isn't she?" Simon said behind her. "Gah! Shit! Baby, what did he do to you?"

"Are you all right?" Marley asked, concerned.

"I'll heal, but look at my *knife*."

"Holy crap, Branwyn!" exclaimed Howl, and Branwyn turned around. Her little brother had remained in the booth for the entire encounter. He was holding onto Rhianna's shirt, as if he'd been worried she was going to join in. "Holy crap. How did you *do* that, man?" He pushed Rhianna away and slid out to join Simon.

The monster hunter stared disconsolately at what had been his knife. Now it was black, pitted slag.

Branwyn set her jaw and plucked it out of his hand, moving back to their booth.

"Hey!" Simon protested.

"Shut up. Rhianna, deal with them." She nodded at the crowd gathering now that the fight was over, a combination of other patrons and restaurant staff. More than one of them was on the phone. "Maybe Simon has a *license for this taser*."

"It's not a taser," said Simon sulkily. "It's a channel. *I'm* the taser. Oh," he said, catching on. "I do have—" and he fumbled out his wallet. Rhianna and Marley both converged on him.

Branwyn tuned them all out, focusing on the ruined weapon. She couldn't save the woman. She was useless with people. But she could damn well do something about broken things.

She concentrated on the weapon, activating all her cultivated magical senses, and realized with a start that it was made of silver. That made sense when she thought about it, but it must have taken a lot of work to maintain the edge. No wonder Simon loved it so much. How could you help it when something required that degree of care?

Studying the lines of Geometry running through it, she noted where they'd frayed apart and stroked along them, smoothing them back together. It was slow going and her rage at Severin sustained her while she worked. After the basic structure of the weapon was repaired, she paused to consider the rest of it. The lines could be intensified, if she concentrated. She found, when she peered closely, that she could see the sharpness. There was something…

Digging into her pocket, she pulled out the Machine Key, laying it on the table beside the knife. The tendrils of the Machine Key unrolled as she touched them, merging with the surrounding Geometry. One sank into her chest, and one wrapped around the knife.

Branwyn smiled. With the knife side by side with the Machine, she could see just what to do. She pinched the lattice of the knife here and there, until she found the heart of the weapon. It pulsed under her fingers, long, slow, hissing beats. She placed one palm on the knife's heart, and touched a finger to the Machine Key. A spark of light ran up her arm, through her chest, and down into the knife. The tangle of lines under her palm *expanded*—

Somebody shook her by the shoulder, hard. "Branwyn! Branwyn, you've got to put that thing away, or we're going to get into even more trouble." It was Marley. But Branwyn was almost done. She ran her fingers over the node she'd created, smoothing it like the inside of a clay pot.

She was still so angry. The knife was a small thing compared to all that Severin had done. She pressed both hands over the node now, the sharpened blade slicing into her fingers. The knife felt her rage, shared it. It felt the mark on her skin as a brand on its own metal and tasted her hunger to even the scales.

It woke up.

Branwyn's breath hissed out as she felt the flicker of awareness, dim cousin to the demanding, alien intellect of the Machine itself. The hints she'd seen in the lines of the metal had all come together to produce this *awareness*. This *desire*.

Distantly, she heard Rhianna say, "I'll do it, then," and her hand came toward the glowing Key.

That snapped Branwyn out of her creative fugue. "No!" She dropped the knife and snatched up the Key before Rhianna could grab it. The light—the actual light, she realized, visible to anyone who looked—radiating from the Key, the knife, and herself vanished. "Don't touch it. It's powerful. I don't know what it would do to you now."

"It's powerful? Really? We never would have realized. It was *glowing*, Branwyn. And so were you." Rhianna crossed her arms. "Are you done? We need to get out of here, right now."

"Where's Simon?" Branwyn stuffed the Key in her pocket and picked up the knife. To her ordinary vision, it looked just as it had when Simon had first pulled it out. It had a bit more of a shimmer, a bit more of an edge, maybe.

"He'll meet us outside. Can you move?"

"Of course!" said Branwyn indignantly. She stood up and did her best not to sway. It was just that she had been so focused. She hadn't been aware of her surroundings at all.

Rhianna eyed her. "Still want to recover Jaimie?"

"Hell yeah. Did Simon say he knew where to find them?" She thought she remembered something like that, through the fog of emotion Severin had raised.

"Yes, he did." As they moved toward the door, watched by a number of extremely curious people, Rhianna said, "People got videos. Hope you're looking forward to being famous."

Branwyn stretched her shoulders as they stepped outside. "The net is clogged with videos of people doing amazing things right now. A glow is nothing. A kid's CG club project."

Darkly, Rhianna said, "We'll see. It looked pretty spooky to me."

"Well, it'll fit right in with all the faerie videos, then."

"Is this what you've been learning on the other side of the door? With your faerie friend?"

Branwyn shrugged. "Yes. Indirectly." And as Branwyn said it, she realized for the first time that she'd been working as if she was in her studio in Underlight. In the Backworld, where manipulating the dreams of matter was much easier than manipulating matter itself. When she'd tried to work on the acrylic casing of Hunter's Machine fragment in the real world before, she'd had no traction. Either she was getting better, or working on the Key was changing her.

Miracle rescue
Views: 1,567,892

It's a windy, cloudy day over a grey river. There's a bridge just at the top of the frame, and the old railing has been bent out. There are people shouting nearby. A man's voice behind the camera says, "Oh my god. A minivan just went off the bridge. We saw it fall. It just sank. The water is so cold. This woman, this woman, she just stood up from beside the river and walked into the water. She didn't even swim. I don't know, I don't know..." There's a siren in the distance, getting closer. The camera is jostled and lowered for a moment. There's splashing, then more splashing, then somebody shouts.

The camera is jerked up again. A diver that had just waded into the water is backing out again. There are ripples on the river surface. First one head, then another rises out of the water. "Holy Mother of God," says the cameraman's voice. Two women slowly climb out of the river, walking rather than swimming. One of them is wearing torn clothes and looks dazed. Her nose and forehead well with blood. She is holding the hand of the other woman. That woman is smiling faintly, and in her free arm, she's holding a sleeping baby while another child clings to her back. None of them are gasping for breath.

The child slides down, crying, and the woman

hands the baby to a uniformed man before turning and kissing the mother she saved on the forehead. Then she looks around, as if startled by all the attention, pulls away from grabbing hands, and vanishes into the growing crowd. The video drops to the ground, then cuts to black.

-twenty-one-

I've thought of a problem," announced Marley. The five of them lurked near a hedge outside the square three-story building that Simon swore was where Rime was taking her victims. And Simon insisted it was "victims," not just Jaimie. It looked bland and soulless to Branwyn, almost completely indistinguishable from the buildings around it.

Branwyn winced. "Of course you did. Lay it on us."

"Well, I was thinking of this poem. *La Belle Dame sans Merci*. It's about a knight enchanted by a faerie. And even when she's left him, he's unable to do anything else but wait for her."

Simon crouched nearby, looking at his knife. He hadn't stopped ogling it since Branwyn had handed it back to him and she wasn't sure whether to be flattered or creeped out. But now he glanced up. "Hey, Keats."

Marley nodded, then her thought process visibly derailed. "Did you know him?"

"Naw, but his daughter's a sweetie." Simon glanced at Branwyn, then hurriedly said, "So, uh, yeah. What about La Belle Dame sans Merci?"

"Well, if she's enchanted Jaimie, won't he just go back to her if we drag him away?"

"Oh." He considered. "Yeah, probably."

"How do we get the enchantment off him, then?" Branwyn demanded, looking between Simon and Marley. "There has to be a way to break it."

"Well, what you have to do is disrupt her power. Kill her via a spirit tether, or mess her up enough that she can't maintain the enchantments anymore." He surveyed the building. "Could be tricky if we're looking to get her hostages out alive and you want to do this right now. Give me a couple of months to stalk her and it'd be much easier."

"We're not waiting a couple of months to get Jaimie back," said Rhianna flatly. "There must be another way."

"Well," Simon drawled slowly, clearly hesitant to suggest a long shot. "You could always... ask her? Convince her to let him go? She can remove her own enchantments whenever she wants."

"Can't you do something, Marley?" appealed Branwyn. "Like you did with Penny?"

"Because *that* worked out so well," said Marley darkly. "And I don't know. What the angel did to Penny wasn't an enchantment or a charm. He was *inhabiting* her until Penny wouldn't let him attack me directly. There was a constant flow of energy between them that my magic interrupted. And for all we know, she still loves him now. In any case, I can't do *anything* unless the target wants me to," she finished bitterly, glaring at Branwyn.

Branwyn stuck out her tongue. "If we have to fight, lots of people will be screaming for help, me included. You'll have your chance. All right, we'll try talking to her. Rhianna—" she looked at her sister, "Uh, never mind, you hate her too much. I guess I'll talk to her. Marley and Simon can cover me. Rhianna, you and Howl find Jaimie and see if you can at least convince him to get out of the building."

Howl asked quietly, "What about the rest of the band?"

"What?" Branwyn blinked at her little brother.

"It's a recording studio, Branwyn, not a penthouse. She's got Jaimie, she's probably got the rest of the band. Are we just going to leave them there?"

Branwyn swore and chewed on her lip, staring at the building. "Well, see if you can get them all outside." She stood up and brushed herself off. The weight of the Key in her pocket was a comforting reminder that she could *do* things now. She wasn't just a bystander. She'd gotten involved as an actor instead of a pawn.

There were consequences, of course.

She would just have to deal with them.

She headed into the building, the others following her. The ground floor was an elevator lobby with only a pair of people talking earnestly at one of the couches. Seeing them made Branwyn uneasy somehow; one was raggedly dressed, with wild hair and a silver flute that he twiddled between his fingers as he listened to his companion, a long-haired man in a plaid shirt who was gesticulating wildly. She didn't know either of them.

The button plate in the elevator declared that the second floor was the home of Coastal Professional Audio. She stabbed it, then had to hold the door open as Howl lagged getting onboard. "What now?"

"Those guys—"

"I know."

"How many—"

"*I know.*" The doors slid closed and Branwyn tried not to think of the face of the hostess whom Severin had dragged off.

A moment later, the elevator doors opened onto another lobby area. This one was smaller, heavily decorated with band memorabilia. It was also crowded full of musicians. They lounged on the black leather couches and tuned their instruments in stray corners and crammed around a buffet set up along the line of darkened windows.

Branwyn gritted her teeth and stepped out of the elevator, ignoring the sounds of dismay from behind her as they saw what she had. So there were a *lot* of people in Rime's studio. That didn't mean they were all being magically compelled. She was there for Jaimie.

Then she paused to take in the room again, spending a few minutes watching more closely this time.

Most of the inhabitants of the couches seemed to be sleeping rather than just lounging, like they were so exhausted they'd dropped off where they were, or hadn't been allowed to go home. And it wasn't just people with musical instruments there, either; she saw several people toting video cameras and a couple with extremely large laptop computers. Every so often, somebody got up and walked through one of the four doors lining the wall opposite the window. Once, someone came out and immediately went to an occupied couch, where she curled up at the end and passed out.

"I don't see them," whispered Rhianna. "Do you?"

"Nope," said Branwyn. "I do see the receptionist, though." She made her way across the room to where a receptionist's high desk had been turned into a dessert bar. A woman sat on the other side of the brownie platter, watching something on her phone. She didn't look up until Branwyn said, "Hey!" but she smiled once she noticed Branwyn.

"Oh, hi. I thought you were here for the brownies. Can I help you with something?"

"What's the party for?"

"It is kind of crazy, isn't it? A producer rented out the whole floor for a massive collaborative project. It's all hush-hush, but there's some nice sounds coming out of the studios." She laughed. "I'm one of the only regulars here this week. So what can I do for you?"

"You know if there's a woman around here who goes by Rime?"

The receptionist looked pleased. "Yep, that's one of the producers. She's in Studio Three right now."

"Thanks," said Branwyn and turned away. Then she turned back. "She might not like the message I have, so if you hear any screaming, that's probably what it is. I suggest staying out of her way for a while."

"Exciting!" said the receptionist, leaning on her elbow to watch Branwyn instead of her phone.

Branwyn beckoned the others after her, aware that she probably shouldn't have said anything to the woman. She'd wanted to tell her to get out of the building right now, but that rarely worked on receptionists. Her compromise wasn't doing much better.

There was a light over the door of Studio Three that said Recording In Progress. As Branwyn glanced up at it, it blinked out. That was a shame; she didn't want Rime to think she'd waited politely until the recording was done. Oh well; if she couldn't be really rude, she'd settle for stealing Jaimie back again. She threw the door open.

Beyond was a large, dimly lit studio, with Jaimie and his band in the center of the open floor. They'd clearly just finished performing and were chatting with each other as they cooled down. It was disconcerting. They didn't seem like they'd been enchanted by a faerie. Branwyn wasn't entirely sure what she'd expected, but it was something along the lines of large feather fans, peeled grapes, and loincloths, not an analysis of that last bridge Jaimie had played. Rime was in the booth, standing behind two technicians, and they hardly seemed aware of her.

Irritated at the lack of attention, Branwyn put her hands on her hips and took a deep breath.

Howl called, "Jaimie!" and pushed past her to lope over to their stepfather. Marley squeezed around her as well, following him. Annoyed at her own hesitation, Branwyn stepped into the room before Rhianna could show her up. As she did, Rime looked up from her conversation and saw Branwyn. A smile curved the faerie lady's mouth, and she nodded a greeting.

Scowling, Branwyn stalked over to the booth, Rhianna trailing her. As she approached, she overheard Rime say, "This is excellent. The hook is perfect. With this done—ah."

The two technicians glanced at Branwyn as she entered, then quickly busied themselves with their work. Rime, though, said, "Welcome, Branwyn. Have you come to join me? Tarn is a bore, isn't he?"

Branwyn clenched her teeth over her first response, then uncracked her jaw enough to say, "I've come to ask you to release Jaimie and the band."

Rime gave her a surprised look. "Release?"

"You've enchanted them, you and I both know it."

Rime glanced into the farthest corner of the booth and Branwyn realized with a start that there was another person in the small room, lounging in the shadows like he was part darkness himself. Another faerie, Branwyn realized, so he probably *was* part shadow.

"You're welcome to try and convince them to leave," said Rime with a sweet smile. "Ah, I see the boy is already doing just that. But you know, with me they really have a chance to stretch their wings. And to find the, ah, appreciation they've always craved. It would be unkind, even selfish, to take that away from them, don't you think?"

"Take your enchantments off them and we'll have that discussion, sure."

Rime tilted her head to one side, studying Branwyn. "No, I don't think so. They're all happier here with me than they ever were at their previous homes. I'm sorry to say this about your mother, truly I am, but she isn't the right mate for a musician like Jaimie. A speech pathologist, really? What kind of muse is that?"

Branwyn caught Rhianna's wrist as the shadow in the corner shifted. Rhianna made a noise, then relaxed, pivoting slightly to watch the shadow. "Oh," she whispered, and Branwyn glanced at her sharply. The familiar look on Rhianna's face both worried and reassured her: her sister had identified something she found both important and interesting.

Rime looked at the shadow again, then away. "When you hear what I have here—" she tapped the recording console, "—you'll see what I mean."

Blowing out her breath, Branwyn repeated, "Take your enchantments off." She didn't know what else to say to convince the faerie woman. "Look, we didn't come alone. You've got something going on here, I can see that. You don't want trouble. Give us back Jaimie and the band and we'll get out of—"

"No," said Rhianna sharply. "They're *all* enchanted, Branwyn."

Branwyn winced, thinking once again of Severin and the hostess.

"They were all perfectly willing to be enchanted," said Rime, sharpness touching her sweet tones. "They are being paid in more ways than one for their service, and they are being *valued* far more than most of them value themselves." She settled herself, running her hands over her silver skirt. "Besides, your sister lies. They aren't all enchanted, except perhaps by promises."

Branwyn shook her head. "But Jaimie is. We can see the magic."

"Yes, I can see that," said Rime, and tapped her lip with a long, blue-burnished fingernail. "You are so *persistent*. I suppose it's part of what makes you special. What to do, what to do."

"Let him go?" suggested Branwyn brightly. Rhianna clutched her arm as the faerie in the shadowy corner shifted, leaning forward, and Branwyn wondered what her sister had noticed about him. Branwyn herself couldn't spare attention from Rime to give him a good look.

"Don't be silly. He's mine. Let's see. You have a role yet to play, so I *should* just send you on your way with your little entourage. But you're like a little yapping dog, aren't you? Bark, bark, bark, and you've even shown me your teeth. No, I didn't miss your clumsy attempt at a meaningless threat, little thing. There must be discipline."

Branwyn sneered. "Oh, please."

Rime looked around the studio. "All protected, I see. Ah—" and she smiled and put her palm on the clear panel separating the booth from the recording area. Branwyn could feel the pulse of magic that poured off her and turned to follow Rime's gaze. She inhaled sharply as she realized that not everybody who had come with her had protection against malicious magic.

Howl, standing with Jaimie and the band, slowly raised his head and looked over at Rime, his eyes extremely wide. Smirking, she crooked her finger and he ran toward her, straight into the clear panel. As he reeled backwards, clutching his head, she giggled delicately, like tiny ice crystals shattering, and turned her attention back to Branwyn. "So—"

"Hell with *that*!" Branwyn launched herself at Rime, pulling the Key out of her pocket as she did. The faerie woman stumbled backward into the recording console, throwing her hand up as her eyes widened. Branwyn pushed Rime's hand aside and slammed the Key against the faerie's chest. "I tried to talk. I tried to *negotiate*. I did. God knows I'm not good at it. But you had to go and fuck with my little brother."

She ground the Key against Rime's skin, feeling it expand and change under her fingers in response to her rage. "Nobody does that but me. Now take your nasty magic off of them—*all* of them—before I convince this Machine it wants to be inside your heart." She saw fear in Rime's eyes and felt only a vengeful satisfaction.

"Branwyn—" squeaked Rhianna in a strangled voice, and—

"Lord—" whimpered Rime and—

The shadow in the corner moved. Branwyn saw it only from the corner of her eye but she *felt* it pass over her; it was the same kind of psychic domination she'd felt twice before. The flavor was different, though. New. It was not Severin or Hunter, but somebody else.

Ebony hands reached past her and plucked at Rime. One came away with a palm full of light, while the other had a fistful of darkness. Rime gasped, then her face froze like a statue's and she fell away.

At first, Branwyn thought she was just collapsing, but it was more than that: she was literally crumbling to dust. Whatever had animated her body was gone, and without it, she wasn't going to even leave a corpse. With an inarticulate cry, Branwyn pulled her hands away from the faerie remains. She swung around, the Key still held like a weapon in her outstretched fist, reacting even as she struggled to keep up with what had happened.

The man from the shadows stood to her side, his hands out. The palmful of light spread around his hand as she moved; he hurled the fistful of darkness into the air. Something rushed past Branwyn up through the ceiling. Then the violet-haired, silver-eyed man moved his hand out to catch Branwyn's fist. "Careful," he said. His voice was deep and sonorous. "We don't want to damage the Key."

"You mean you don't want it to damage you," Branwyn snarled. She finally realized why Rhianna had been watching him so closely. He was the faerie from some of the videos that had been going around.

The Duke of Nightwell raised his eyebrows. "Do you think it is infinitely powerful? Or is it only that Tarn has misinformed you?" He moved his hand from Branwyn's fist to the shaft of the Key jutting out, hooking two fingers around it. Touching it didn't seem to bother him. He certainly didn't turn to dust, even when Branwyn ground the Key against his fingers.

"Well, it certainly wasn't healthy for Rime, so—"

"It wasn't," agreed the Duke of Nightwell. "You surprised her. It would have damaged her greatly, and she would have distorted the Key. We couldn't have that. So I tore her free of its grip and sent her back to the elements. She will reform in time."

Branwyn frowned up at him, replaying the last thirty seconds in her mind. "You mean you killed her?"

"Ladies, things are getting weird out here!" came Simon's shout from outside the studio.

"Ah," said Nightwell. "Her pets. Let me just—" and without unhooking his fingers from around the Key, he waved his other hand. The light still limning it vanished, sinking into his skin. "As for you, my little Artificer—" He gave her an appraising look. "I can see you're quite disturbed by my vassal's choice in pets. We have taken what we needed from the band beyond, and I don't share her tastes. So I will release them back to you. But you must promise to complete your work swiftly." He let go of the Key and chucked Branwyn under the chin gently, as if she was a child.

She mastered her rage enough to say, "What about the rest of them?"

He smiled lazily. "We'll see. Now do run along before I change my mind."

Branwyn drew in a deep breath. It was clear that just as Rime had, he valued her, or what she was doing for Tarn. That was leverage. She could—

Rhianna grabbed her arm and pulled her hard. "Come on."

"What? Rhianna—"

"*Come on,*" Rhianna said between her teeth. "Marley, help me get her out of here before somebody else gets killed."

Marley grabbed Branwyn's other arm and the two of them started to hustle Branwyn out of the booth. After a brief internal struggle, Branwyn opted for dignity and turned to walk between them. It was that or be dragged backward, looking into the Duke of Nightwell's laughing eyes.

-twenty-two-

Howl went home with the band in their van, since from their perspective, the gig was done and he'd told Jaimie about the "misunderstanding" he needed to sort out with Holly. Dark-eyed and with a headache, Howl said they'd stop for flowers along the way. Meanwhile, Rhianna and Marley escorted Branwyn to Marley's car and stayed with her. She was in the back seat. They were in the front. It wasn't the most empowering of configurations, but it suited Branwyn. She had thinking to do.

She looked out the car window and listened to Rhianna and Marley talk about her. It was clear they were worried. She didn't know why. Sure, they'd dragged her away from a confrontation with a half-unleashed creature of unknown power who thought it was reasonable to strip the free will away from dozens and dozens of people. Sure, they'd forced her to flee with only her loved ones, like a coward. Sure, they'd tried to make a choice for her.

But she wasn't angry, no matter what they thought.

At least, she wasn't angry at *them*.

"I'd like to go see Penny," she said as they passed near the hospital. "You can drop me off here."

Marley tried to catch her eyes in the rearview mirror, but Branwyn looked out the window again. "What are you going to do now, Branwyn?"

"Go see Penny," Branwyn repeated patiently.

Marley sighed, pulled the car over, then turned around to look into the back seat. "You're not done with the faeries yet, are you?"

Branwyn laughed humorlessly. "How can we ever be done? With faeries or monsters or angels or nephilim?" Marley flinched but Branwyn wasn't sorry. "This is the world we live in. The only way to be done would be to be dead, and even then I'm not convinced."

"There was a balance at least, before the faeries started coming back," said Rhianna. Branwyn shot her a glance, wondering once again what exactly her organization knew. Hell, what exactly her organization *was* and what her sister's place was in it all.

"Maybe that was true, but it wasn't a balance that humans were involved in."

"I really think some humans—" began Marley.

"*I wasn't,*" said Branwyn sharply. She caught herself, stuffed her emotions back down again, recaptured the voice of calm reason. "Try not to worry, Marley. Why should you? Don't you know what's happening?" She held out a hand to her friend. "What do you see?"

"I don't *know,*" said Marley tightly. "There's a lot of bad that could happen and a lot of bad that already has and I haven't been able to stop *any* of it. I don't think you're going to die, but that's hardly the worst thing that could happen to you." Branwyn remembered Hunter and nodded involuntarily. Marley went on. "Tell me what you're going to do. That helps focus my vision."

"I wasn't joking about going to see Penny, you know. After that, I… don't know." It wasn't exactly a lie.

"It isn't a gift, you know," said Marley, subdued. "It's never worked to give me concrete information. I only ever know 'something bad may happen.' It's a curse. The only *useful* thing I can do is *protect.*"

"You helped get Jaimie back. And you were ready to rescue me from Hunter." Branwyn wrapped her hand around Marley's. "That matters."

Marley squeezed her hand hard for a long moment, then let go. "I'll go try to put kindergarten charms on everybody back at your mom's house. I don't trust that guy from the videos. Call me if… you know. I can help."

Branwyn turned to her little sister. "You heard her. Whatever I do is going to be dangerous. Do you have any advice for me? Any tips? Any secret handshakes?"

Rhianna gazed at her with a studied innocence. "I don't know. Given that I don't want any more of those bastards on the streets, should I be trying to stop you?"

"I haven't thought about it," said Branwyn casually. Then she added, "But maybe."

Rhianna toyed with something in her hand. Then she said, "I trust you," and opened her fingers. In her palm was the silver courtkey that allowed Branwyn to open her own doors to Underlight. She held it up, offering it back to Branwyn.

Branwyn snatched it up, growling under her breath. Unabashed, Rhianna said, "I'm going back to work soon. They want me to bring back souvenirs. But I'll just pick up some postcards."

"Wait," said Branwyn. She pulled out her mundane, day-to-day keychain and unclipped the key to her old studio. Then she pulled out the Machine key and concentrated for a while. When she was done, the old studio key had the same kind of nascent node that she'd given Simon's knife. It was very small, but she thought perhaps it would eventually be good for unlocking very small things. She offered it to Rhianna. "Give them that."

Rhianna hesitated, then wrapped her fingers around Branwyn's and the key. "I don't know what they'll do with it."

Branwyn found a little smile somewhere. "Unpredictable, are they? A bit like the faeries, I guess."

Her sister smiled back. "Maybe a bit. Thank you." She took the key and tucked it away.

Branwyn slid out of the car, walking briskly away. For a moment, the world around her brightened, and she felt safe, like she had as a little girl curled up in her mother's bed. She looked back over her shoulder, at Marley looking out at her. Marley shrugged sheepishly and Branwyn turned and kept walking, ignoring the pleasant light. About a block from the car, which stayed still, the brightness tingeing the world faded back to dull normalcy. She could suddenly smell the smog. And she felt like an adult again, making her own choices, alone against the world.

Well, almost alone. Friends mattered, even without magic.

She went to see Penny. There was a new bunch of flowers in the vase, and a fresh edition of *Eclipse* beside the bed. Penny's mother's perfume lingered in the room, but only Penny was there, pale and shallowly breathing. The monitor beeped, very slowly. Branwyn didn't make a long visit of it, and when she was done, she knew what she had to do next.

She made her way to her old studio. The fact that she'd just given the studio key away turned out to be a mild inconvenience, but it took only a little work to open the door. There was probably a lesson there about making spontaneous symbolic gestures, but Branwyn didn't regret it.

She dug around in her store of materials until she found what she needed. Then she set to work. It took particular concentration, but not nearly as much time as it once would have, When she was done, she collapsed into the sagging couch in the center of her studio and fell asleep.

She was exhausted and she slept a long time. When she woke up, it was the middle of the next day. The only message on her phone was a new video from the channel she'd subscribed to. She watched it contemplatively, then looked out the window at the sky for a long moment. Eventually she turned away, back to packing up her work.

The silver key to Underlight didn't open the door the way it used to. It slid in easily, and when she turned it, she could feel it catch—but the door seemed stuck. Branwyn frowned and focused her Sight on the door. She could see the double entity: the magic door to Underlight, and the prosaic door to her family's home. It wasn't anything like as complex as the sealed portal in Tarn's gallery, and Branwyn had no patience for its moods. "Don't make me fix you," she warned it. "I've got a package explicitly requested by your master and I'm going to deliver it, whether or not you want to allow it."

The door relented and stopped clinging to its frame. Although it wasn't the door, was it? That was just a thing imbued with celestial magic. It was the realm itself that had been resisting her presence. Tarn was trying to avoid her again.

Tough luck for him. Branwyn opened the door and went through.

He was waiting for her. But before he could speak, she swung the package she'd brought out from under her arm. It was quite large and flat. "Here you go," she said. "You commissioned this, back at the beginning of this adventure. I don't think you really cared about it, but I don't like loose ends."

Wordlessly, Tarn accepted the package, pulling away the paper wrappings. Within was a mirror set into an iron frame. The mirror itself was half the height of a man. The frame was simple, but carefully made, with restrained scrollwork at each corner. Tarnished silver ornamentation, starting with the phases of the moon and moving on to more esoteric symbols, had been welded to the frame. Branwyn had gone with whatever her imagination could provide.

"I figured out what to do," Branwyn went on. "I mean—I used the Machine Key as a template to wake it up. It's sleeping now, but I think it will grow into something. I tried to give it suggestions. It might help to put it in the moonlight when the full moon comes around again."

Tarn looked at the mirror for a long moment, his fingers brushing the decoration, then touching the place in the center of the mirror where Branwyn had gathered the Geometry lattice into a living node. "Branwyn," he finally said, looking at her. "What does this mean?"

Branwyn shrugged and repeated, "I don't like loose ends."

"I see," he said gravely. "It is well done. I shall treasure it."

Branwyn tensed for another little earthquake, but none came. Perhaps he was telling the truth. Or maybe she'd never understood the earthquakes, not really. Privately, she thought she could have done better with the mirror's design, but she'd wanted to finish it and he'd given her so few guidelines. Because, of course, he hadn't wanted it in the first place. It had always been about the Machine Key.

William materialized out of the darkness to take the mirror from his master's hands. Branwyn did a double-take. "You're alive!"

He gave her a familiar cool look, but didn't say anything. Tarn put his hand on William's shoulder. "Did you doubt? Take the mirror to my private chamber, William."

William vanished as silently as he'd appeared and Tarn crossed his arms, gazing at Branwyn calmly.

Branwyn looked back at him. After a moment, she said, "So, where's the third Machine I need to finish the Key?"

Tarn frowned. "You wish to finish it? Even now?"

"And after I just said I don't like loose ends." She snapped her fingers. "Come on, come on. Out with it."

His face lost all expression, but he didn't waste her time with any more pointless questions. "I know of one place certain to have what you need. It is extremely well-guarded, but contains many Machine fragments."

"You're not talking about Heaven, are you?" she said lightly.

He didn't smile. "No. I'm talking about Senyaza."

Branwyn swore, then stared at his serious face, then swore again. "Senyaza?"

"Senyaza. Stronghold of the nephilim. The force that thwarted the Deluge and bound the angels to the Hush. Sometimes, they kill monsters," Tarn reminded her helpfully. "They've collected many Machine fragments over the centuries. Part of their Repository is stored in the facility in your city."

"Okay then. And you have an in? You've convinced Senyaza to give up a fragment for the Key?" Branwyn said, equal parts hopeful and disbelieving.

"No. This is my last resort. My only 'in,' as you put it, is you, Branwyn."

Branwyn gave him a sharp look. "What are you talking about?"

He shrugged elegantly. "You are friends with Senyaza, or at least some of its people. Use them to get to the Machine fragments." When she looked at him askance, he half turned away. "Or do not. I know how you value your friends."

She'd already committed to doing this. She couldn't back down. But for a moment, she shied and wondered if storming Heaven would be preferable. *There must be another way*, she thought. But this *was* the other way. She was trying to make a complex tool tailored to perform a specific task, a task most people believed was impossible. Too often there was *no* way. She had to take this opportunity.

But it was up to her how she went about it.

"How about I steal a fragment without betraying my friends?" Branwyn suggested. "You could help me get in from the Backworld, the same way I got to Hunter's place."

He smiled grimly. "If it was possible to break into the Repository via the Backworld, it would have long ago been emptied. No. It is

244244 chrysoula tzavelas

protected. No earthly body can arrive that way."

"The front door, then." As she said it, she remembered Antonio the security guard and his *special talents*.

"It is protected that way, too. You *must* use your connections, or else there is no way forward."

Branwyn shrugged. "We'll see."

He looked appalled by her reaction. It seemed like everybody eventually gave her that look, which just demonstrated people were the same no matter whether they were human, nephilim, or celestial. "Branwyn, you cannot just *walk into* Senyaza's Repository."

She sighed at his negativity. "I've found, oh trapped faerie lord, that it isn't usually getting into places that's the problem." She rapped her knuckles on the door behind her. "It's getting out again."

Swear to God this happened
Views: 26,019
Sorry it's only a slideshow, didn't know how to take a video. It really happened, though!

A slideshow set to harp music;

1.) Broad white stone steps climbing a hill lead to a civic building at the top. People are climbing the steps and sitting on them.

2.) Closeup of a flight of pigeons on the steps.

3.) Closeup of a woman feeding the pigeons. She's delicate, in a simple white dress with a sheet of black hair. It's a great picture.

4.) Another shot of the woman, not so good. She's moving, her face away from the camera.

5.) Another shot. The pigeons are flying around her as she walks along a step.

6.) She's bending over somebody sitting on the steps. No pigeons. It's a homeless man, unshaven and dressed in layers of rags despite the sunshine.

7.) He's looking up at her as she holds out her hand to him.

8.) Almost the same shot, but there's no homeless man. A pigeon perches on her hand. There's a blur near her.

9.) The woman is surrounded by pigeons, with her hands raised to the sky. Again, a really great shot.

-twenty-three-

Admittedly, getting in wasn't as smooth as Branwyn had hoped. Basic security in the private parts of the building involved keycards and name badges, all keyed to biometric impressions like the thumbprint they'd taken when she came to visit Corbin. It would have been easier if she'd gotten Simon to help her get past Antonio and the reception desk, at least. But he'd helped her save Jaimie. She couldn't do that to him. She considered talking to Howl about technological solutions, but that seemed like it would take more time and planning than she was interested in.

In the end, she relied on that most time-honored way of circumventing security: she found the little keycarded back door that employees used to take their smoke breaks and loitered with a cigarette until she could slip in behind somebody. It didn't take very long before a middle-aged man—human, she saw, with filled nodes just like her—glanced at her as he headed inside. "Coming in?"

"I guess I should," she said and followed him in, glancing up at the camera over the door as she did. That gave her access to the back corridors and, one elevator ride later, after talking to the middle-aged man enthusiastically about hair dye, she was inside the private part of Senyaza Titan One.

After that, she had some time to kill. She explored the private elevator system until she found the underground floor with the

Repository. It required keycard access just to push the button. That was okay, though. She waited until after business hours, when most of the employees went home, then went out to the fire stairs.

That entrance to the Repository level also required a keycard. But when she didn't need to watch out for anybody coming up behind her, keycards were just an inconvenience. At least, they were compared to the Door in the gallery.

She knelt before the lock panel and studied its Geometric structure for a few moments. Then she stroked a finger along one of the cobwebby lines embedding it into the door. For a moment, she could taste the magnetism in her teeth, cobalt and sweet. There was a pop and a whir and the lock disengaged.

Before the Geometry could reassert itself, she hauled the door open and darted inside. The lights in the hall beyond had been dimmed and the floor was quiet save for the hum of distant electronics. She went past the elevators to the reception desk, which was located in front of a big wall inset with a single heavy door and one large picture window. Beyond the window there was another room, one with a collection of filing cabinets and shelves, with two tables in the center of the space.

At least, that's what she saw with her normal vision. What she saw with the Sight made her wonder why they thought it was a good idea to put so many Machine fragments in such close proximity. They reinforced each other, pressing on the local Geometry, warping and weakening it with the weight of their presence. The fragments were tucked away inside the filing cabinets, but they shone through the enclosures like stars wrapped in tissue paper, like the morning sun washing away a dream. Without will, the worldly objects could barely maintain their integrity against the light.

Branwyn smiled and put her hands on the glass of the window. It was cool and solid under her fingers, but she slid her hands apart and the Geometric web of the glass parted. The glass fell into two smooth-edged halves with a Branwyn-sized circle in the middle. As she swung herself into the room, an alarm went off somewhere.

She ignored it, surveying the room. Heavy oak cabinets formed a semicircle around the pair of tables, with shelves between each cabinet. Many, many binders and bins, untidily arranged, occupied the shelves. "Hello, children," she said. "Who wants to open a lock?" She strolled along the circle of cabinets, inspecting each Machine fragment, looking at its nature, sensing its inclinations. When she pulled open one of the cabinets, a loud clattering indicated further security measures activating. A steel grate had descended from the ceiling to block off the wall containing the door and the split window. Branwyn only glanced at it for an instant before looking back at the cabinet.

The Machine fragment was in a metal box that, in turn, was nestled within a mess of papers, folders, discs, and memory sticks. The box wasn't locked in any way, which suggested either an odd lapse on the part of Senyaza's security designer, or the triumph of reason. She opened it and pulled out the fragment, then kept walking. She counted fourteen fragments in total, including one she'd interacted with before, the children's toy she'd reshaped into a weapon for Marley. She frowned at the Lullaby Spear and almost took it as well; she felt like it was hers or Marley's, not Senyaza's. But in the end she left it behind, choosing only three of the fragments to help her.

She set to work.

When security showed up, she was sitting at one of the tables flipping through one of the binders. Four men in helmets and black battledress thundered in, arrayed themselves beyond the split window, and leveled large guns at her.

"Step away from the table!" one of them barked. "Hands in the air!"

She blinked at them, then stood up and said, "How intimidating." She made a show of raising her empty hands into the air.

"Excuse me, gentlemen," said a different voice. The security team rearranged themselves to let a thin man in an exquisite pearl-grey suit approach the window. He had an older face, and a clean pate, and he was a nephil. His nodes contained complex charms, and the auras at his head and feet burned with white radiance.

He looked Branwyn over with faint interest. "Good evening, Miss Lennox. I am Mr. Black. Would you come with me, please?"

"Nice tie," Branwyn commented. It was black silk, speckled with the stars of the Milky Way. "Very modern wizard." He looked down at his chest in surprise, then looked up with an amused smile that lingered as Branwyn kept talking. "Where is it you'd like me to go?"

"Oh, to my office. It's not far."

Branwyn considered the request. "I could do that. But I can't stay long."

His amusement didn't flicker. "We shall see." He addressed the security force in a very different tone of voice. "Make sure she's clean. A librarian will be along soon to restore the artifacts to their proper locations."

The grate separating Branwyn from the others rattled up and the door buzzed open. While two of the team kept their weapons trained on her, the other two entered, ready to frisk her. Branwyn lowered her hands slowly and held up one finger. "Let me get those for you." She reached into the pocket of her cargo pants and pulled out a handkerchief. She carefully unfolded it to reveal two Machine fragments: a shard of blue glass with red veins trailing from the angled ends, and a thin lavender needle with a bent hollow tip.

She held out the handkerchief to one of the men. "Careful," she said. "They bite the unwary."

The man took the cloth and inspected its contents with a healthy caution. "Where's the third artifact?"

"Ah," she said. "That one stays with me."

"Bullshit," said the man, and nodded at his companion.

Before the second man could move, Branwyn said pleasantly, "Have you any idea about the contents of the room you're standing in, gentlemen? You think of them as artifacts, yes? Relics of another time, a faraway place. But in the right hands, each and every one of them is a weapon. Your hands are not the right hands. Mine are. And the truth is? I don't even need to use my hands."

The guard holding the handkerchief jerked in surprise, staring down at his palm in horror. The shard of blue glass had changed, the red tendrils extending from it growing just a little bit longer. The second guard hesitated.

"Put it on the table," Branwyn suggested. "Let the librarian handle it. That's what she's paid for."

The guard hurriedly did as she said and Branwyn smiled. This seemed to annoy the second guard, who said, "Put the third artifact on the table yourself, then."

"It wants to come with me," Branwyn said. "It kills angels. Do you really want to argue with it?" The little golden disc nestled against her left breast, under her bra, warm and eager to work.

With a touch of impatience, Mr. Black called from beyond the door, "Must I do this myself?"

"Sir, she—"

"Check her for weapons, then bring her. Let her retain the artifact for now. It will be an instructive exercise."

Branwyn allowed this, although she repressed a smile at how half-hearted the pat-down was. When they decided she was free of mundane weapons, she walked between them out of the Repository and into the elevator, which took her up to the above-ground part of the building, a few floors above the main entrance.

Mr. Black had a corner office overlooking the street below, tucked up close to the public part of the tower. It was quite large, with a grouping of couches as well as a desk near the window with a hard wooden chair across from it. When the guards escorted her into the room, Mr. Black was waiting. He gestured Branwyn to the loveseat and, once she was seated, moved to the sofa. "Thank you," he said to the guards. "Please wait outside. Would you like a drink, Miss Lennox?"

"No, thank you," said Branwyn, just as polite. It turned out she *was* capable of it, when it entertained her. That was just so rare. "So, your men checked me for guns and knives and the like."

"As I asked. It makes them feel useful," Mr. Black confided. "They do like that."

"What would you do if I had a weaponized charm, though?"

He sat down on the couch, chuckling. "You are such an innocent, Miss Lennox. So new to our world, and so ignorant."

Branwyn became less entertained. "So educate me."

"Aren't I doing just that? Let us say that I am not without protection of my own, and sometimes the best defense is a good offense." The smile he gave her was positively jolly. His confidence was starting to get on Branwyn's nerves. "Be easy, my dear. As long as you behave yourself, no harm will come to you."

Branwyn concentrated on not letting her irritation show and waited quietly for him to get to the point. He clearly had one. They'd caught her in their secured facility, playing with their toys, and they'd neither shot her nor turned her over to the ordinary authorities.

Mr. Black leaned back, lacing his fingers together in front of him. "We've been watching you. You first came to this tower in the company of my grandson. After he went abroad, you attached yourself to Simon. Yet you snuck in here today without any assistance from him."

"Oh, he wouldn't help me," lied Branwyn. "I asked but he wouldn't even consider it. He warned me it was a bad idea." She shook her head. "If only I'd listened."

"Very loyal," Mr. Black said, and Branwyn wasn't sure if he was talking about Simon, or her transparent lie. He paused, studying her. Branwyn returned the favor, looking for a resemblance to Corbin in his face. She couldn't see it. "I've been watching almost since you walked in the side door. We were very curious about your goals and methods. There are obviously holes we'll have to plug."

"If you knew I was here from the beginning, it seems like you've got security well in hand," Branwyn pointed out.

"Oh, Miss Lennox, give yourself more credit. We may have watched you as you loitered in the lounge reading the newspaper, but we didn't open any doors for you. We certainly didn't give you access to the Repository. It was really quite a good demonstration of your skills."

Branwyn sighed. "Thank you." She thought about trying to hurry things along, but there was no point. Some things took time.

"My theory," confided the elder nephil, "is that you *wanted* to get caught. You needed a way to get out of helping the faeries. If we had you, not only would you be unable to complete their task, but we'd protect you from them."

"Close. Even plausible," said Branwyn. She bared her teeth in what was nominally a smile. "But not correct. Care to try again?"

Mr. Black's expression sharpened. "No? Well. The end result is the same, no matter your motivation. You will work for us now. We will pay you well, of course—"

"In exchange for the Machine fragment known as the Golden Memory? That seems like a fair exchange. I've already begun." Branwyn noticed with some satisfaction Mr. Black's increased agitation; it reflected her own irritation nicely.

"Don't be tedious, girl. You will not be permitted to retain the Machine beyond this room, and you will certainly not be permitted to further aid humanity's enemies. Working for us will be satisfying and rewarding. You will be protected from dangers and—" He paused. "What do you mean, you've already begun?"

Branwyn stretched. "You really don't want me working for you, you know. Not as a permanent employee. The Queen of Stone can look through my eyes whenever she wants, and there's an asshole kaiju who already thinks he owns me. I'm pretty sure there's not *room* for Senyaza as well. It certainly wouldn't be secure. But I'm totally open to specific commissions. When I get home, I'll write up a rate sheet for you."

And now Mr. Black's voice had an edge. "What did you mean, you've already begun?"

Glancing at the walls, Branwyn said, "And here I thought you said you were watching me the whole time. Oh right." She smiled again, sharper this time. "You haven't had access to a real Artificer— it's a human ability, you know, comes from humans with a faerie education—for centuries." She stood. "I woke up the Repository, Mr. Black. I woke up a few other things, too, just to see if I could. And right now the Machines in the Repository are accelerating the growth of the loci I made. They're so cute, don't you think? The door has a node, just like we do."

Mr. Black stared at her, thinking over what she said. "All right—"

Branwyn stood up and spoke over him. "Just like we do. Except you and I, we have charms. So I gave the door a copy of one of my charms. Just like Corbin did for me once! It wasn't the same, of course; I had to use a Machine to help. They're very helpful to anybody who tries to understand them. Well, to humans."

Mr. Black's eyes narrowed and Branwyn could tell he was scanning her charms, trying to guess which one she'd given the door. She gave him a brilliant smile. "I gave it the charm for opening a passage into the Backworld. And I made a request. If I haven't walked out of here with the Golden Memory by the time it wakes up all the way, it's going to use the charm." She tapped her chin thoughtfully. "Now, because it's a room and not a person, I think it may work a little differently. I'm just guessing, but I think what's going to happen is that the room is going to swap places with whatever's in the Backworld right there. I don't know what that is, although apparently faeries and monsters are afraid of it! Even if that's just an urban legend, the contents of the

Repository will be in the Backworld, all unguarded." She put her hand on the wall behind the sofa and felt the thrum as the awakened bones of the building carried her touch to the Repository.

She was surprised when Mr. Black said, "You're bluffing." She'd told the absolute truth, after all.

"Go and see, then. Or ask your librarian to look. Tell her it might be best if she didn't open the door, though."

With an ugly twist of his mouth, he pulled a phone out of his jacket pocket and speed-dialed a number. Less than thirty seconds later, he murmured, "I see," and put the phone away. His gaze was trained on Branwyn's hand.

"Oh, sorry, is this making you nervous? We wouldn't want that." She pulled her hand away from the wall. Mischievously, she added, "As long as you behave yourself, no harm will come to you." He glared at her and suddenly she could see the resemblance to Corbin. Before she could feel a pang of regret, she went on. "So what's it going to be? Am I going to walk out of here or is something awkward going to happen? What *is* on the other side of the curtain down there?"

"Nothing we wish to see in the human world," Mr. Black said.

He gave her a look she thought she recognized and hurriedly, she said, "There's no advantage in killing me."

"This is hardly behaving," he pointed out. "But yes, that would also be... awkward." He hesitated, then slowly shook his head. "I *cannot* let you take the Machine. You may leave without it and we will pretend this never happened."

"I need it," said Branwyn flatly.

"To free humanity's enemies, those who have already wreaked havoc on your own family. Really, girl, I would have expected better."

Sourly, Branwyn said, "Shouldn't humanity have a say? A lot of people seem to quite like what they've seen of the faeries."

"Is that what this is?" he asked incredulously. "A pettish fit because we have the *temerity* to protect humanity from the monsters? And, yes, even from its own dangerous desires? Oh, the *audacity!*" He added acidly, "I should have retired decades ago and let you silly brats destroy yourselves."

Branwyn glared at him. "I never said that. You seem to be okay at managing the monsters, although there's a few I wish you'd focus on. But you didn't exile the faeries, did you? That was the work of the angels. They're the *angels'* enemies. They locked them away three times. Parole them and perhaps they'll help you out. If they don't, leave the final lock in place."

He frowned. "You are ignorant. Don't be stupid, too."

Branwyn crossed her arms. "And now we're on to name-calling. All right, I'm done. I'm going to walk out that door and take the elevator now. Anybody stops me and there will be, and maybe I mean this literally, Hell to pay. Goodbye." She walked past him toward the door, every muscle quivering with tension.

He watched her silently. As she reached the door, she saw his posture change from the corner of her eye.

Suddenly she wanted to run, very badly.

She resisted. She opened the door and stepped out. The security team standing in the hall shifted in surprise, but when Mr. Black said, "Let her go," they fell back. They trusted him.

Branwyn didn't.

She sped up, and took the stairs down instead of the elevator. There was no lock on the ground floor exit; they were emergency stairs, after all. As she emerged from the stairwell, she saw Simon walking across the empty shopping court. He paused when he saw her. "Branwyn! What are you doing here?"

"Leaving," she said. "Working late?"

"Mr. Black called me," he said. "He wanted to see me immediately. Said he had a task for me. Something for me to hunt down. A big, immediate threat he's just discovered."

Branwyn's heart, already racing, skipped a beat. Simon cocked his head, then froze. "Oh." He met her gaze and she checked her long stride. "Go," he said softly.

"Simon—" She had no idea what she had been going to say.

"I haven't got any orders yet, except to see the boss. I don't know what you're up to. You said you were leaving? Leave, already." He started walking toward the elevators again. As he passed her, she heard him mutter, "You should probably run."

Once she left the building, she did.

-twenty-four-

Branwyn went home. To her own home, not her family's home—to the apartment she shared with Marley. It was the middle of the night, but Marley was still awake, curled on the couch with a book. She always had a book. Branwyn was pretty sure it had been the same one for the last few weeks, too.

Without preamble, she said, "I think Simon may show up any minute and try to kill me. Can you protect me from him while I do what I need to do?" She locked the front door behind her.

Marley scrambled off the couch. "What the hell?"

Branwyn fished the disc-shaped Machine fragment out of her bra and held it up. "From Senyaza's Repository. Their chief of security didn't appreciate my ingenuity as much as he thought he would. And apparently he's got a vicious sense of humor." She smiled bitterly. "Corbin's grandpa, you know." She felt the gentle brightness of the shield close around her even as Marley goggled at her.

"You're doing it, then? Finishing the Key?"

"I'm doing it for Penny," Branwyn said, then hesitated. "And for me." She ran to Marley's bedroom and pulled the unfinished Key out from the box of books she'd hidden it in.

Ignoring Marley's frown, she sat down on the floor with the Key and the disc of Golden Memory arrayed in front of her. According to the notes she'd scanned while waiting for the security team to liberate her from the Repository, it often raised forgotten or nearly forgotten memories when the bearer concentrated on it. It hadn't done that for Branwyn, and she wondered if it still would after she'd incorporated it into the Key.

She stared at the pieces in front of her, but she couldn't focus. Marley moved between the window and the couch restlessly, and Branwyn kept wondering what would happen when Simon showed up. She wondered if the Repository was behaving itself now that she'd left the building. She thought they should be able to communicate with it somehow, get it on their side. But they might need her help for that.

Branwyn shook herself. "This isn't working. I need to get out of here." She picked up her materials and tucked them away.

"Where?" asked Marley instantly.

"My workroom at Underlight, I think."

"I'm driving."

At her family's house, they ran into a problem: a party was in progress. Branwyn vaguely remembered her mother mentioning it. This one was a lot more crowded than the last, with music and light spilling out into the night. The front door stood open to the breeze and several of Jaimie and Holly's friends were on the porch. Branwyn hesitated, then ducked behind the band van, pulling Marley after her. She activated the charms Zachariah had given her for opening a gate on her own. Immediately, she saw that the entire property was a soft spot in the curtain. Tearing open her own hole in the curtain while hidden behind the band van was easy.

But she didn't expect Tarn to appear. He filled the window, his appearance so startling and his face so bleak that she scrambled backward. "Get in here," he said, reaching out of the window and yanking her through by her arm. The gap sealed behind her and she felt Marley's protection vanish.

He put his hand on the wall in Underlight, and Branwyn's still-active charm recoiled off a suddenly diamond-hard curtain. "You acquired a Machine," he said grimly.

Branwyn brushed herself off. "It turns out that the best way to get out of a cage is to get *them* to open the doors. Did you have to be so abrupt? I wanted Marley here, too. Although I suppose you can keep

Simon off my back just as well."

He stared at her, apparently speechless, then held out his hand. "Give me the Key."

"I haven't finished it yet." She moved toward her workshop.

"And you won't," he said fiercely. The long hall became longer, an impossible distance between her and the door to her workshop.

Branwyn turned on her heel to give Tarn a disbelieving look. "Have you lost it? You arranged everything so this would happen. Underlight needs the door to be opened. You told me you want this!"

"I changed my mind," he growled and stalked toward her, murder in his eyes. "Underlight will recover eventually. Your family deserves better than the attentions of Rime and her kind."

Penny doesn't have that long. She'd seen that yesterday, in the slow beeping of the monitor. Planting her feet, Branwyn crossed her arms. "Go ahead. Tell me you don't want me to finish this Key."

"I don't want you to finish the Key," he said as he reached for her. The room trembled at his words. He stumbled.

"I thought so," said Branwyn. She turned and ran down the hall. The shaking grew more agitated and knocked her down; when she bounced to her feet again, the workshop door was right in front of her.

Tarn caught her arm again as she opened the door. "It's complicated," he said softly.

"I know," said Branwyn, and kicked him away before darting into her workshop and slamming the door behind her. She locked it with the courtkey.

This place might have been carved out of Underlight, out of a faerie's realm, but it was hers now. She'd made it hers, reaching into the substance of the world and reshaping it over and over again. It responded to her whim.

"Keep him out," she said, and the door merged with the wall. Almost immediately, light flashed where the door had been, settling into a burning glow. Her whim against his command. She didn't have much time.

She set to work, and here she could concentrate. Here, it was easy. She took the partial Key and introduced it to the golden disc. With barely a touch of her finger and her will, they reached inside of her and merged together, becoming one whole thing. It was like they'd been made for this purpose, shed from the cosmic Machines so they could come together in this final shape, for this ultimate purpose. It just needed a bit of guidance.

The door fell away. Tarn loomed out of the mist that curled through the door. Branwyn opened her hand, revealing the large key formed of twisted metal strands in her palm.

Tarn's shoulders slumped. "You finished it." He raised his gaze to her face, his eyes flashing. "You idiot."

Branwyn quirked her mouth to one side, studying the Key. "Yes. I had to work from memory, though." What she was about to do weighed heavily on her. She'd originally thought of the faeries as long-lived humans. That had been easier, at first. She knew now they were something else. Angels, once, who dreamt of being other than how they were made. Personalities bound to primal forces. And despite not being human, they were still people, still individuals. They deserved individual attention, not exile as a class.

But Tarn himself had repeatedly said the faeries thought in terms of centuries. Maybe eventually something could be done that would let people protect themselves from predatory fae without imprisoning all of them. They could work that out later. But Penny wouldn't last until later.

When she thought of it like that, it was an easy decision. The faeries could *wait*.

"Will it open the door?" Tarn demanded harshly. Then he answered himself. "Yes, of course it will. I could feel it when you completed it."

Closing her fingers over the key, Branwyn raised her gaze to his face. "Yes. I know the door too well. But that's not what it's for. I lied. I'm sorry, Tarn. I need to get this to Penny."

Tarn ran his hands through his dark hair, as if she'd driven him to the edge of reason. The world shook, and Branwyn wondered how he was lying now.

"You feel that?" he said. "*Everybody* bound to the Covenant could feel it when you completed the Key. All Faerie trembles in anticipation."

Alarmed, Branwyn pulled her hand close to her body. "It's for Penny. Why should they care? It's not like it would have truly freed you. It was just one of two remaining."

Almost gently, he said, "You are so human. Branwyn, the Duke of Nightwell has been working on the other lock since the first one was broken."

Blankly, Branwyn asked, "How? Not Machines...?"

"Something to do with music. I don't know the details, only that what he has created will work. I could feel it. It works on the lock even now."

"Music. Oh." She remembered Rime and the Duke of Nightwell speaking quietly in the recording studio. She remembered Rime saying *Music opens doors.* "Oh." She put her hand with the Key behind her back. It was childish, but instinctive. "So I'm all that's standing between you and complete freedom."

"Yes," he said deliberately. "And we *did* make a deal."

"Was it a deal? I think it was more of an informal arrangement, really. And my sources tell me you can't carry out your side of the arrangement. That saving Penny without her soul isn't saving her at all."

"Do you really think that all of those leashed outside the world are going to let you change your mind? He is coming, even now."

"I didn't make the deal with him!"

"*He doesn't care.*"

Branwyn stared at Tarn in bewilderment. "Do you? If you're trying to get me to give it to you—"

"I don't care about the damn Key!" This time, the ground stayed rock-stable. "I care about making sure your mad head stays on your shoulders. I care about making sure my people aren't fully unleashed on yours without at least time to prepare."

"That's new," said Branwyn, subdued and wary.

Tarn spread his hands helplessly. "I wasn't a Duke when last we were free. I thought the imprisonment had hardened me, but I've been watching your family all this time—" He shook his head. "Doubt is dangerous for a lord of Faerie, so I tried to ignore it. That wasn't the answer."

"Well, congratulations on developing a conscience, I guess," Branwyn said. "What about Nightwell and the others?"

"If you hand over the Key, they'll let you live. If you don't, they'll take it."

"And your conscience is going to just let them do that?"

"No! Don't you listen? Is your head stuffed with cotton? I don't know how to save you now that you finished it. The door has drained Underlight so much. The Key can't be destroyed, can it?"

Branwyn sighed. "Possibly. But that's not going to happen. How much time do we have? Can his lock be closed? How does music open a door?"

Tarn's gaze went far away. "It is a song, with a video attached. Each time the song is played, the lock temporarily opens. It remains unlocked as long as the song is being sung. And he is putting the song on your internet."

"Oh no." Branwyn thought of all the video sites out there. "Is it catchy?"

His gaze flickered back to her, hard and unfriendly. "What do you think?"

"All right." She caught Tarn's hand and squeezed it. "It's okay. I just have to get to Penny, and it will be all okay. Or at least no worse than if your lock had opened and theirs hadn't."

He stared at her in astonishment. "What are you going to do with Penny?" The world shook again, ringing like a bell, and she gave him a sharp look. But he only said, "He's here. William!"

William materialized behind his master. Tarn pulled Branwyn past him and thrust her at the changeling. "Take her. Get her to her friend's bedside. I have a guest to greet. Go quickly! He will only let me delay him so long." He took a step and vanished. The hall behind William lengthened again, an endless dark and light with cracks running down the walls.

William grimaced. "Come." He started running down the hall, towing Branwyn after him like she was a misbehaving child. She bit back a complaint and focused on getting her feet under her. After a moment, William said, without apparent effort, "You are *slow*. He is changing the realm for you, to move us closer to your precious Penny, but soon he will have to fight Nightwell directly. When he does that, we'll be ejected into Faerie main. We'll have to find the right path. Don't do anything stupid, like letting go of my hand."

Branwyn, concentrating on running, only nodded.

"Already," he said. "Now." The hall peeled away around them, dropping them into a verdant field dotted with carnelian flowers that reached to Branwyn's thighs. She stumbled in the transition and almost fell, dragging against William's hand. The light shifted around them, becoming the aquamarine of an underwater world. Her eyes and lungs burned. "Not here," said William, his words hollow. The light changed again, the thistle-grey of stormclouds. "Here. Move!"

Instead, Branwyn, soaking wet from the dip into the wet light, gagged on the saltwater that had flooded her mouth and nose during the moment before. She tried to move forward, even though she could barely tell where the ground was.

"I hate mortals," William grumbled, and slung her over his shoulder. After only a few leaping steps, the water had been jarred right out of her system and she had enough sense back to be aware of the absolute indignity of being carried from an enemy over an ally's shoulder. It was nearly intolerable. It was everything she wanted to avoid.

It was also, she thought, the best way. William was actually moving faster now that he was carrying her. They ran through a shallow marsh, William leaping from hummock to hummock under a sky that danced with lightning. The only way Branwyn would be able to keep up was by letting him carry her for now. She thought she was okay with help—hadn't she asked Marley for help in the end?—but it still rankled.

Oh well. At least he'd been human once, and made a choice as a human. He didn't like her at all, but he loved Tarn and he was helping her because Tarn wished it, and how much more human could you get?

"Are we almost there?"

"Shut up," he said. "There's—" and darkness burst out of the ground in front of them. A figure, tall and slender with wild purple hair, advanced from within the maelstrom of shadows.

William dropped Branwyn into some mud and moved in front of her. "Get out of here. I'll—"

Branwyn activated the charm to tear the veil before William finished speaking, but nothing happened. It was the same smoothed and hardened curtain she'd encountered when Tarn had yanked her into Underlight. She was trapped in the Backworld.

Scrambling to her feet, she started running. There was a clash and thud behind her, and a very human cry of pain from William, and

Branwyn stopped short. She knew she ought to keep moving until she outran the curtain-hardening effect, but it was the second time William had been damaged on her behalf, the second time she'd heard that cry. How many times had he died already?

She turned around in time to see Nightwell fling William aside and smile at her. She scowled at him and opened her palm to show him the Key. It was heavy in her palm, and the light it shed made the dreary landscape seem like a momentary bad mood rather than a real place. He gestured, and the landscape compressed, bringing her closer to him. But the Key dragged against the land. He couldn't take it from her without killing her, she could tell.

Then, rising up from where William's body lay, came Tarn, a long slim blade in one hand. "No," he said.

"So you're fool enough to abandon Underlight," said Nightwell, surprised. "You sacrifice everything for a human's whim."

"I abandon nothing that is mine. Branwyn, get out of here. Open a door." His sword, glowing like a distant star, cut through Nightwell's darkness.

Branwyn opened her mouth to explain she couldn't, then caught her breath as she looked at what she held. "Oh." She reached into the Backworld with the Key and twisted it.

The curtain melted away around her. She tumbled out into the world.

-twenty-five-

She fell six feet, landing on the roof of a car and rolling off heavily. As she sprawled on the pavement, she tried to figure out where she was. A parking lot beside a busy city street. It was familiar. She limped to the shadow of the nearby building and worked to turn the sense of familiarity into an actual place. Her head was fuzzy. She still held the Key, but it was excited by the recent use, and it sang to her. It was ready to open bigger things.

"No," she whispered to it. "Maybe later. There's something else now." She blinked in the early morning light and realized she was only a few blocks from Penny's hospital, at a strip mall with a bank and a coffee shop. William had almost gotten her there. She just had to stagger across the street and there she was. Easy.

Except that the coffee shop down the street was playing music out over the sidewalk tables, and a new song had begun. Branwyn recognized the chords she'd heard Jaimie practicing days ago, and a moment later, heard his voice singing. Up and down the sidewalk, people appeared out of thin air. Tall, slender, beautiful people. They'd been in all the videos lately, showing off magic that faded whenever their leashes snapped them back to their prison. And as one, they turned to the Key Branwyn clutched tightly.

No time to stagger, then. Branwyn ran to the curb, ignoring the pain that screamed in her ankle and knee. Even this early, there were too many cars to ignore; she'd be flattened. She punched the crosswalk button, then, in desperation, pushed the Key into the light post—it sank in like the post was an illusion—and twisted it the other direction. The light controlling traffic flickered from green to red without pausing at yellow. A moment later, traffic going both directions was at a standstill and Branwyn limped across the street, waving at the puzzled drivers.

She was limping; the faeries were not. It wouldn't do. She ran as she'd never run before, sure she heard the sound of dogs baying behind her. It was a game, she realized. They didn't know where she was going, or why. So when she zagged into the door of the hospital as a man stepped out, they didn't expect it. She grabbed the door from the man leaving and pulled it shut, then locked it behind her before staggering to the elevator and using the Key to demand priority service. It was a useful tool and she was really going to miss it.

In the elevator, she caught her breath for a moment. She was going to make it. They weren't going to stop her. She was almost there.

Then she walked into Penny's room, and came face to face with Simon and Marley.

They were glaring at each other, but Branwyn hardly noticed, unable to imagine any reason for Simon being there other than stopping her at Senyaza's behest. "What—No! Get out of my way! Marley, help me!"

Simon blinked and looked away from Marley, who was hovering protectively over Penny's bedside. "Bran—" he began.

Then all hell broke loose.

Darkness flooded the room as Nightwell arrived. A hand reached out of the shadows for Branwyn and a dimly radiant blade batted it away as Tarn rose from the floor. The hospital room was suddenly much too crowded and Branwyn dropped to the ground to get past them. She felt Marley's shield drop over her as her friend grabbed her and pulled her into the tiny space where she was wedged between the IV stand and the hospital bed.

"What did you *do*, Branwyn?" shouted Simon. He had his knife out, and it flickered with an electric glow as he stared at the two faerie lords battling. As a sword almost clipped him, he ducked and swore.

It started to rain in the hospital room. At first, Branwyn thought it was a sprinkler system accidentally set off, but she could smell the freshness of the rain. An alarm went off, and another one. "Protect Penny," she told Marley urgently. "I need some time to work, so if you can—" she gave the chaos in the room a speaking glance, then crouched beside Penny. Her friend's breathing was rapid and shallow.

Marley said, "Right. I'll do what I can." The visual brightness vanished and Penny's breathing stabilized. Then Marley stepped between Branwyn and the rest of the room.

Branwyn laid the Key on Penny's chest. "Souls are key," she whispered. AT had said that. *Music opens doors*, Rime had said. There were probably fewer figures of speech in the world than people thought. Or at least, there would be with faeries around.

Her own breathing quickening, Branwyn tried to shut out the chaos and look at Penny with maker's eyes. She'd done this the last time she visited, when she saw that the two-part key wouldn't be enough. Now, with the complete tripartite key, the Key that could open any door, she looked at Penny's ravaged soul. The fit wasn't perfect, not yet. She thought, when dealing with a prosthetic soul, the fit should probably be perfect. She had to work. She had to *concentrate*.

The noise in the room was incredible. Even on their worst days, her family had never been this bad. Some of the hospital staff had shown up to add to the noise. There was screaming, and Simon cursing, and probably the gnashing of teeth, too.

"Will you all just *be quiet!*" she shouted, unable to stop herself.

The mark on her collarbone burned, and silence fell across the room like a switch had been flipped. Severin said, his voice cutting across the silence like a bad dream, "I'm here to help, cupcake. You've served me admirably, after all."

Branwyn looked around, wild-eyed. Everybody seemed frozen. She spotted the kaiju, standing amidst panicking medical staff at the entrance to the room. He touched three of them on the foreheads in rapid succession and they collapsed. She met his bright gaze, then looked with panic at the two faeries. They were moving very slowly, as if caught underwater.

"Ah, well, I didn't think it would last. Work fast, cupcake." Then everything sped up again, sans alarm and screaming humans. Severin insinuated himself between Nightwell and Tarn like a dancer, flung

Nightwell away with a quiet, "Mine," then turned and knocked Tarn flat on his back. Nightwell bounced off the wall and sprang forward again, then seemed to realize that Severin had stolen his opposition and turned toward Branwyn.

"And what are you doing?" Nightwell asked, almost politely, but Branwyn couldn't spare any attention for him. She couldn't seem to pull her gaze from Tarn and Severin. Severin straddled Tarn's chest, kneeling with his hands on both sides of Tarn's head, his forehead pressed against the faerie's. Severin's teeth were bared in savage glee, while Tarn had his eyes closed. He wasn't struggling at all, but the clashing of celestial auras rose, the black diamond rain damping for a moment even the thrum of the Key Branwyn still held. Something warm and oceanic flickered around Tarn, then faded under the dark onslaught.

Strands of light glowed to life around Tarn, tying him down. Something glinted in Severin's hand, and Marley said in a hushed voice, "He's actually going to kill him for real."

Something tickled Branwyn's throat. She didn't want Tarn to die, not because he'd stepped out of safety, not because she'd been Severin's pawn, not because of *her*. The tickling grew to a burning and she screamed, "No!"

Simon, who'd been standing stock still alongside the wall, glanced down at the knife in his hand. Then he shrugged, stepped forward, grabbed Severin's head by a handful of dark hair, and dragged the lightning-sparking knife across his throat.

There was a thunderclap that rattled the IV stand, and for the second time, almost everything froze.

The kaiju's black diamond aura throbbed twice, like a beating heart, then vanished as blood gushed out over Simon's hand. Severin twitched, turning his head. Then his body collapsed, freezing and crumbling just as Rime's had.

The white light binding Tarn vanished and he scrambled backward, out from under the disintegrating statue. He caught something that fell amid the dust, and pulled his own sword out of nowhere.

"Damn thing's been after me to do that since you fixed it," muttered Simon. "It told me he'd be here."

Something dark twisted painfully within Branwyn. She looked

down at Penny and crushed her feelings away. She had work to do.

"Very interesting," said Nightwell courteously. "But I'd like the Key now. Don't make me kill you. You're a treasure. It would be a shame."

Branwyn raised her head again.

Tarn said, just as politely, "Go ahead, Branwyn. What you're doing does look very interesting." Then he connected the glittering thing he'd taken from Severin's remains to his sword and pressed the flat of the blade against Nightwell's abdomen, wrapping his arm around him from behind. "I'm feeling generous, cousin. Nobody should die the Machine death today. So just stay quiet and watch. Or go home. I don't really care."

Nightwell stiffened, his gaze sweeping across Marley and Simon. Branwyn stopped watching, then. She turned her attention back to the Key. It lay quiescent, a multidimensional piece of celestial machinery folded into a shape made for opening doors. It could do other things, too. It could do this.

Working carefully and slowly, she touched the Machine here and there. She introduced it to Penny, showed it Penny's ragged soul. Silently, she told it about Penny, about Penny's reaction to her first kiss, and her feelings about her mother. It responded. It knew what to do.

Then, gently, she started transferring the tendrils the Key sank into her into Penny, drawing them snug. It was detailed, complicated work. But as she worked, the Key began to work as well and for a few endless moments, she and Penny were connected to each other. She saw Penny's dreams and caught her breath in grief.

But with time, Penny could heal. The Machine would see to that, see she had time, see she would heal if she chose to. Branwyn was sure she would. And so, delicately, she moved the last connection from her chest to Penny's and the Key sank into Penny's torso. The glow that spread out from Branwyn's hands faded and, wearily, she lifted them away.

She was sitting in a chair beside Penny's bed. Not much time had passed, she supposed; almost everybody was still there. Nightwell had vanished, and Tarn stood at the door chatting quietly with some people just beyond. He looked, she thought muzzily, like a doctor. He had more magic now, and more freedom, despite the fact that she'd used the Key for something else. Rhianna wouldn't be happy about that.

The pile of dust on the floor that had been Severin was gone.

Marley touched her shoulder and offered her a glass of water. She looked as tired as Branwyn felt. "Are you okay?"

Branwyn drank the water, then stretched stiff shoulders. "That depends. How is she?"

"I don't know. You did something, I can see that, but—"

"Ah, but you can't expect something like that to work all at once. It was amazing, but you're not a miracle-worker, Branwyn," said Simon.

Tarn turned, closing the door behind him. "Actually, I think she is."

"Nope. She can't be. Mortal hands, right there."

With a faintly amused smile, Tarn shrugged. "I owe you my life, so I won't argue with you."

Simon rose from where he was sprawled on the couch. "He'll be back, you know. That wasn't anywhere *near* permanent. He'll be back and he'll *remember*." He sighed.

"Does it worry you?" asked Tarn.

"I'd be an idiot if it didn't," said Simon bluntly. "I don't usually like to do such a poor job of things. It's dangerous. The question is, who's he going to be angriest at? You? Me? Her?"

An odd expression crossed Tarn's face. "Me, certainly. He might hunt you down, I suppose. Not her."

"You think? Possibly so. Still, she made the knife awfully angry at him. I couldn't have hurt him enough without it, not so quickly. I wouldn't have been here, either. Damn thing knew where he'd be. Strangest thing." Simon shook his head.

"She's an Artificer," said Tarn. "It's what they do."

Marley reached over and squeezed Branwyn's hand. "Don't worry about him."

"I'm not," said Branwyn, and meant it. She never had been. She was much more worried about her own ambiguous feelings about the kaiju. Then, because Marley was looking at her with a thoughtful gaze she didn't like, she said, "I'm a little worried about Nightwell, though. Will he or other faeries come after Penny?"

"That *will* be interesting," said Tarn, with unexpected cheer. "I think she may be able to defend herself if they do."

Branwyn focused on Tarn and realized something. "You're here. What's happening in Underlight? What's happened to the door?"

He held her gaze steadily as he said, "The door is drifting unanchored through the mists of the Backworld. And Underlight will reform. If you would return the courtkey to me, that would help quite a bit." He held out his hand, his fingers closed over something. "We can trade."

"Of course," she said, and, "I'm sorry," as she found the courtkey in her pocket and offered it to him.

He took it and said, "Doubt is deadly for a faerie lord, Branwyn. But life is beautiful. I'm glad to be reminded of that." Then he deposited what he'd been holding into her now-empty hand.

She stared down at it. It looked very much like an actual black diamond and it whispered like a Machine fragment. "Where—?"

"*He* had it, as well as the spirit tethers. The Destroyer. He was *very* determined that I die. I wish I could remember why." Regret moved over his face, and a hint of a profound sadness. But it was gone so quickly Branwyn might have dreamt it. Lightly, he finished, "I have no idea where he got it. But I thought you might find it useful."

Branwyn hesitated, thinking about the kaiju, then tucked the black diamond away. "Yes, I will."

She transferred her gaze to Simon. "Are you supposed to kill me for stealing from Senyaza?"

"Nope," he said. He yawned, like somebody who'd been up all night.

"Nope?" she asked suspiciously.

"Nope. I'm supposed to kill you to stop you from freeing the faerie scourge. You might want to—" and he stopped talking, suddenly.

There was movement under the blanket below Branwyn and Marley's linked hands. Branwyn's breath caught in her throat and she looked down.

With a little sound, Penny opened her eyes.

For a long moment, she stared up at Branwyn. Then her eyebrows furrowed. "Branwyn? What are you doing in my—" She looked around and said, "Oh. Oh. What happened?" She coughed and Marley gave her some water. "I remember going to sleep after my date with Jeremy." Her face darkened. "I had dreams."

Branwyn smiled and stood up, pushing Marley into the chair. "Marley will tell you all about it." She leaned over and gave Penny a hug.

"Where are you going?" Marley demanded.

"I've got to write up a rate sheet for Senyaza," Branwyn said cheerfully. "And fill in my siblings. And maybe sleep a little. Busy, busy." Marley scowled at her, and Penny looked at her in just-woken-up bemusement. "Besides, your mom is going to be here soon. You know how I hate crying moms." She winked and walked out the door Tarn had just opened, the whole world ahead of her.

acknowledgments

Without whom this book would not exist:

My editors, Kate and Sarah:
thanks for pushing me past my comfort zone.

My beta readers, Michelle, Angie, Jenna, Beth, Stacy and Suzanne:
I'm so glad you were there when I needed you.

The denizens of the War Room:
how would I get anything done without your support?

Raymond, who is endlessly patient.

Kevin: see elsewhere.

Robin: you make it all worth it.

about the author

Chrysoula Tzavelas went to twelve schools in twelve years while growing up as an Air Force brat, and she never met a library she didn't like. She now lives near Seattle with cats, dogs, adults, and children. They graciously allow her a few hours to write every day and one day she'll have time to do other things again, too.

She likes combed wool, bread dough, and gardens, but she also likes technology, games, and space. This probably goes hand in hand with liking Jane Austen, Terry Pratchett, and Iain Banks.

follow the author

www.dreamfarmer.net
Twitter: @chrysouladreams
Facebook: facebook.com/chrysoula.tzavelas
Google+: plus.google.com/u/0/103166129089211811271/posts
Goodreads: goodreads.com/author/show/5049815.Chrysoula_Tzavelas

www.ingramcontent.com/pod-product-compliance
Lightning Source LLC
Chambersburg PA
CBHW030324200626
46816CB00006BA/1919